MONSTERS BEWARE!

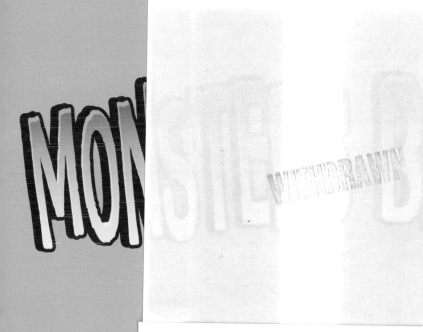

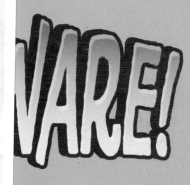

For my wife, Darlene, who's always been my cheerleader —R.R.

For my mother, Rosita, who taught me to be polite, but stubborn.
In other words, she accidentally raised a writer —J.A.

We would both like to thank our editor, Mark Siegel, for his continuing guidance, support, and patience. Thanks, Mark! Thank you to the talented and hardworking crew at First Second Books: Calista Brill, Gina Gagliano, Robyn Chapman, Kiara Valdez, and Danielle Ceccolini. Thank you, Darlene Rosado, for your social media help. *Gracias a* Raul Rosado for your early design work. Thank you, John Novak, for another extraordinary job at coloring our books. Rafael would like to once again thank Dee Dee Sue, Amelia, and Avery for their love and support. Jorge would like to thank Carla, Diego, Pablo, and Luna, who prevent him from navel-gazing too much. And a special thanks to all the librarians and educators around the country who have championed Claudette's adventures all these years.

— Jorge & Rafael

First Second

Text copyright © 2018 by Jorge Aguirre
Art copyright © 2018 by Rafael Rosado
Published by First Second
First Second is an imprint of Roaring Brook Press, a division of Holtzbrinck Publishing Holdings Limited Partnership
175 Fifth Avenue, New York, New York 10010

Library of Congress Control Number: 2017941159

ISBN: 978-1-62672-180-7

Our books may be purchased in bulk for promotional, educational, or business use. Please contact your local bookseller or the Macmillan Corporate and Premium Sales Department at (800) 221-7945 ext. 5442 or by e-mail at MacmillanSpecialMarkets@macmillan.com.

First edition, 2018
Book design by Gordon Whiteside and Rob Steen
Printed in China by 1010 Printing International Ltd., North Point, Hong Kong.
10 9 8 7 6 5 4 3 2 1

MONSTERS BEWARE!

WRITTEN BY
JORGE AGUIRRE

ART BY
RAFAEL ROSADO

STORY BY
JORGE AGUIRRE &
RAFAEL ROSADO

COLOR BY
JOHN NOVAK

:01
First Second
New York

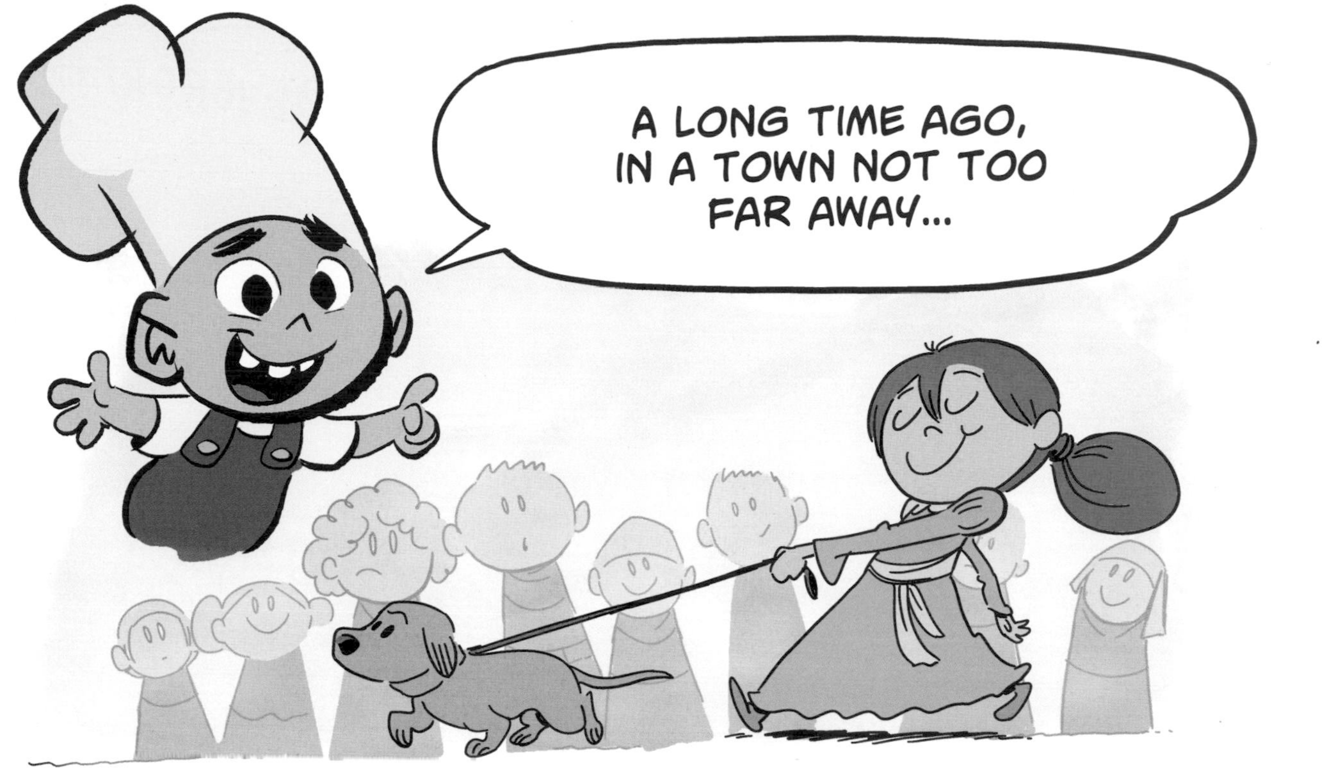
A LONG TIME AGO, IN A TOWN NOT TOO FAR AWAY...

A YOUNG GIRL FROM THE ***MOUNTAIN CITADEL*** MOVED TO ***MONT PETIT PIERRE***.

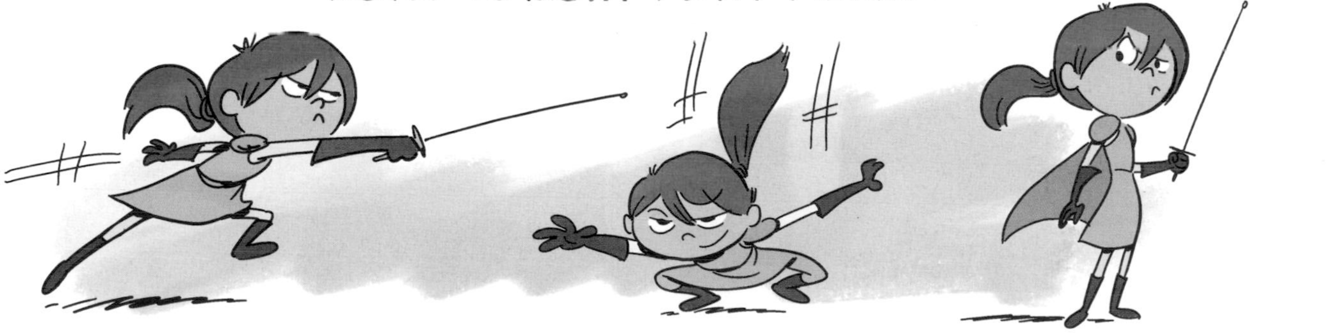

BECAUSE OF HER UNDENIABLE BATTLE SKILLS...

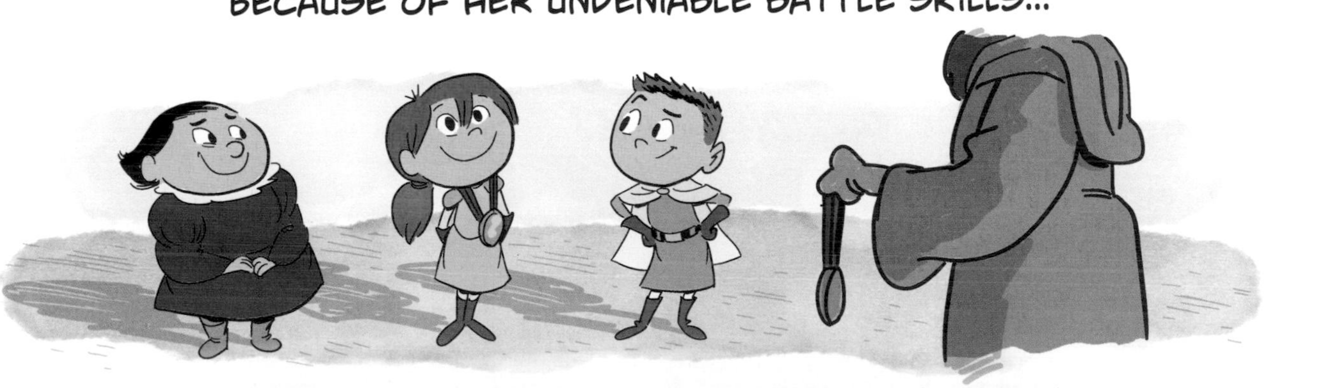

...SHE WAS CHOSEN TO REPRESENT THE TOWN IN THE ELITE ***WARRIOR GAMES***. ALONG WITH A BOY NAMED AUGUSTINE AND A YOUNG MARQUIS.

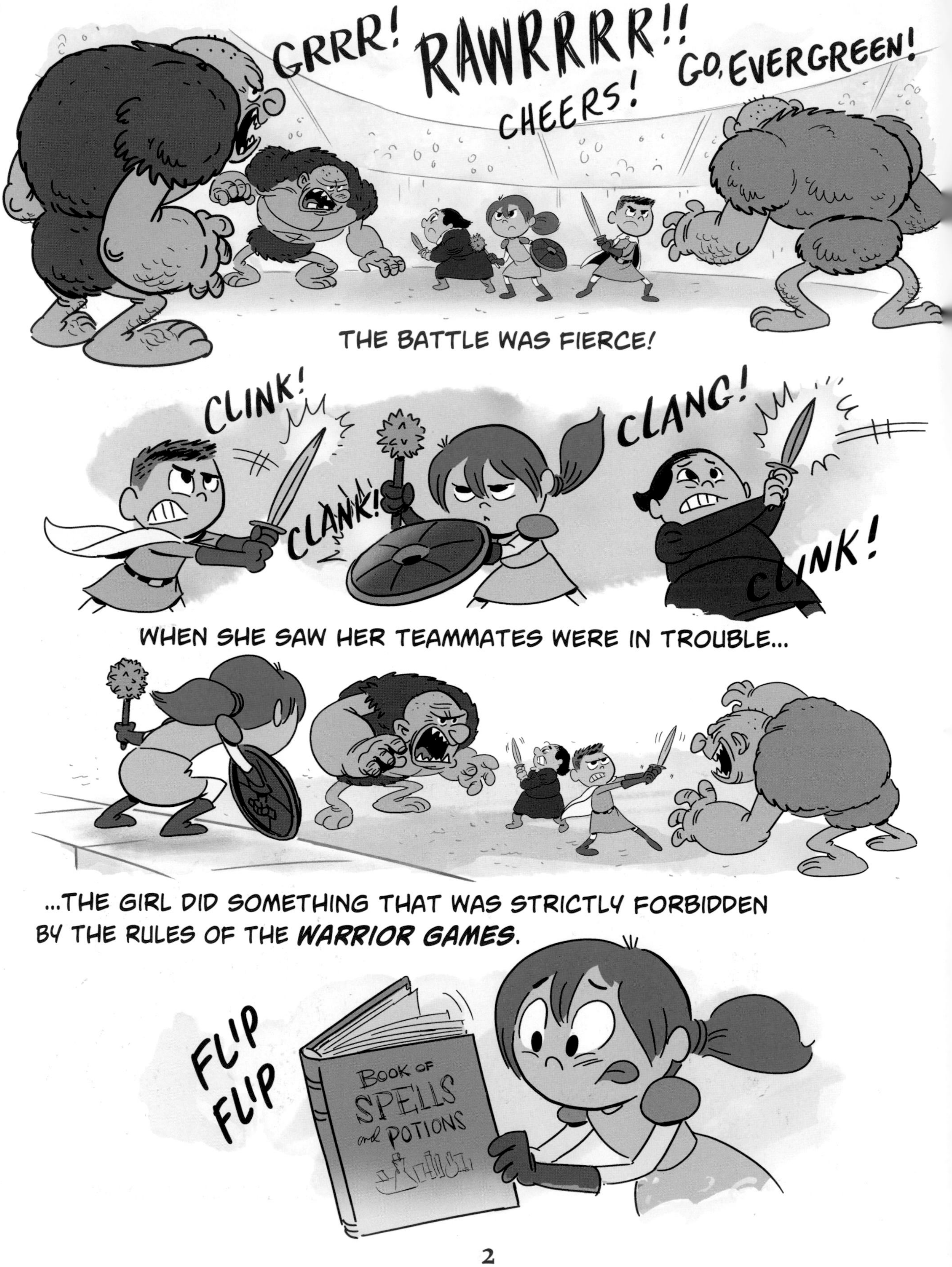
GRRR!
RAWRRRR!!
CHEERS!
GO, EVERGREEN!
THE BATTLE WAS FIERCE!
CLINK!
CLANK!
CLANG!
CLINK!
WHEN SHE SAW HER TEAMMATES WERE IN TROUBLE...
...THE GIRL DID SOMETHING THAT WAS STRICTLY FORBIDDEN BY THE RULES OF THE *WARRIOR GAMES*.
FLIP FLIP
BOOK OF SPELLS and POTIONS

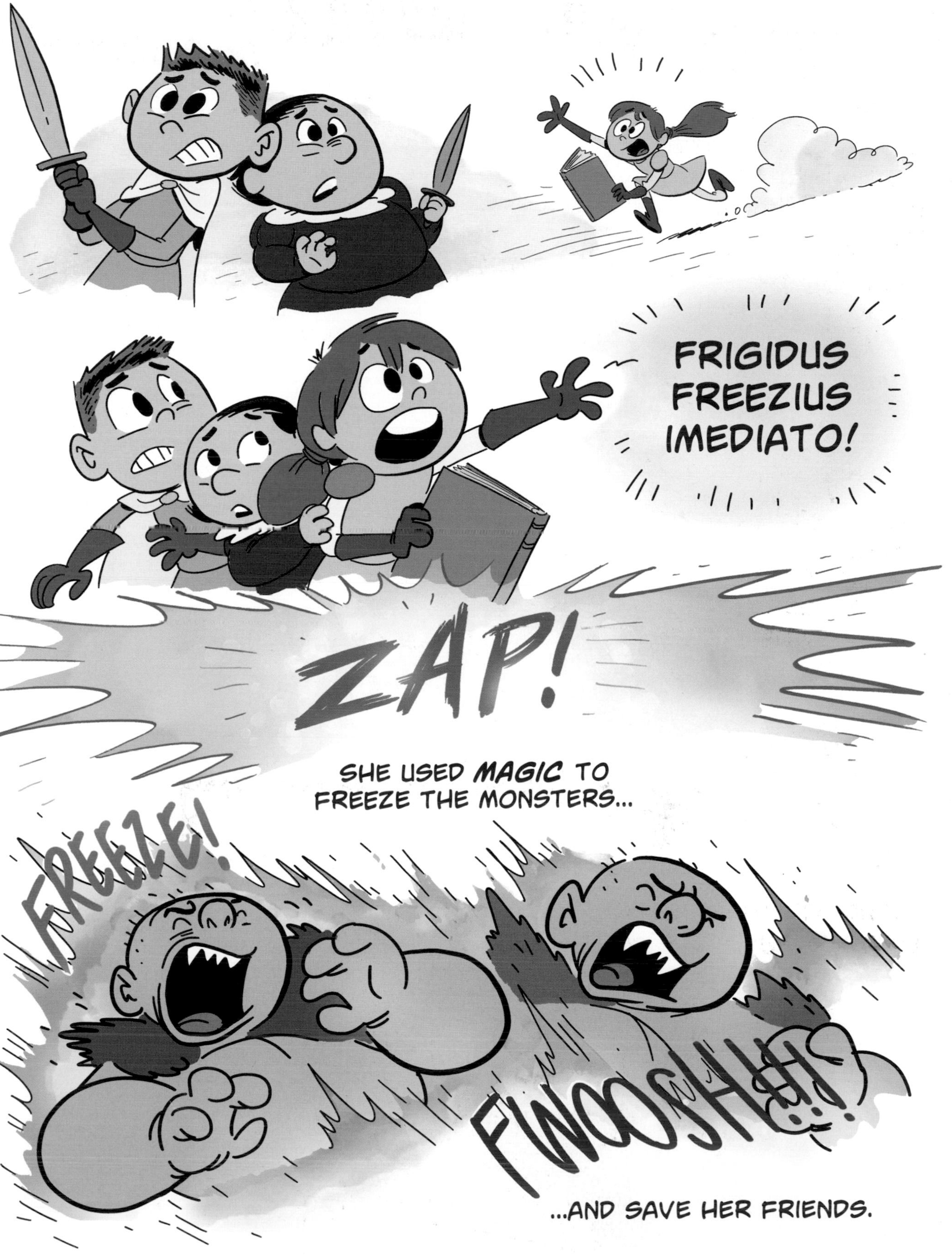
FRIGIDUS FREEZIUS IMEDIATO!
ZAP!
SHE USED MAGIC TO FREEZE THE MONSTERS...
FREEZE!
FWOOSH!!!
...AND SAVE HER FRIENDS.

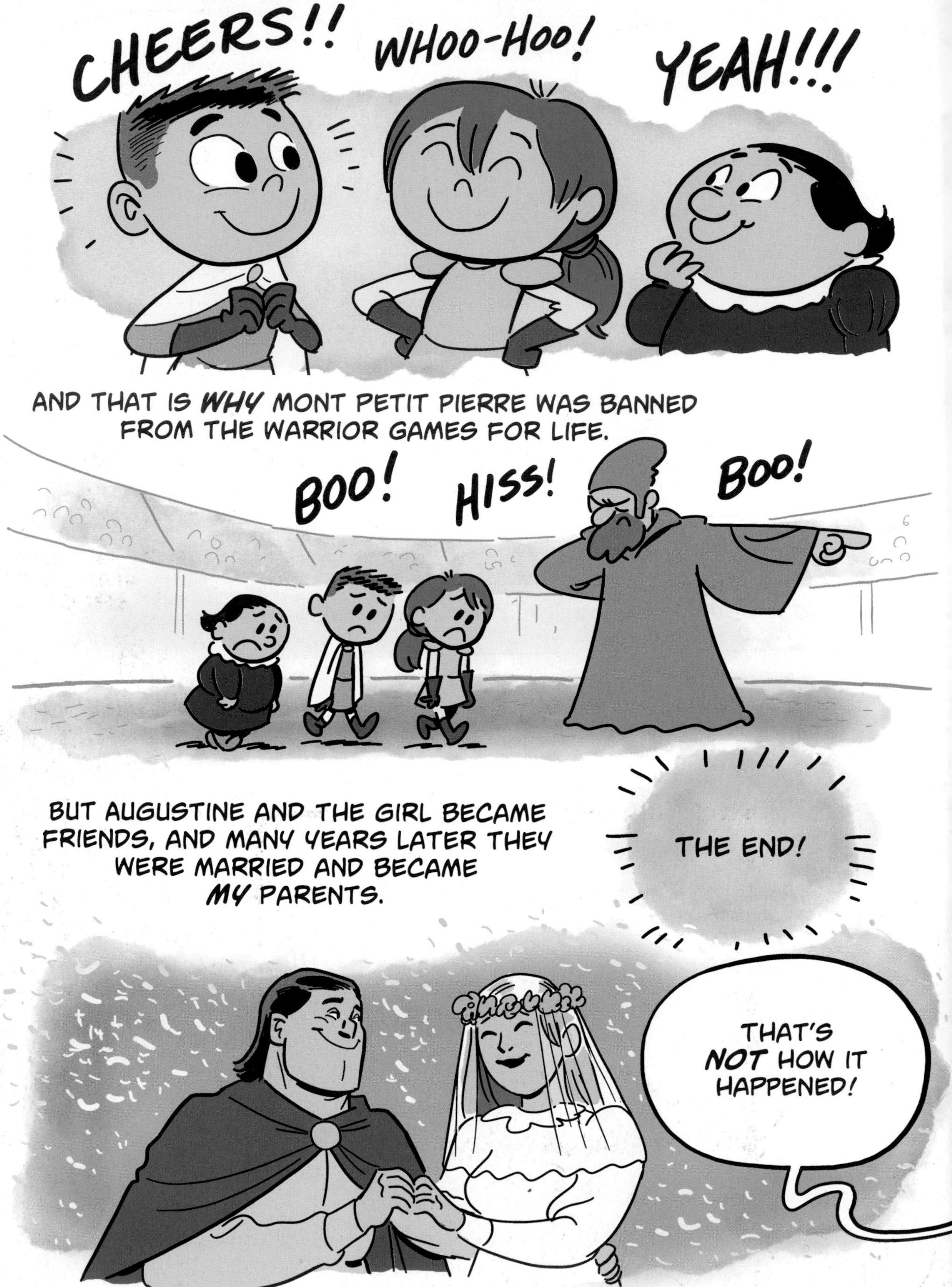
CHEERS!!
WHOO-HOO!
YEAH!!!
AND THAT IS *WHY* MONT PETIT PIERRE WAS BANNED FROM THE WARRIOR GAMES FOR LIFE.
BOO!
HISS!
BOO!
BUT AUGUSTINE AND THE GIRL BECAME FRIENDS, AND MANY YEARS LATER THEY WERE MARRIED AND BECAME *MY* PARENTS.
THE END!
THAT'S *NOT* HOW IT HAPPENED!

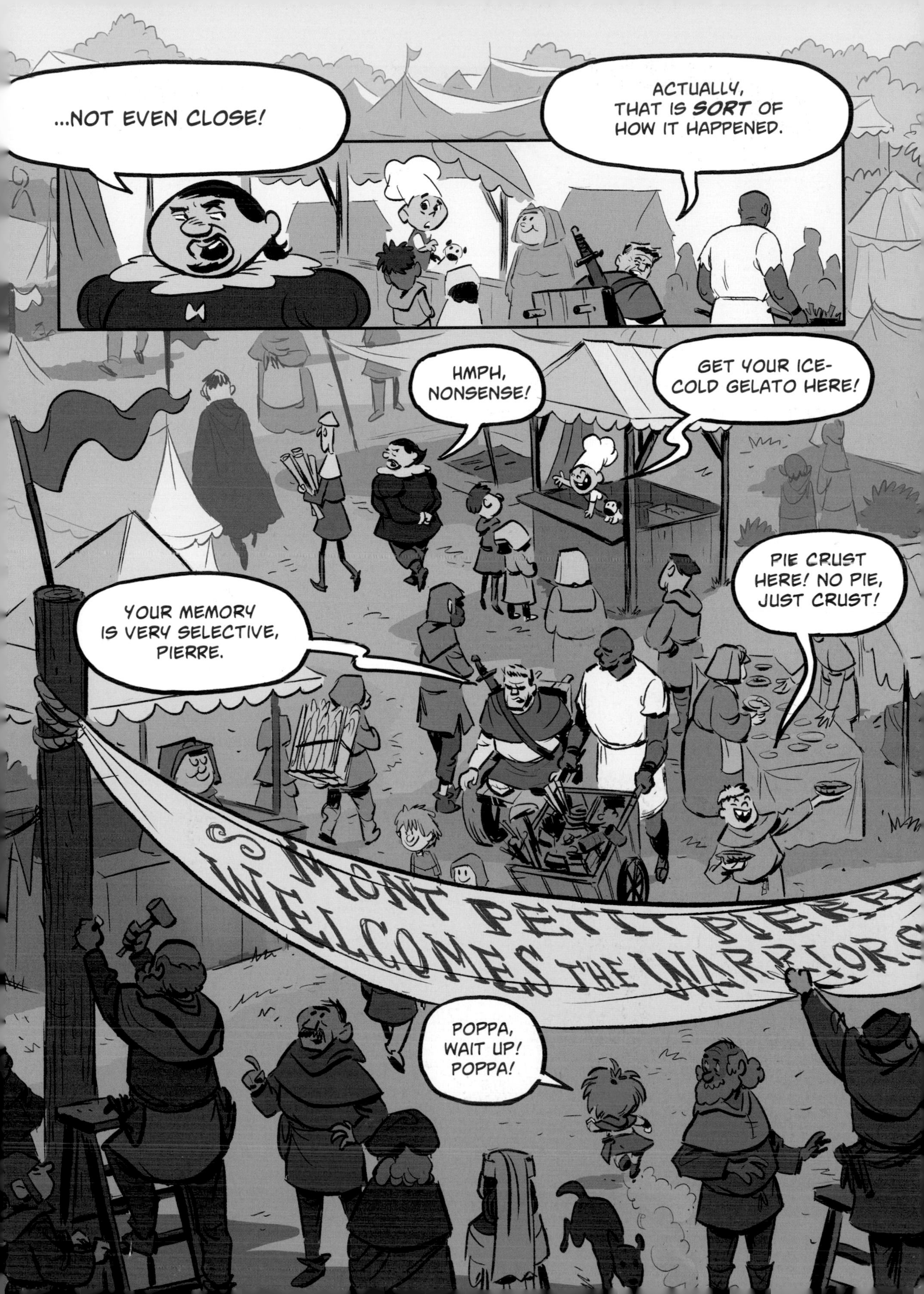

...NOT EVEN CLOSE!
ACTUALLY, THAT IS **SORT** OF HOW IT HAPPENED.
HMPH, NONSENSE!
GET YOUR ICE-COLD GELATO HERE!
PIE CRUST HERE! NO PIE, JUST CRUST!
YOUR MEMORY IS VERY SELECTIVE, PIERRE.
MONT PETIT PIERRE WELCOMES THE WARRIORS
POPPA, WAIT UP! POPPA!

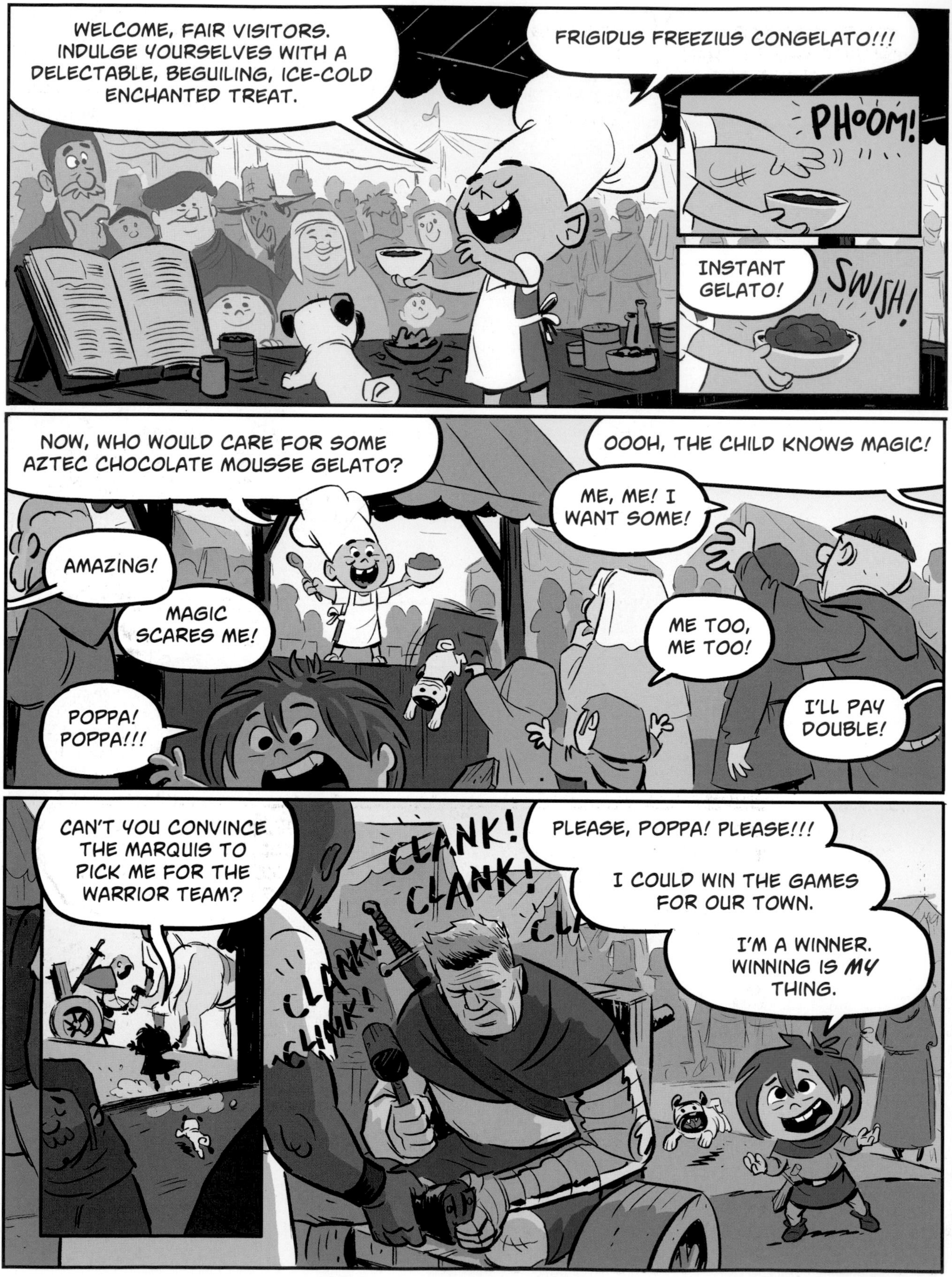
WELCOME, FAIR VISITORS. INDULGE YOURSELVES WITH A DELECTABLE, BEGUILING, ICE-COLD ENCHANTED TREAT.
FRIGIDUS FREEZIUS CONGELATO!!!
PHOOM!
INSTANT GELATO!
SWISH!
NOW, WHO WOULD CARE FOR SOME AZTEC CHOCOLATE MOUSSE GELATO?
OOOH, THE CHILD KNOWS MAGIC!
ME, ME! I WANT SOME!
AMAZING!
MAGIC SCARES ME!
ME TOO, ME TOO!
POPPA! POPPA!!!
I'LL PAY DOUBLE!
CAN'T YOU CONVINCE THE MARQUIS TO PICK ME FOR THE WARRIOR TEAM?
CLANK! CLANK!
CLANK! CLANK!
PLEASE, POPPA! PLEASE!!!
I COULD WIN THE GAMES FOR OUR TOWN.
I'M A WINNER. WINNING IS *MY* THING.

THERE ARE MORE IMPORTANT THINGS THAN WINNING, CLAUDETTE.

SURE...

THERE'S ALSO HONOR, GLORY, AND BASHING MONSTERS FOR THE FUN OF IT.

BUT WINNING IS MY *MAIN* THING.

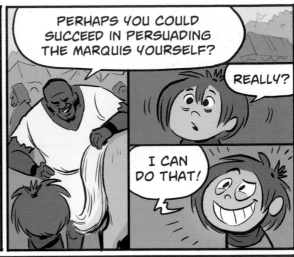

PERHAPS YOU COULD SUCCEED IN PERSUADING THE MARQUIS YOURSELF?

REALLY?

I CAN DO THAT!

HEY, MARQUIS, PICK ME FOR THE WARRIOR TEAM. PICK ME, PICK ME, PICK ME, PICK ME!

WE CAN PUT THE DAIS RIGHT HERE...

PICK *YOU* TO REPRESENT OUR TOWN IN THE WARRIOR GAMES? NO, I WILL NEVER, EVER PICK YOU.

SO THERE'S ROOM FOR COMPROMISE, RIGHT?

OH, MISGUIDED CLAUDETTE...

IT WAS DIFFICULT ENOUGH FOR ME TO CONVINCE THE TRIBUNAL TO ALLOW OUR TOWN TO COMPETE AGAIN.

OF COURSE, IT HELPED THAT I PROMISED TO BUILD THE *GREATEST* COLISEUM THE GAMES HAVE EVER BEEN HELD IN.

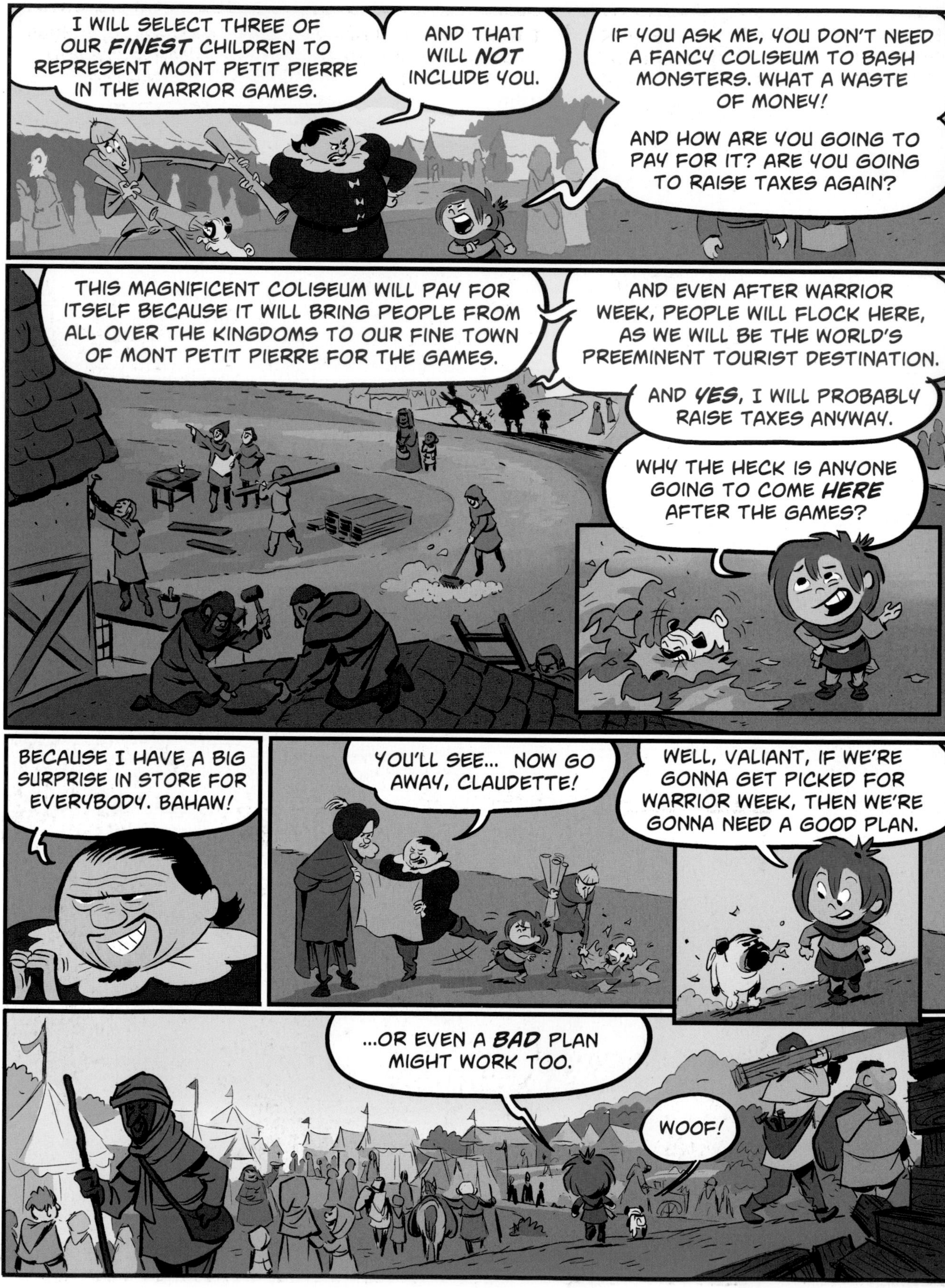
I WILL SELECT THREE OF OUR FINEST CHILDREN TO REPRESENT MONT PETIT PIERRE IN THE WARRIOR GAMES.
AND THAT WILL NOT INCLUDE YOU.
IF YOU ASK ME, YOU DON'T NEED A FANCY COLISEUM TO BASH MONSTERS. WHAT A WASTE OF MONEY!
AND HOW ARE YOU GOING TO PAY FOR IT? ARE YOU GOING TO RAISE TAXES AGAIN?
THIS MAGNIFICENT COLISEUM WILL PAY FOR ITSELF BECAUSE IT WILL BRING PEOPLE FROM ALL OVER THE KINGDOMS TO OUR FINE TOWN OF MONT PETIT PIERRE FOR THE GAMES.
AND EVEN AFTER WARRIOR WEEK, PEOPLE WILL FLOCK HERE, AS WE WILL BE THE WORLD'S PREEMINENT TOURIST DESTINATION.
AND YES, I WILL PROBABLY RAISE TAXES ANYWAY.
WHY THE HECK IS ANYONE GOING TO COME HERE AFTER THE GAMES?
BECAUSE I HAVE A BIG SURPRISE IN STORE FOR EVERYBODY. BAHAW!
YOU'LL SEE... NOW GO AWAY, CLAUDETTE!
WELL, VALIANT, IF WE'RE GONNA GET PICKED FOR WARRIOR WEEK, THEN WE'RE GONNA NEED A GOOD PLAN.
...OR EVEN A BAD PLAN MIGHT WORK TOO.
WOOF!

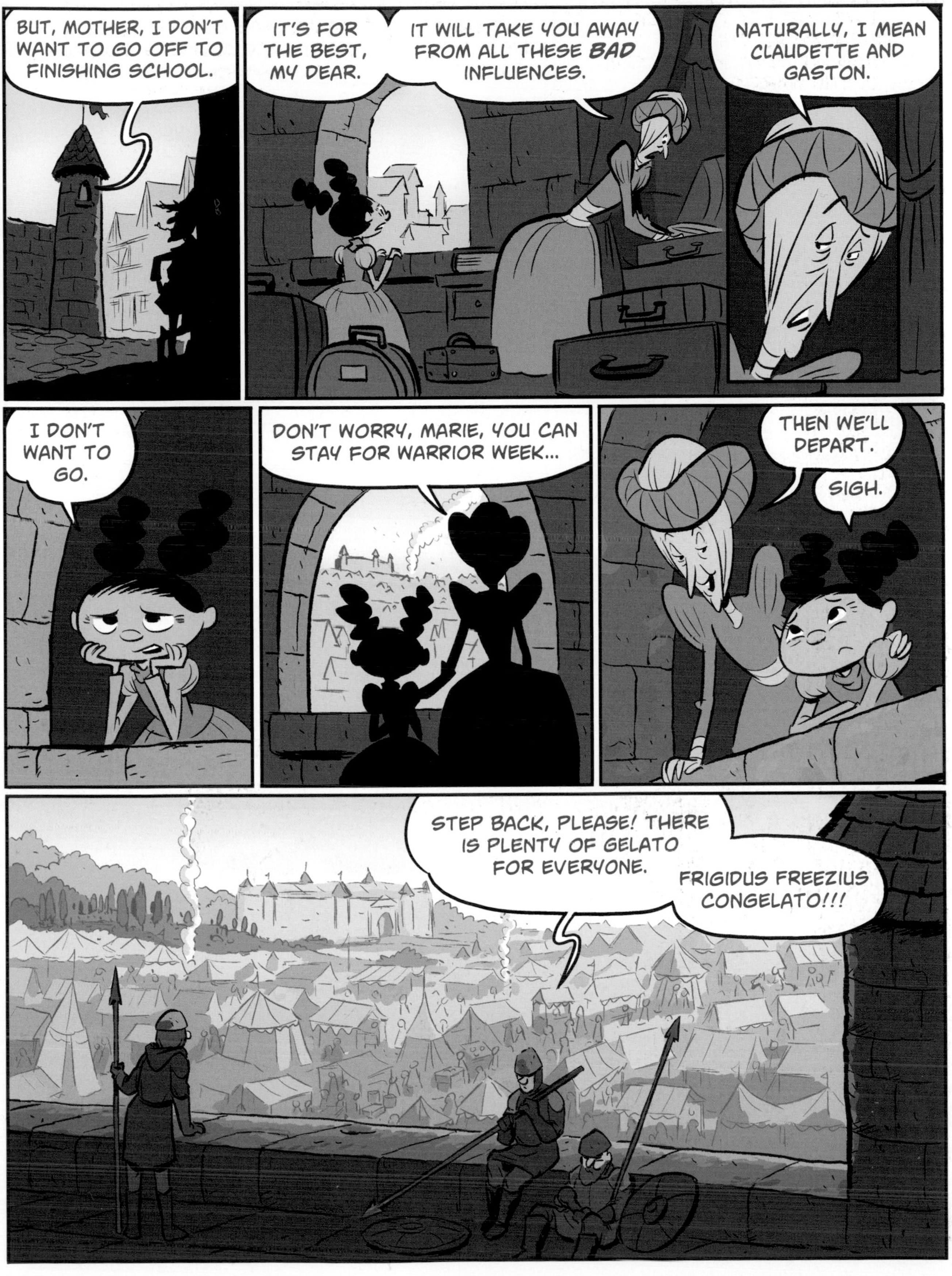
BUT, MOTHER, I DON'T WANT TO GO OFF TO FINISHING SCHOOL.
IT'S FOR THE BEST, MY DEAR.
IT WILL TAKE YOU AWAY FROM ALL THESE *BAD* INFLUENCES.
NATURALLY, I MEAN CLAUDETTE AND GASTON.
I DON'T WANT TO GO.
DON'T WORRY, MARIE, YOU CAN STAY FOR WARRIOR WEEK...
THEN WE'LL DEPART.
SIGH.
STEP BACK, PLEASE! THERE IS PLENTY OF GELATO FOR EVERYONE.
FRIGIDUS FREEZIUS CONGELATO!!!

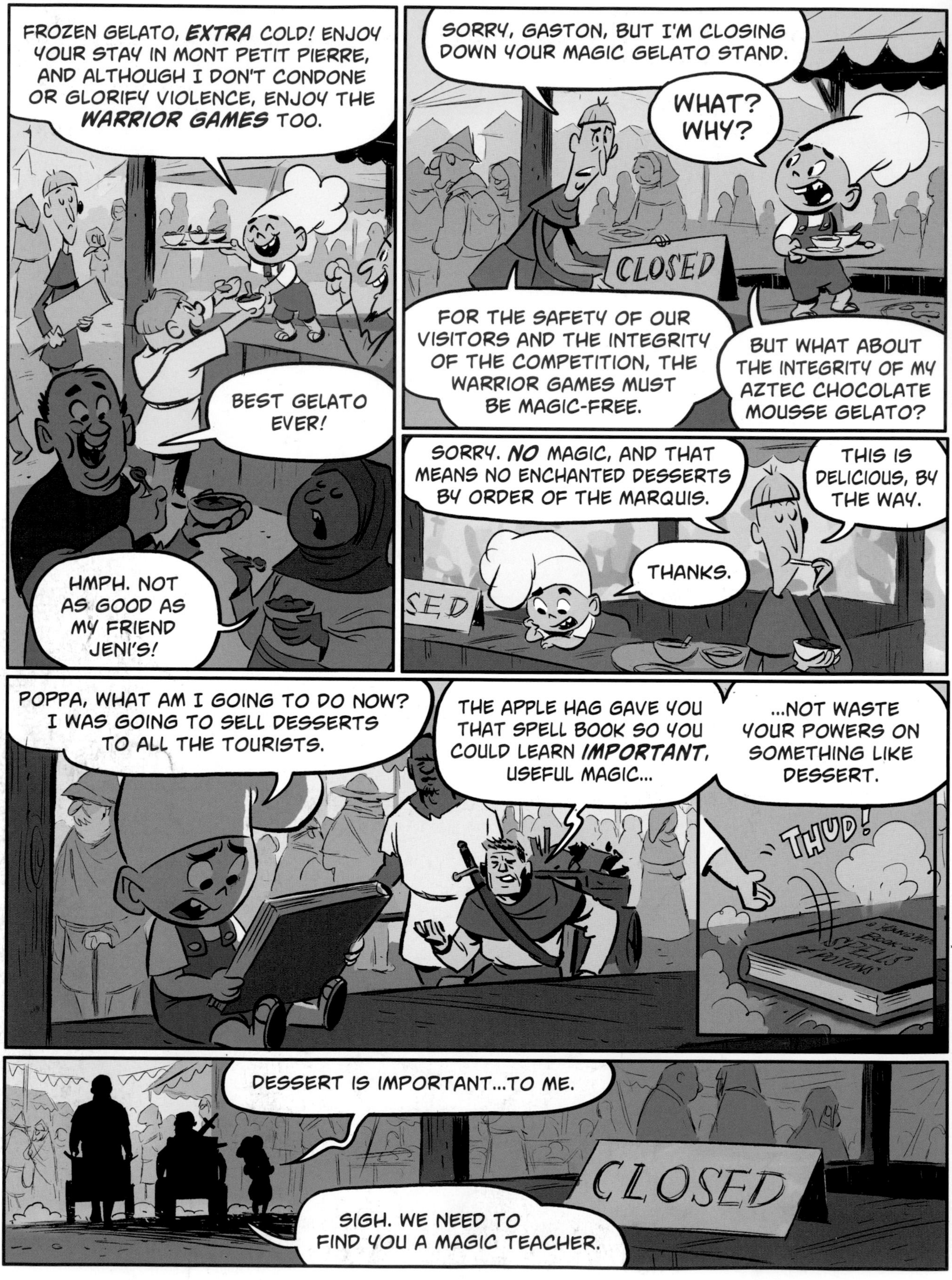
FROZEN GELATO, ***EXTRA*** COLD! ENJOY YOUR STAY IN MONT PETIT PIERRE, AND ALTHOUGH I DON'T CONDONE OR GLORIFY VIOLENCE, ENJOY THE ***WARRIOR GAMES*** TOO.
BEST GELATO EVER!
HMPH. NOT AS GOOD AS MY FRIEND JENI'S!
SORRY, GASTON, BUT I'M CLOSING DOWN YOUR MAGIC GELATO STAND.
WHAT? WHY?
CLOSED
FOR THE SAFETY OF OUR VISITORS AND THE INTEGRITY OF THE COMPETITION, THE WARRIOR GAMES MUST BE MAGIC-FREE.
BUT WHAT ABOUT THE INTEGRITY OF MY AZTEC CHOCOLATE MOUSSE GELATO?
SORRY. ***NO*** MAGIC, AND THAT MEANS NO ENCHANTED DESSERTS BY ORDER OF THE MARQUIS.
THIS IS DELICIOUS, BY THE WAY.
SED
THANKS.
POPPA, WHAT AM I GOING TO DO NOW? I WAS GOING TO SELL DESSERTS TO ALL THE TOURISTS.
THE APPLE HAG GAVE YOU THAT SPELL BOOK SO YOU COULD LEARN ***IMPORTANT***, USEFUL MAGIC...
...NOT WASTE YOUR POWERS ON SOMETHING LIKE DESSERT.
THUD!
DESSERT IS IMPORTANT...TO ME.
CLOSED
SIGH. WE NEED TO FIND YOU A MAGIC TEACHER.

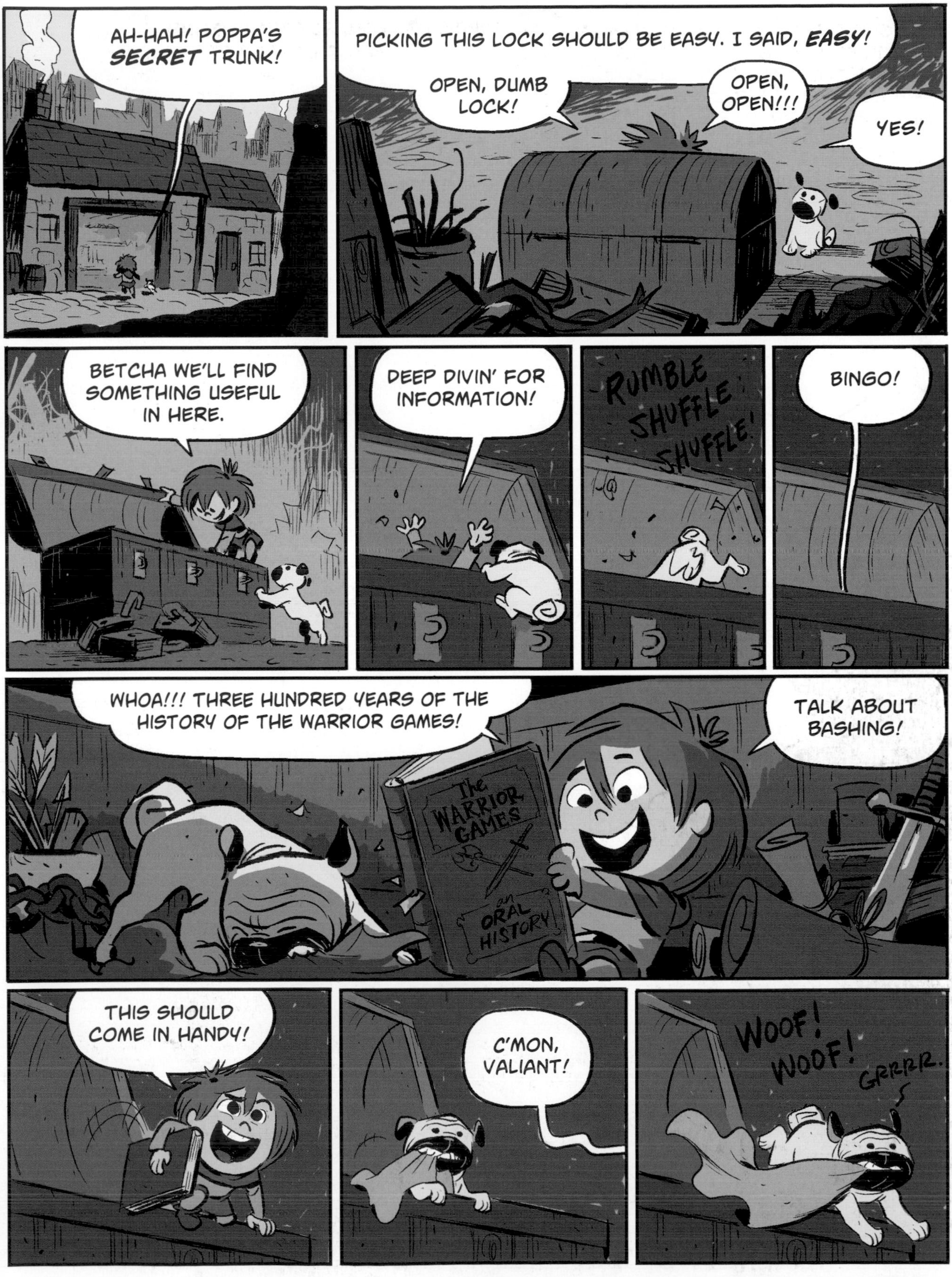
AH-HAH! POPPA'S SECRET TRUNK!
PICKING THIS LOCK SHOULD BE EASY. I SAID, EASY!
OPEN, DUMB LOCK!
OPEN, OPEN!!!
YES!
BETCHA WE'LL FIND SOMETHING USEFUL IN HERE.
DEEP DIVIN' FOR INFORMATION!
RUMBLE SHUFFLE SHUFFLE!
BINGO!
WHOA!!! THREE HUNDRED YEARS OF THE HISTORY OF THE WARRIOR GAMES!
The WARRIOR GAMES
an ORAL HISTORY
TALK ABOUT BASHING!
THIS SHOULD COME IN HANDY!
C'MON, VALIANT!
WOOF! WOOF!
GRRRR.

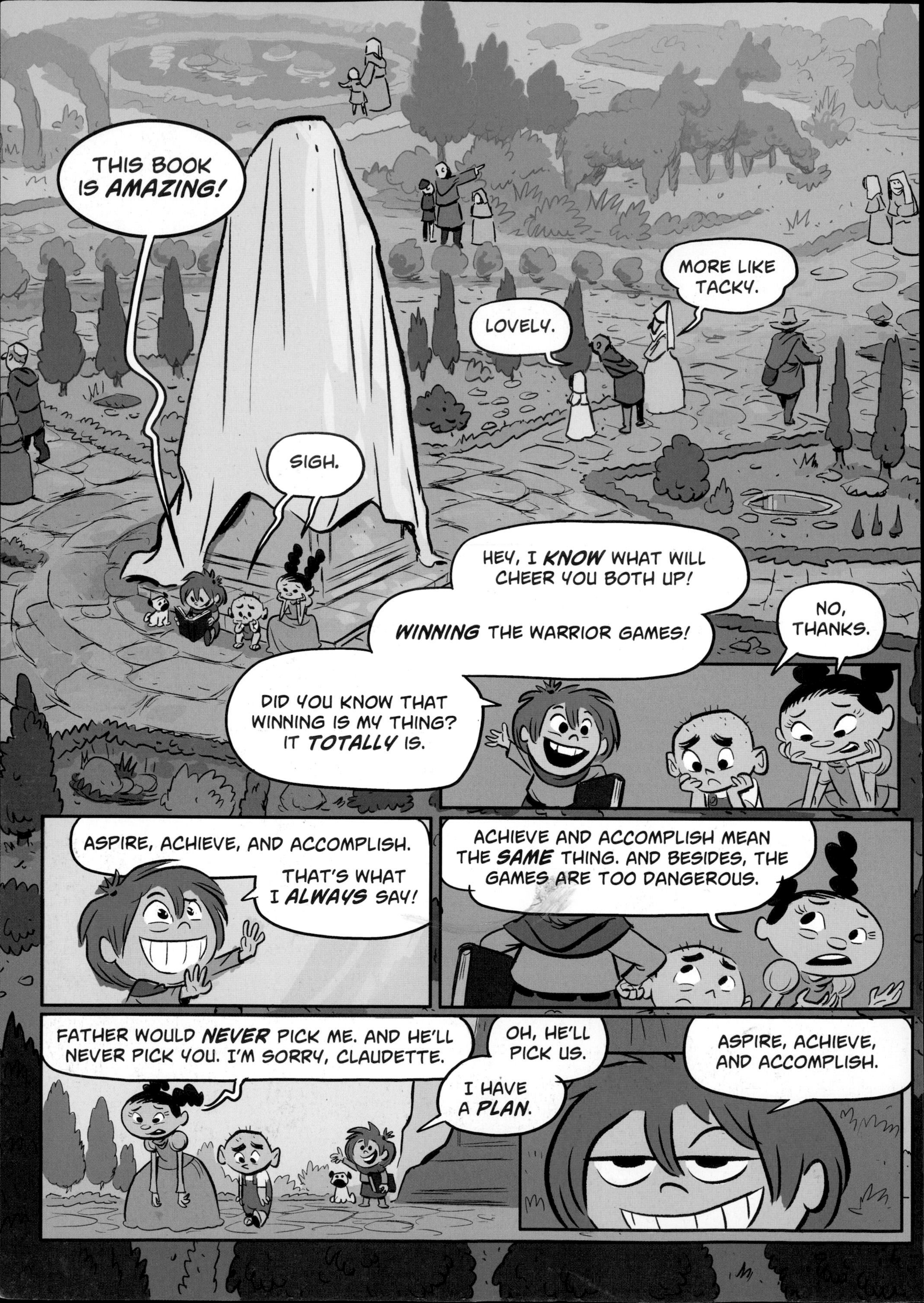
THIS BOOK IS AMAZING!
SIGH.
LOVELY.
MORE LIKE TACKY.
HEY, I KNOW WHAT WILL CHEER YOU BOTH UP!
WINNING THE WARRIOR GAMES!
DID YOU KNOW THAT WINNING IS MY THING? IT TOTALLY IS.
NO, THANKS.
ASPIRE, ACHIEVE, AND ACCOMPLISH.
THAT'S WHAT I ALWAYS SAY!
ACHIEVE AND ACCOMPLISH MEAN THE SAME THING. AND BESIDES, THE GAMES ARE TOO DANGEROUS.
FATHER WOULD NEVER PICK ME. AND HE'LL NEVER PICK YOU. I'M SORRY, CLAUDETTE.
OH, HE'LL PICK US.
I HAVE A PLAN.
ASPIRE, ACHIEVE, AND ACCOMPLISH.

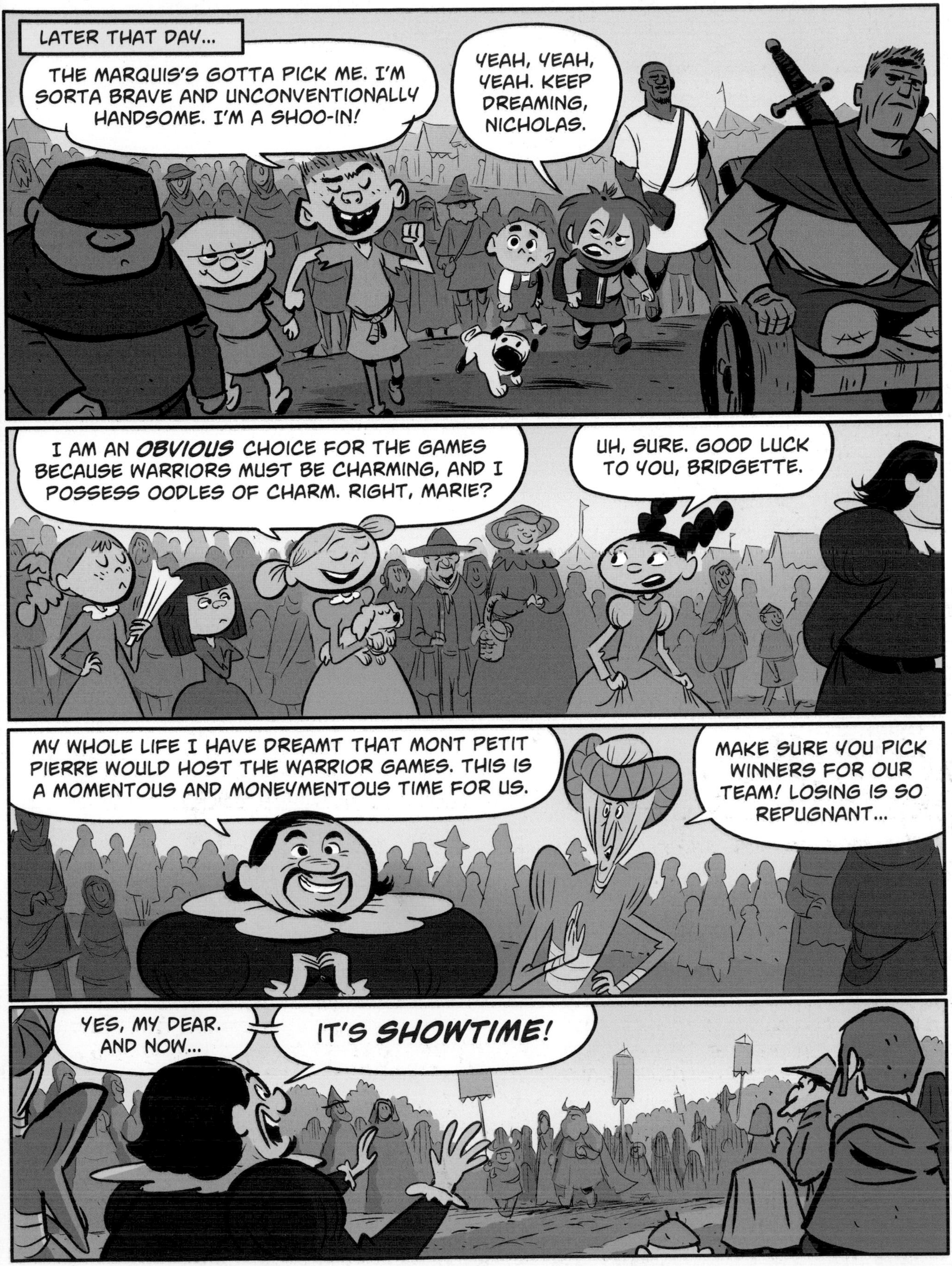
LATER THAT DAY...
THE MARQUIS'S GOTTA PICK ME. I'M SORTA BRAVE AND UNCONVENTIONALLY HANDSOME. I'M A SHOO-IN!
YEAH, YEAH, YEAH. KEEP DREAMING, NICHOLAS.
I AM AN *OBVIOUS* CHOICE FOR THE GAMES BECAUSE WARRIORS MUST BE CHARMING, AND I POSSESS OODLES OF CHARM. RIGHT, MARIE?
UH, SURE. GOOD LUCK TO YOU, BRIDGETTE.
MY WHOLE LIFE I HAVE DREAMT THAT MONT PETIT PIERRE WOULD HOST THE WARRIOR GAMES. THIS IS A MOMENTOUS AND MONEYMENTOUS TIME FOR US.
MAKE SURE YOU PICK WINNERS FOR OUR TEAM! LOSING IS SO REPUGNANT...
YES, MY DEAR. AND NOW...
IT'S *SHOWTIME*!

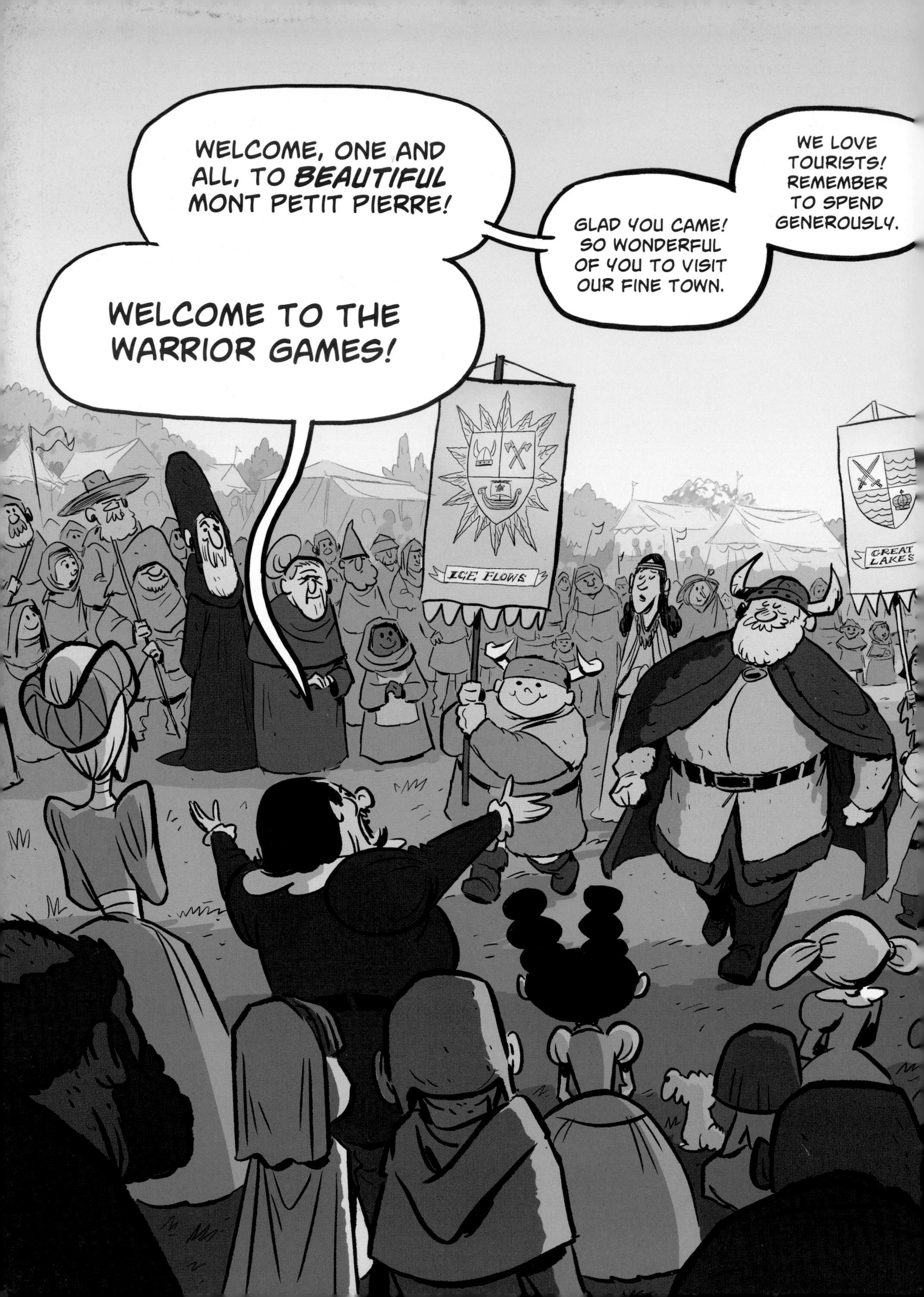
WELCOME, ONE AND ALL, TO *BEAUTIFUL* MONT PETIT PIERRE!
WELCOME TO THE WARRIOR GAMES!
GLAD YOU CAME! SO WONDERFUL OF YOU TO VISIT OUR FINE TOWN.
WE LOVE TOURISTS! REMEMBER TO SPEND GENEROUSLY.
ICE FLOWS
GREAT LAKES

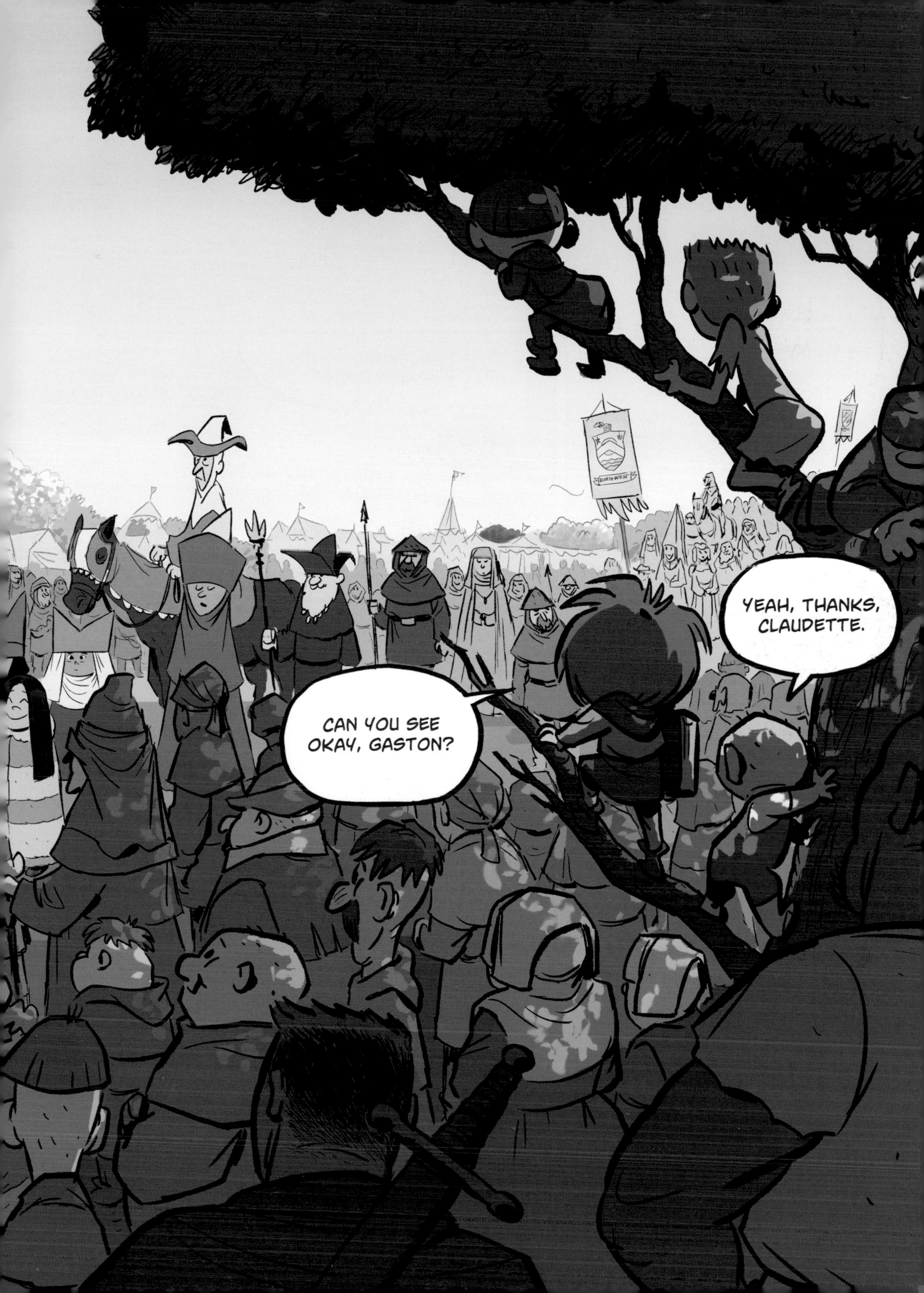
YEAH, THANKS, CLAUDETTE.
CAN YOU SEE OKAY, GASTON?

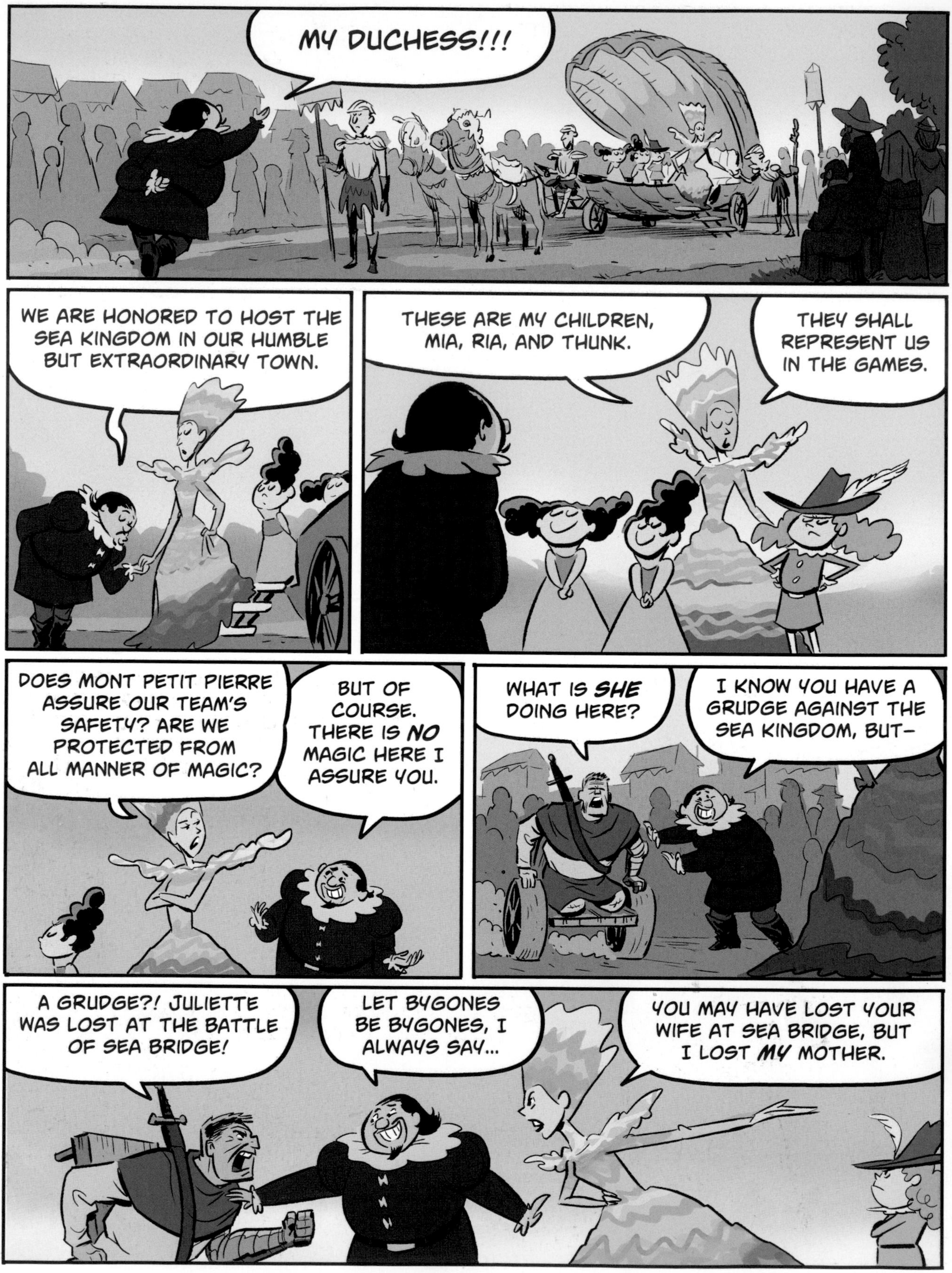

MY DUCHESS!!!
WE ARE HONORED TO HOST THE SEA KINGDOM IN OUR HUMBLE BUT EXTRAORDINARY TOWN.
THESE ARE MY CHILDREN, MIA, RIA, AND THUNK.
THEY SHALL REPRESENT US IN THE GAMES.
DOES MONT PETIT PIERRE ASSURE OUR TEAM'S SAFETY? ARE WE PROTECTED FROM ALL MANNER OF MAGIC?
BUT OF COURSE. THERE IS *NO* MAGIC HERE I ASSURE YOU.
WHAT IS *SHE* DOING HERE?
I KNOW YOU HAVE A GRUDGE AGAINST THE SEA KINGDOM, BUT–
A GRUDGE?! JULIETTE WAS LOST AT THE BATTLE OF SEA BRIDGE!
LET BYGONES BE BYGONES, I ALWAYS SAY...
YOU MAY HAVE LOST YOUR WIFE AT SEA BRIDGE, BUT I LOST *MY* MOTHER.

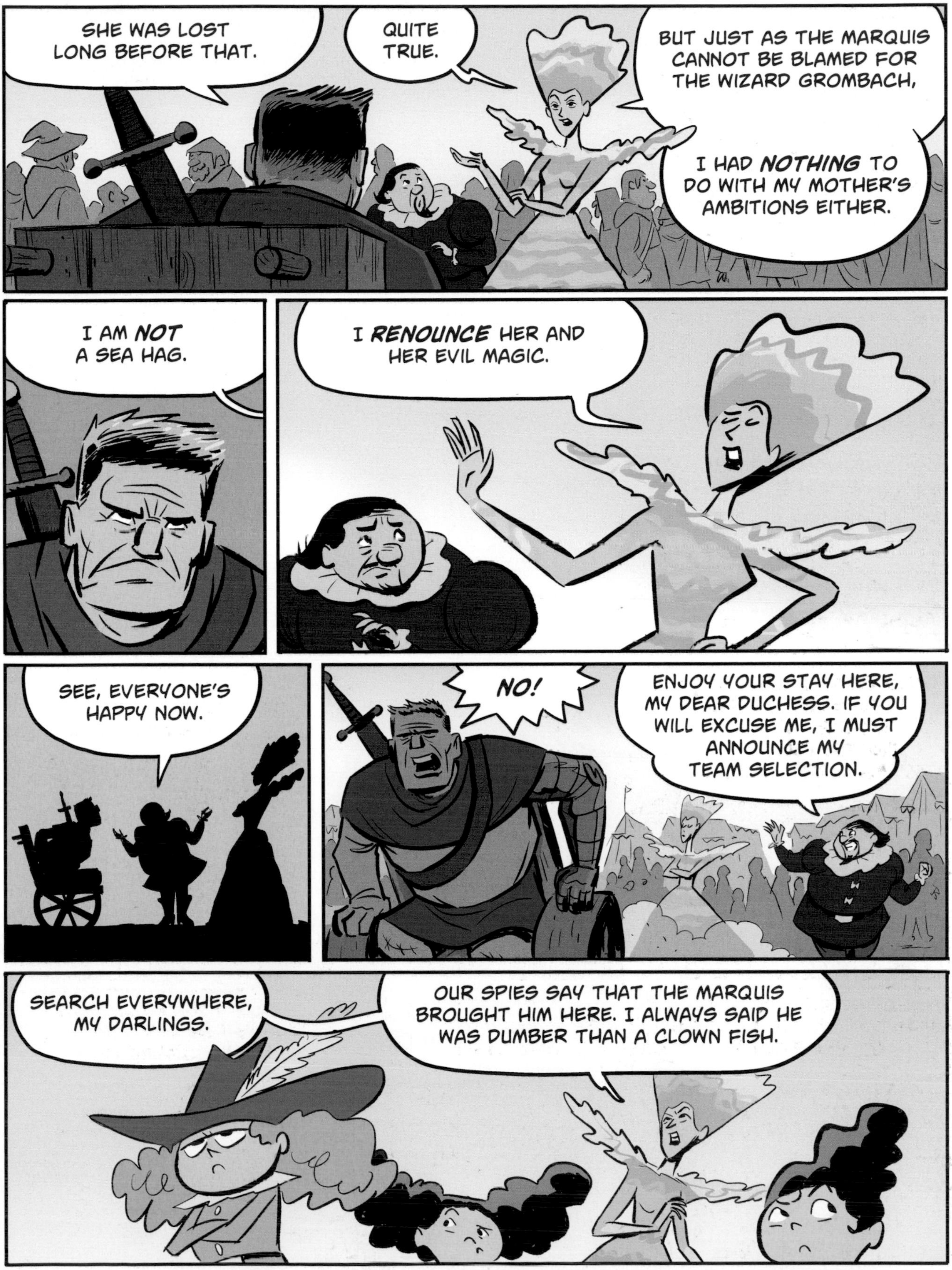
SHE WAS LOST LONG BEFORE THAT.
QUITE TRUE.
BUT JUST AS THE MARQUIS CANNOT BE BLAMED FOR THE WIZARD GROMBACH,
I HAD ***NOTHING*** TO DO WITH MY MOTHER'S AMBITIONS EITHER.
I AM ***NOT*** A SEA HAG.
I ***RENOUNCE*** HER AND HER EVIL MAGIC.
SEE, EVERYONE'S HAPPY NOW.
NO!
ENJOY YOUR STAY HERE, MY DEAR DUCHESS. IF YOU WILL EXCUSE ME, I MUST ANNOUNCE MY TEAM SELECTION.
SEARCH EVERYWHERE, MY DARLINGS.
OUR SPIES SAY THAT THE MARQUIS BROUGHT HIM HERE. I ALWAYS SAID HE WAS DUMBER THAN A CLOWN FISH.

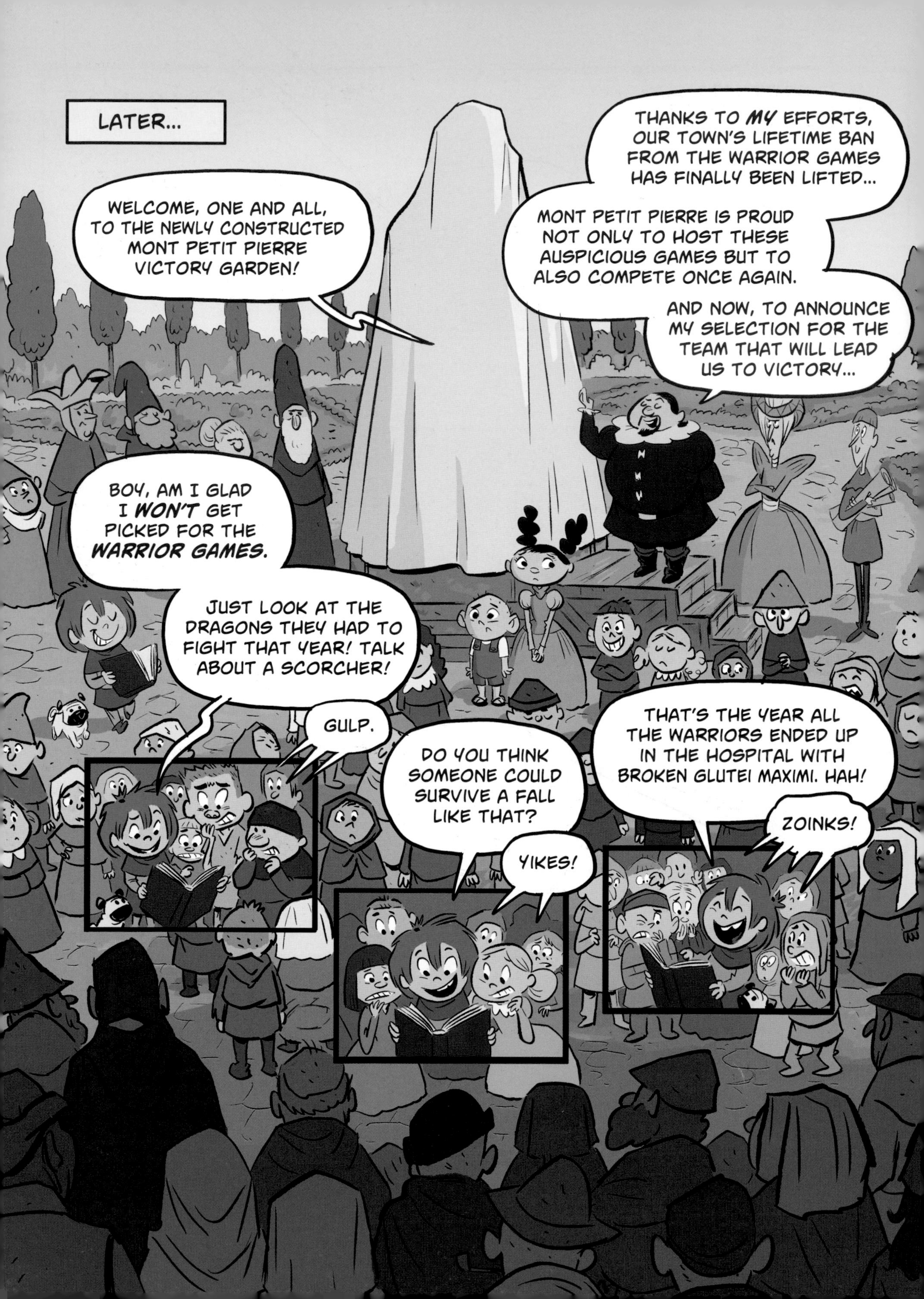
LATER...
WELCOME, ONE AND ALL, TO THE NEWLY CONSTRUCTED MONT PETIT PIERRE VICTORY GARDEN!
THANKS TO MY EFFORTS, OUR TOWN'S LIFETIME BAN FROM THE WARRIOR GAMES HAS FINALLY BEEN LIFTED...
MONT PETIT PIERRE IS PROUD NOT ONLY TO HOST THESE AUSPICIOUS GAMES BUT TO ALSO COMPETE ONCE AGAIN.
AND NOW, TO ANNOUNCE MY SELECTION FOR THE TEAM THAT WILL LEAD US TO VICTORY...
BOY, AM I GLAD I WON'T GET PICKED FOR THE WARRIOR GAMES.
JUST LOOK AT THE DRAGONS THEY HAD TO FIGHT THAT YEAR! TALK ABOUT A SCORCHER!
GULP.
DO YOU THINK SOMEONE COULD SURVIVE A FALL LIKE THAT?
YIKES!
THAT'S THE YEAR ALL THE WARRIORS ENDED UP IN THE HOSPITAL WITH BROKEN GLUTEI MAXIMI. HAH!
ZOINKS!

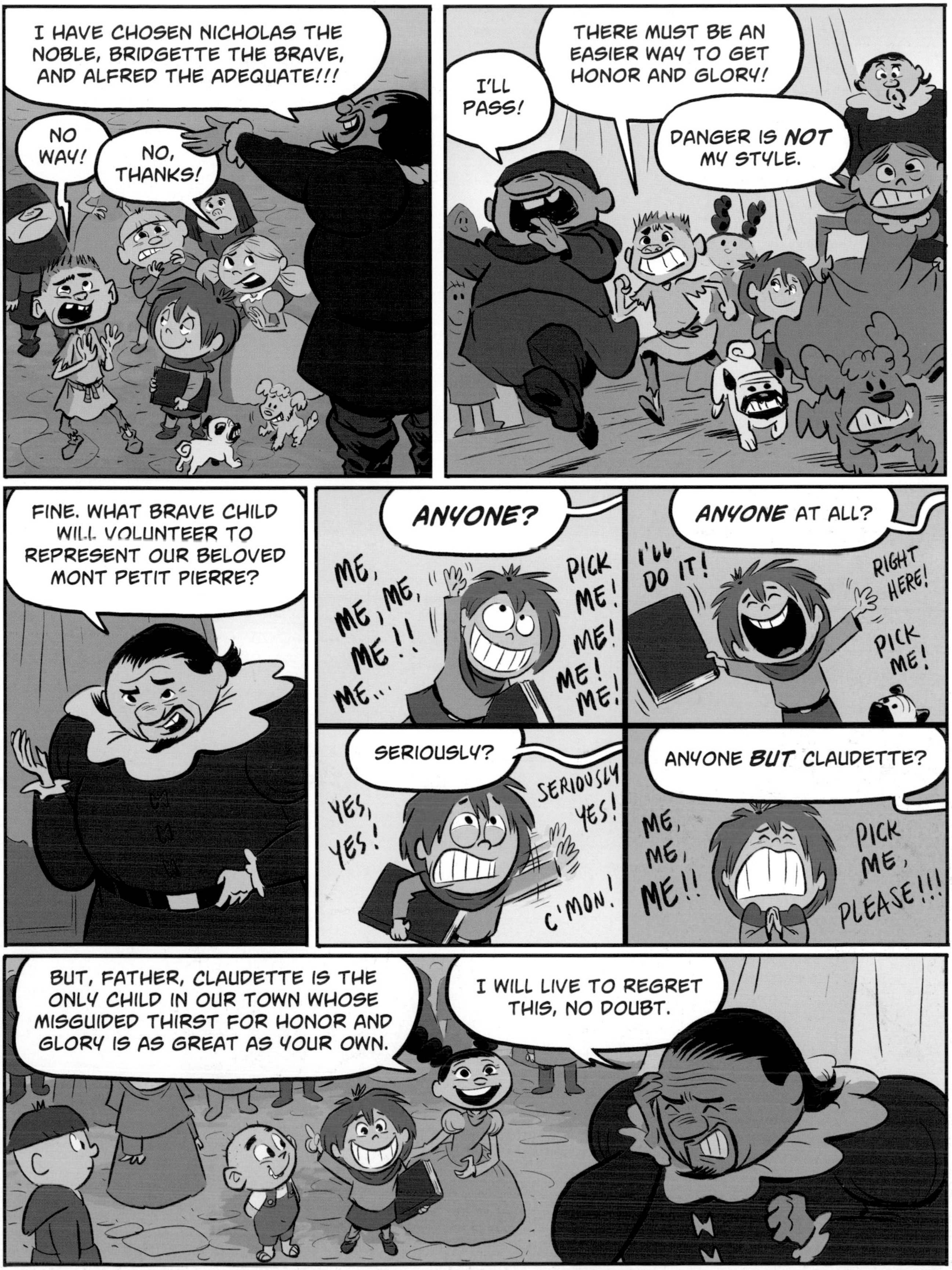
I HAVE CHOSEN NICHOLAS THE NOBLE, BRIDGETTE THE BRAVE, AND ALFRED THE ADEQUATE!!!
NO WAY!
NO, THANKS!
I'LL PASS!
THERE MUST BE AN EASIER WAY TO GET HONOR AND GLORY!
DANGER IS NOT MY STYLE.
FINE. WHAT BRAVE CHILD WILL VOLUNTEER TO REPRESENT OUR BELOVED MONT PETIT PIERRE?
ANYONE?
ME, ME, ME, ME!! ME...
PICK ME! ME! ME! ME!
ANYONE AT ALL?
I'LL DO IT!
RIGHT HERE!
PICK ME!
SERIOUSLY?
YES, YES!
SERIOUSLY YES!
C'MON!
ANYONE BUT CLAUDETTE?
ME, ME, ME!!
PICK ME, PLEASE!!!
BUT, FATHER, CLAUDETTE IS THE ONLY CHILD IN OUR TOWN WHOSE MISGUIDED THIRST FOR HONOR AND GLORY IS AS GREAT AS YOUR OWN.
I WILL LIVE TO REGRET THIS, NO DOUBT.

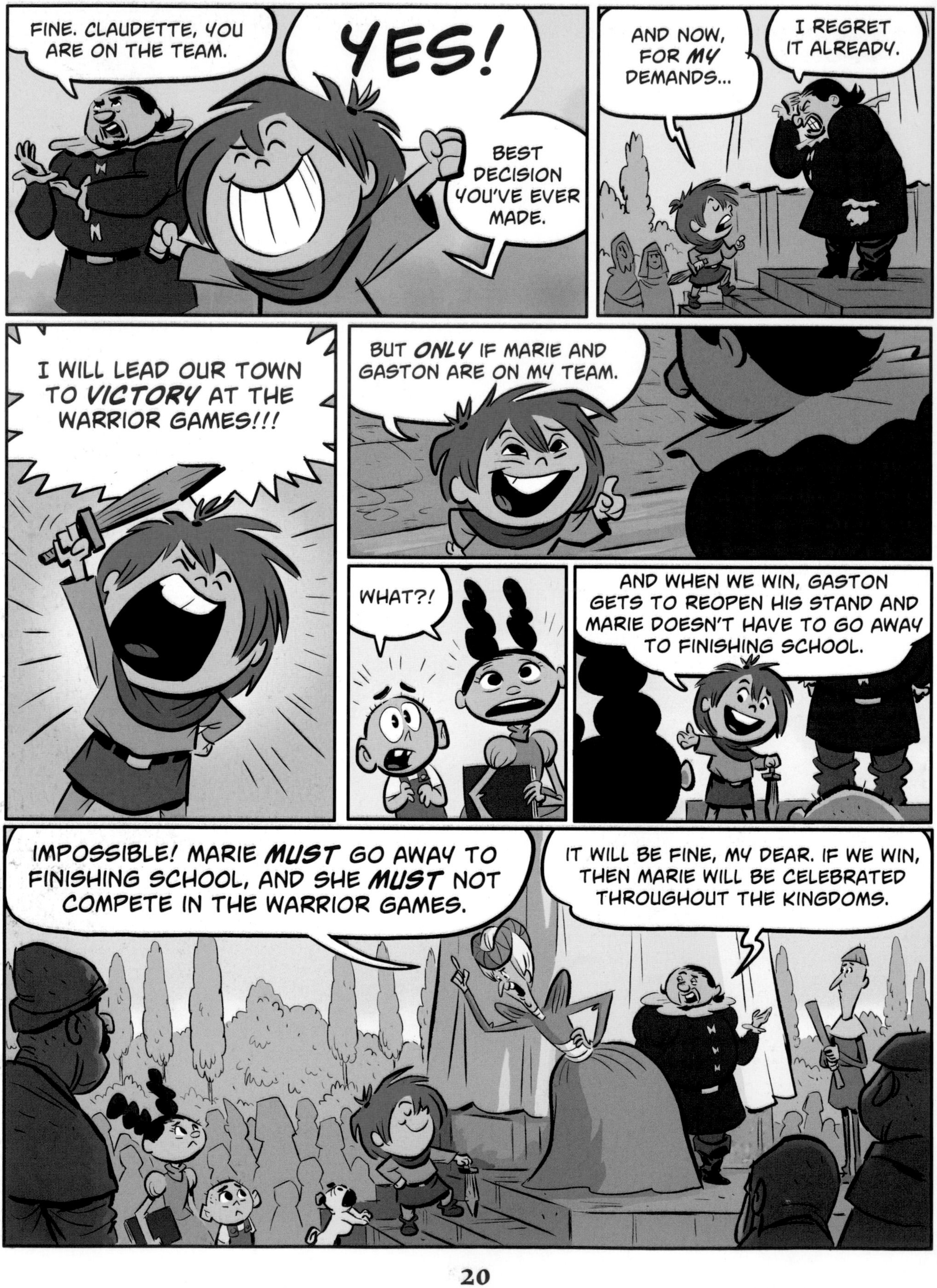
FINE. CLAUDETTE, YOU ARE ON THE TEAM.
YES!
BEST DECISION YOU'VE EVER MADE.
AND NOW, FOR MY DEMANDS...
I REGRET IT ALREADY.
I WILL LEAD OUR TOWN TO VICTORY AT THE WARRIOR GAMES!!!
BUT ONLY IF MARIE AND GASTON ARE ON MY TEAM.
WHAT?!
AND WHEN WE WIN, GASTON GETS TO REOPEN HIS STAND AND MARIE DOESN'T HAVE TO GO AWAY TO FINISHING SCHOOL.
IMPOSSIBLE! MARIE MUST GO AWAY TO FINISHING SCHOOL, AND SHE MUST NOT COMPETE IN THE WARRIOR GAMES.
IT WILL BE FINE, MY DEAR. IF WE WIN, THEN MARIE WILL BE CELEBRATED THROUGHOUT THE KINGDOMS.

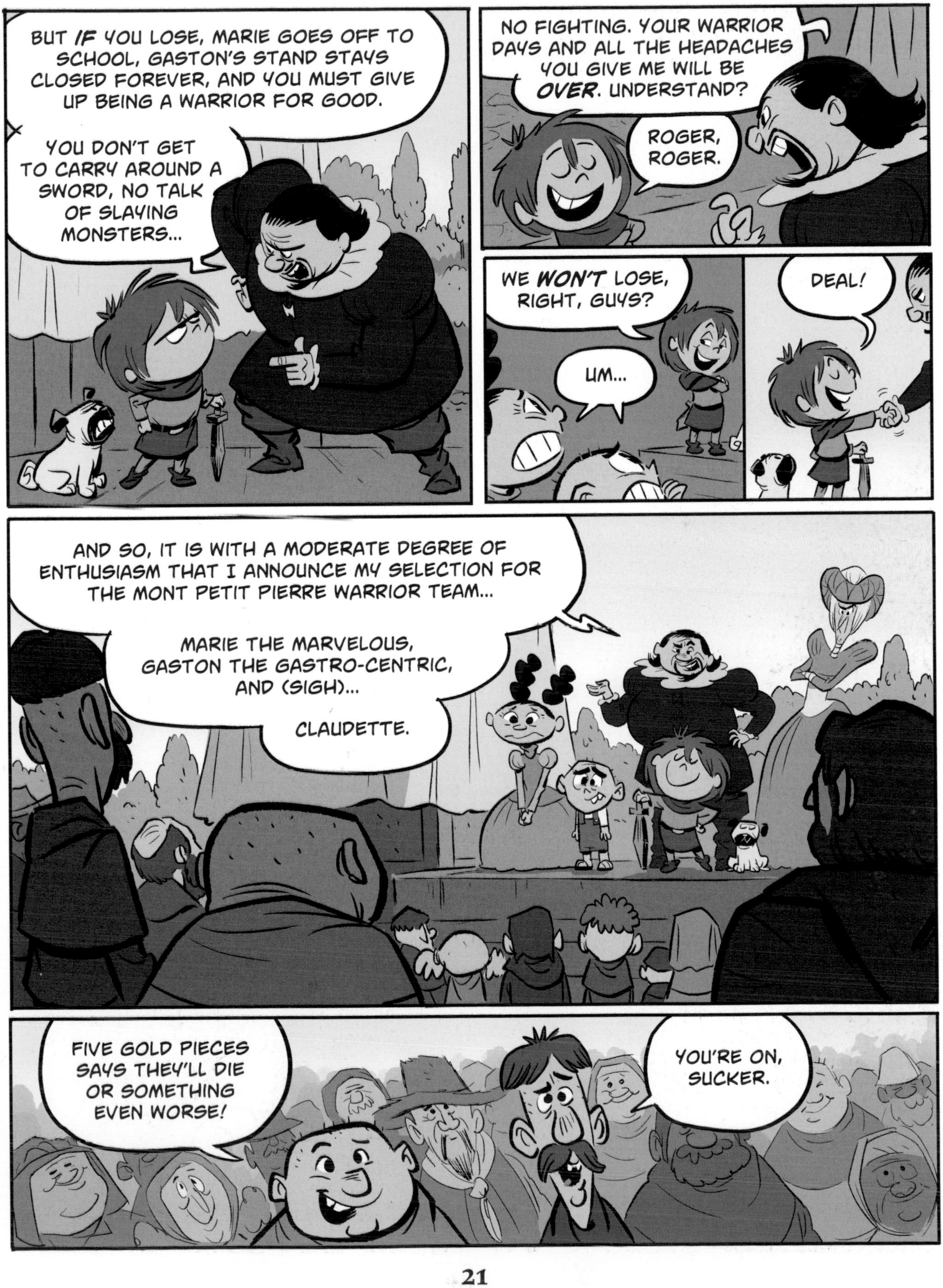
BUT IF YOU LOSE, MARIE GOES OFF TO SCHOOL, GASTON'S STAND STAYS CLOSED FOREVER, AND YOU MUST GIVE UP BEING A WARRIOR FOR GOOD.
YOU DON'T GET TO CARRY AROUND A SWORD, NO TALK OF SLAYING MONSTERS...
NO FIGHTING. YOUR WARRIOR DAYS AND ALL THE HEADACHES YOU GIVE ME WILL BE OVER. UNDERSTAND?
ROGER, ROGER.
WE WON'T LOSE, RIGHT, GUYS?
UM...
DEAL!
AND SO, IT IS WITH A MODERATE DEGREE OF ENTHUSIASM THAT I ANNOUNCE MY SELECTION FOR THE MONT PETIT PIERRE WARRIOR TEAM...
MARIE THE MARVELOUS, GASTON THE GASTRO-CENTRIC, AND (SIGH)...
CLAUDETTE.
FIVE GOLD PIECES SAYS THEY'LL DIE OR SOMETHING EVEN WORSE!
YOU'RE ON, SUCKER.

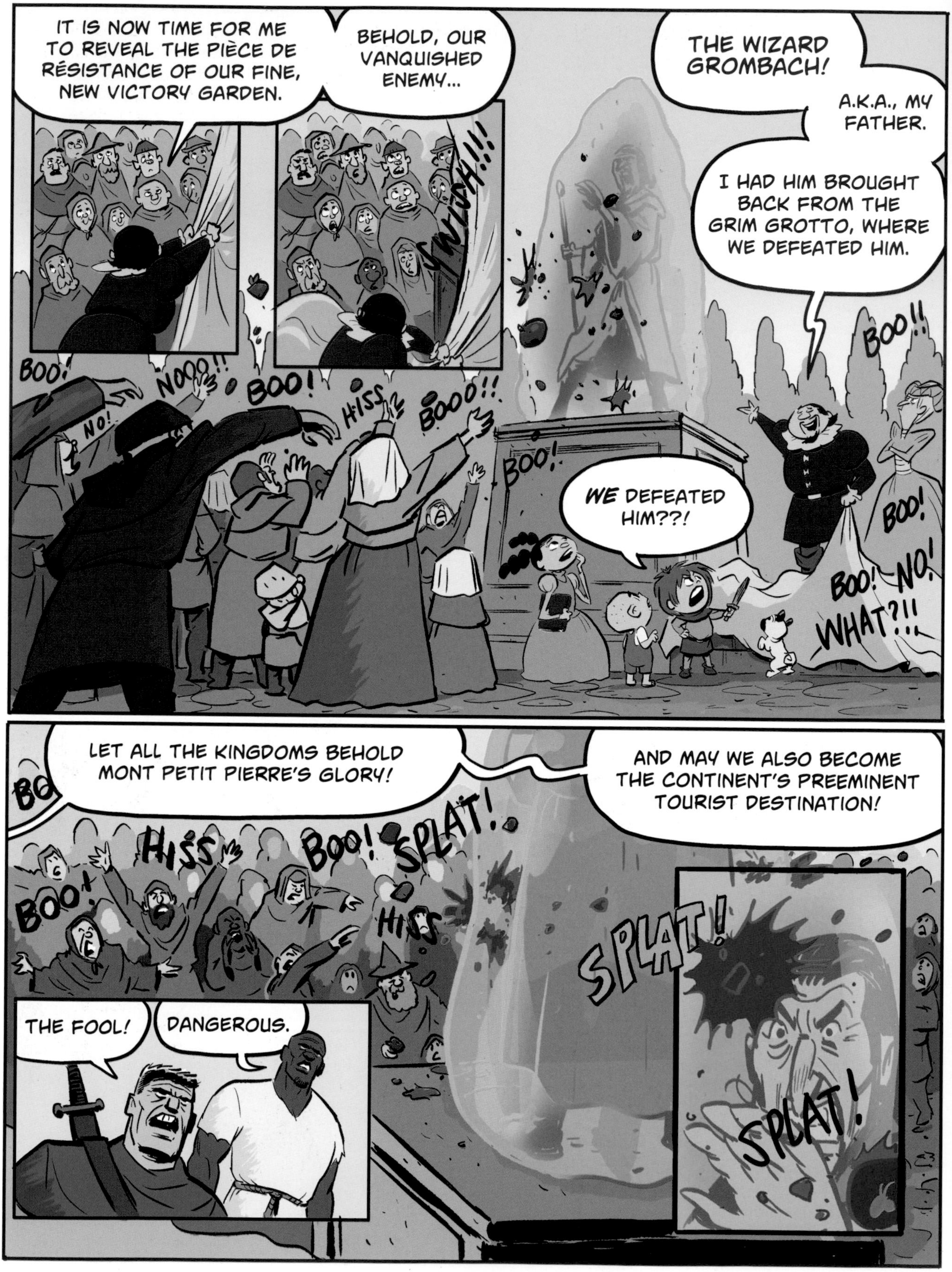
IT IS NOW TIME FOR ME TO REVEAL THE PIÈCE DE RÉSISTANCE OF OUR FINE, NEW VICTORY GARDEN.
BEHOLD, OUR VANQUISHED ENEMY...
SWISH!!!
THE WIZARD GROMBACH!
A.K.A., MY FATHER.
I HAD HIM BROUGHT BACK FROM THE GRIM GROTTO, WHERE WE DEFEATED HIM.
BOO!
NOOO!!
NO!
BOO!
HISS
BOOO!!
BOO!
BOO!!
WE DEFEATED HIM??!
BOO!
BOO! NO!
WHAT?!!
LET ALL THE KINGDOMS BEHOLD MONT PETIT PIERRE'S GLORY!
AND MAY WE ALSO BECOME THE CONTINENT'S PREEMINENT TOURIST DESTINATION!
HISS
BOO! SPLAT!
BOO!
HISS
SPLAT!
THE FOOL!
DANGEROUS.
SPLAT!

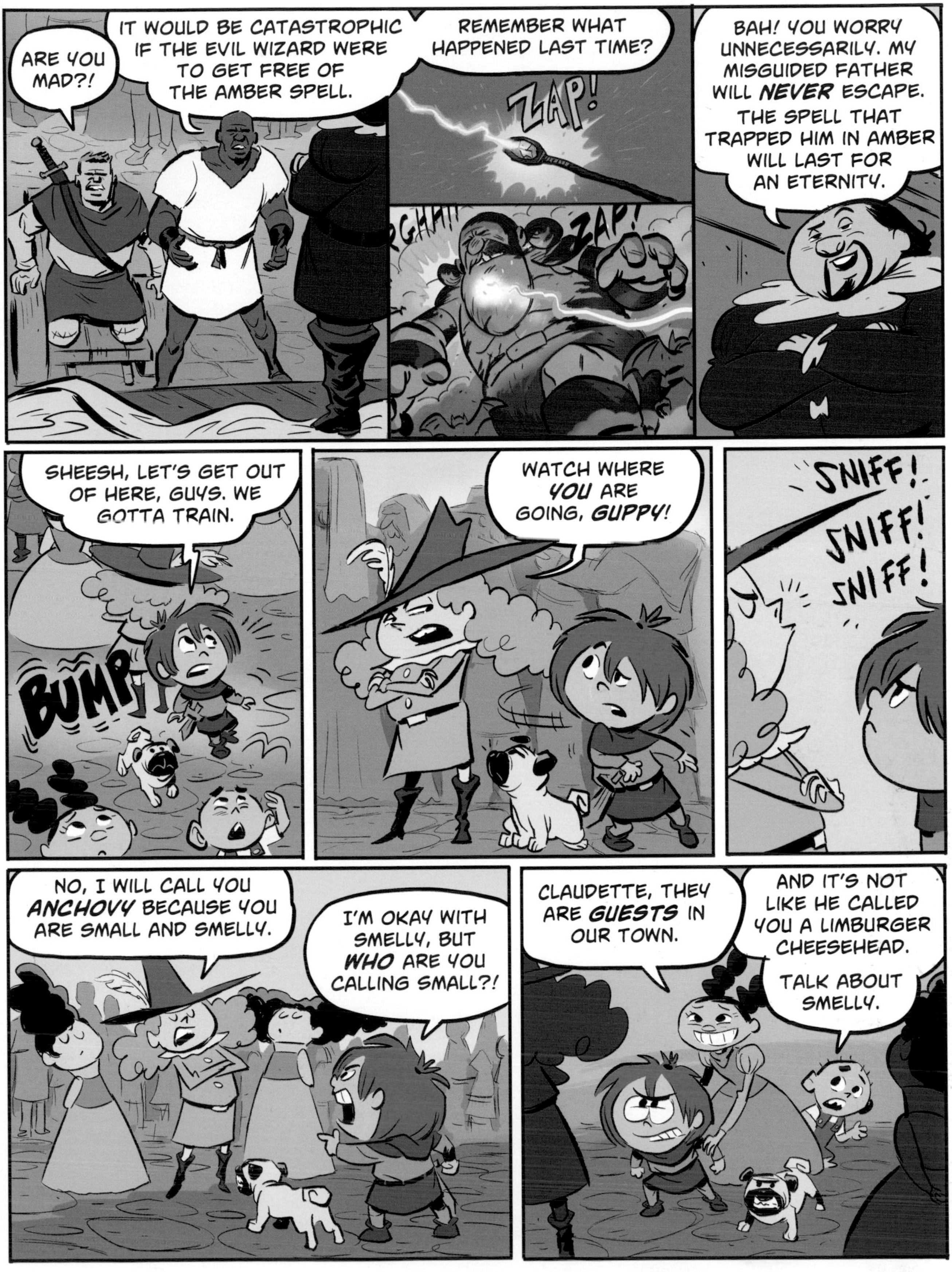
ARE YOU MAD?!
IT WOULD BE CATASTROPHIC IF THE EVIL WIZARD WERE TO GET FREE OF THE AMBER SPELL.
REMEMBER WHAT HAPPENED LAST TIME?
ZAP!
ZAP!
BAH! YOU WORRY UNNECESSARILY. MY MISGUIDED FATHER WILL NEVER ESCAPE.
THE SPELL THAT TRAPPED HIM IN AMBER WILL LAST FOR AN ETERNITY.
SHEESH, LET'S GET OUT OF HERE, GUYS. WE GOTTA TRAIN.
BUMP
WATCH WHERE YOU ARE GOING, GUPPY!
SNIFF!
SNIFF!
SNIFF!
NO, I WILL CALL YOU ANCHOVY BECAUSE YOU ARE SMALL AND SMELLY.
I'M OKAY WITH SMELLY, BUT WHO ARE YOU CALLING SMALL?!
CLAUDETTE, THEY ARE GUESTS IN OUR TOWN.
AND IT'S NOT LIKE HE CALLED YOU A LIMBURGER CHEESEHEAD.
TALK ABOUT SMELLY.

OOOH, WE *LOVE* YOUR HAIR!

HOW DO YOU KEEP IT UP LIKE THAT?

WELL, IT'S *NOT* EASY.

LET ME TELL YOU *ALL* ABOUT MY HAIR...

VICTORY WILL BE MINE, ANCHOVY.

NOT *IF* IT'S MINE FIRST, LIMBURGER BREATH!

OOOH, GOOD BURN!

HOW *COULD* YOU PICK MARIE? THE GAMES ARE DANGEROUS AND LETHAL!

SHE IS NO WARRIOR!

SHE IS A PRINCESS-IN-TRAINING!

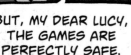

BUT, MY DEAR LUCY, THE GAMES ARE PERFECTLY SAFE.

SIR, WHERE SHOULD WE PUT THE FEROCIOUS *WARRIOR-EATING* MONSTERS WE NEED FOR THE GAMES?

AWRAAAAAA!!!!

TAKE THE CREATURES BACK TO THEIR HOMELANDS. WE DON'T NEED THEM.

NOT TO WORRY, MY LOVE. I WILL MAKE CERTAIN THAT THE GAMES TRIBUNAL MAKES AN "ADJUSTMENT" TO THIS YEAR'S COMPETITION. MARIE WILL *NOT* BE IN *ANY* DANGER.

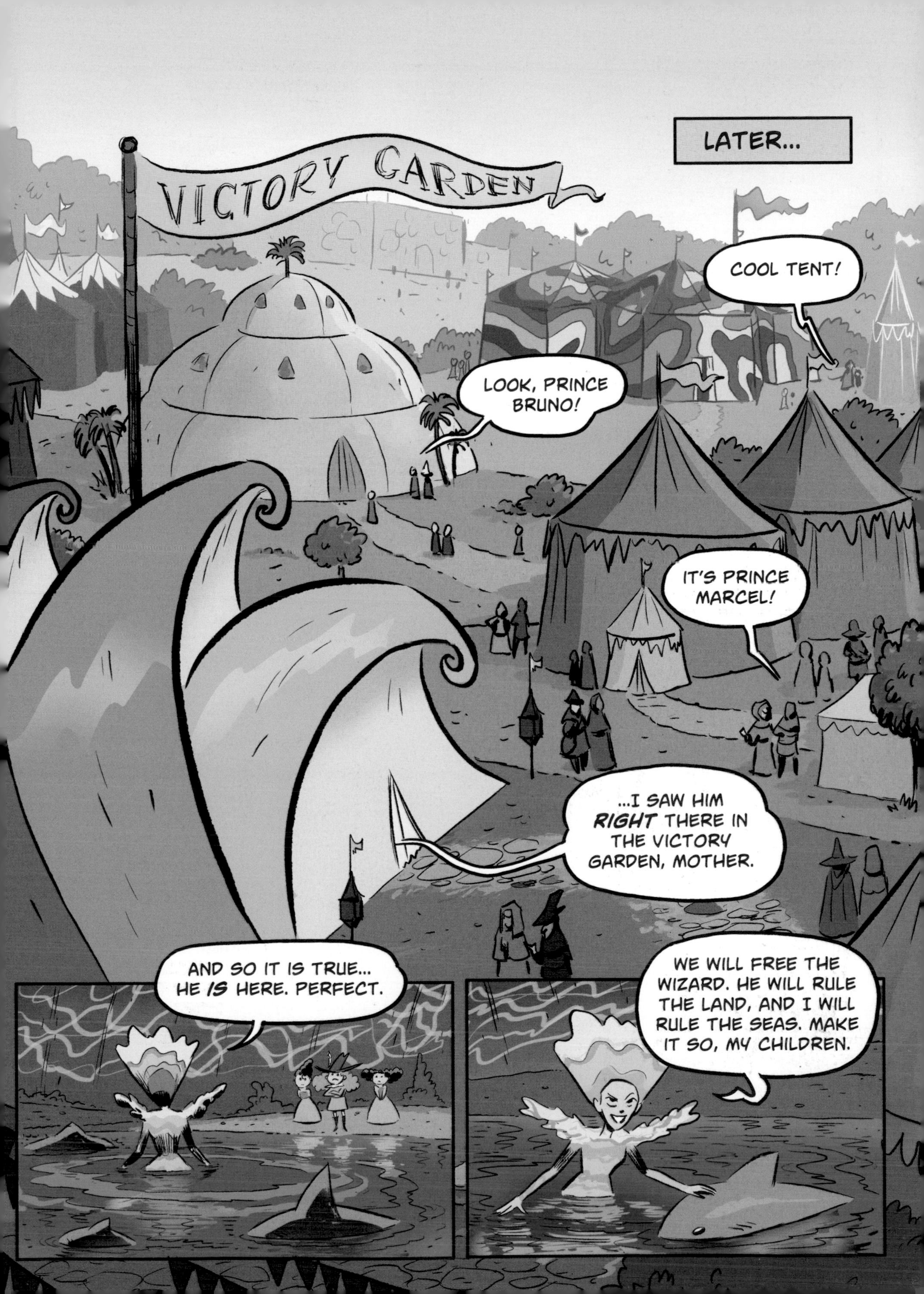
LATER...
VICTORY GARDEN
COOL TENT!
LOOK, PRINCE BRUNO!
IT'S PRINCE MARCEL!
...I SAW HIM RIGHT THERE IN THE VICTORY GARDEN, MOTHER.
AND SO IT IS TRUE... HE IS HERE. PERFECT.
WE WILL FREE THE WIZARD. HE WILL RULE THE LAND, AND I WILL RULE THE SEAS. MAKE IT SO, MY CHILDREN.

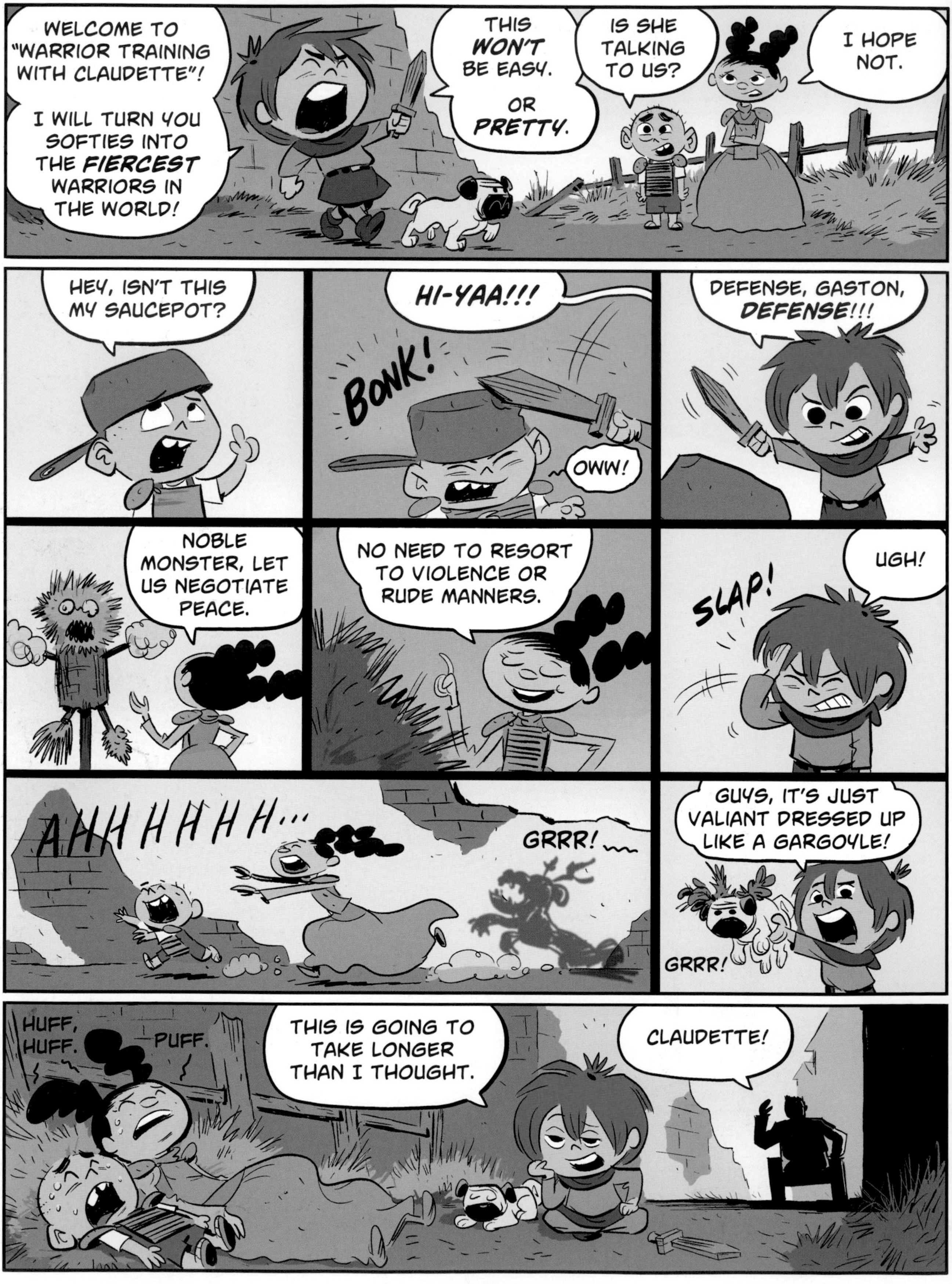

WELCOME TO "WARRIOR TRAINING WITH CLAUDETTE"!
I WILL TURN YOU SOFTIES INTO THE *FIERCEST* WARRIORS IN THE WORLD!
THIS *WON'T* BE EASY.
OR *PRETTY*.
IS SHE TALKING TO US?
I HOPE NOT.
HEY, ISN'T THIS MY SAUCEPOT?
HI-YAA!!!
BONK!
OWW!
DEFENSE, GASTON, *DEFENSE*!!!
NOBLE MONSTER, LET US NEGOTIATE PEACE.
NO NEED TO RESORT TO VIOLENCE OR RUDE MANNERS.
UGH!
SLAP!
AHHHHHHH...
GRRR!
GUYS, IT'S JUST VALIANT DRESSED UP LIKE A GARGOYLE!
GRRR!
HUFF, HUFF.
PUFF.
THIS IS GOING TO TAKE LONGER THAN I THOUGHT.
CLAUDETTE!

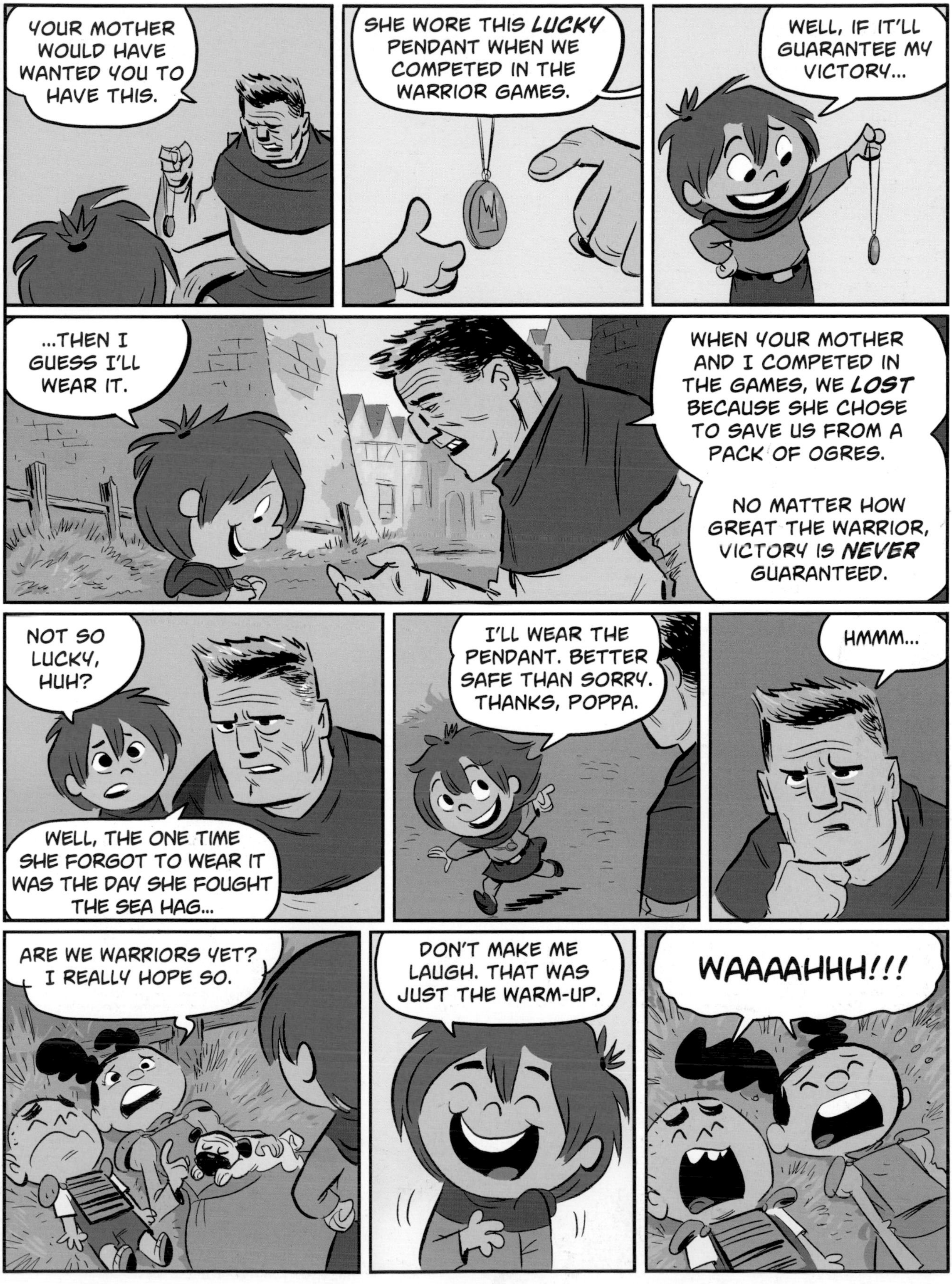
YOUR MOTHER WOULD HAVE WANTED YOU TO HAVE THIS.
SHE WORE THIS LUCKY PENDANT WHEN WE COMPETED IN THE WARRIOR GAMES.
WELL, IF IT'LL GUARANTEE MY VICTORY...
...THEN I GUESS I'LL WEAR IT.
WHEN YOUR MOTHER AND I COMPETED IN THE GAMES, WE LOST BECAUSE SHE CHOSE TO SAVE US FROM A PACK OF OGRES.
NO MATTER HOW GREAT THE WARRIOR, VICTORY IS NEVER GUARANTEED.
NOT SO LUCKY, HUH?
WELL, THE ONE TIME SHE FORGOT TO WEAR IT WAS THE DAY SHE FOUGHT THE SEA HAG...
I'LL WEAR THE PENDANT. BETTER SAFE THAN SORRY. THANKS, POPPA.
HMMM...
ARE WE WARRIORS YET? I REALLY HOPE SO.
DON'T MAKE ME LAUGH. THAT WAS JUST THE WARM-UP.
WAAAAHHH!!!

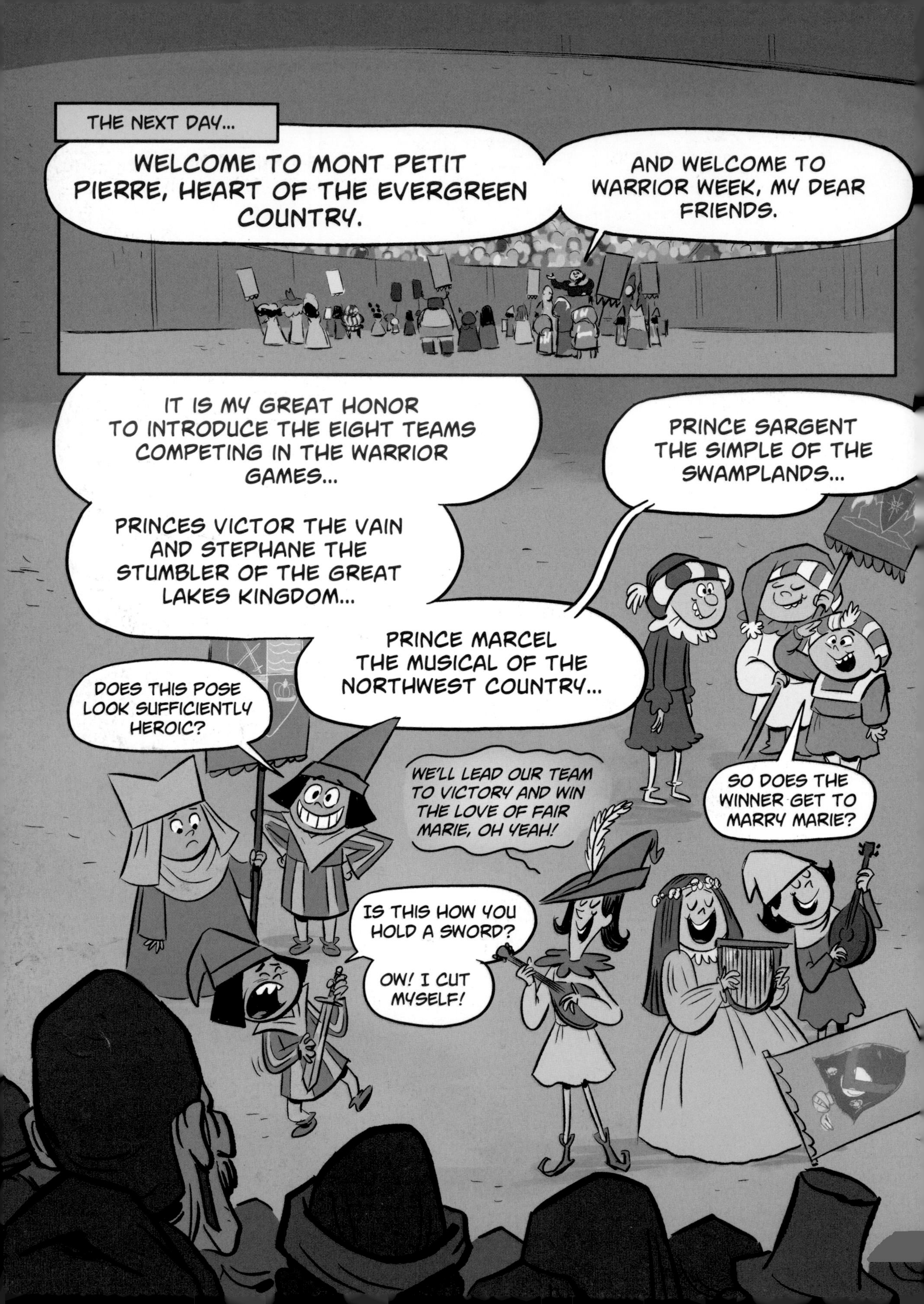
THE NEXT DAY...
WELCOME TO MONT PETIT PIERRE, HEART OF THE EVERGREEN COUNTRY.
AND WELCOME TO WARRIOR WEEK, MY DEAR FRIENDS.
IT IS MY GREAT HONOR TO INTRODUCE THE EIGHT TEAMS COMPETING IN THE WARRIOR GAMES...
PRINCES VICTOR THE VAIN AND STEPHANE THE STUMBLER OF THE GREAT LAKES KINGDOM...
PRINCE SARGENT THE SIMPLE OF THE SWAMPLANDS...
PRINCE MARCEL THE MUSICAL OF THE NORTHWEST COUNTRY...
DOES THIS POSE LOOK SUFFICIENTLY HEROIC?
WE'LL LEAD OUR TEAM TO VICTORY AND WIN THE LOVE OF FAIR MARIE, OH YEAH!
SO DOES THE WINNER GET TO MARRY MARIE?
IS THIS HOW YOU HOLD A SWORD?
OW! I CUT MYSELF!

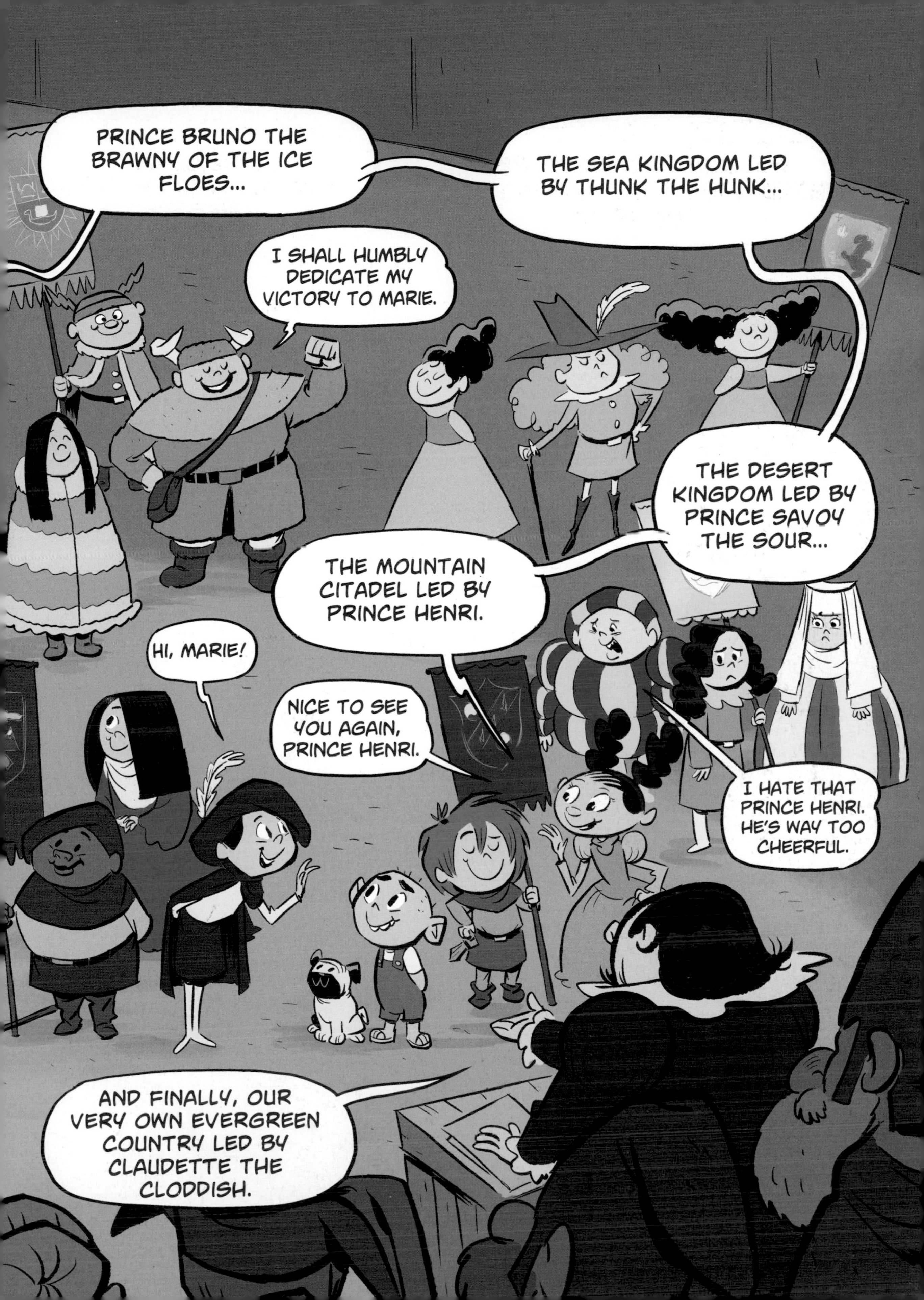
PRINCE BRUNO THE BRAWNY OF THE ICE FLOES...
THE SEA KINGDOM LED BY THUNK THE HUNK...
I SHALL HUMBLY DEDICATE MY VICTORY TO MARIE.
THE DESERT KINGDOM LED BY PRINCE SAVOY THE SOUR...
THE MOUNTAIN CITADEL LED BY PRINCE HENRI.
HI, MARIE!
NICE TO SEE YOU AGAIN, PRINCE HENRI.
I HATE THAT PRINCE HENRI. HE'S WAY TOO CHEERFUL.
AND FINALLY, OUR VERY OWN EVERGREEN COUNTRY LED BY CLAUDETTE THE CLODDISH.

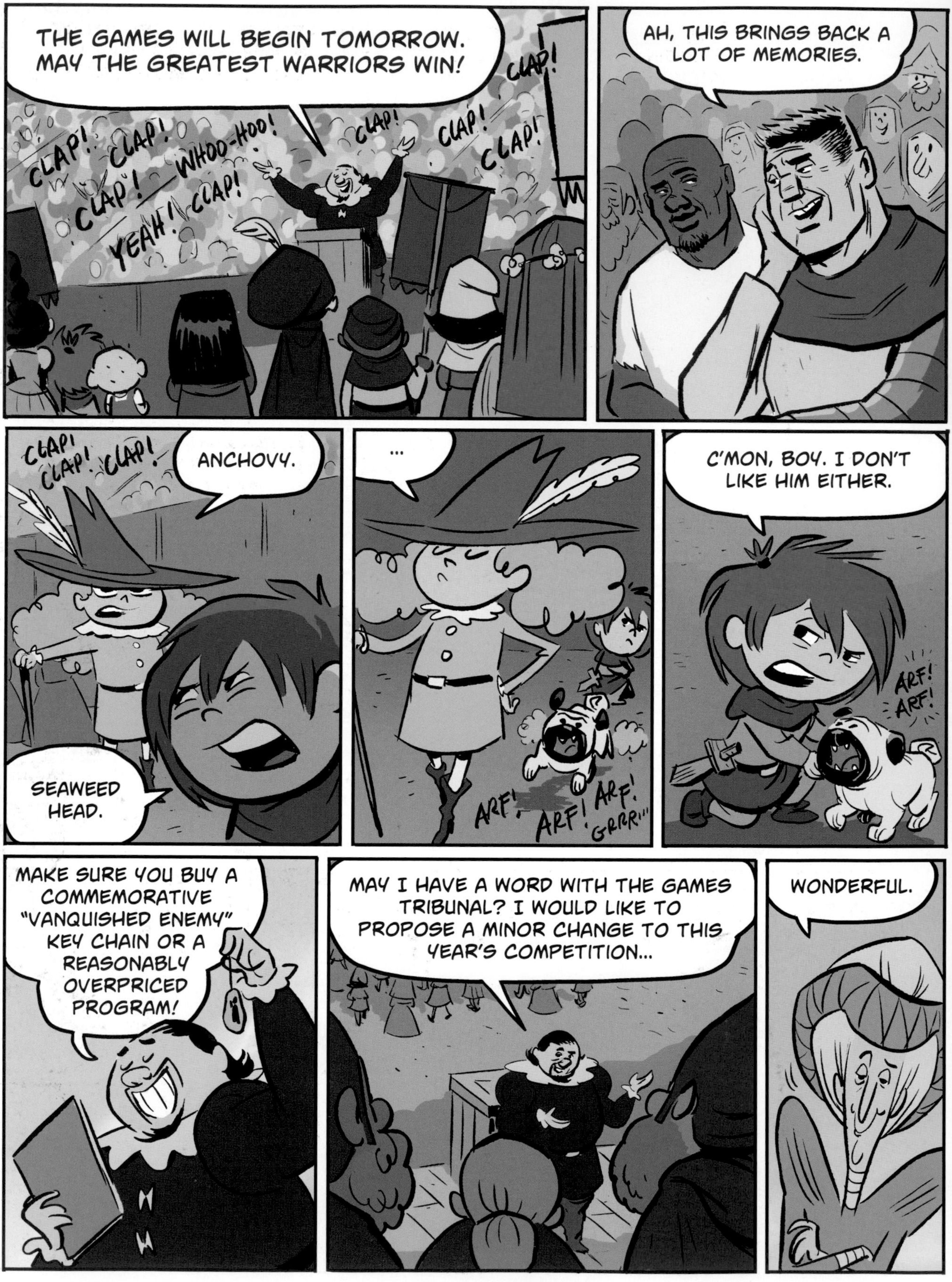
THE GAMES WILL BEGIN TOMORROW. MAY THE GREATEST WARRIORS WIN!
CLAP! CLAP! CLAP! WHOO-HOO! YEAH! CLAP! CLAP! CLAP! CLAP! CLAP!
AH, THIS BRINGS BACK A LOT OF MEMORIES.
CLAP! CLAP! CLAP!
ANCHOVY.
SEAWEED HEAD.
...
ARF! ARF! ARF! GRRR...
C'MON, BOY. I DON'T LIKE HIM EITHER.
ARF! ARF!
MAKE SURE YOU BUY A COMMEMORATIVE "VANQUISHED ENEMY" KEY CHAIN OR A REASONABLY OVERPRICED PROGRAM!
MAY I HAVE A WORD WITH THE GAMES TRIBUNAL? I WOULD LIKE TO PROPOSE A MINOR CHANGE TO THIS YEAR'S COMPETITION...
WONDERFUL.

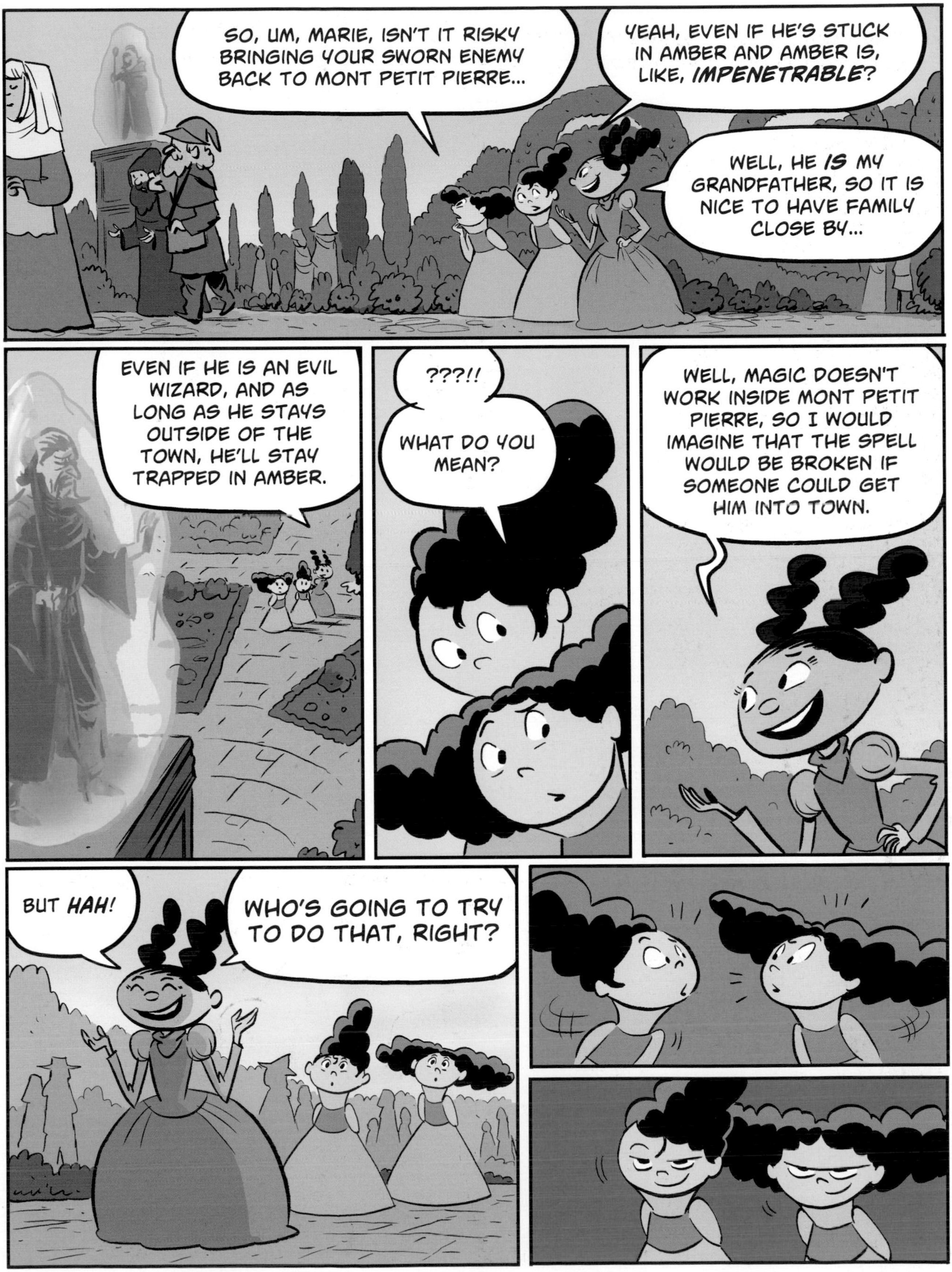
SO, UM, MARIE, ISN'T IT RISKY BRINGING YOUR SWORN ENEMY BACK TO MONT PETIT PIERRE...
YEAH, EVEN IF HE'S STUCK IN AMBER AND AMBER IS, LIKE, *IMPENETRABLE*?
WELL, HE *IS* MY GRANDFATHER, SO IT IS NICE TO HAVE FAMILY CLOSE BY...
EVEN IF HE IS AN EVIL WIZARD, AND AS LONG AS HE STAYS OUTSIDE OF THE TOWN, HE'LL STAY TRAPPED IN AMBER.
???!!
WHAT DO YOU MEAN?
WELL, MAGIC DOESN'T WORK INSIDE MONT PETIT PIERRE, SO I WOULD IMAGINE THAT THE SPELL WOULD BE BROKEN IF SOMEONE COULD GET HIM INTO TOWN.
BUT *HAH*!
WHO'S GOING TO TRY TO DO THAT, RIGHT?

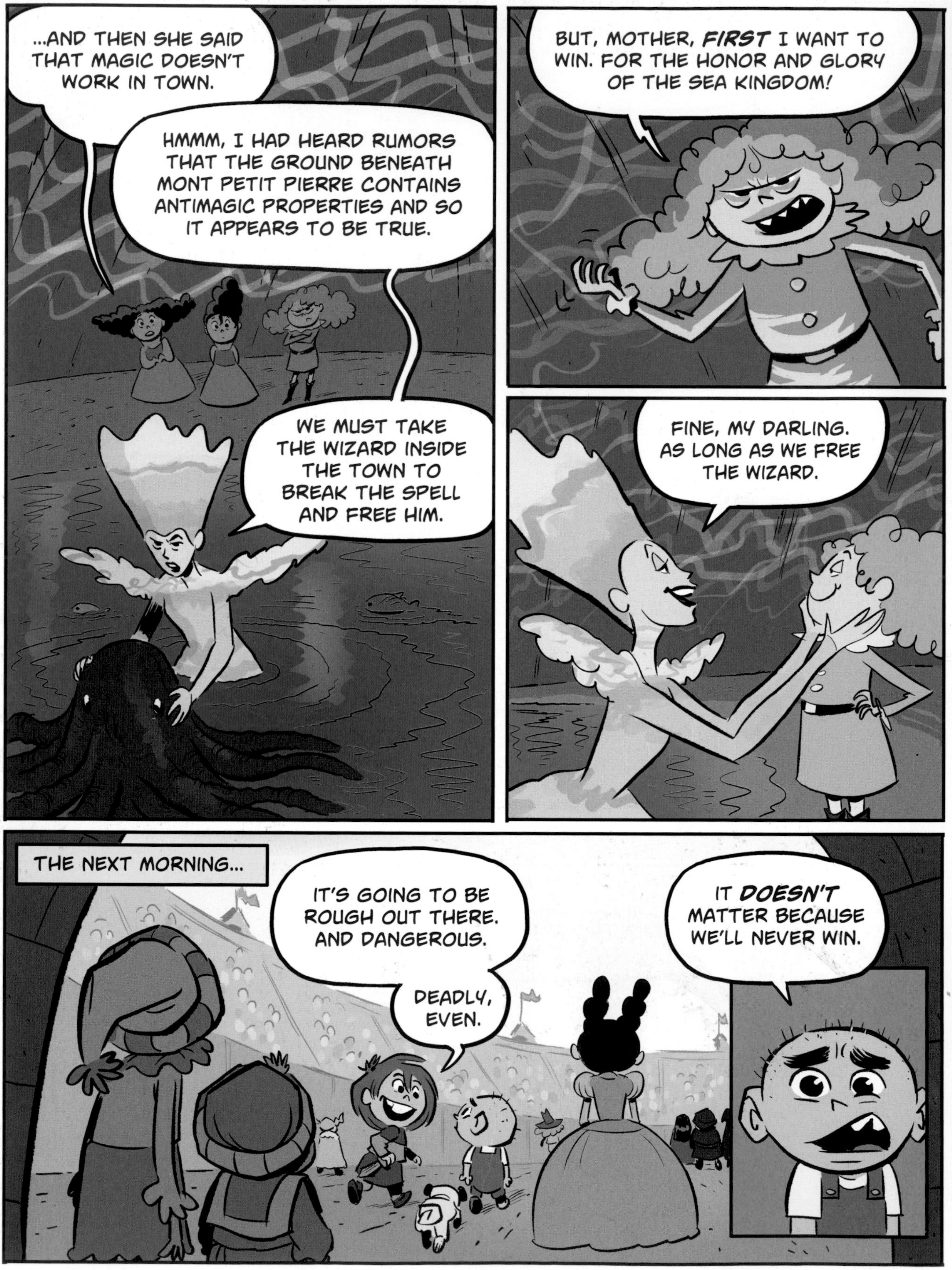
...AND THEN SHE SAID THAT MAGIC DOESN'T WORK IN TOWN.
HMMM, I HAD HEARD RUMORS THAT THE GROUND BENEATH MONT PETIT PIERRE CONTAINS ANTIMAGIC PROPERTIES AND SO IT APPEARS TO BE TRUE.
WE MUST TAKE THE WIZARD INSIDE THE TOWN TO BREAK THE SPELL AND FREE HIM.
BUT, MOTHER, FIRST I WANT TO WIN. FOR THE HONOR AND GLORY OF THE SEA KINGDOM!
FINE, MY DARLING. AS LONG AS WE FREE THE WIZARD.
THE NEXT MORNING...
IT'S GOING TO BE ROUGH OUT THERE. AND DANGEROUS.
DEADLY, EVEN.
IT DOESN'T MATTER BECAUSE WE'LL NEVER WIN.

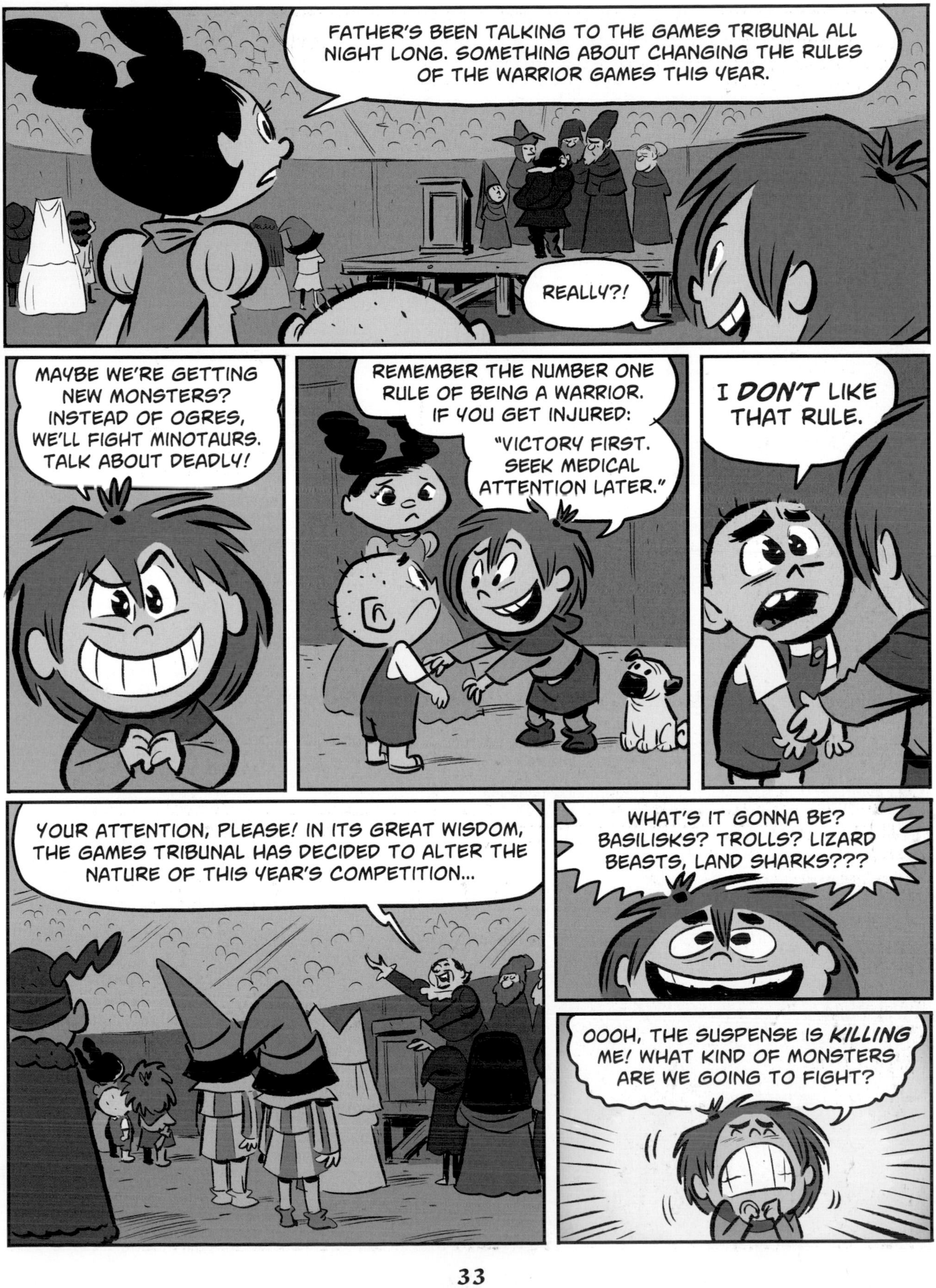
FATHER'S BEEN TALKING TO THE GAMES TRIBUNAL ALL NIGHT LONG. SOMETHING ABOUT CHANGING THE RULES OF THE WARRIOR GAMES THIS YEAR.
REALLY?!
MAYBE WE'RE GETTING NEW MONSTERS? INSTEAD OF OGRES, WE'LL FIGHT MINOTAURS. TALK ABOUT DEADLY!
REMEMBER THE NUMBER ONE RULE OF BEING A WARRIOR. IF YOU GET INJURED:
"VICTORY FIRST. SEEK MEDICAL ATTENTION LATER."
I DON'T LIKE THAT RULE.
YOUR ATTENTION, PLEASE! IN ITS GREAT WISDOM, THE GAMES TRIBUNAL HAS DECIDED TO ALTER THE NATURE OF THIS YEAR'S COMPETITION...
WHAT'S IT GONNA BE? BASILISKS? TROLLS? LIZARD BEASTS, LAND SHARKS???
OOOH, THE SUSPENSE IS KILLING ME! WHAT KIND OF MONSTERS ARE WE GOING TO FIGHT?

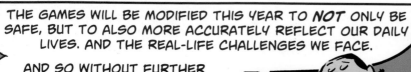

THE GAMES WILL BE MODIFIED THIS YEAR TO **NOT** ONLY BE SAFE, BUT TO ALSO MORE ACCURATELY REFLECT OUR DAILY LIVES. AND THE REAL-LIFE CHALLENGES WE FACE.

AND SO WITHOUT FURTHER ADO, I AM PROUD TO ANNOUNCE OUR FIRST ACTION-PACKED COMPETITION...

I DON'T LIKE WHERE HE'S GOING WITH THIS...

THE FIRST GAME WILL BE...

BUTTER CHURNING!

MOO
MOO
MOOO
MOO
MOOO
MOO
MOOO
MOO
MOOO

WHAAAT?!

HAPPY, MY DEAR?

THE FIRST TEAM TO FILL THEIR BUCKETS WITH COW'S MILK AND CHURN IT INTO BUTTER WILL BE DECLARED THE WINNER. MAY THE **BEST** CHURNER WIN!

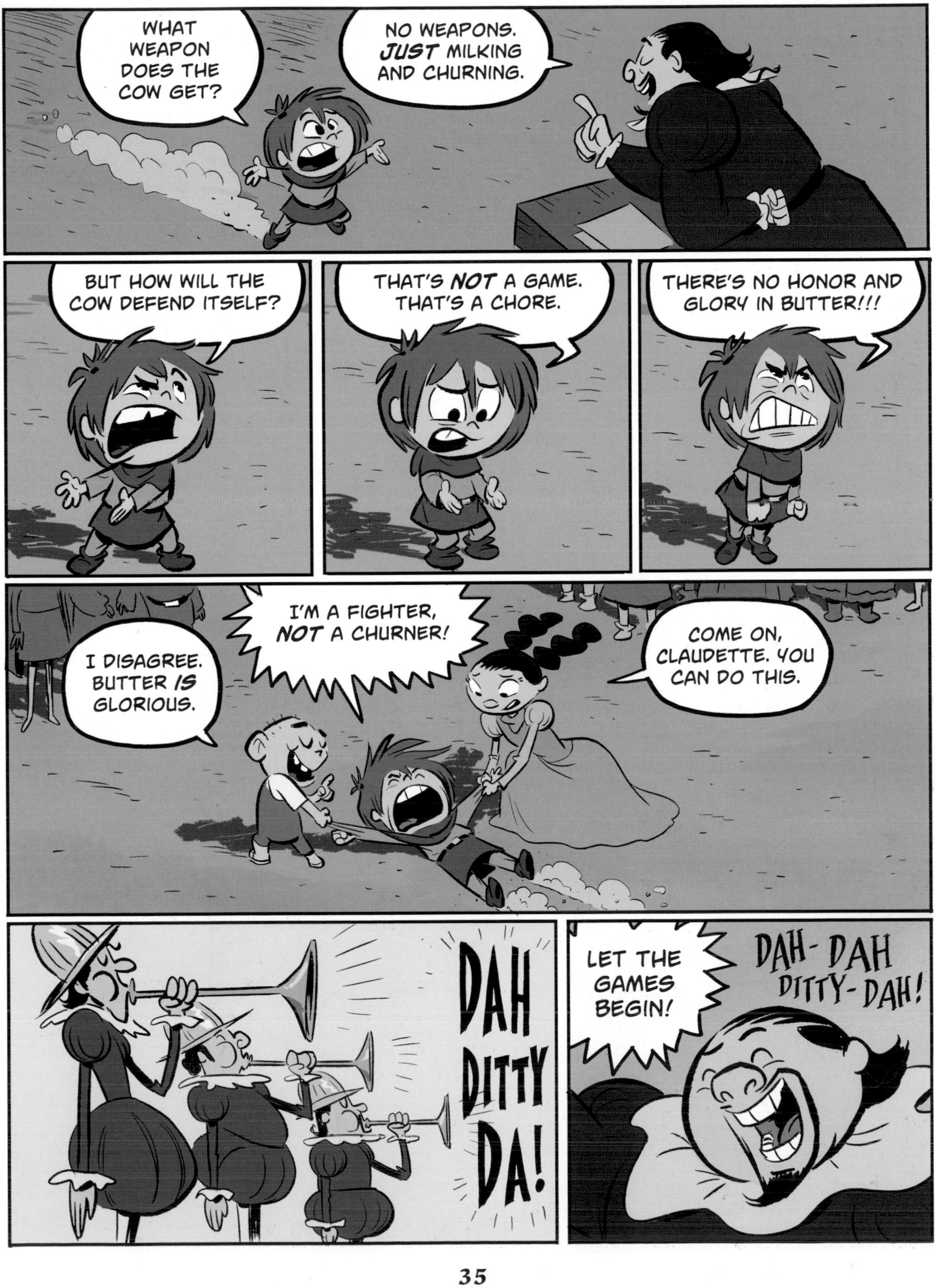
WHAT WEAPON DOES THE COW GET?
NO WEAPONS. JUST MILKING AND CHURNING.
BUT HOW WILL THE COW DEFEND ITSELF?
THAT'S NOT A GAME. THAT'S A CHORE.
THERE'S NO HONOR AND GLORY IN BUTTER!!!
I'M A FIGHTER, NOT A CHURNER!
I DISAGREE. BUTTER IS GLORIOUS.
COME ON, CLAUDETTE. YOU CAN DO THIS.
DAH DITTY DA!
LET THE GAMES BEGIN!
DAH-DAH DITTY-DAH!

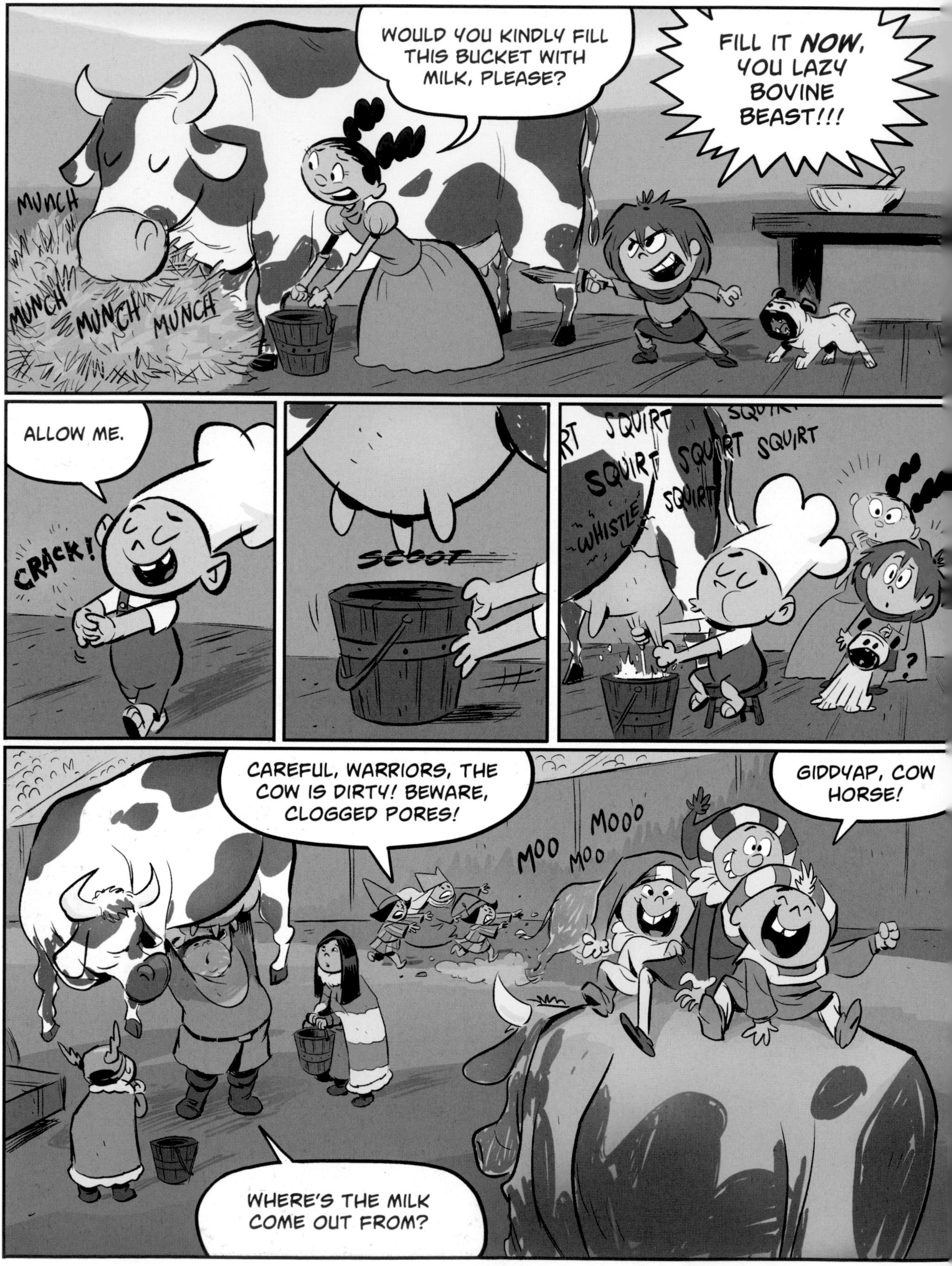
WOULD YOU KINDLY FILL THIS BUCKET WITH MILK, PLEASE?
FILL IT NOW, YOU LAZY BOVINE BEAST!!!
MUNCH
MUNCH MUNCH MUNCH
ALLOW ME.
CRACK!
SCOOT
SQUIRT SQUIRT SQUIRT SQUIRT SQUIRT SQUIRT
WHISTLE
?
CAREFUL, WARRIORS, THE COW IS DIRTY! BEWARE, CLOGGED PORES!
GIDDYAP, COW HORSE!
MOO MOO MOOO
WHERE'S THE MILK COME OUT FROM?

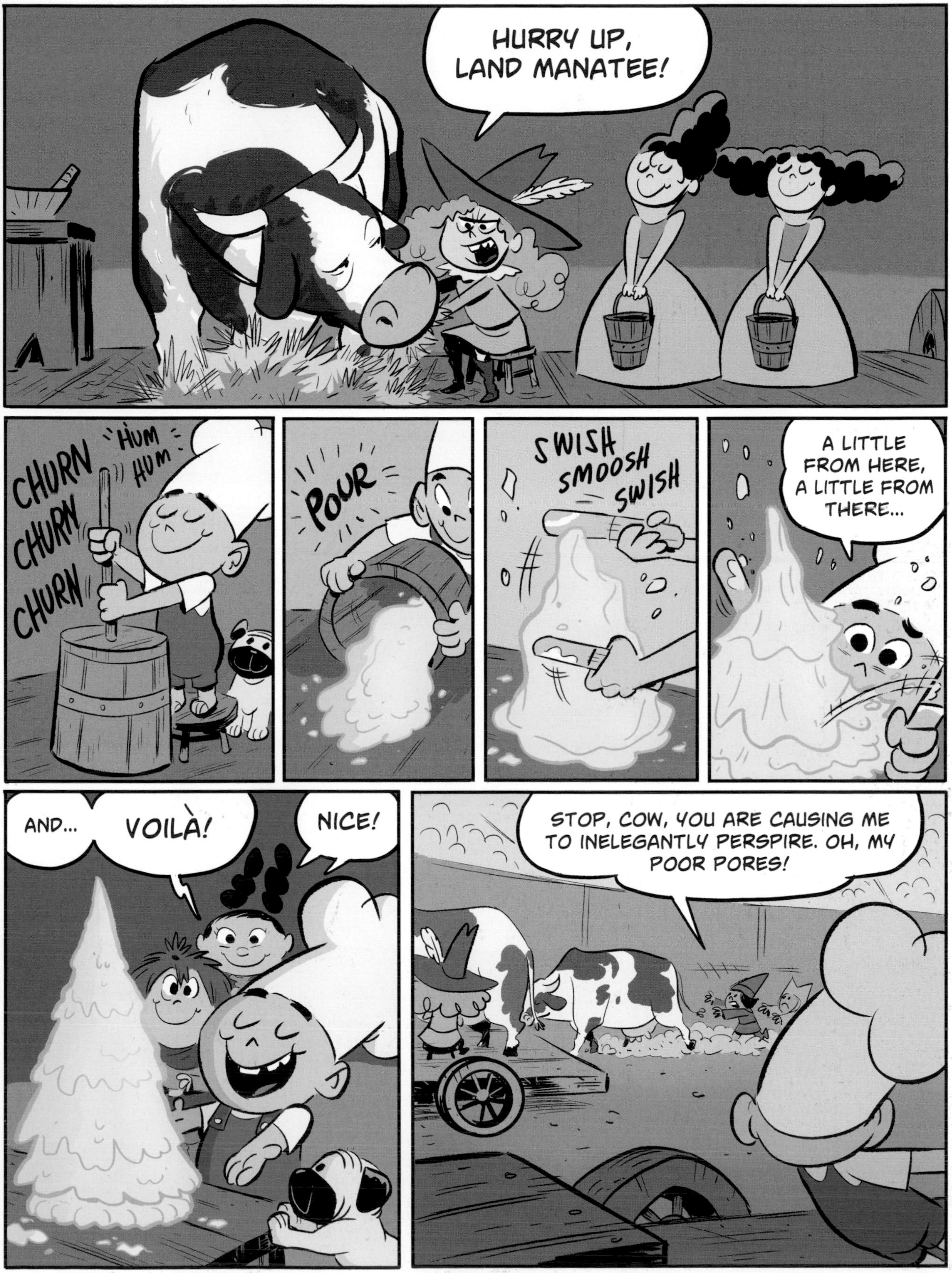
HURRY UP, LAND MANATEE!
CHURN CHURN CHURN
HUM HUM
POUR
SWISH SMOOSH SWISH
A LITTLE FROM HERE, A LITTLE FROM THERE...
AND...
VOILÀ!
NICE!
STOP, COW, YOU ARE CAUSING ME TO INELEGANTLY PERSPIRE. OH, MY POOR PORES!

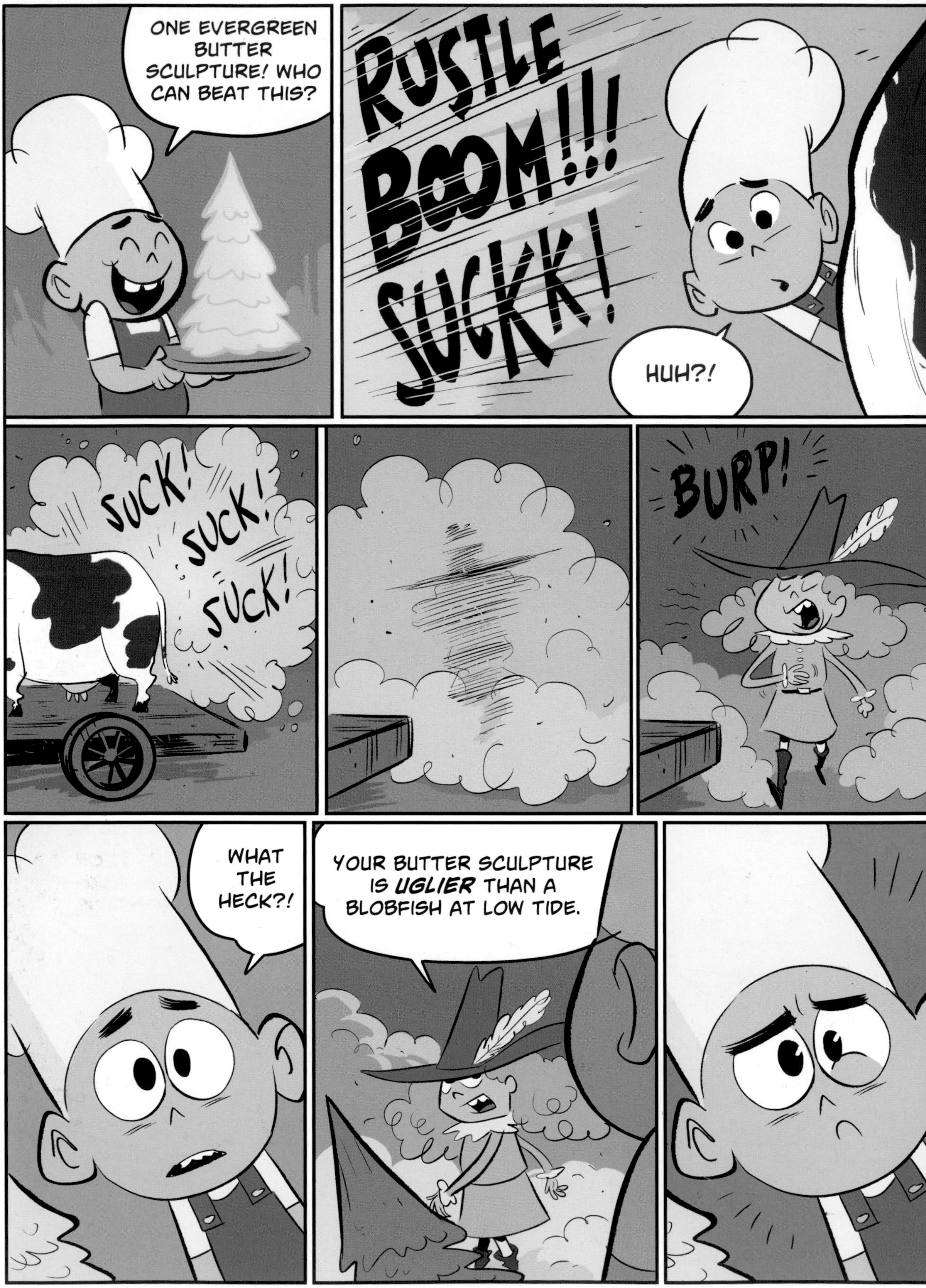

ONE EVERGREEN BUTTER SCULPTURE! WHO CAN BEAT THIS?
RUSTLE BOOM!!! SUCKK!
HUH?!
SUCK! SUCK! SUCK!
BURP!
WHAT THE HECK?!
YOUR BUTTER SCULPTURE IS *UGLIER* THAN A BLOBFISH AT LOW TIDE.

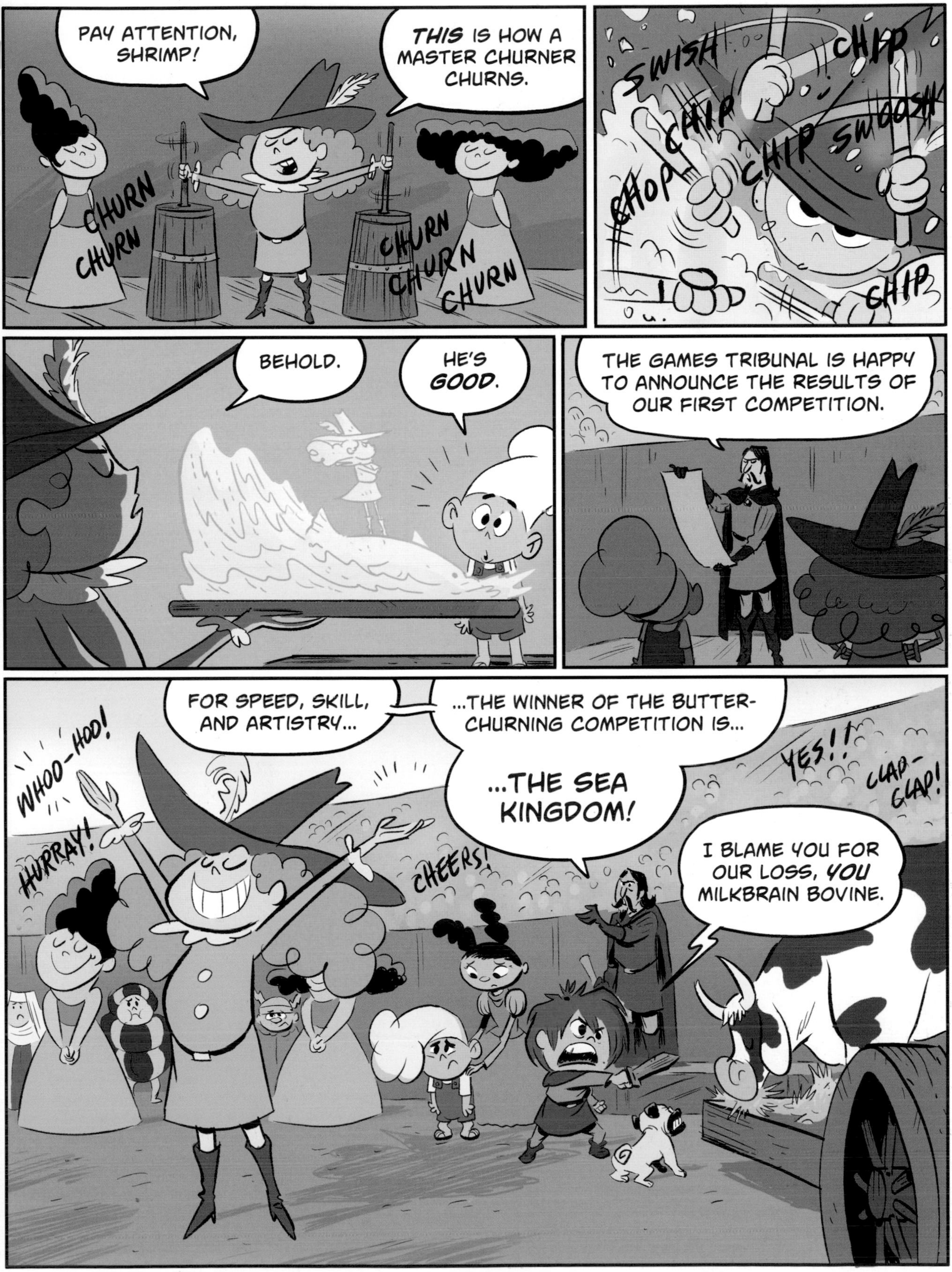
PAY ATTENTION, SHRIMP!
THIS IS HOW A MASTER CHURNER CHURNS.
CHURN CHURN
CHURN CHURN CHURN
SWISH
CHIP
CHOP
CHIP
CHIP
SWOOSH
CHIP
BEHOLD.
HE'S GOOD.
THE GAMES TRIBUNAL IS HAPPY TO ANNOUNCE THE RESULTS OF OUR FIRST COMPETITION.
FOR SPEED, SKILL, AND ARTISTRY...
...THE WINNER OF THE BUTTER-CHURNING COMPETITION IS...
...THE SEA KINGDOM!
WHOO-HOO!
HURRAY!
CHEERS!
YES!!
CLAP-CLAP!
I BLAME YOU FOR OUR LOSS, YOU MILKBRAIN BOVINE.

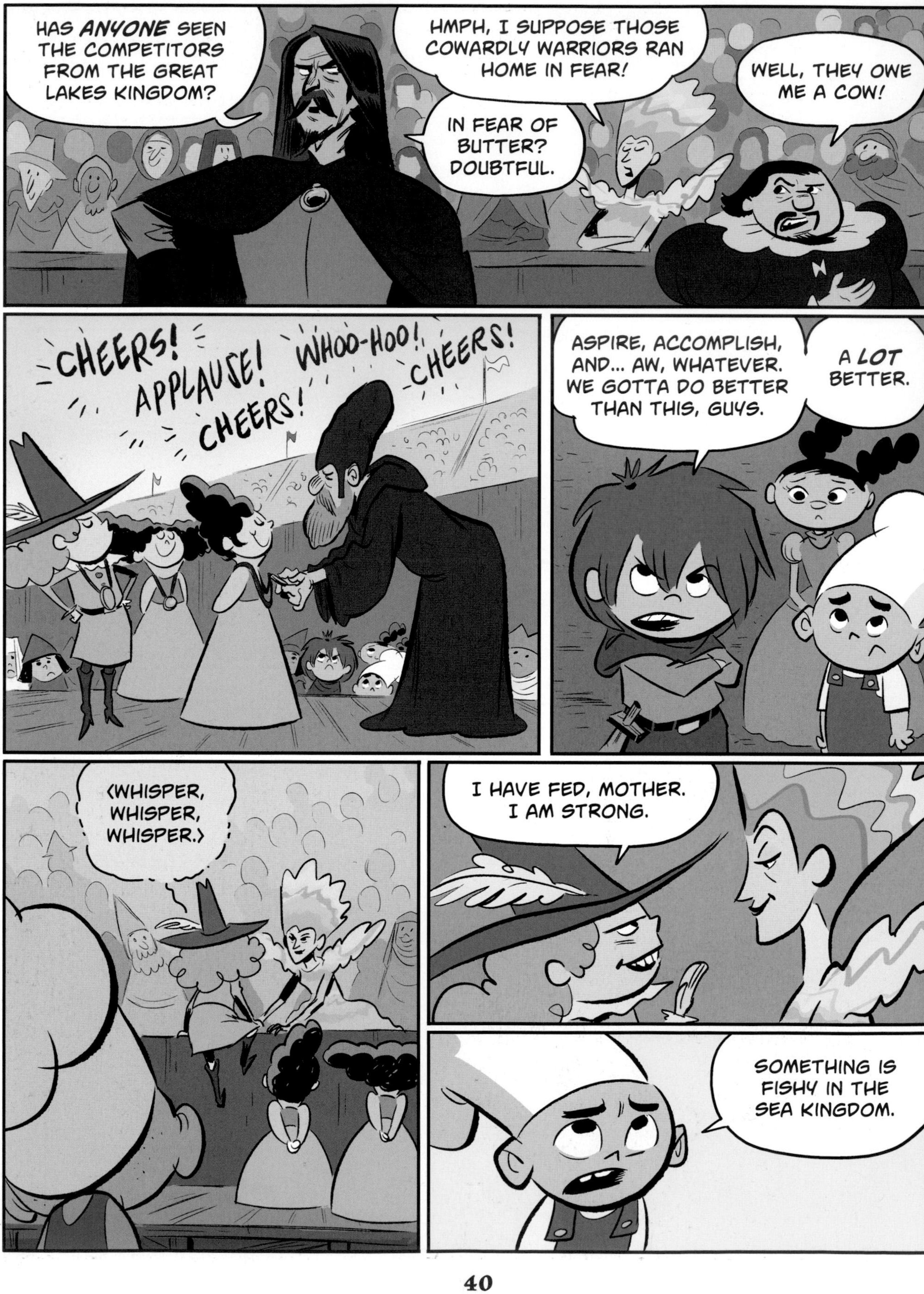
HAS ANYONE SEEN THE COMPETITORS FROM THE GREAT LAKES KINGDOM?
HMPH, I SUPPOSE THOSE COWARDLY WARRIORS RAN HOME IN FEAR!
IN FEAR OF BUTTER? DOUBTFUL.
WELL, THEY OWE ME A COW!
CHEERS! APPLAUSE! WHOO-HOO! CHEERS! CHEERS!
ASPIRE, ACCOMPLISH, AND... AW, WHATEVER. WE GOTTA DO BETTER THAN THIS, GUYS.
A LOT BETTER.
‹WHISPER, WHISPER, WHISPER.›
I HAVE FED, MOTHER. I AM STRONG.
SOMETHING IS FISHY IN THE SEA KINGDOM.

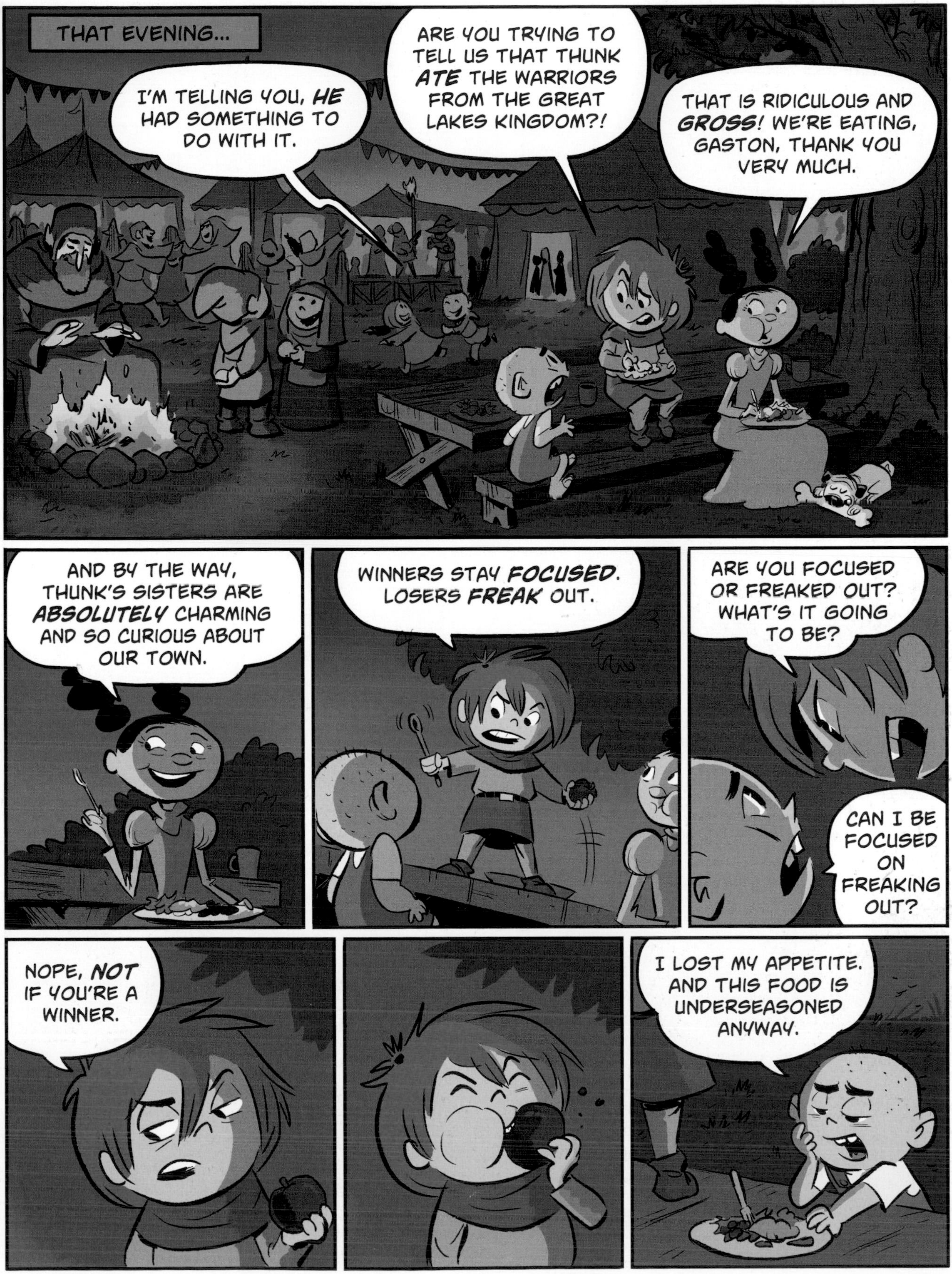

THAT EVENING...
I'M TELLING YOU, **HE** HAD SOMETHING TO DO WITH IT.
ARE YOU TRYING TO TELL US THAT THUNK **ATE** THE WARRIORS FROM THE GREAT LAKES KINGDOM?!
THAT IS RIDICULOUS AND **GROSS**! WE'RE EATING, GASTON, THANK YOU VERY MUCH.
AND BY THE WAY, THUNK'S SISTERS ARE **ABSOLUTELY** CHARMING AND SO CURIOUS ABOUT OUR TOWN.
WINNERS STAY **FOCUSED**. LOSERS **FREAK** OUT.
ARE YOU FOCUSED OR FREAKED OUT? WHAT'S IT GOING TO BE?
CAN I BE FOCUSED ON FREAKING OUT?
NOPE, **NOT** IF YOU'RE A WINNER.
I LOST MY APPETITE. AND THIS FOOD IS UNDERSEASONED ANYWAY.

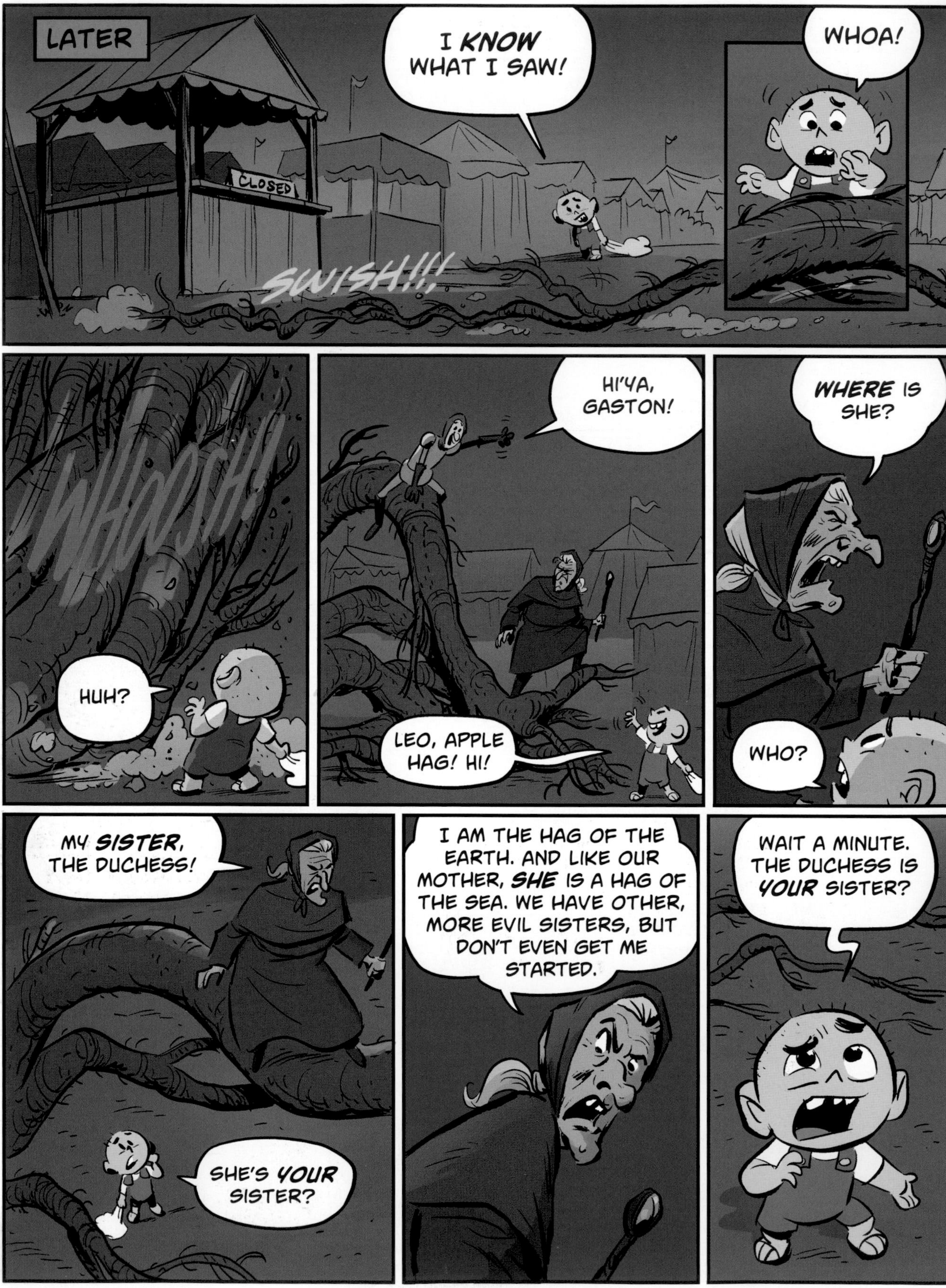
LATER
CLOSED
I KNOW WHAT I SAW!
SWISH!!!
WHOA!
WHOOSH!
HUH?
HI'YA, GASTON!
LEO, APPLE HAG! HI!
WHERE IS SHE?
WHO?
MY SISTER, THE DUCHESS!
SHE'S YOUR SISTER?
I AM THE HAG OF THE EARTH. AND LIKE OUR MOTHER, SHE IS A HAG OF THE SEA. WE HAVE OTHER, MORE EVIL SISTERS, BUT DON'T EVEN GET ME STARTED.
WAIT A MINUTE. THE DUCHESS IS YOUR SISTER?

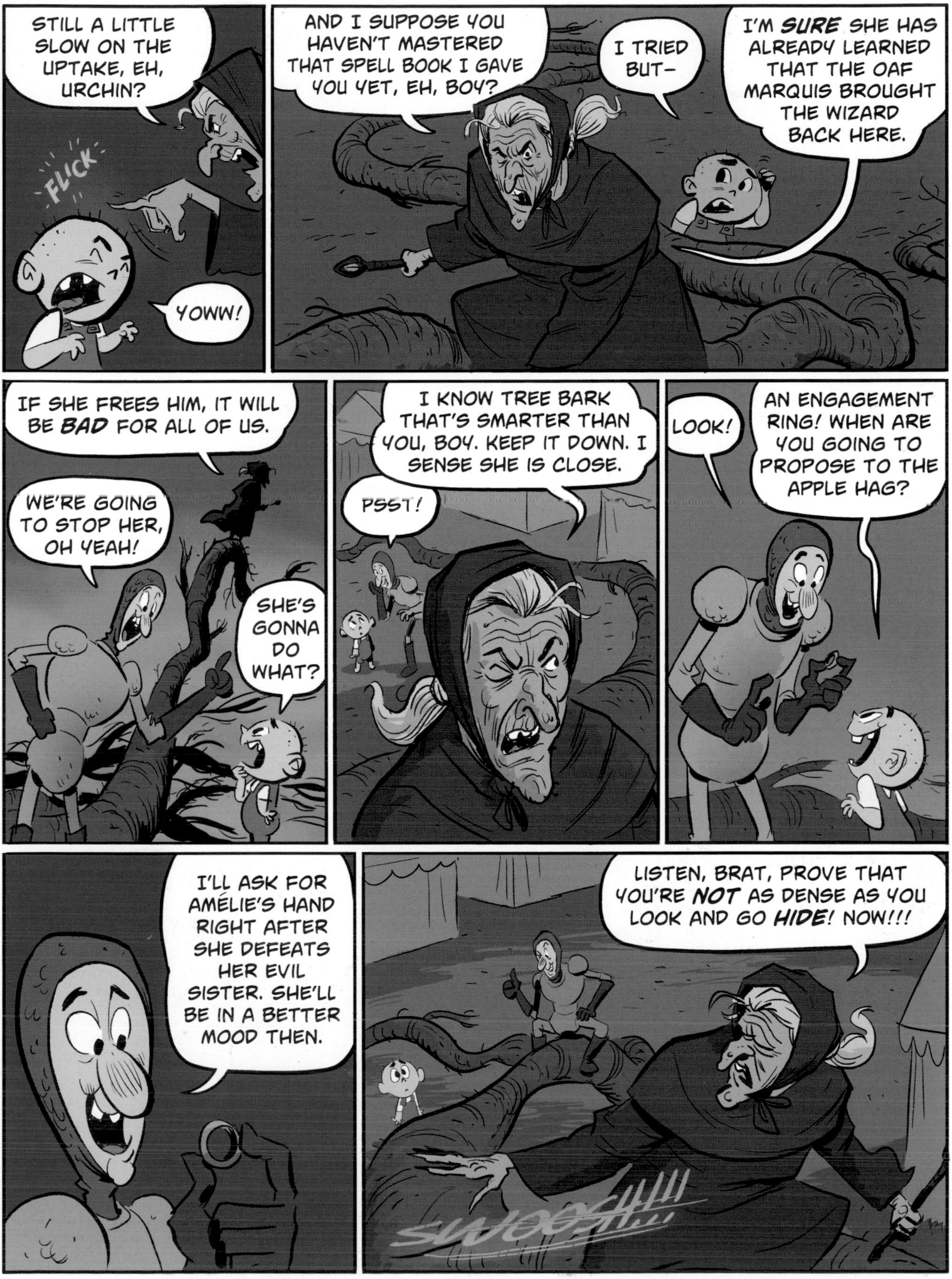

STILL A LITTLE SLOW ON THE UPTAKE, EH, URCHIN?
FLICK
YOWW!
AND I SUPPOSE YOU HAVEN'T MASTERED THAT SPELL BOOK I GAVE YOU YET, EH, BOY?
I TRIED BUT–
I'M SURE SHE HAS ALREADY LEARNED THAT THE OAF MARQUIS BROUGHT THE WIZARD BACK HERE.
IF SHE FREES HIM, IT WILL BE BAD FOR ALL OF US.
WE'RE GOING TO STOP HER, OH YEAH!
SHE'S GONNA DO WHAT?
I KNOW TREE BARK THAT'S SMARTER THAN YOU, BOY. KEEP IT DOWN. I SENSE SHE IS CLOSE.
PSST!
LOOK!
AN ENGAGEMENT RING! WHEN ARE YOU GOING TO PROPOSE TO THE APPLE HAG?
I'LL ASK FOR AMÉLIE'S HAND RIGHT AFTER SHE DEFEATS HER EVIL SISTER. SHE'LL BE IN A BETTER MOOD THEN.
LISTEN, BRAT, PROVE THAT YOU'RE NOT AS DENSE AS YOU LOOK AND GO HIDE! NOW!!!
SWOOSH!!!

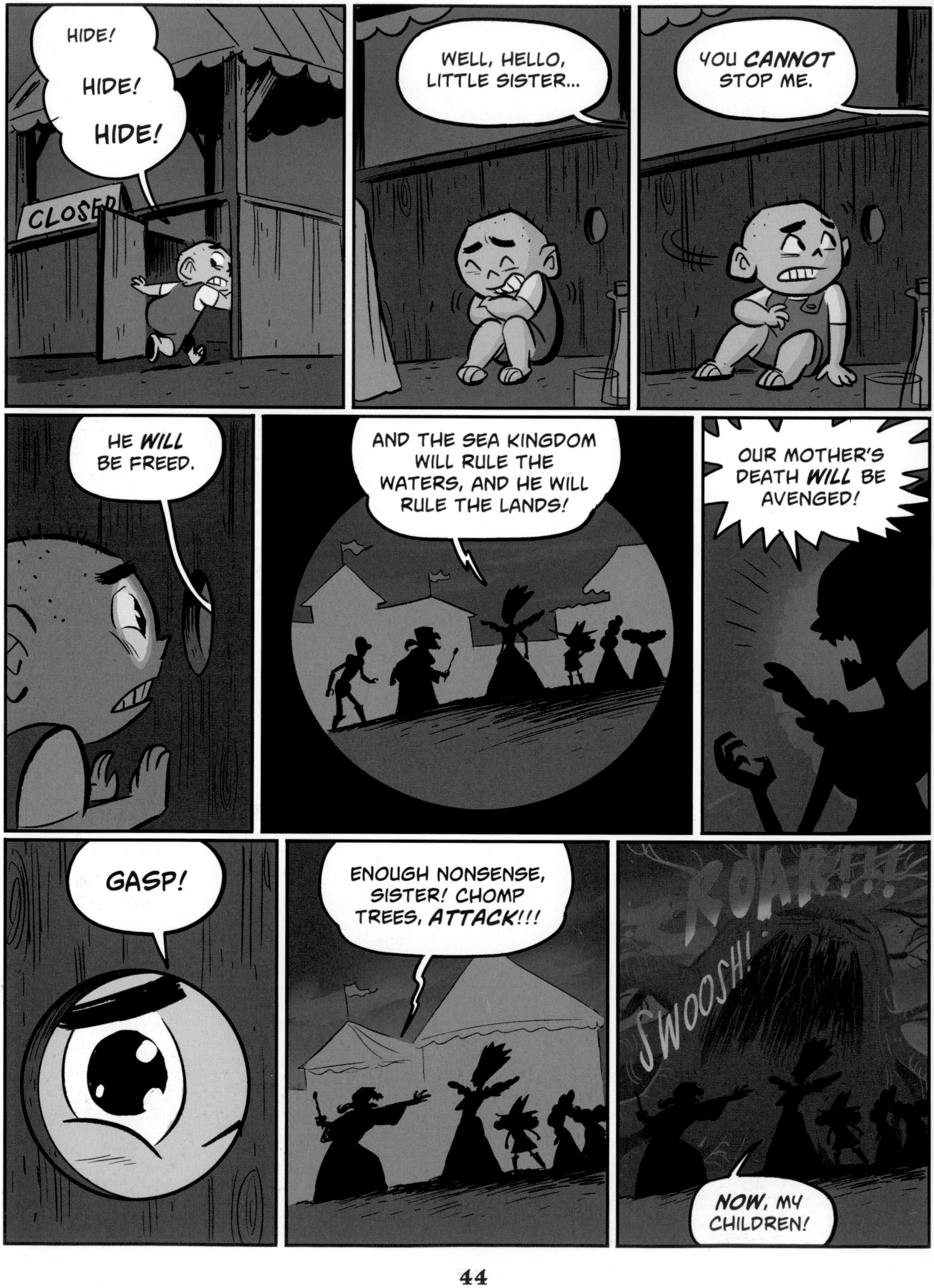
HIDE!
HIDE!
HIDE!
CLOSED
WELL, HELLO, LITTLE SISTER...
YOU CANNOT STOP ME.
HE WILL BE FREED.
AND THE SEA KINGDOM WILL RULE THE WATERS, AND HE WILL RULE THE LANDS!
OUR MOTHER'S DEATH WILL BE AVENGED!
GASP!
ENOUGH NONSENSE, SISTER! CHOMP TREES, ATTACK!!!
ROAR!!!
SWOOSH!
NOW, MY CHILDREN!

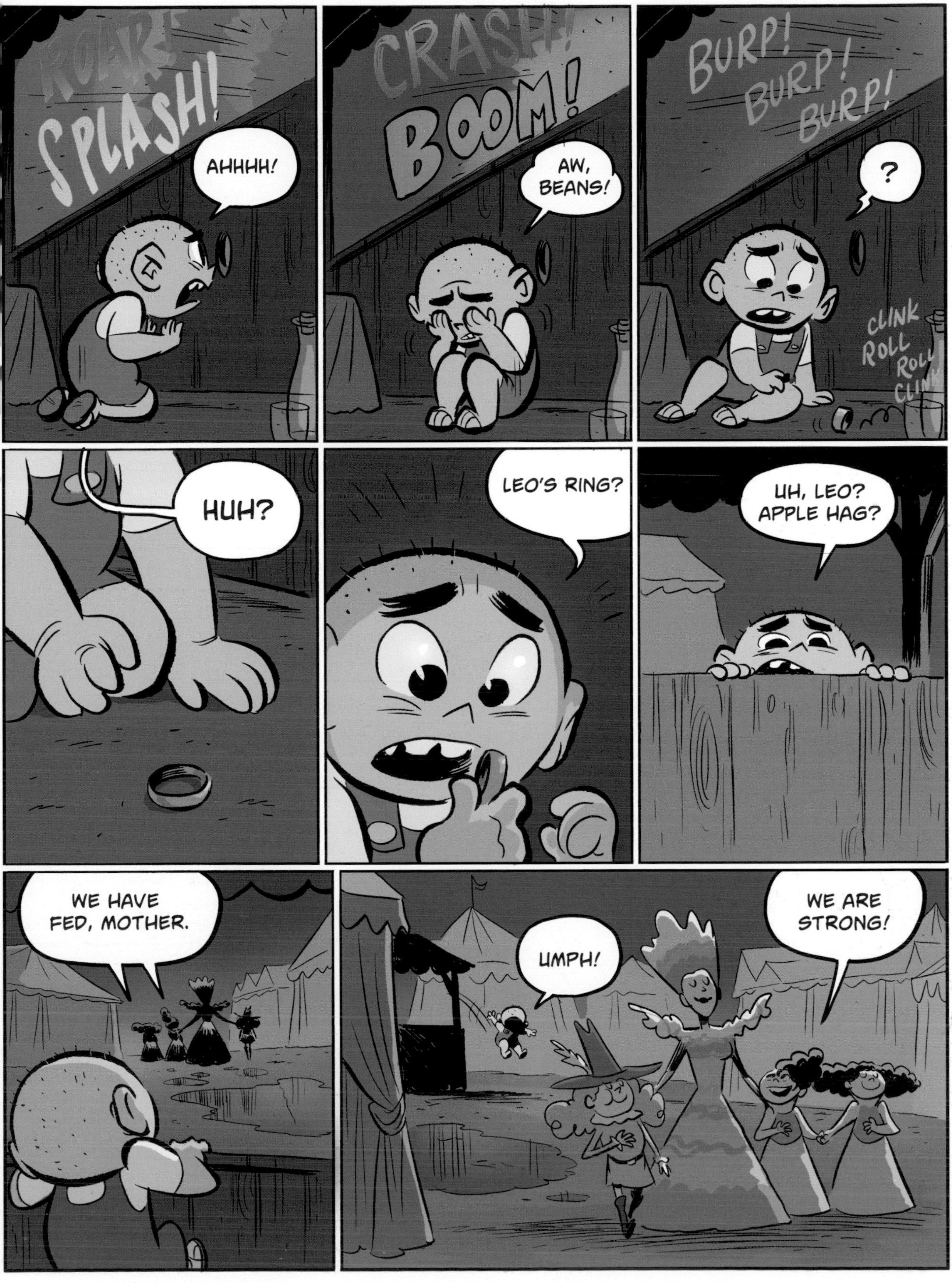
ROAR!
SPLASH!
AHHHH!
CRASH!
BOOM!
AW, BEANS!
BURP! BURP! BURP!
?
CLINK ROLL ROLL CLINK
HUH?
LEO'S RING?
UH, LEO? APPLE HAG?
WE HAVE FED, MOTHER.
UMPH!
WE ARE STRONG!

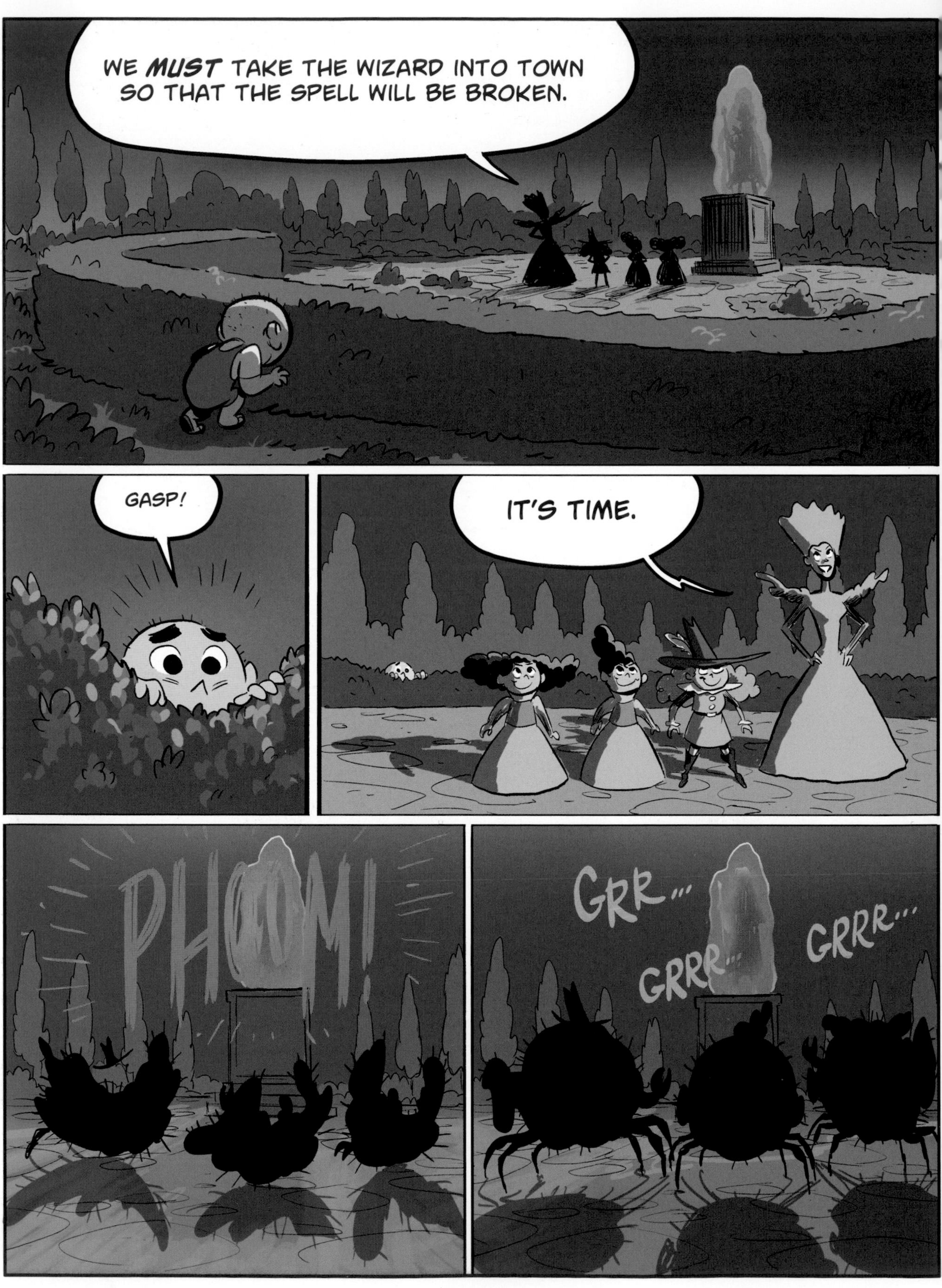
WE *MUST* TAKE THE WIZARD INTO TOWN SO THAT THE SPELL WILL BE BROKEN.
GASP!
IT'S TIME.
PHOOM!
GRR...
GRRR...
GRRR...

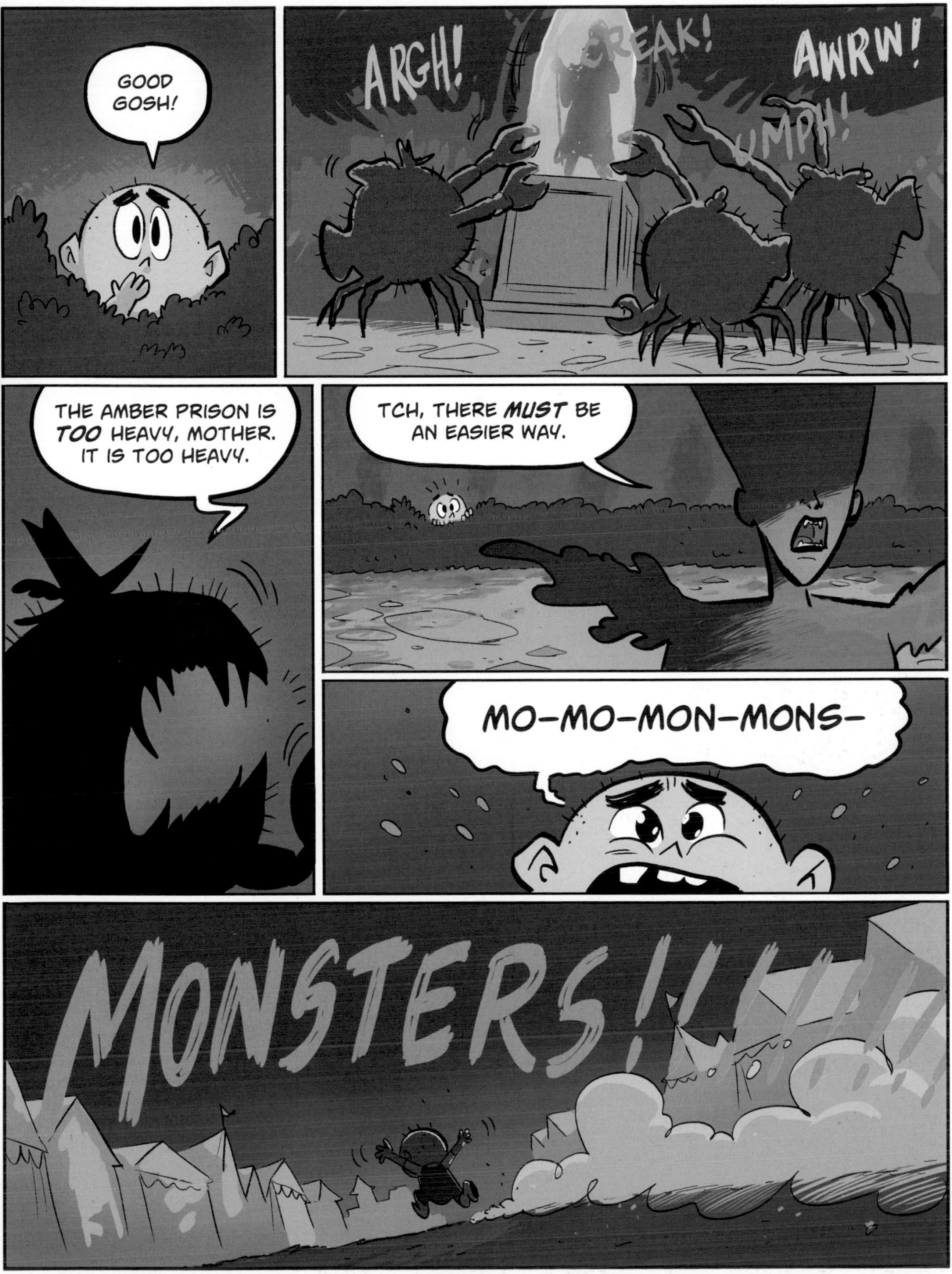
GOOD GOSH!
ARGH!
CREAK!
AWRW!
UMPH!
THE AMBER PRISON IS *TOO* HEAVY, MOTHER. IT IS TOO HEAVY.
TCH, THERE *MUST* BE AN EASIER WAY.
MO-MO-MON-MONS-
MONSTERS!!!!!

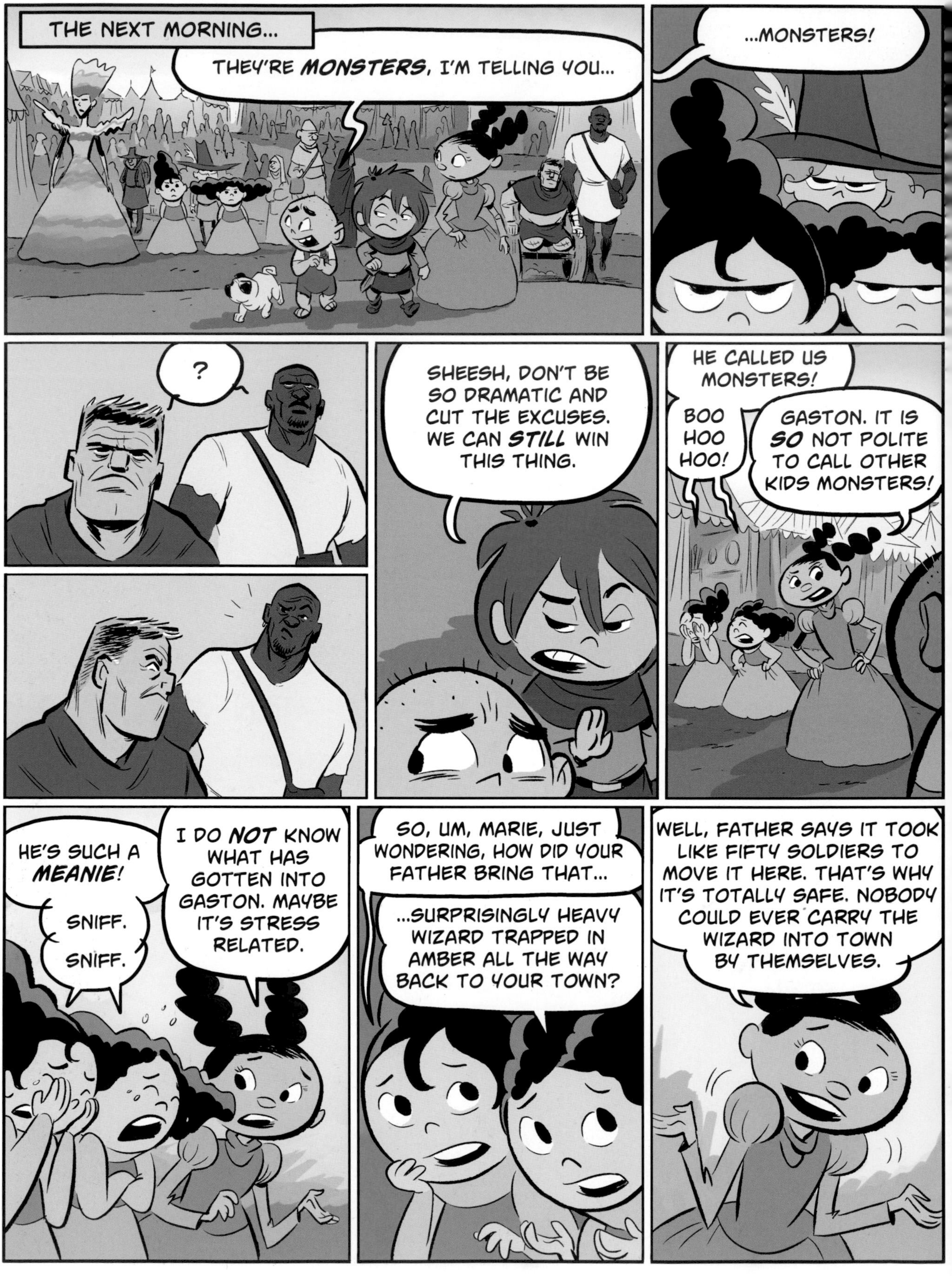
THE NEXT MORNING...
THEY'RE MONSTERS, I'M TELLING YOU...
...MONSTERS!
?
SHEESH, DON'T BE SO DRAMATIC AND CUT THE EXCUSES. WE CAN STILL WIN THIS THING.
HE CALLED US MONSTERS!
BOO HOO HOO!
GASTON. IT IS SO NOT POLITE TO CALL OTHER KIDS MONSTERS!
HE'S SUCH A MEANIE!
SNIFF.
SNIFF.
I DO NOT KNOW WHAT HAS GOTTEN INTO GASTON. MAYBE IT'S STRESS RELATED.
SO, UM, MARIE, JUST WONDERING, HOW DID YOUR FATHER BRING THAT...
...SURPRISINGLY HEAVY WIZARD TRAPPED IN AMBER ALL THE WAY BACK TO YOUR TOWN?
WELL, FATHER SAYS IT TOOK LIKE FIFTY SOLDIERS TO MOVE IT HERE. THAT'S WHY IT'S TOTALLY SAFE. NOBODY COULD EVER CARRY THE WIZARD INTO TOWN BY THEMSELVES.

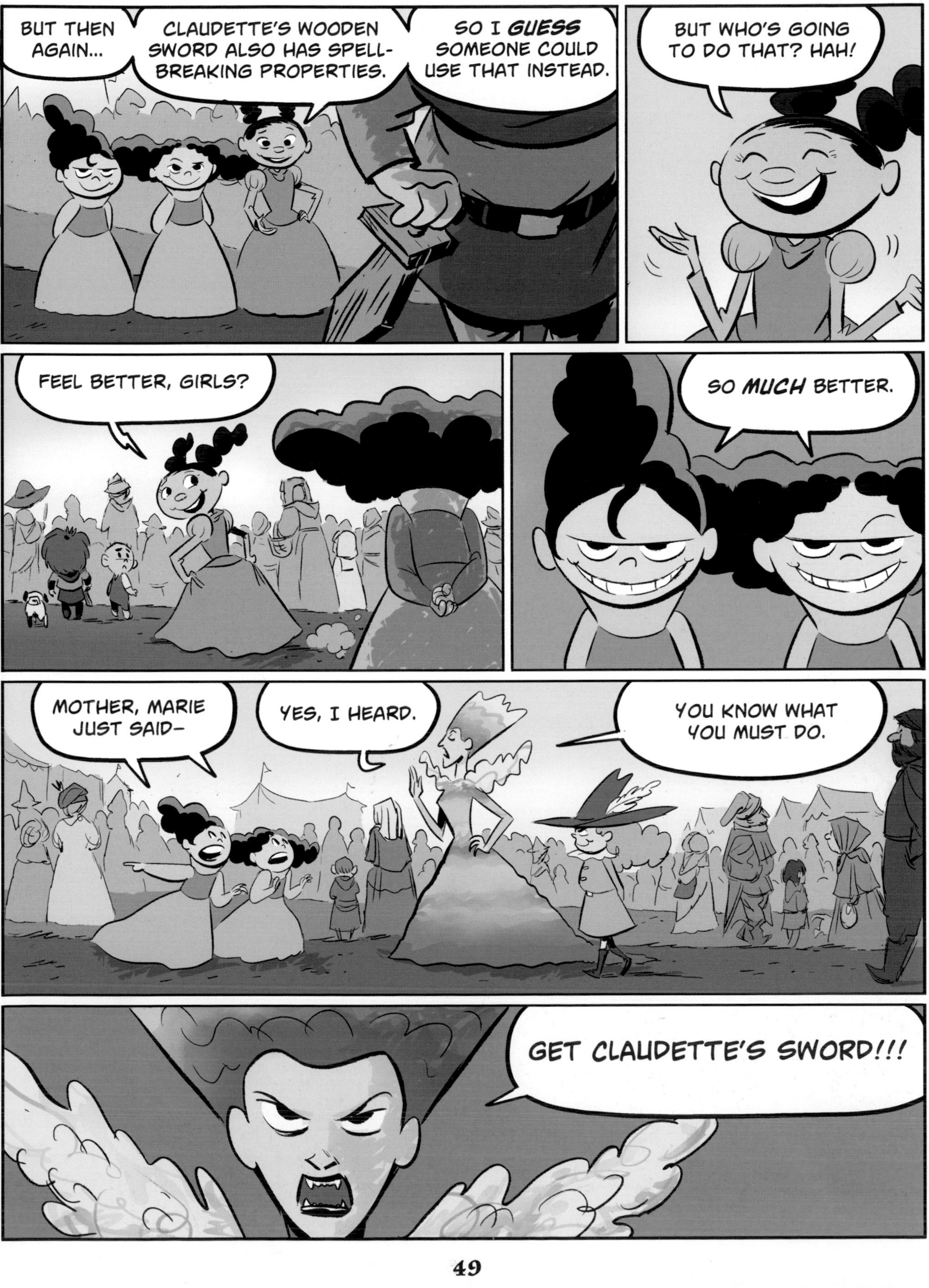

BUT THEN AGAIN...
CLAUDETTE'S WOODEN SWORD ALSO HAS SPELL-BREAKING PROPERTIES.
SO I *GUESS* SOMEONE COULD USE THAT INSTEAD.
BUT WHO'S GOING TO DO THAT? HAH!
FEEL BETTER, GIRLS?
SO *MUCH* BETTER.
MOTHER, MARIE JUST SAID–
YES, I HEARD.
YOU KNOW WHAT YOU MUST DO.
GET CLAUDETTE'S SWORD!!!

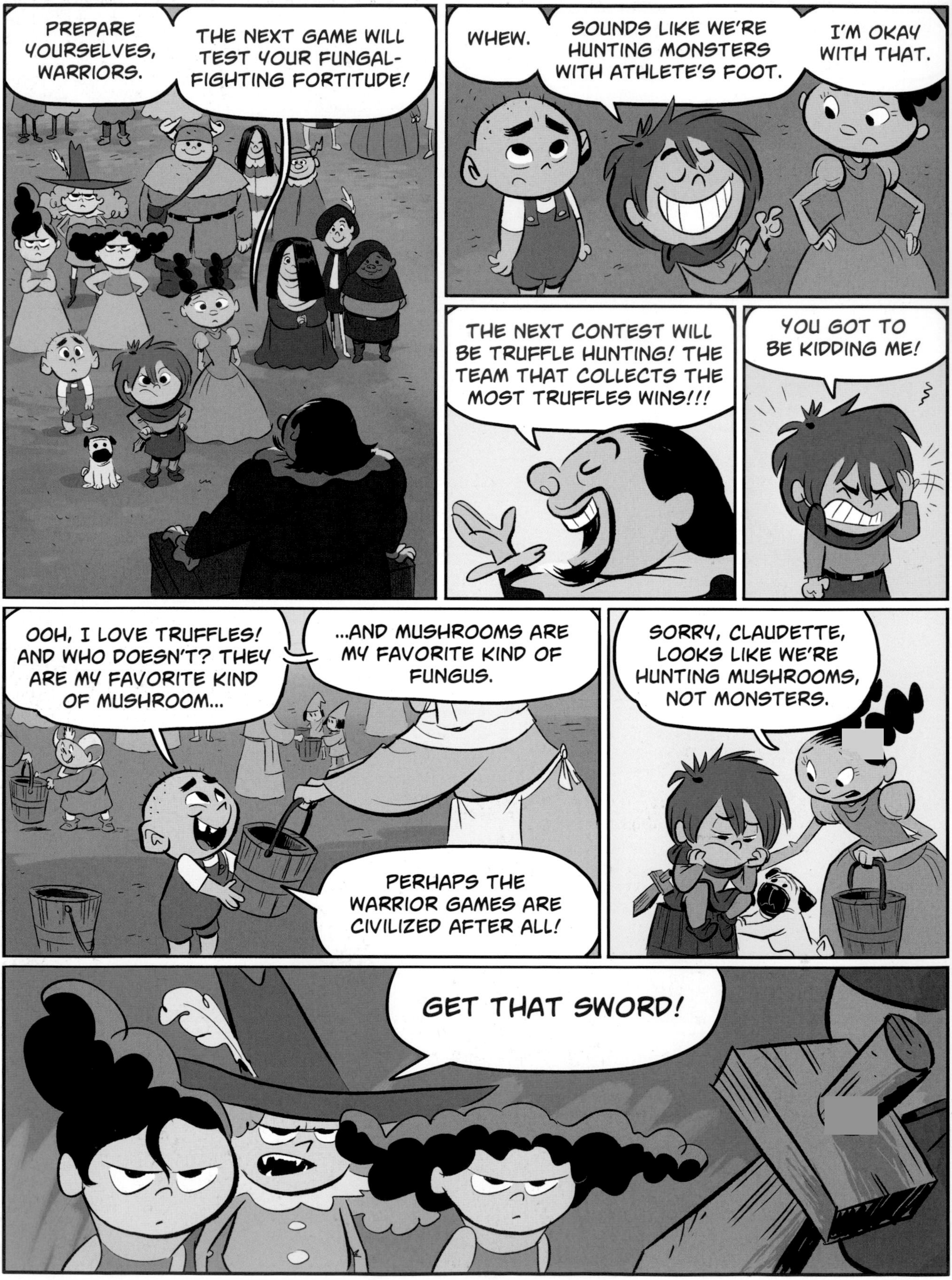
PREPARE YOURSELVES, WARRIORS.
THE NEXT GAME WILL TEST YOUR FUNGAL-FIGHTING FORTITUDE!
WHEW.
SOUNDS LIKE WE'RE HUNTING MONSTERS WITH ATHLETE'S FOOT.
I'M OKAY WITH THAT.
THE NEXT CONTEST WILL BE TRUFFLE HUNTING! THE TEAM THAT COLLECTS THE MOST TRUFFLES WINS!!!
YOU GOT TO BE KIDDING ME!
OOH, I LOVE TRUFFLES! AND WHO DOESN'T? THEY ARE MY FAVORITE KIND OF MUSHROOM...
...AND MUSHROOMS ARE MY FAVORITE KIND OF FUNGUS.
PERHAPS THE WARRIOR GAMES ARE CIVILIZED AFTER ALL!
SORRY, CLAUDETTE, LOOKS LIKE WE'RE HUNTING MUSHROOMS, NOT MONSTERS.
GET THAT SWORD!

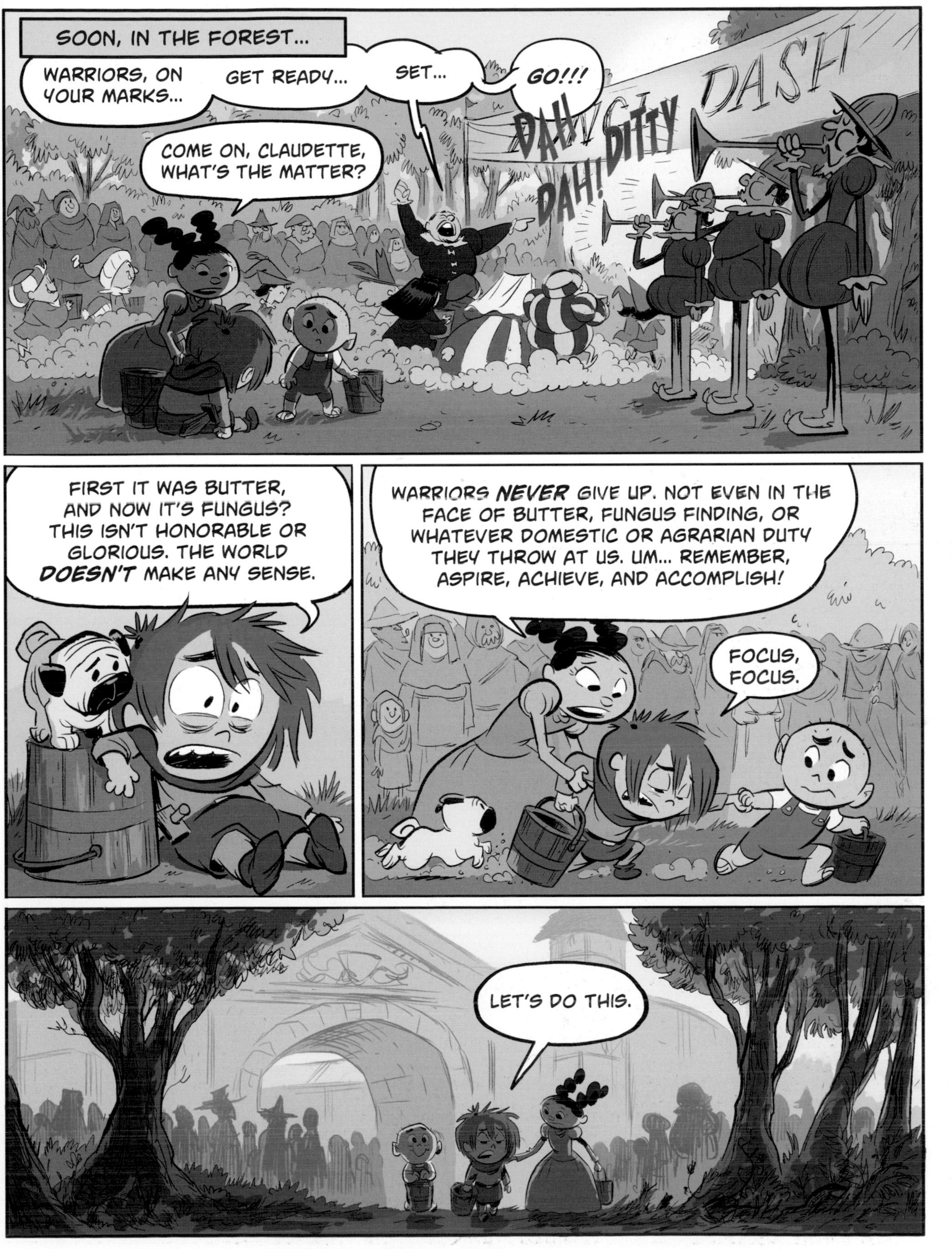
SOON, IN THE FOREST...
WARRIORS, ON YOUR MARKS...
GET READY...
SET...
GO!!!
DASH
DAH DAH! DITTY
COME ON, CLAUDETTE, WHAT'S THE MATTER?
FIRST IT WAS BUTTER, AND NOW IT'S FUNGUS? THIS ISN'T HONORABLE OR GLORIOUS. THE WORLD DOESN'T MAKE ANY SENSE.
WARRIORS NEVER GIVE UP. NOT EVEN IN THE FACE OF BUTTER, FUNGUS FINDING, OR WHATEVER DOMESTIC OR AGRARIAN DUTY THEY THROW AT US. UM... REMEMBER, ASPIRE, ACHIEVE, AND ACCOMPLISH!
FOCUS, FOCUS.
LET'S DO THIS.

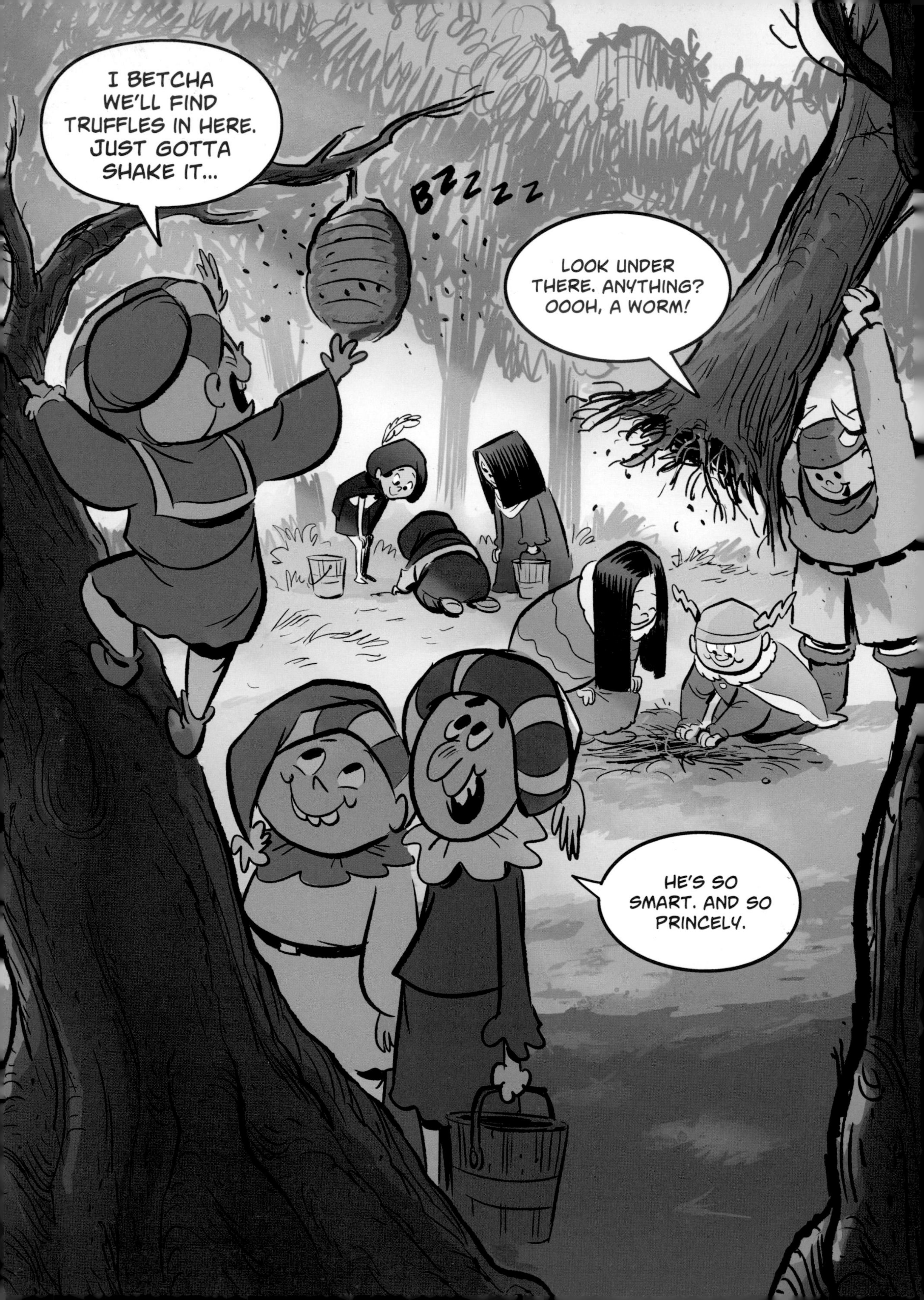
I BETCHA WE'LL FIND TRUFFLES IN HERE. JUST GOTTA SHAKE IT...
BZZZZZ
LOOK UNDER THERE. ANYTHING? OOOH, A WORM!
HE'S SO SMART. AND SO PRINCELY.

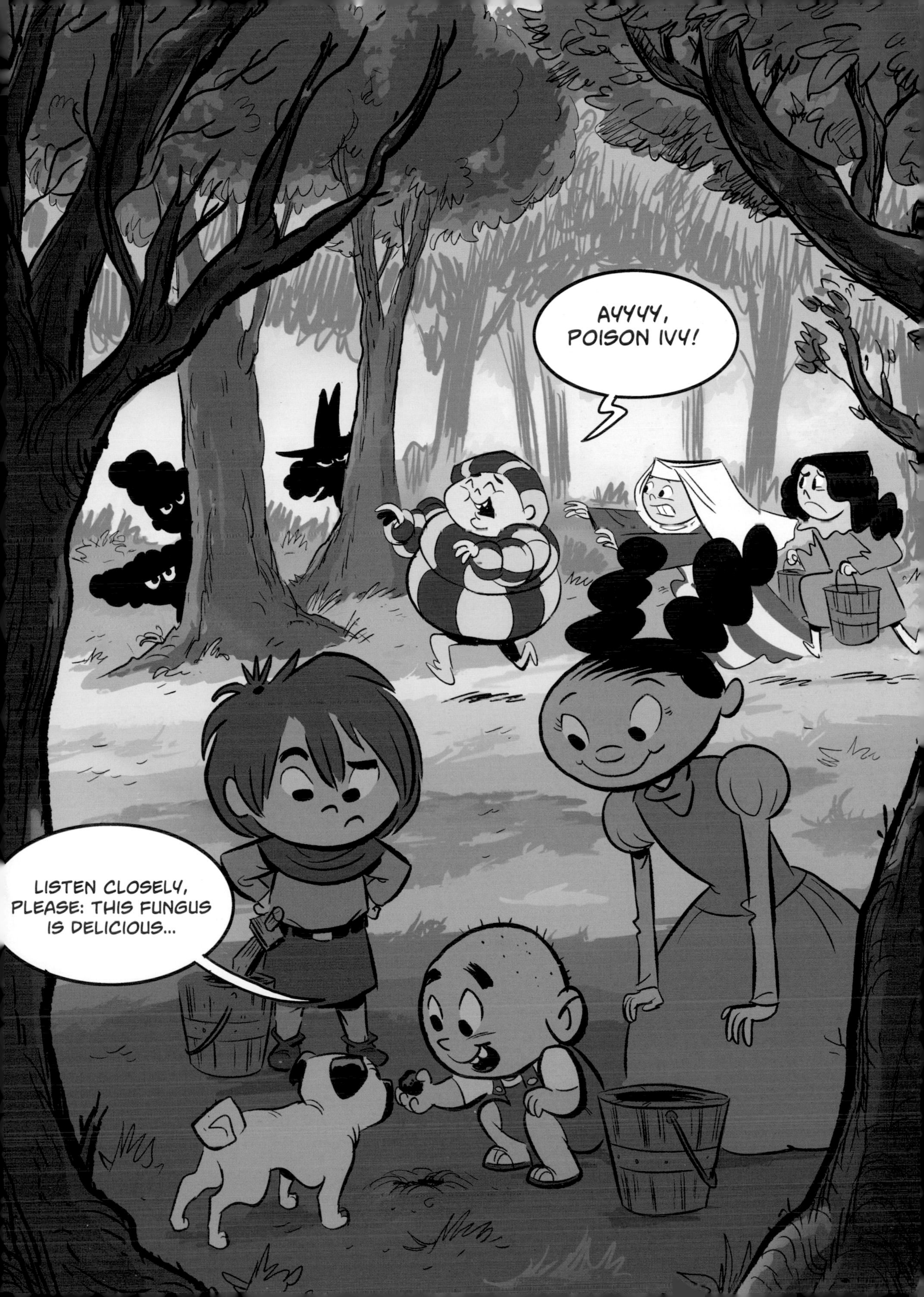
AYYYY, POISON IVY!
LISTEN CLOSELY, PLEASE: THIS FUNGUS IS DELICIOUS...

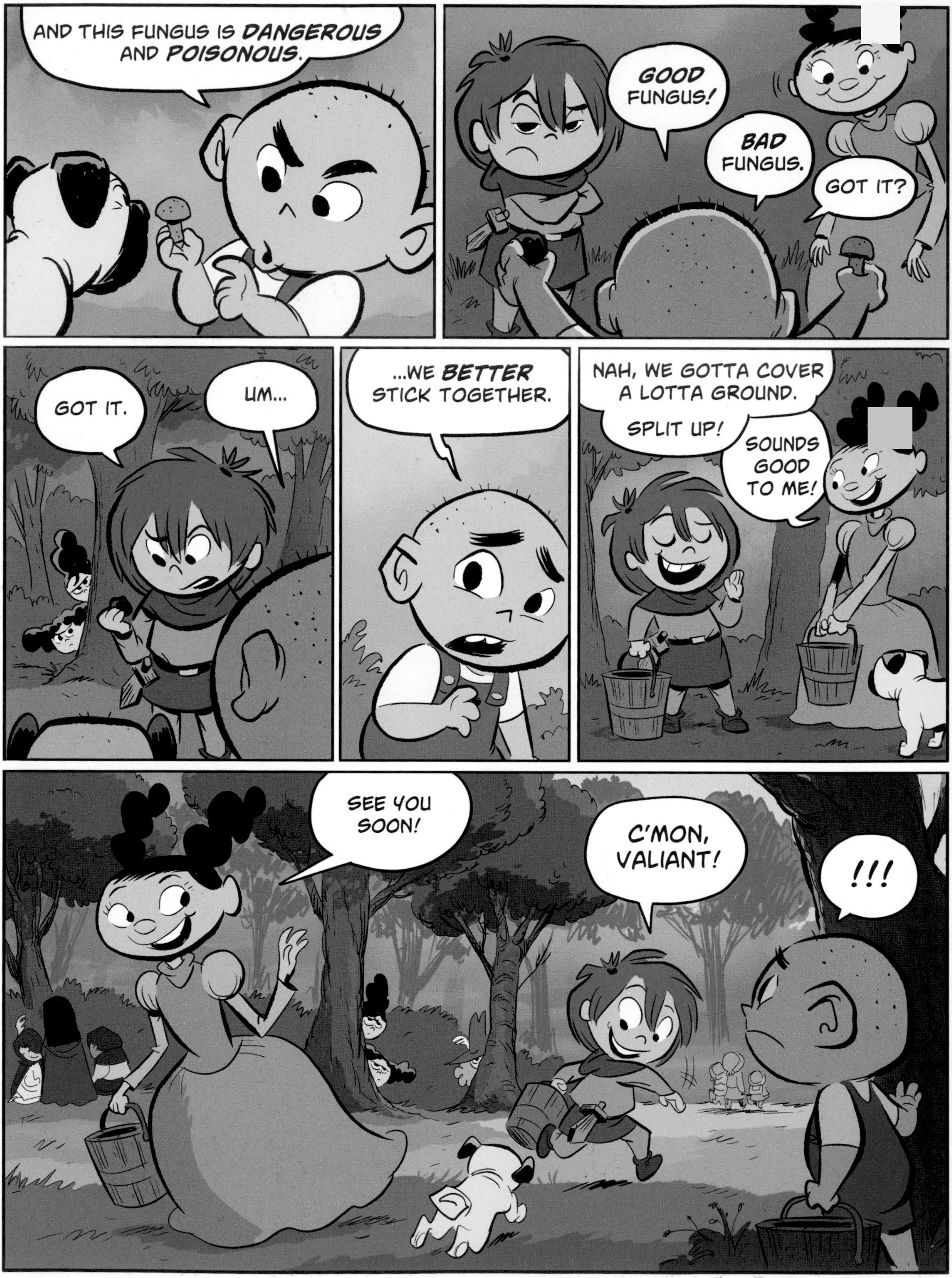
AND THIS FUNGUS IS DANGEROUS AND POISONOUS.
GOOD FUNGUS!
BAD FUNGUS.
GOT IT?
GOT IT.
UM...
...WE BETTER STICK TOGETHER.
NAH, WE GOTTA COVER A LOTTA GROUND.
SPLIT UP!
SOUNDS GOOD TO ME!
SEE YOU SOON!
C'MON, VALIANT!
!!!

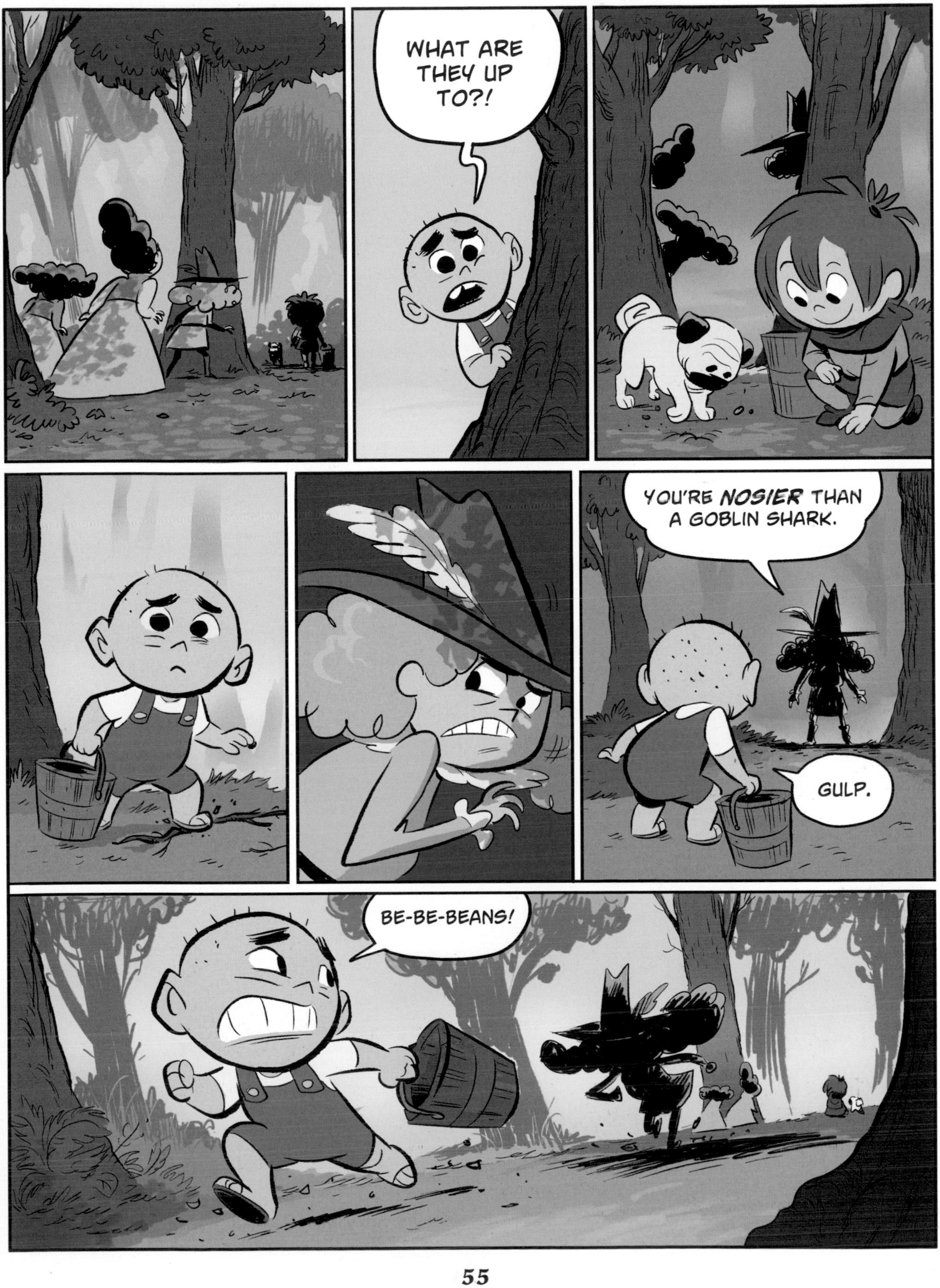
WHAT ARE THEY UP TO?!
YOU'RE **NOSIER** THAN A GOBLIN SHARK.
GULP.
BE-BE-BEANS!

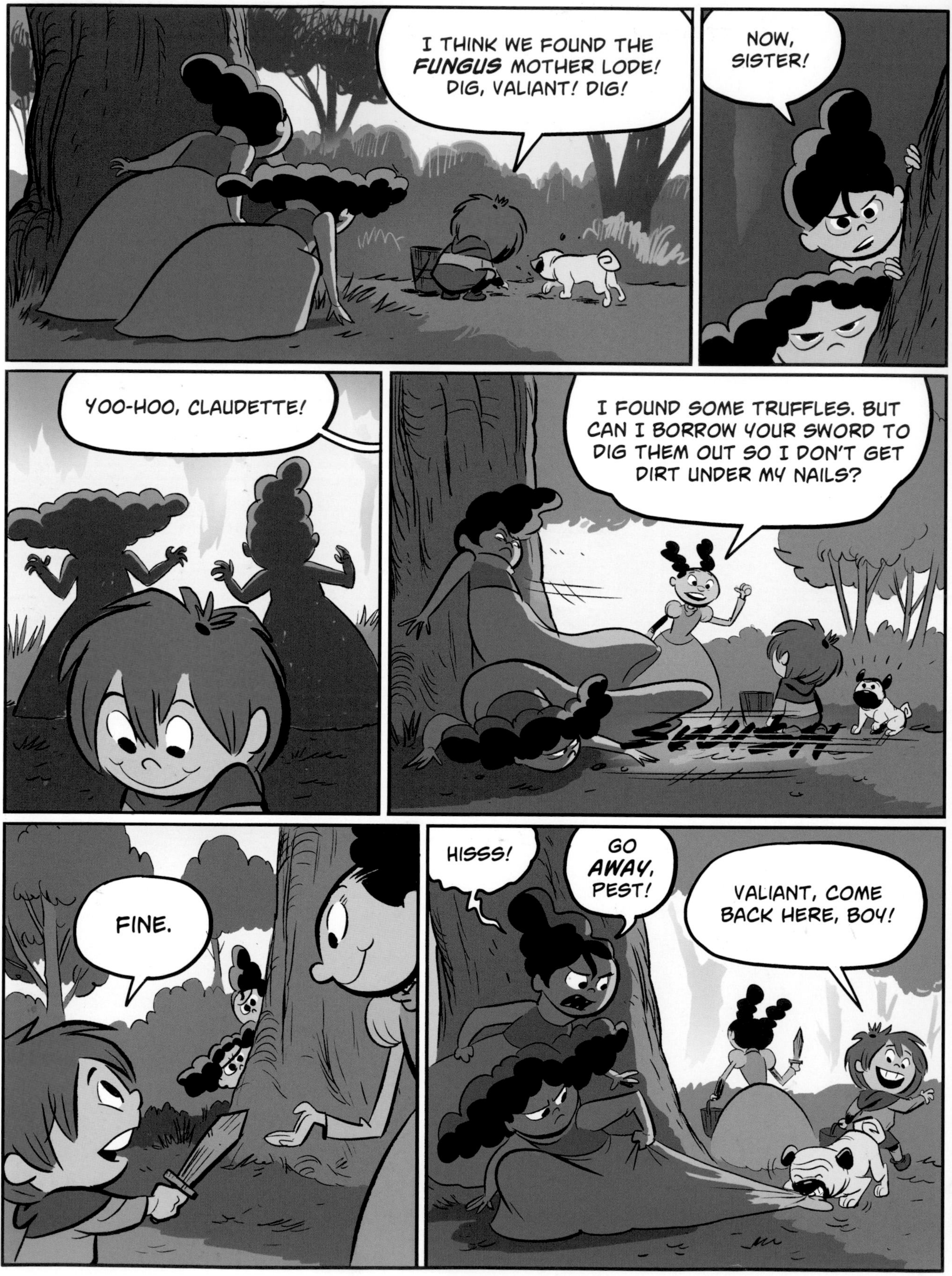
I THINK WE FOUND THE *FUNGUS* MOTHER LODE! DIG, VALIANT! DIG!
NOW, SISTER!
YOO-HOO, CLAUDETTE!
I FOUND SOME TRUFFLES. BUT CAN I BORROW YOUR SWORD TO DIG THEM OUT SO I DON'T GET DIRT UNDER MY NAILS?
FINE.
HISSS!
GO *AWAY*, PEST!
VALIANT, COME BACK HERE, BOY!

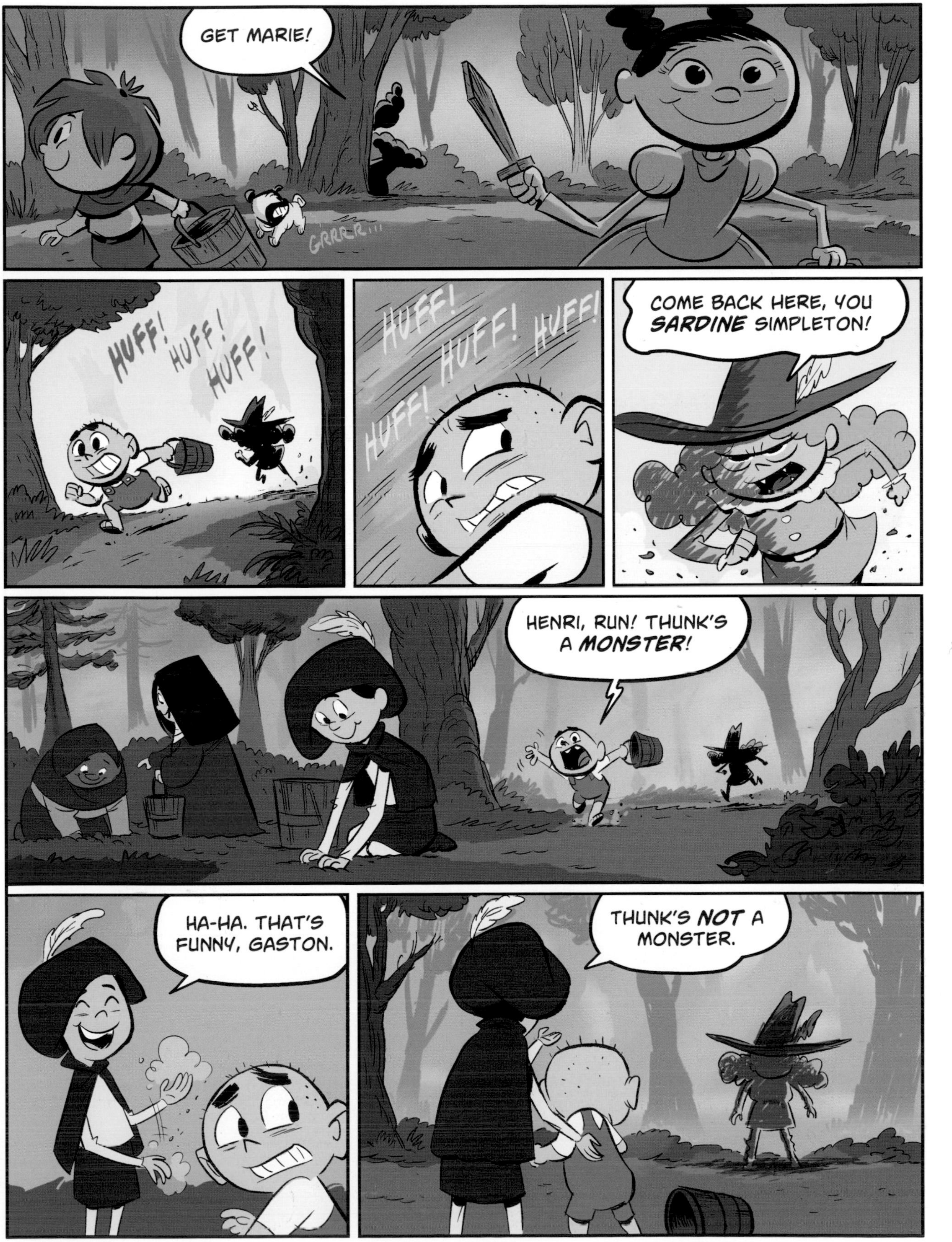
GET MARIE!
GRRRR...
HUFF! HUFF! HUFF!
HUFF! HUFF! HUFF! HUFF!
COME BACK HERE, YOU SARDINE SIMPLETON!
HENRI, RUN! THUNK'S A MONSTER!
HA-HA. THAT'S FUNNY, GASTON.
THUNK'S NOT A MONSTER.

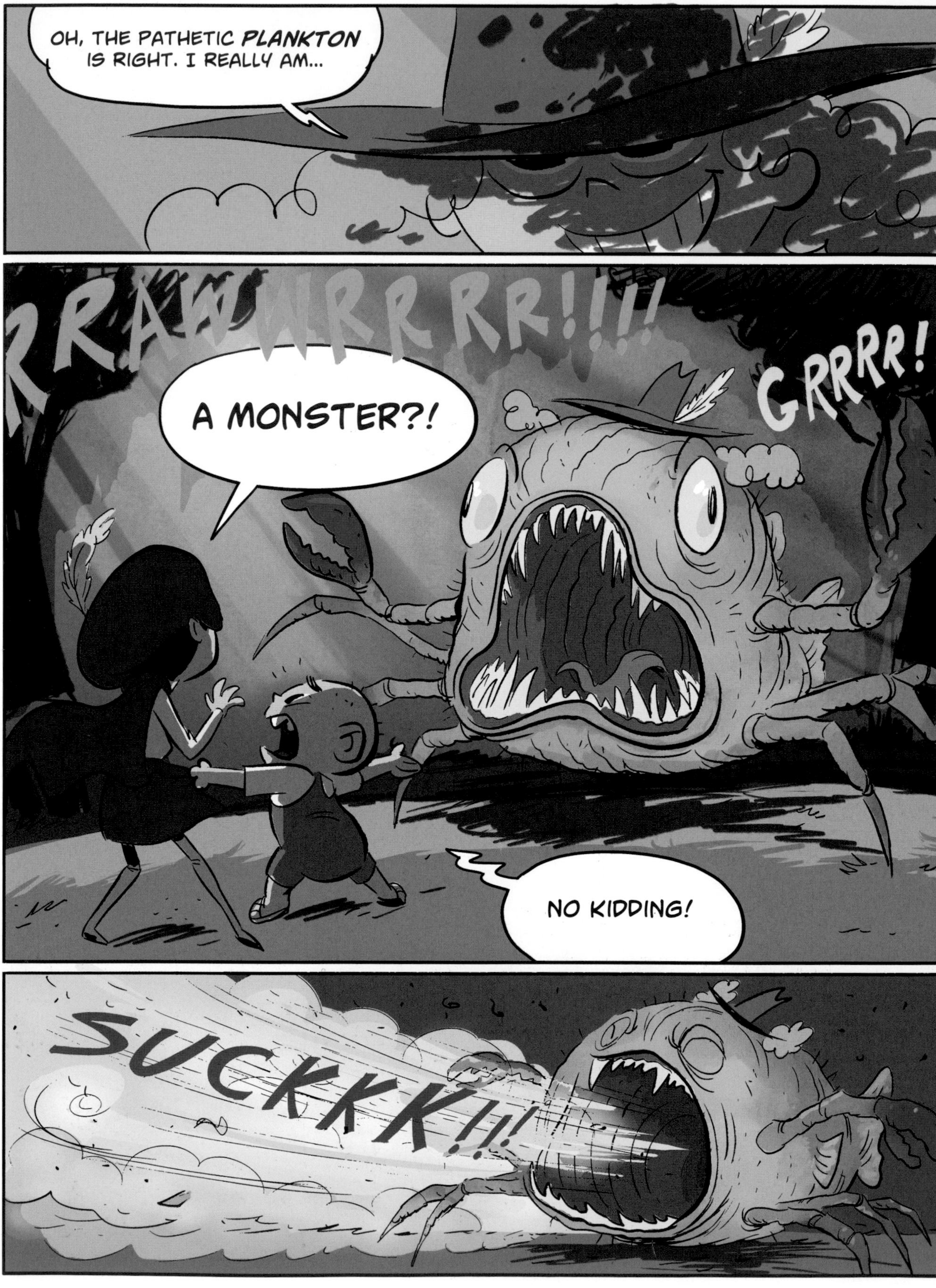
OH, THE PATHETIC *PLANKTON* IS RIGHT. I REALLY AM...
RRAWWRRRRR!!!!
A MONSTER?!
GRRRR!
NO KIDDING!
SUCKKK!!!

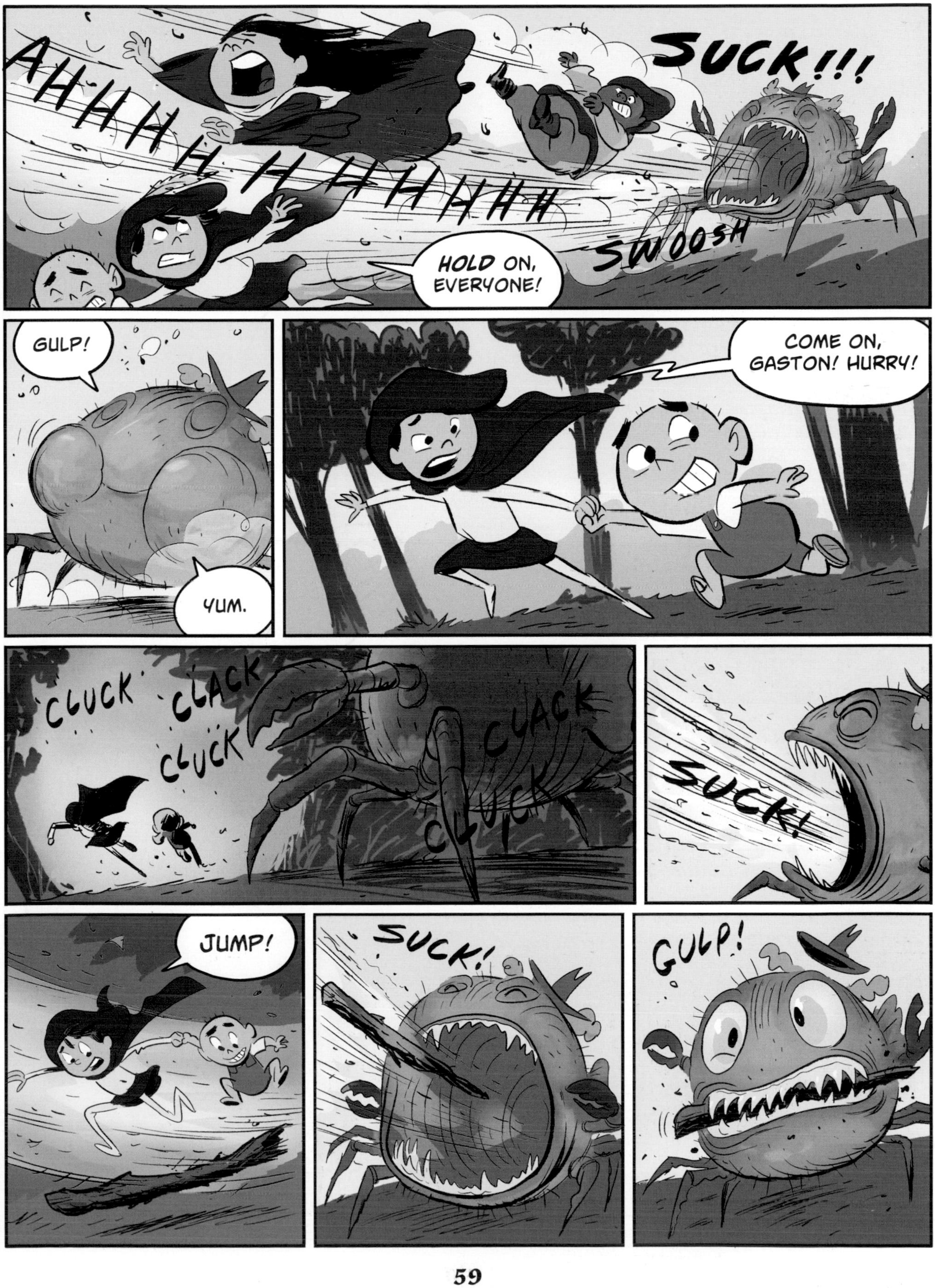
AHHHHHHHHHHHHHH
SUCK!!!
SWOOSH
HOLD ON, EVERYONE!
GULP!
YUM.
COME ON, GASTON! HURRY!
CLUCK
CLACK
CLUCK
CLACK
CLUCK
SUCK!
JUMP!
SUCK!
GULP!

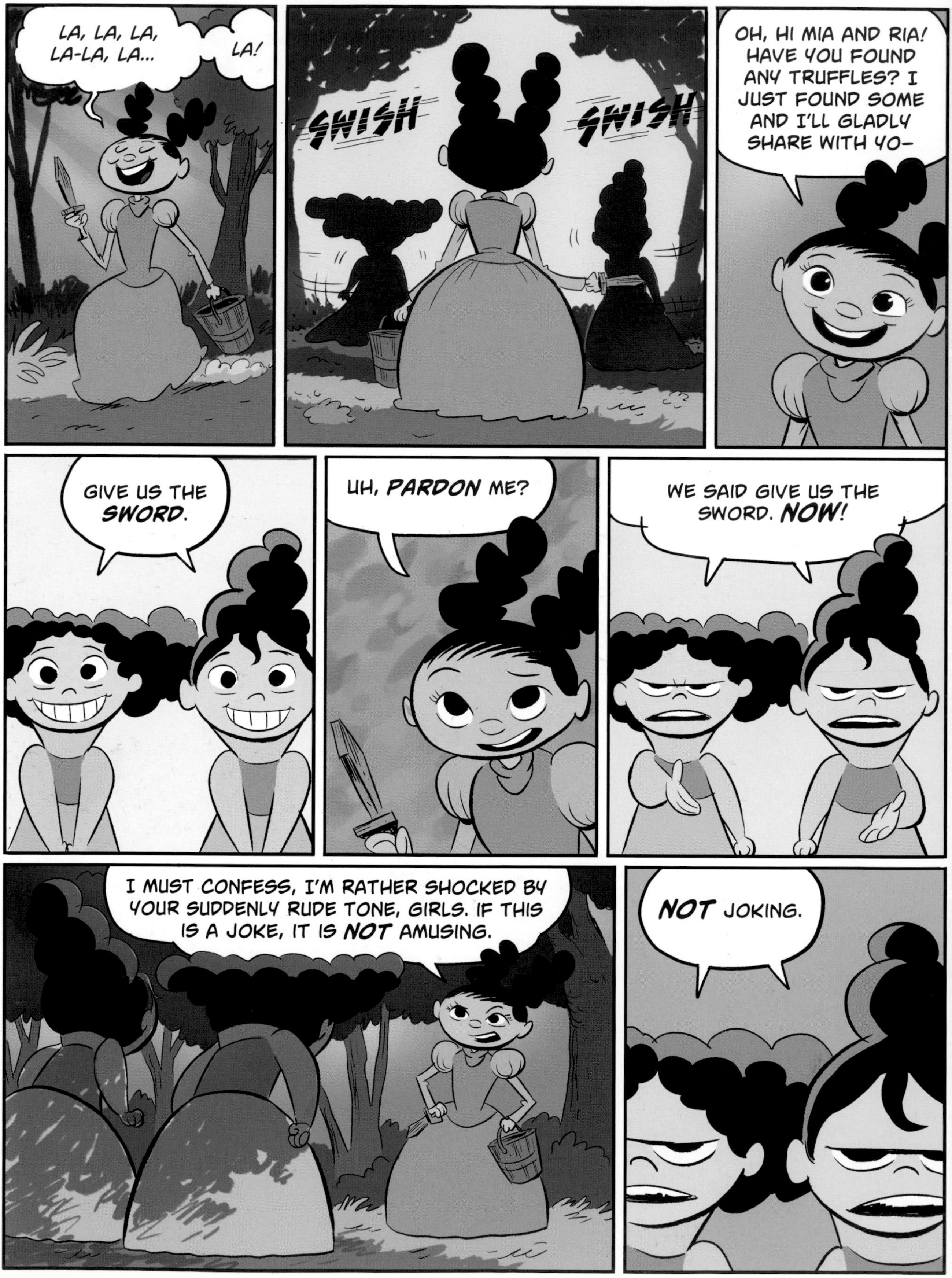
LA, LA, LA,
LA-LA, LA...
LA!
SWISH
SWISH
OH, HI MIA AND RIA! HAVE YOU FOUND ANY TRUFFLES? I JUST FOUND SOME AND I'LL GLADLY SHARE WITH YO–
GIVE US THE SWORD.
UH, PARDON ME?
WE SAID GIVE US THE SWORD. NOW!
I MUST CONFESS, I'M RATHER SHOCKED BY YOUR SUDDENLY RUDE TONE, GIRLS. IF THIS IS A JOKE, IT IS NOT AMUSING.
NOT JOKING.

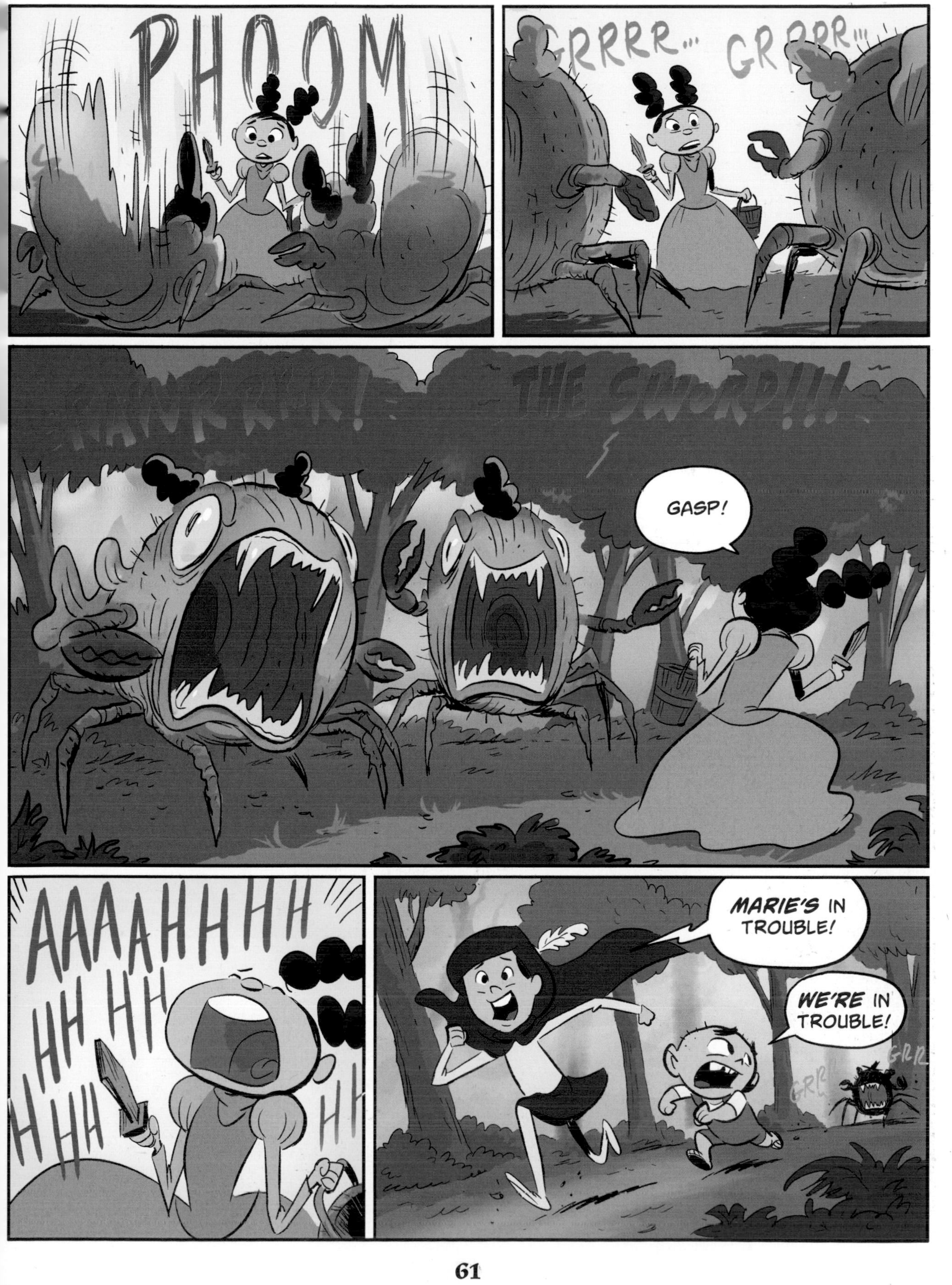
PHOOM
GRRRR...
GRRRR...
RAWRRRR!
THE SWORD!!!
GASP!
AAAAHHHHH HH HH HHH H
MARIE'S IN TROUBLE!
WE'RE IN TROUBLE!
GRR
GRR

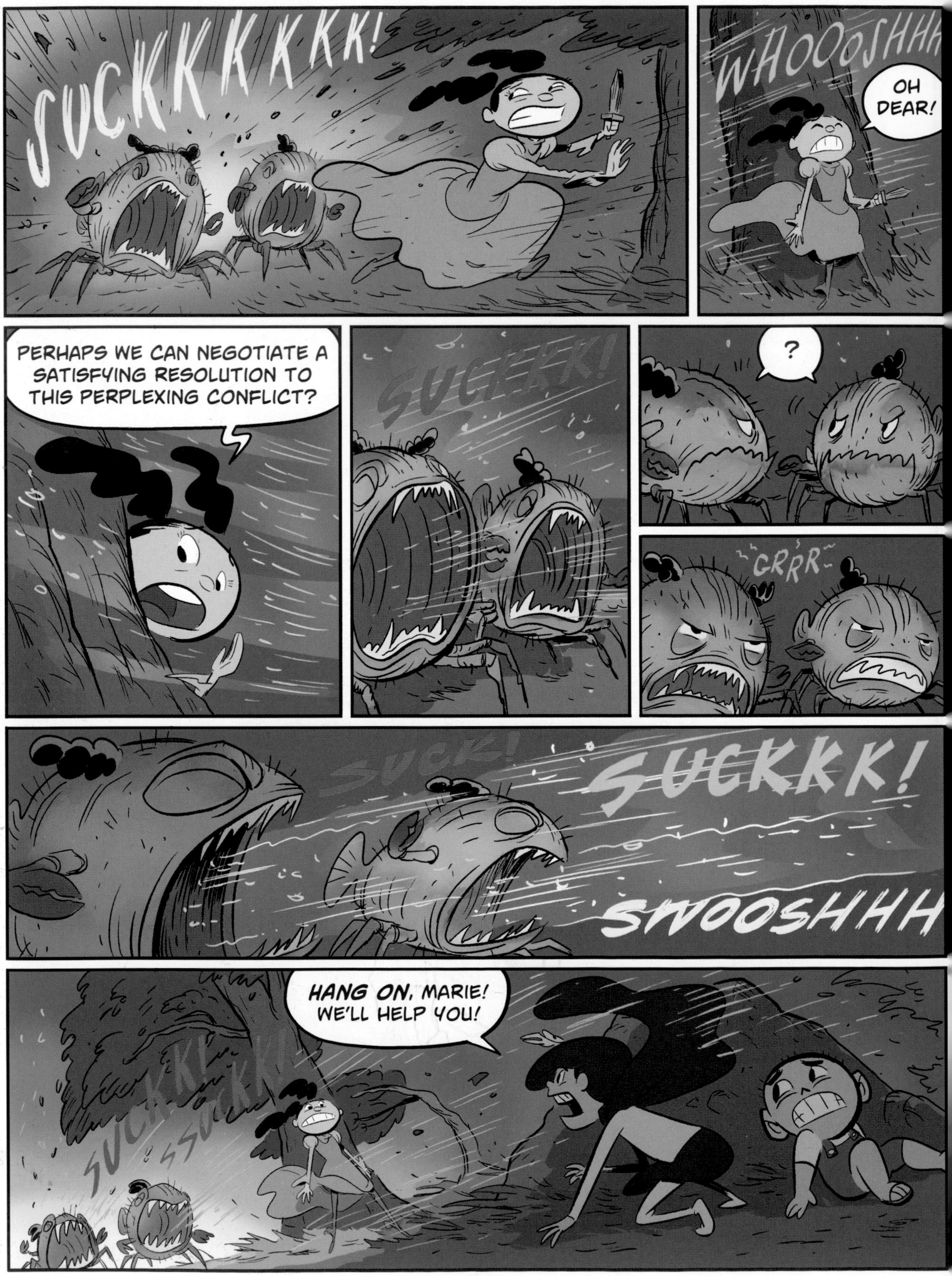
SUCKKKKKK!
WHOOOSHHH
OH DEAR!
PERHAPS WE CAN NEGOTIATE A SATISFYING RESOLUTION TO THIS PERPLEXING CONFLICT?
SUCKKK!
?
GRRR
SUCK!
SUCKKK!
SWOOSHHH
HANG ON, MARIE! WE'LL HELP YOU!
SUCK!
SSUCK!

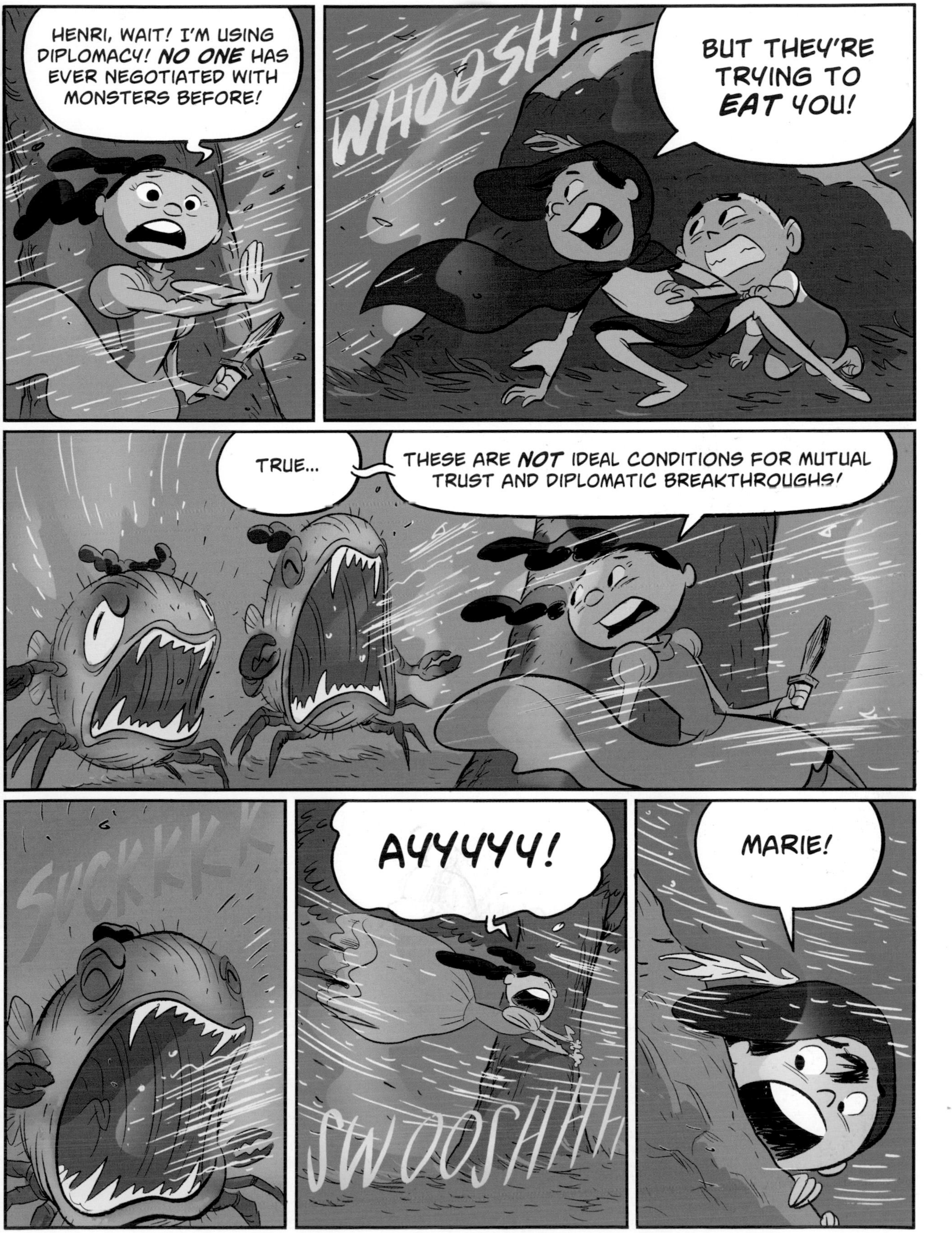
HENRI, WAIT! I'M USING DIPLOMACY! NO ONE HAS EVER NEGOTIATED WITH MONSTERS BEFORE!
WHOOSH!
BUT THEY'RE TRYING TO EAT YOU!
TRUE...
THESE ARE NOT IDEAL CONDITIONS FOR MUTUAL TRUST AND DIPLOMATIC BREAKTHROUGHS!
SUCKKKK
AYYYYY!
SWOOSHHH
MARIE!

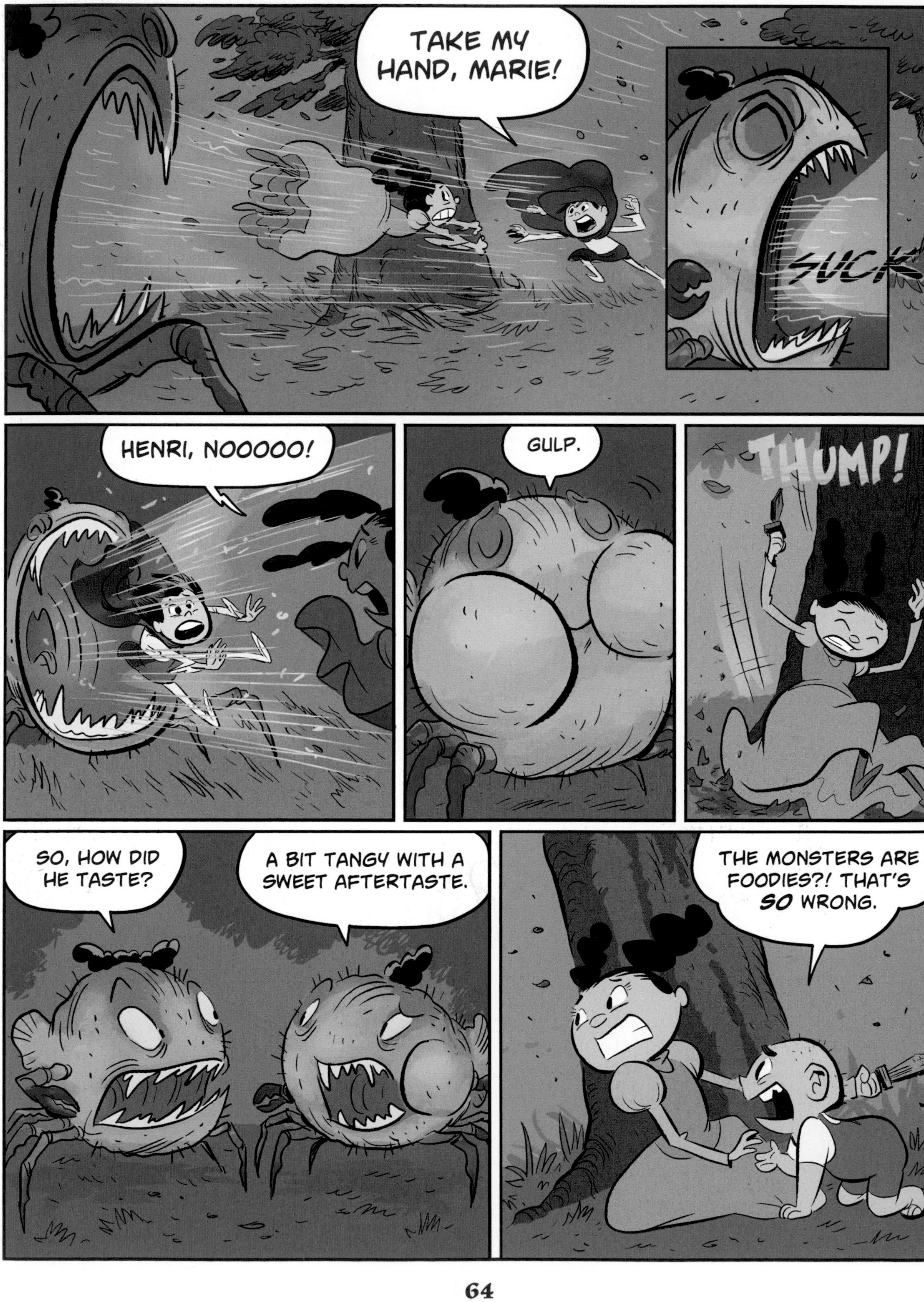
TAKE MY HAND, MARIE!
SUCK!
HENRI, NOOOOO!
GULP.
THUMP!
SO, HOW DID HE TASTE?
A BIT TANGY WITH A SWEET AFTERTASTE.
THE MONSTERS ARE FOODIES?! THAT'S *SO* WRONG.

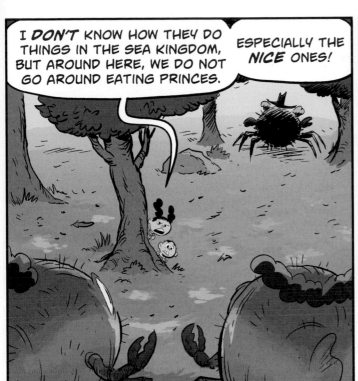

I **DON'T** KNOW HOW THEY DO THINGS IN THE SEA KINGDOM, BUT AROUND HERE, WE DO NOT GO AROUND EATING PRINCES.

ESPECIALLY THE **NICE** ONES!

THAT IS **UNACCEPTABLE** BEHAVIOR!

YEAH, WHAT SHE SAID!

GIVE US THE **SWORD**!

CLAUDETTE'S SWORD?

WHY?

SO THEY CAN FREE THE EVIL WIZARD!

THE WIZARD GROMBACH WILL RULE THE LAND, AND WE WILL RULE THE SEAS!

SUCKK!

MAHHHA

SWOOSHHH!!!

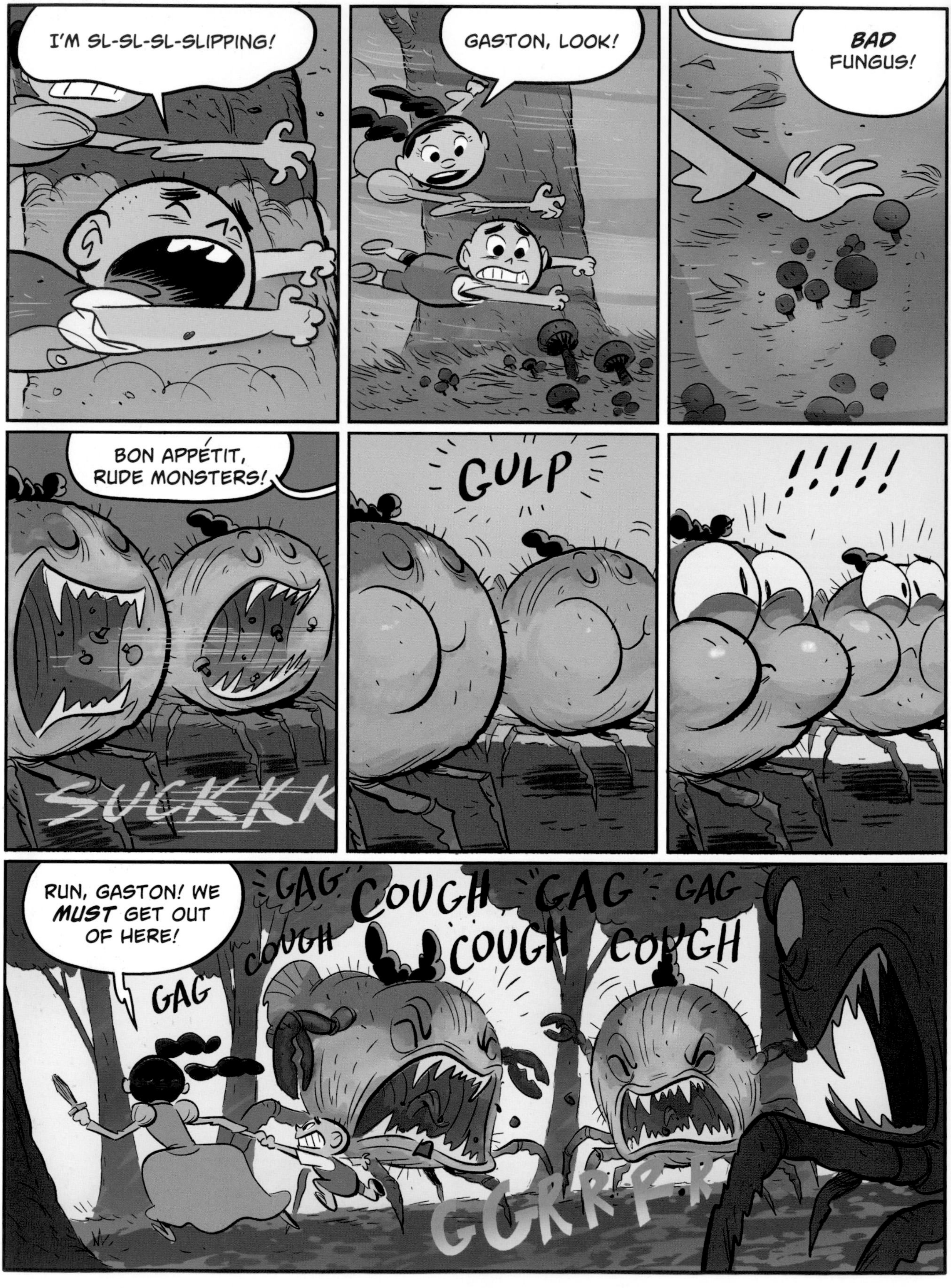
I'M SL-SL-SL-SLIPPING!
GASTON, LOOK!
BAD FUNGUS!
BON APPÉTIT, RUDE MONSTERS!
SUCKKK
GULP
!!!!!
RUN, GASTON! WE MUST GET OUT OF HERE!
GAG
COUGH
GAG
GAG
COUGH
COUGH
COUGH
GAG
GGRRRR

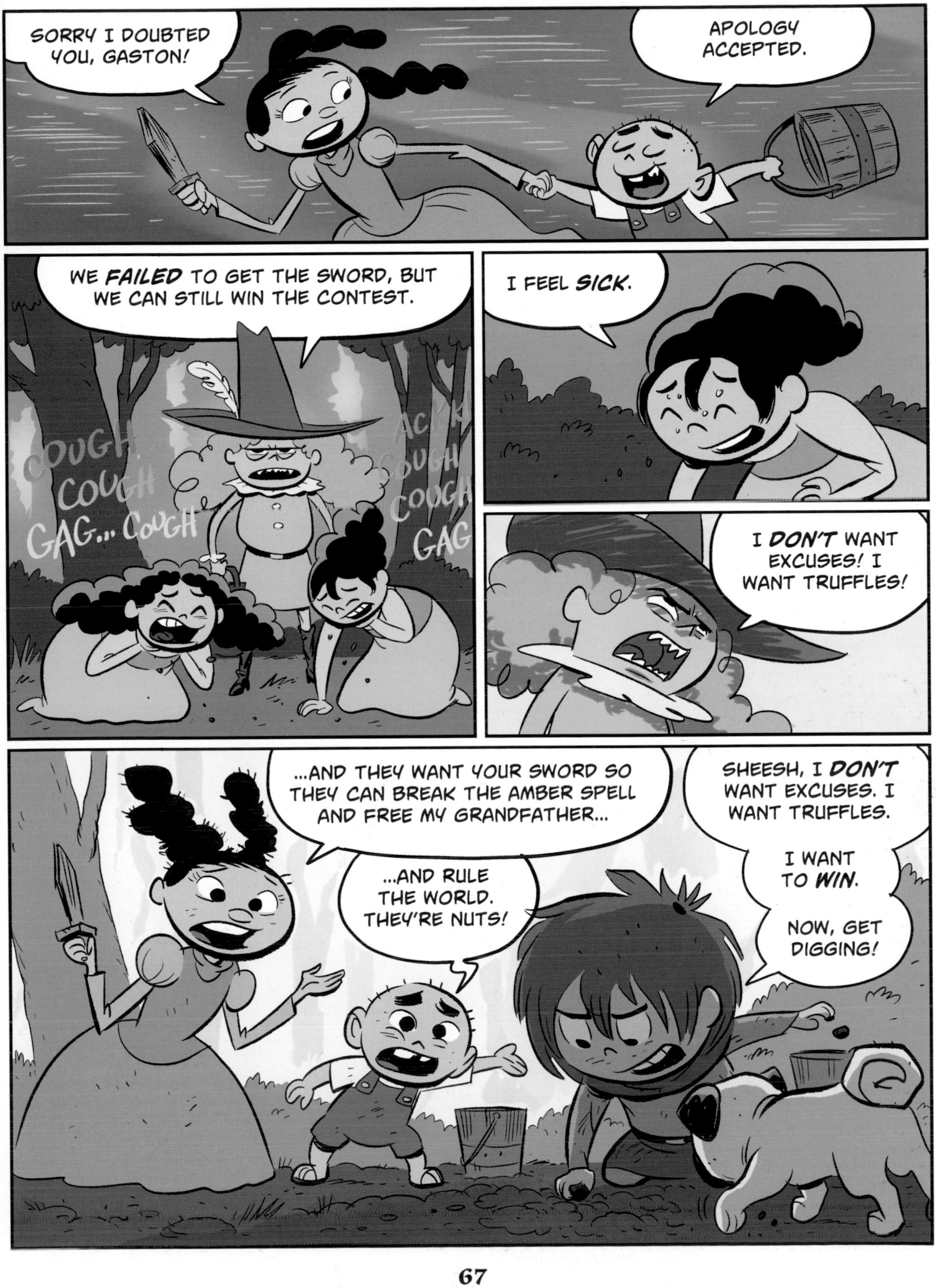
SORRY I DOUBTED YOU, GASTON!
APOLOGY ACCEPTED.
WE FAILED TO GET THE SWORD, BUT WE CAN STILL WIN THE CONTEST.
COUGH COUGH GAG... COUGH
ACKK COUGH COUGH GAG
I FEEL SICK.
I DON'T WANT EXCUSES! I WANT TRUFFLES!
...AND THEY WANT YOUR SWORD SO THEY CAN BREAK THE AMBER SPELL AND FREE MY GRANDFATHER...
...AND RULE THE WORLD. THEY'RE NUTS!
SHEESH, I DON'T WANT EXCUSES. I WANT TRUFFLES.
I WANT TO WIN.
NOW, GET DIGGING!

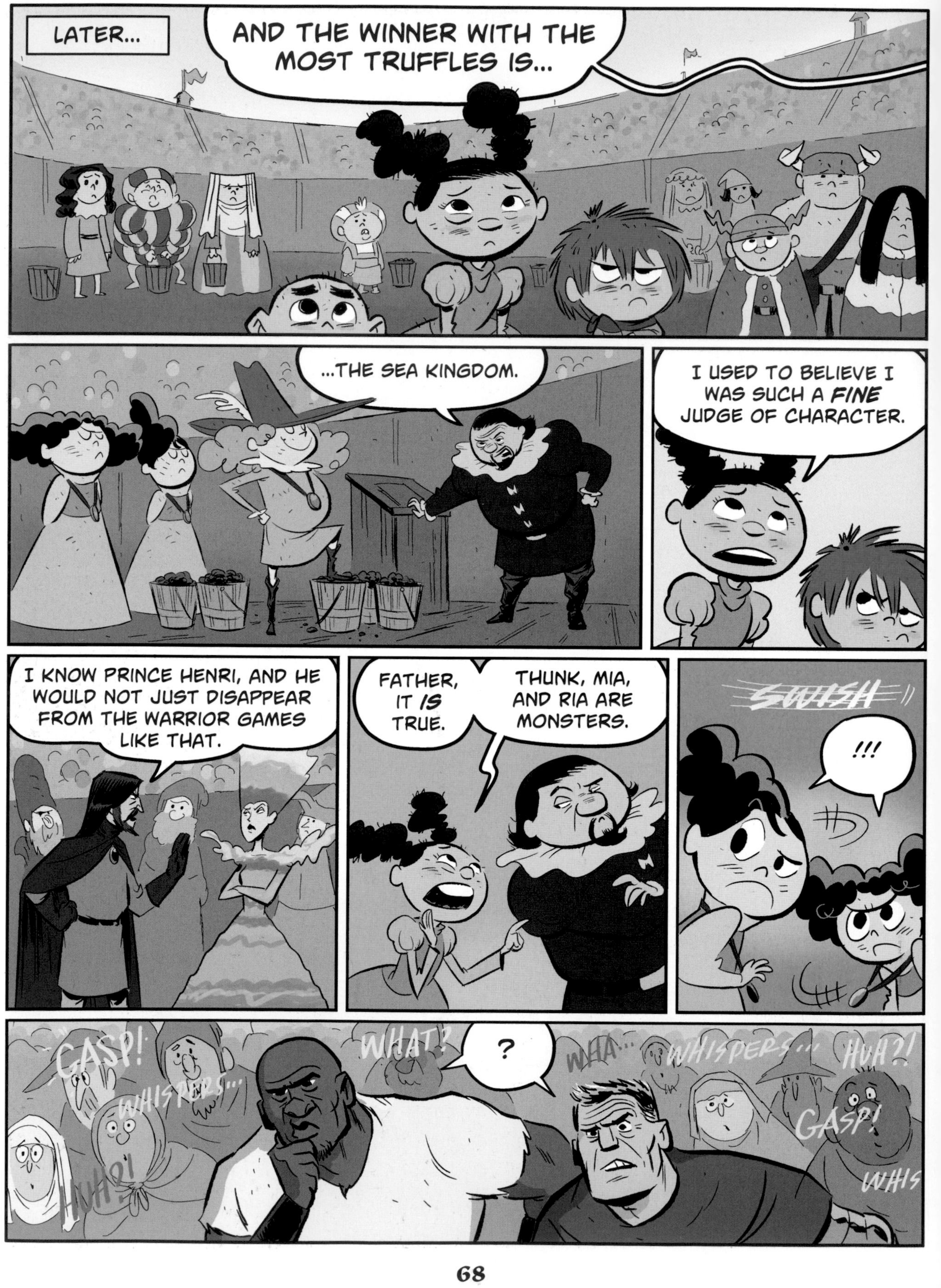
LATER...
AND THE WINNER WITH THE MOST TRUFFLES IS...
...THE SEA KINGDOM.
I USED TO BELIEVE I WAS SUCH A *FINE* JUDGE OF CHARACTER.
I KNOW PRINCE HENRI, AND HE WOULD NOT JUST DISAPPEAR FROM THE WARRIOR GAMES LIKE THAT.
FATHER, IT *IS* TRUE.
THUNK, MIA, AND RIA ARE MONSTERS.
SWISH
!!!
GASP!
WHISPERS...
HUH?!
WHAT?
?
WHA...
WHISPERS...
HUH?!
GASP!
WHIS

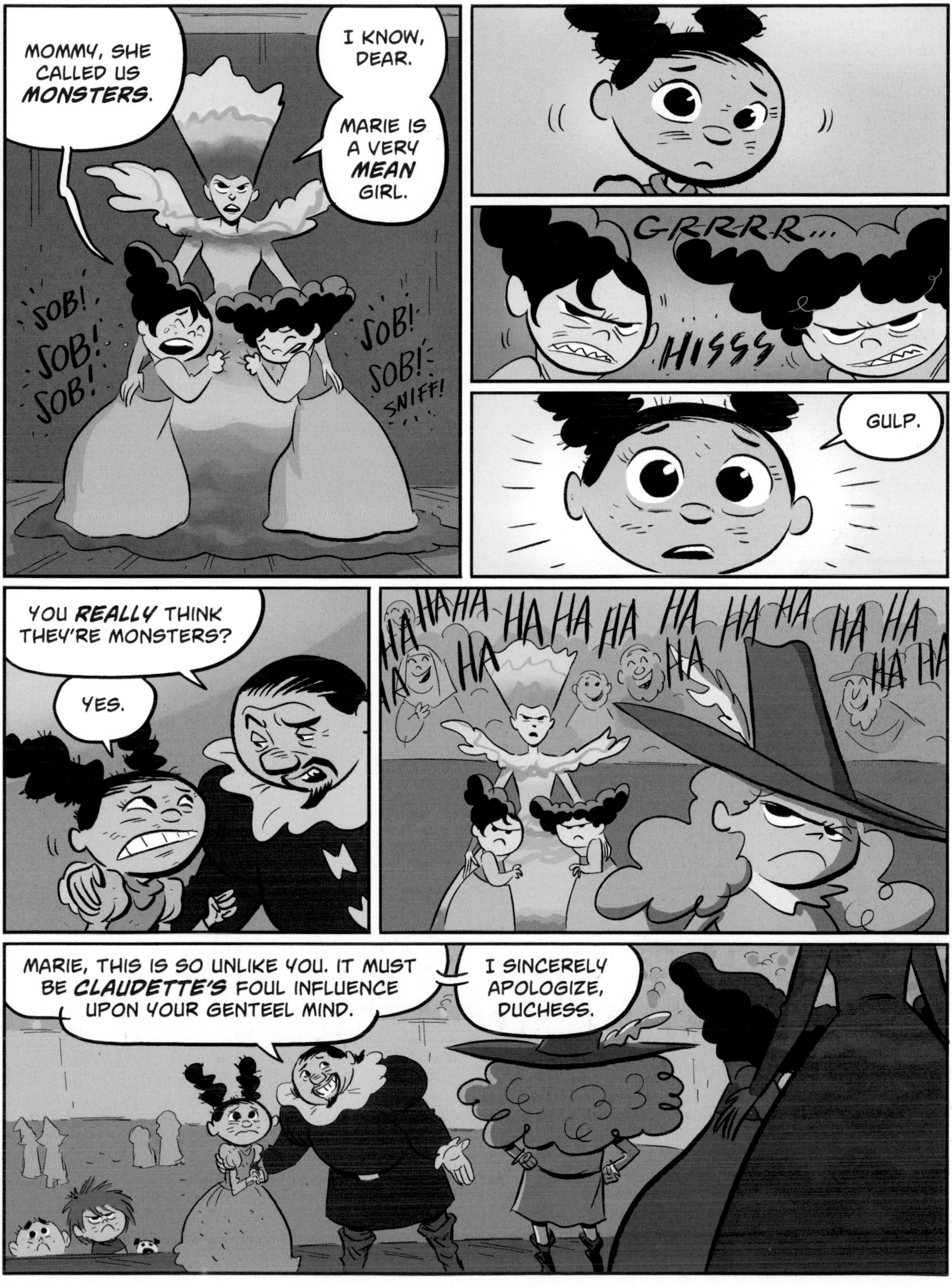
MOMMY, SHE CALLED US MONSTERS.
I KNOW, DEAR.
MARIE IS A VERY MEAN GIRL.
SOB! SOB! SOB!
SOB! SOB! SNIFF!
GRRRR...
HISSS
GULP.
YOU REALLY THINK THEY'RE MONSTERS?
YES.
HA HA HA HA HA HA HA HA HA HA HA HA HA HA HA
MARIE, THIS IS SO UNLIKE YOU. IT MUST BE CLAUDETTE'S FOUL INFLUENCE UPON YOUR GENTEEL MIND.
I SINCERELY APOLOGIZE, DUCHESS.

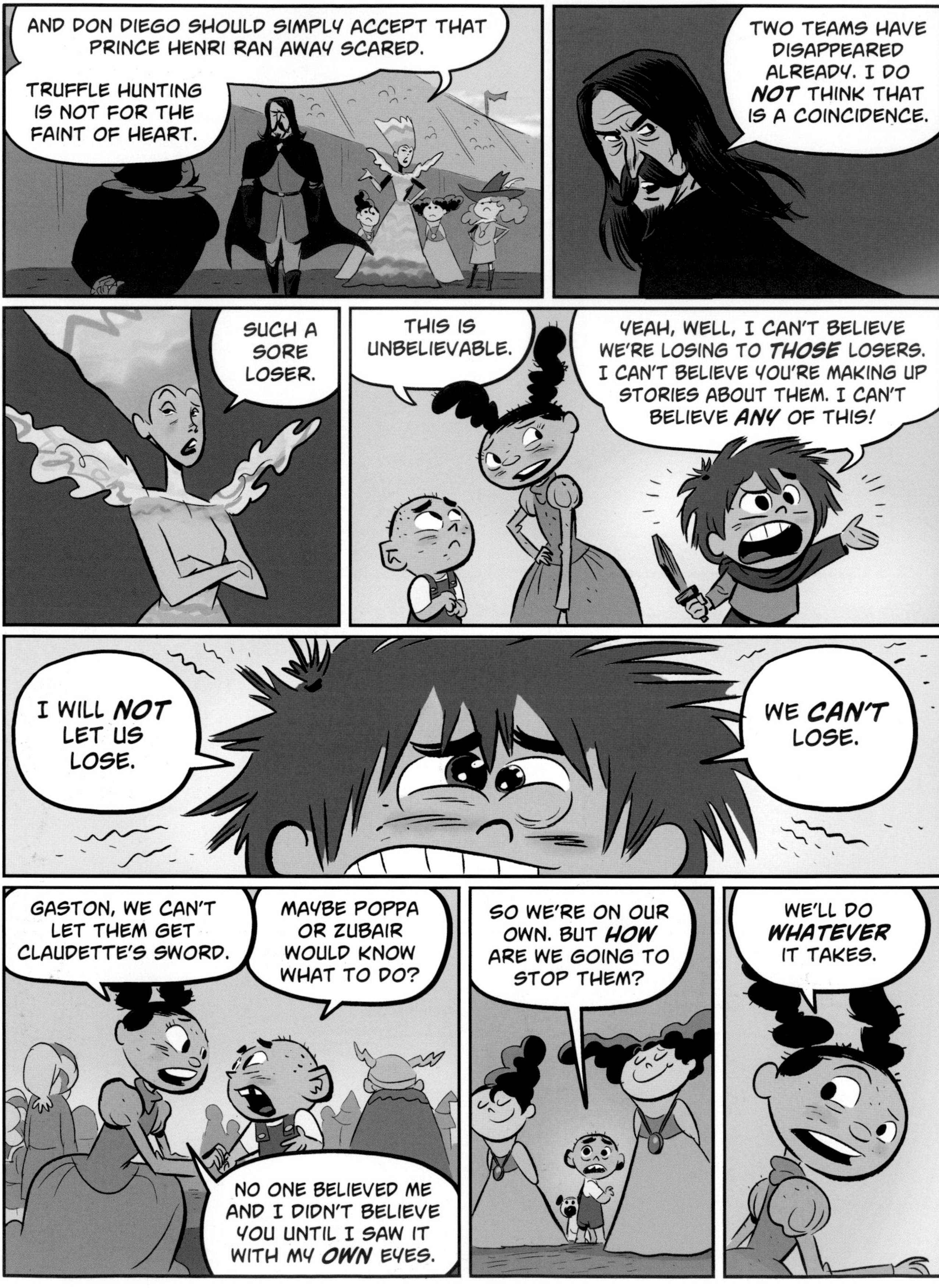
AND DON DIEGO SHOULD SIMPLY ACCEPT THAT PRINCE HENRI RAN AWAY SCARED.
TRUFFLE HUNTING IS NOT FOR THE FAINT OF HEART.
TWO TEAMS HAVE DISAPPEARED ALREADY. I DO NOT THINK THAT IS A COINCIDENCE.
SUCH A SORE LOSER.
THIS IS UNBELIEVABLE.
YEAH, WELL, I CAN'T BELIEVE WE'RE LOSING TO THOSE LOSERS. I CAN'T BELIEVE YOU'RE MAKING UP STORIES ABOUT THEM. I CAN'T BELIEVE ANY OF THIS!
I WILL NOT LET US LOSE.
WE CAN'T LOSE.
GASTON, WE CAN'T LET THEM GET CLAUDETTE'S SWORD.
MAYBE POPPA OR ZUBAIR WOULD KNOW WHAT TO DO?
NO ONE BELIEVED ME AND I DIDN'T BELIEVE YOU UNTIL I SAW IT WITH MY OWN EYES.
SO WE'RE ON OUR OWN. BUT HOW ARE WE GOING TO STOP THEM?
WE'LL DO WHATEVER IT TAKES.

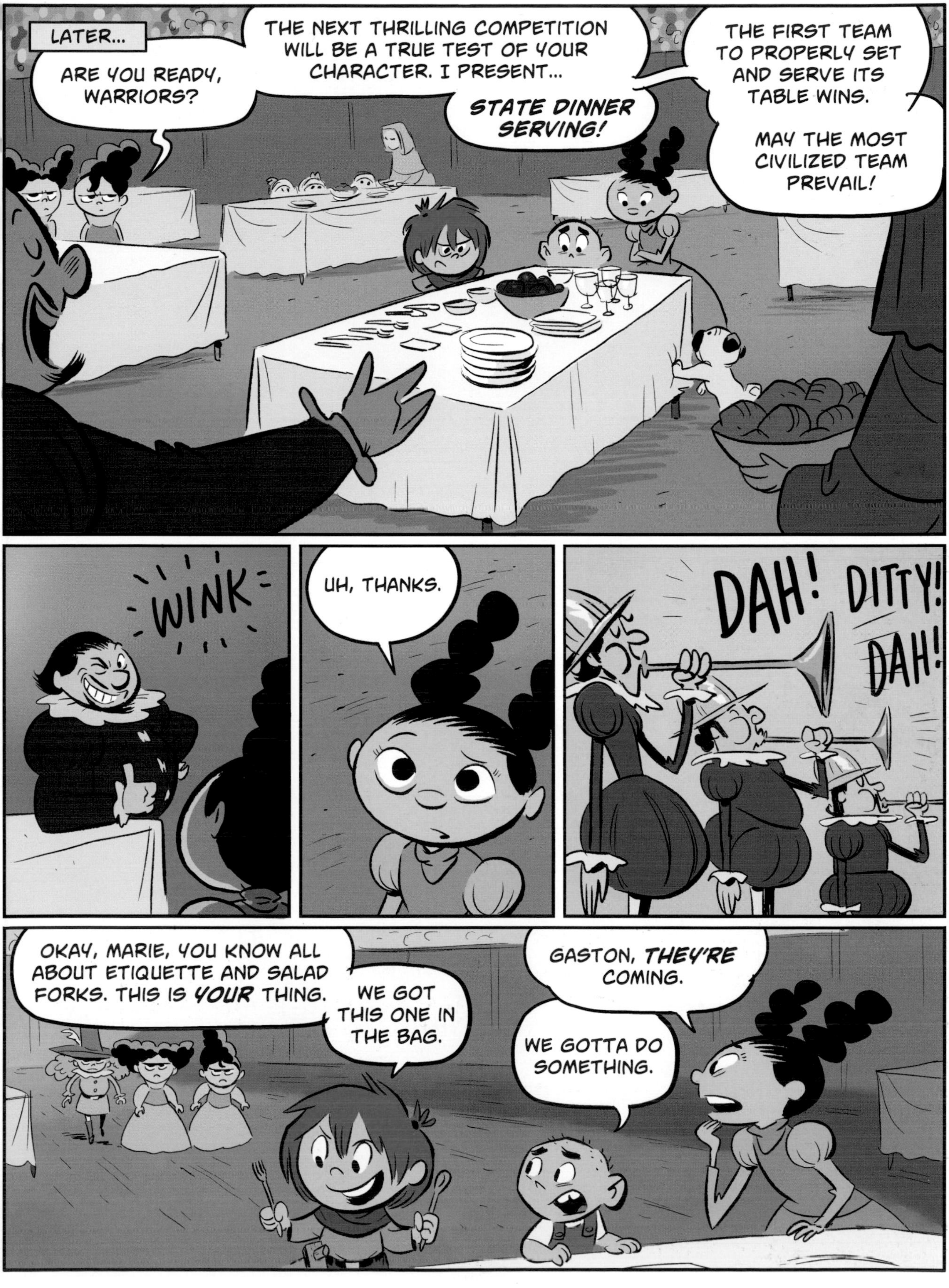
LATER...
ARE YOU READY, WARRIORS?
THE NEXT THRILLING COMPETITION WILL BE A TRUE TEST OF YOUR CHARACTER. I PRESENT...
STATE DINNER SERVING!
THE FIRST TEAM TO PROPERLY SET AND SERVE ITS TABLE WINS.
MAY THE MOST CIVILIZED TEAM PREVAIL!
WINK
UH, THANKS.
DAH! DITTY! DAH!
OKAY, MARIE, YOU KNOW ALL ABOUT ETIQUETTE AND SALAD FORKS. THIS IS YOUR THING.
WE GOT THIS ONE IN THE BAG.
GASTON, THEY'RE COMING.
WE GOTTA DO SOMETHING.

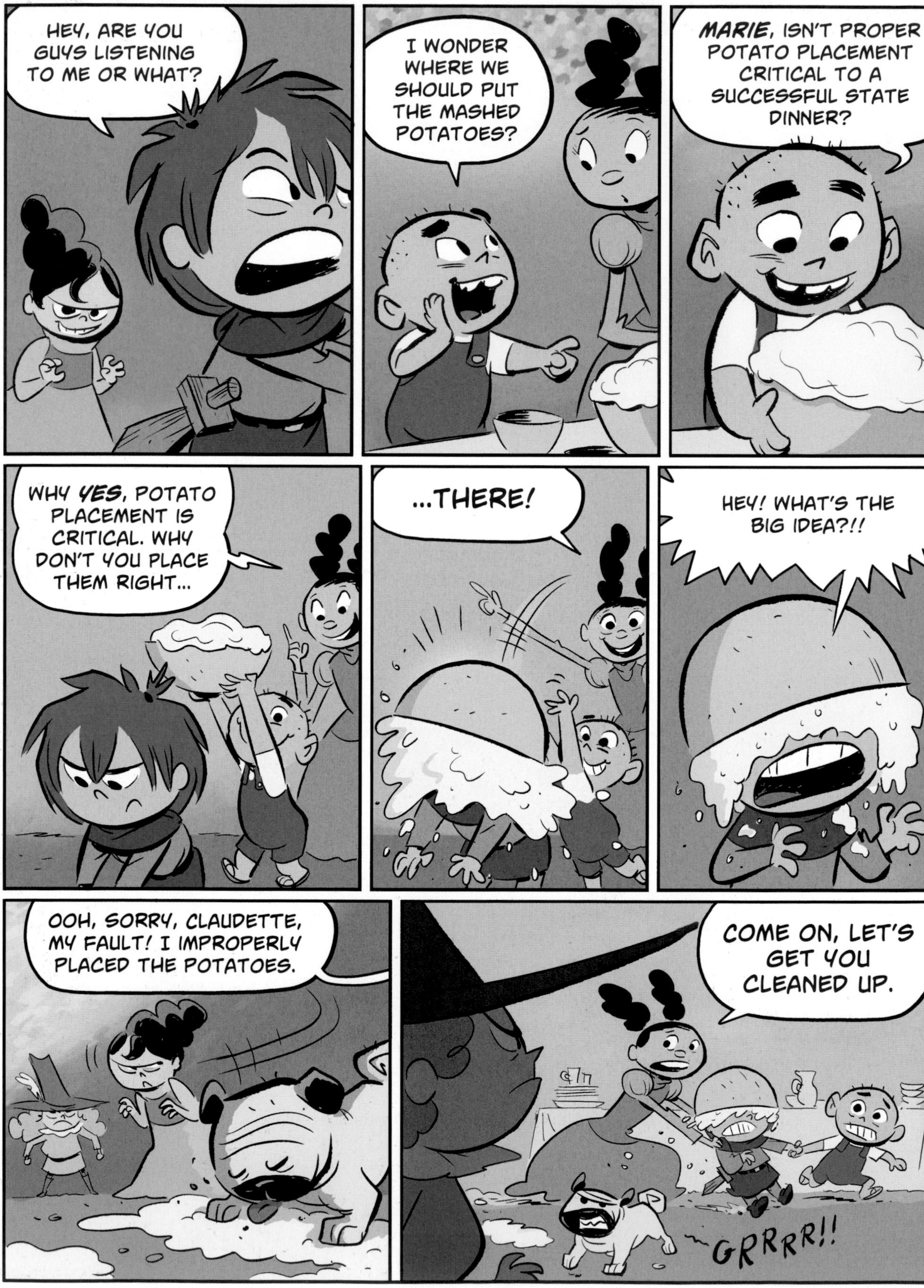

HEY, ARE YOU GUYS LISTENING TO ME OR WHAT?
I WONDER WHERE WE SHOULD PUT THE MASHED POTATOES?
MARIE, ISN'T PROPER POTATO PLACEMENT CRITICAL TO A SUCCESSFUL STATE DINNER?
WHY YES, POTATO PLACEMENT IS CRITICAL. WHY DON'T YOU PLACE THEM RIGHT...
...THERE!
HEY! WHAT'S THE BIG IDEA?!!
OOH, SORRY, CLAUDETTE, MY FAULT! I IMPROPERLY PLACED THE POTATOES.
COME ON, LET'S GET YOU CLEANED UP.
GRRRR!!

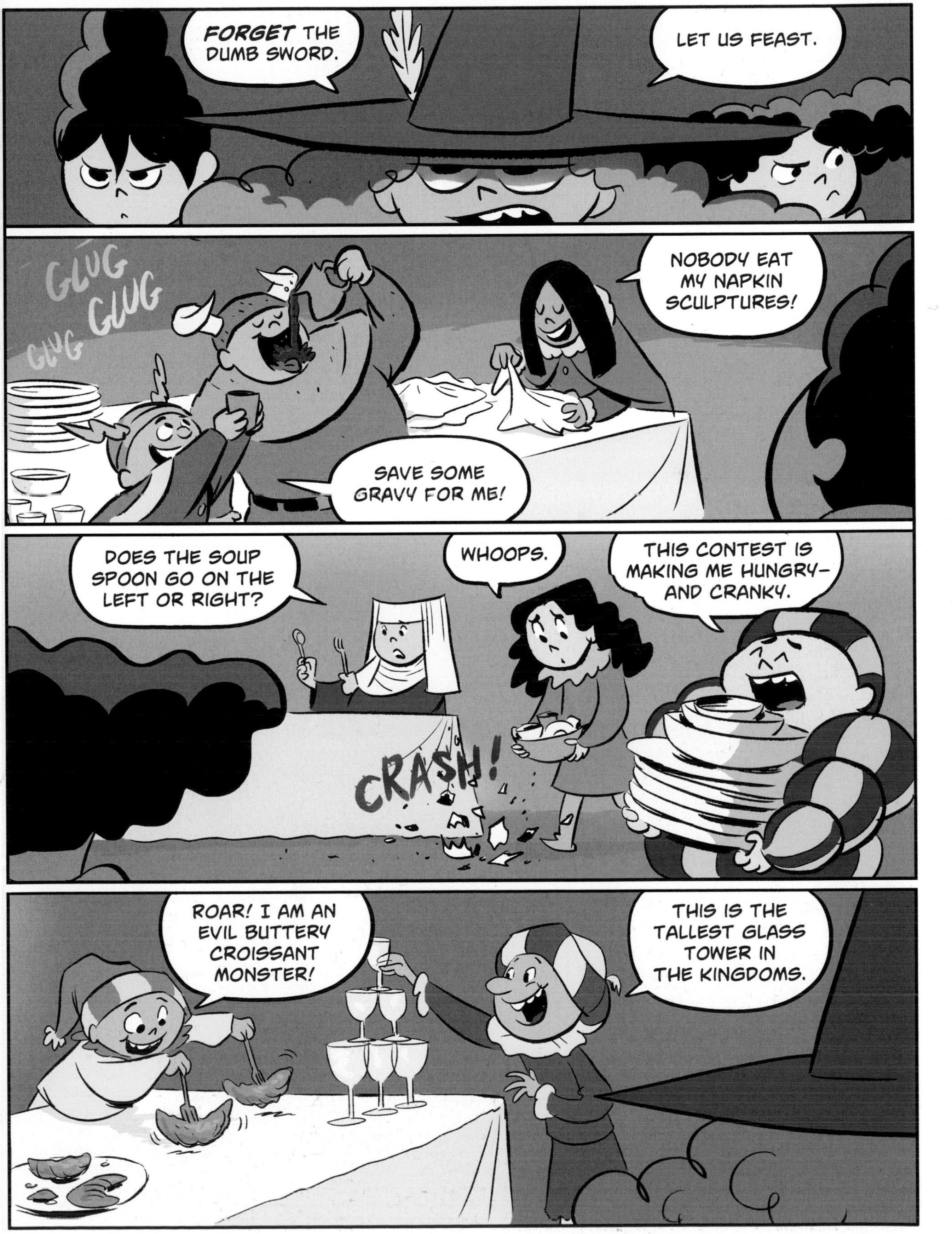
FORGET THE DUMB SWORD.
LET US FEAST.
GLUG GLUG GLUG
NOBODY EAT MY NAPKIN SCULPTURES!
SAVE SOME GRAVY FOR ME!
DOES THE SOUP SPOON GO ON THE LEFT OR RIGHT?
WHOOPS.
THIS CONTEST IS MAKING ME HUNGRY— AND CRANKY.
CRASH!
ROAR! I AM AN EVIL BUTTERY CROISSANT MONSTER!
THIS IS THE TALLEST GLASS TOWER IN THE KINGDOMS.

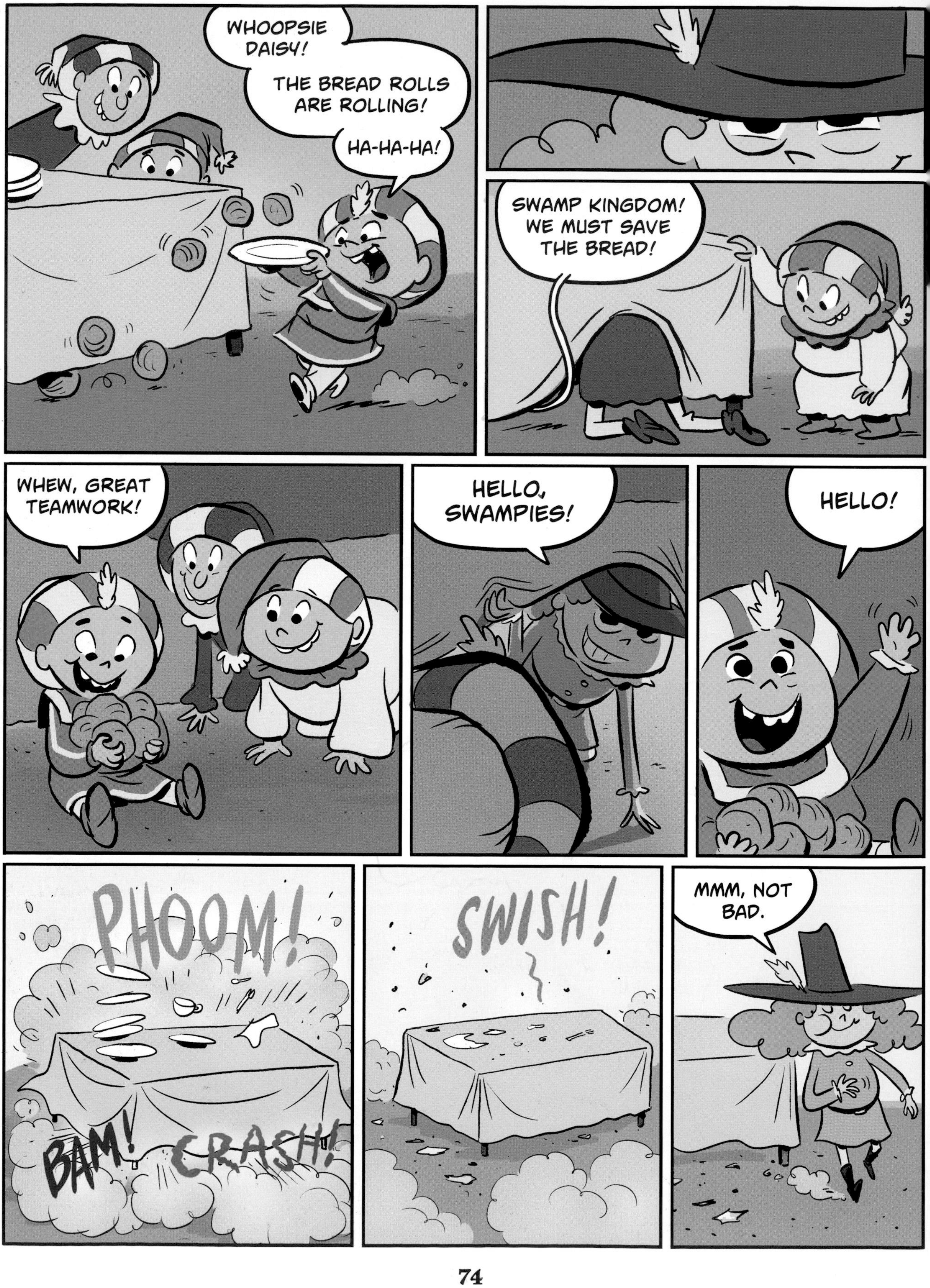
WHOOPSIE DAISY!
THE BREAD ROLLS ARE ROLLING!
HA-HA-HA!
SWAMP KINGDOM! WE MUST SAVE THE BREAD!
WHEW, GREAT TEAMWORK!
HELLO, SWAMPIES!
HELLO!
PHOOM!
BAM!
CRASH!
SWISH!
MMM, NOT BAD.

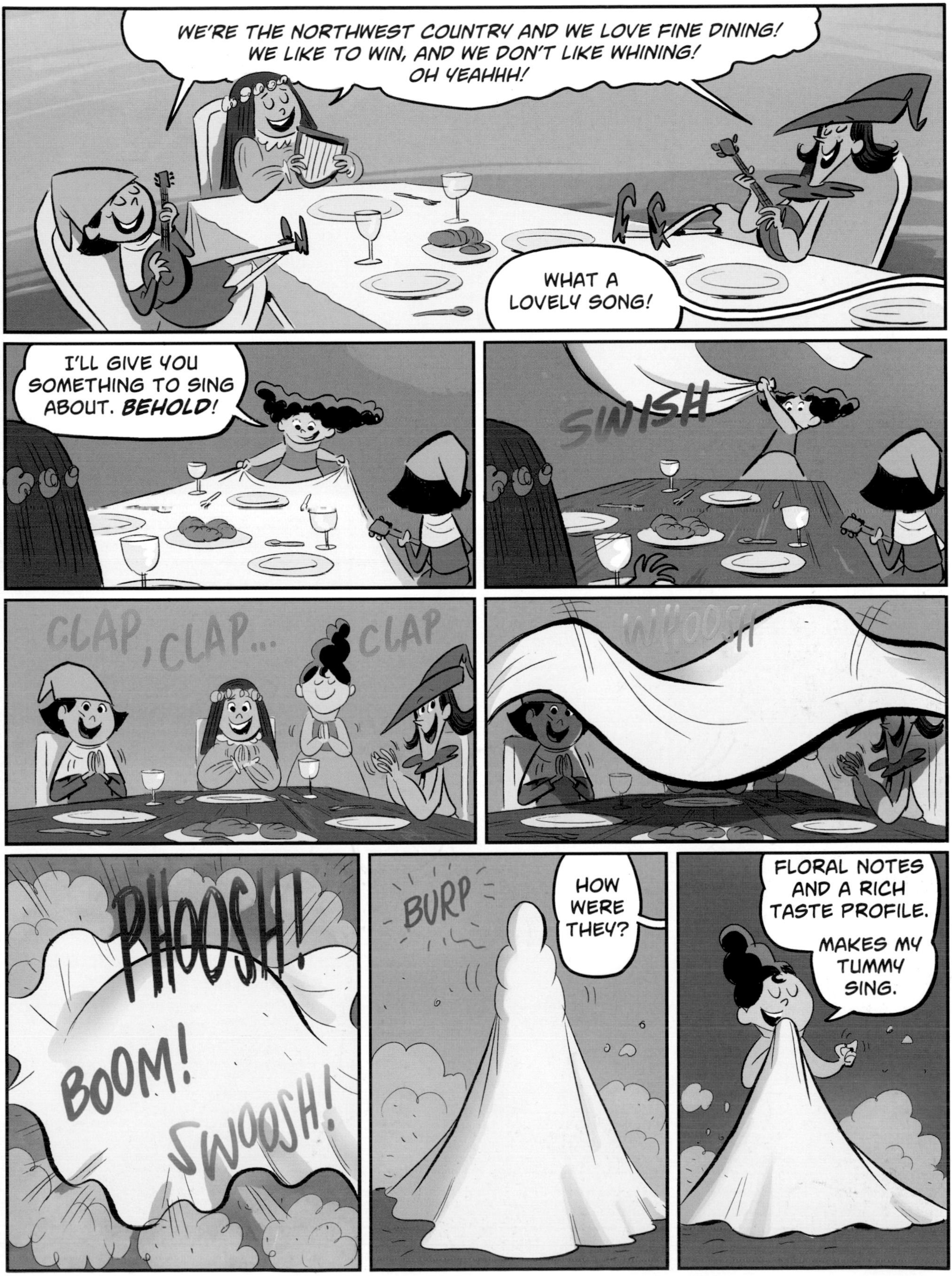
WE'RE THE NORTHWEST COUNTRY AND WE LOVE FINE DINING! WE LIKE TO WIN, AND WE DON'T LIKE WHINING! OH YEAHHH!
WHAT A LOVELY SONG!
I'LL GIVE YOU SOMETHING TO SING ABOUT. BEHOLD!
SWISH
CLAP, CLAP... CLAP
WHOOSH
PHOOSH!
BOOM!
SWOOSH!
BURP
HOW WERE THEY?
FLORAL NOTES AND A RICH TASTE PROFILE.
MAKES MY TUMMY SING.

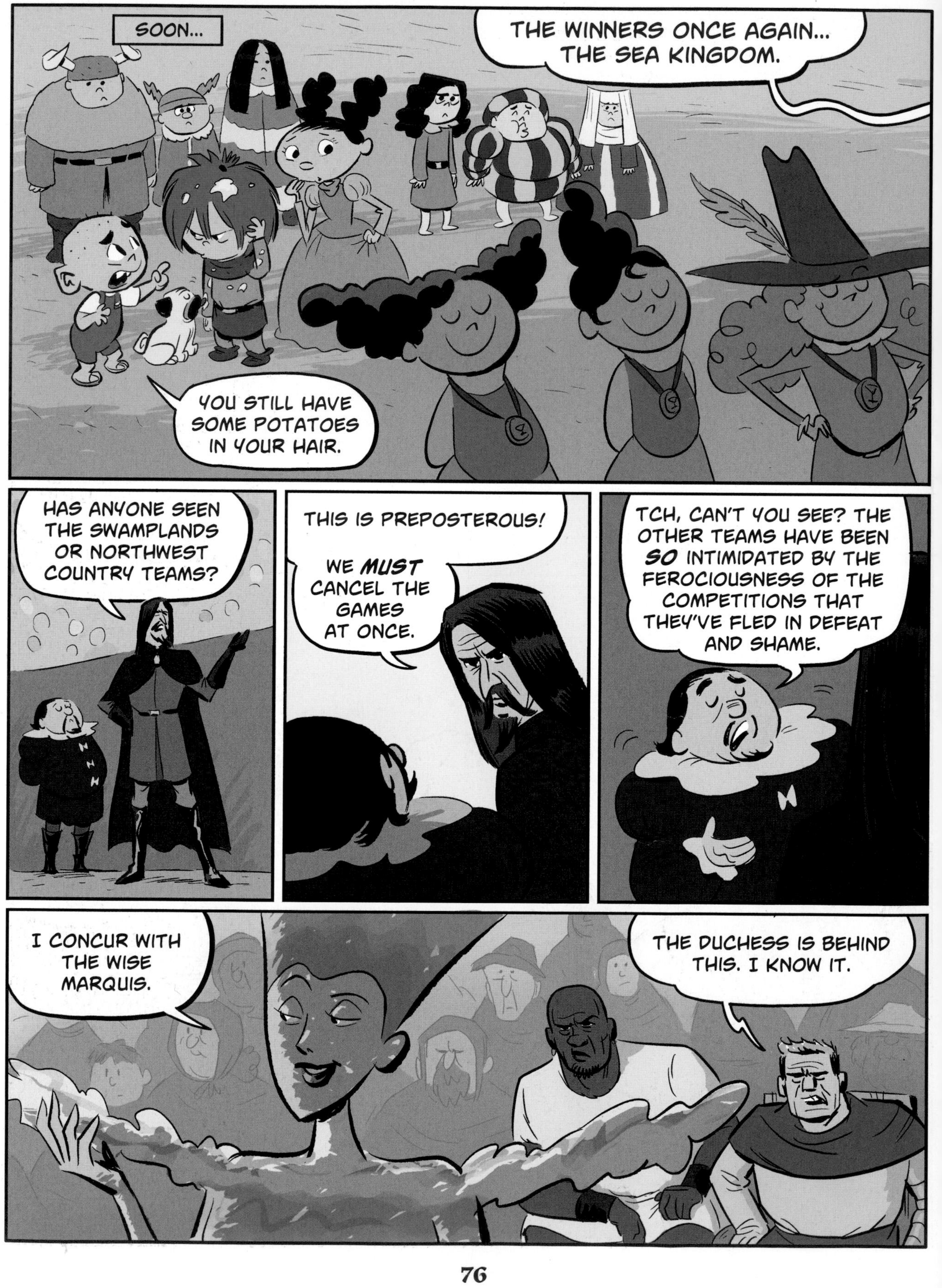
SOON...
THE WINNERS ONCE AGAIN... THE SEA KINGDOM.
YOU STILL HAVE SOME POTATOES IN YOUR HAIR.
HAS ANYONE SEEN THE SWAMPLANDS OR NORTHWEST COUNTRY TEAMS?
THIS IS PREPOSTEROUS!
WE MUST CANCEL THE GAMES AT ONCE.
TCH, CAN'T YOU SEE? THE OTHER TEAMS HAVE BEEN SO INTIMIDATED BY THE FEROCIOUSNESS OF THE COMPETITIONS THAT THEY'VE FLED IN DEFEAT AND SHAME.
I CONCUR WITH THE WISE MARQUIS.
THE DUCHESS IS BEHIND THIS. I KNOW IT.

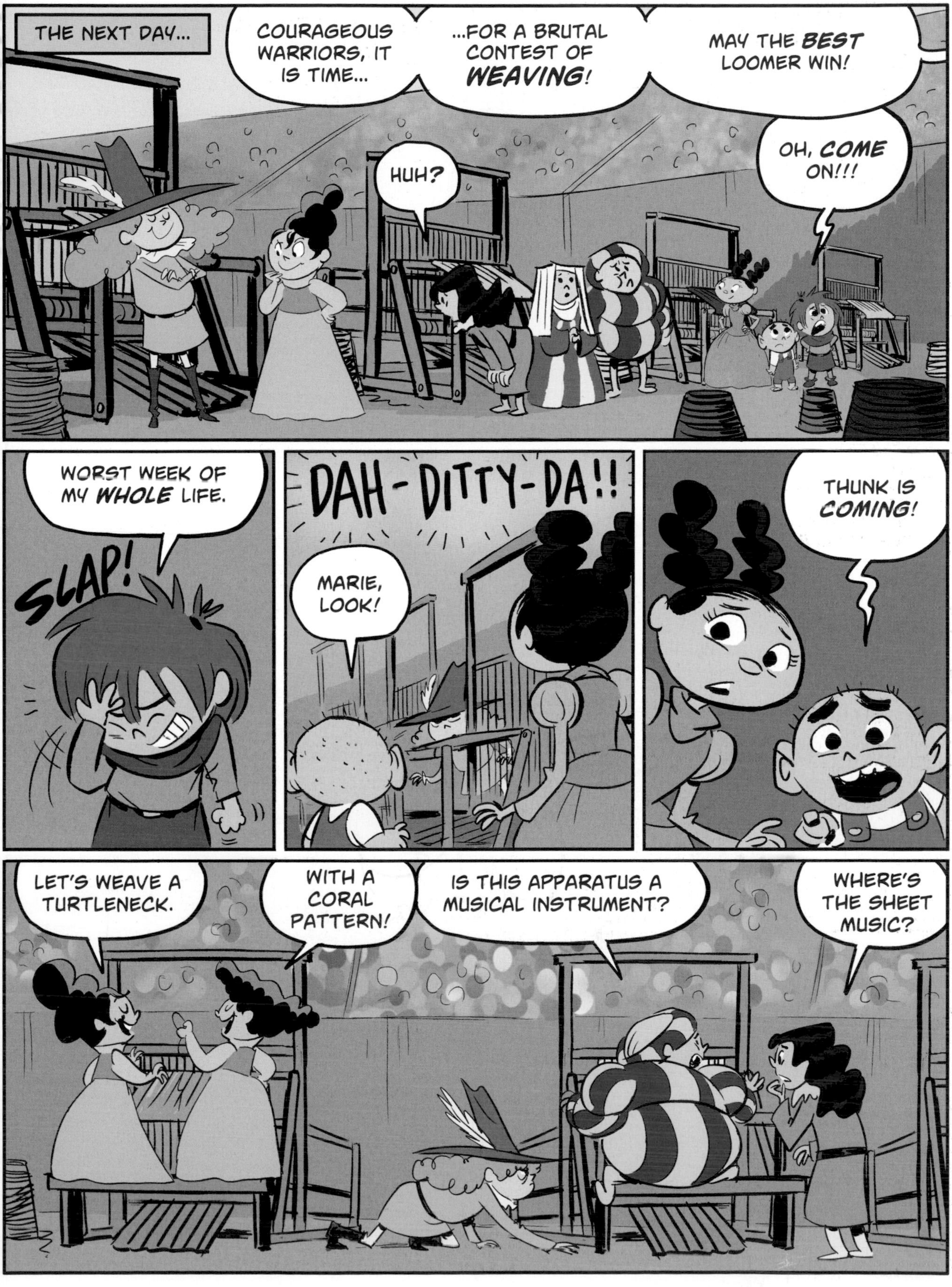
THE NEXT DAY...
COURAGEOUS WARRIORS, IT IS TIME...
...FOR A BRUTAL CONTEST OF WEAVING!
MAY THE BEST LOOMER WIN!
HUH?
OH, COME ON!!!
WORST WEEK OF MY WHOLE LIFE.
SLAP!
DAH-DITTY-DA!!
MARIE, LOOK!
THUNK IS COMING!
LET'S WEAVE A TURTLENECK.
WITH A CORAL PATTERN!
IS THIS APPARATUS A MUSICAL INSTRUMENT?
WHERE'S THE SHEET MUSIC?

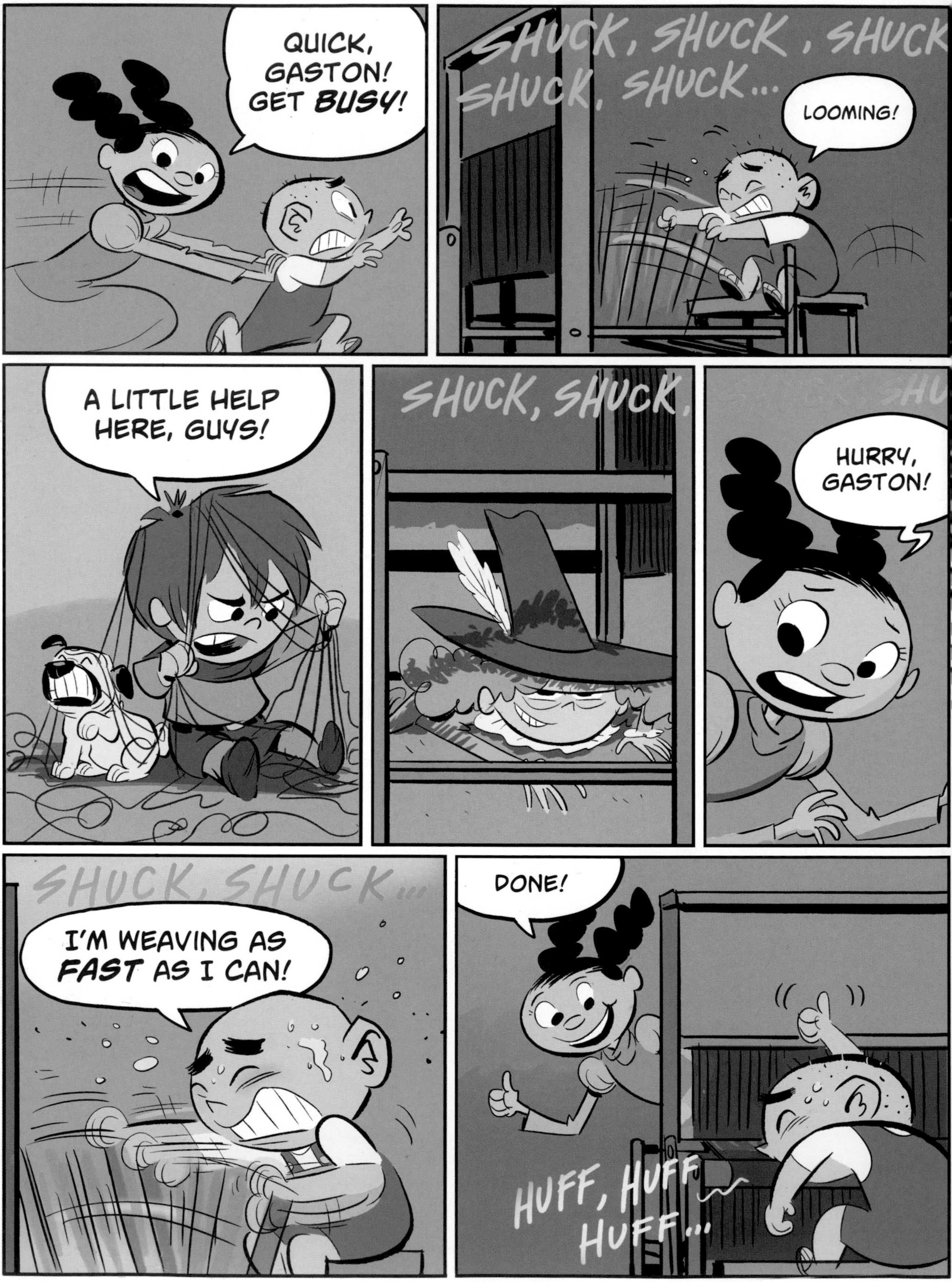
QUICK, GASTON! GET BUSY!
SHUCK, SHUCK, SHUCK
SHUCK, SHUCK...
LOOMING!
A LITTLE HELP HERE, GUYS!
SHUCK, SHUCK,
HURRY, GASTON!
SHUCK, SHUCK...
I'M WEAVING AS FAST AS I CAN!
DONE!
HUFF, HUFF
HUFF...

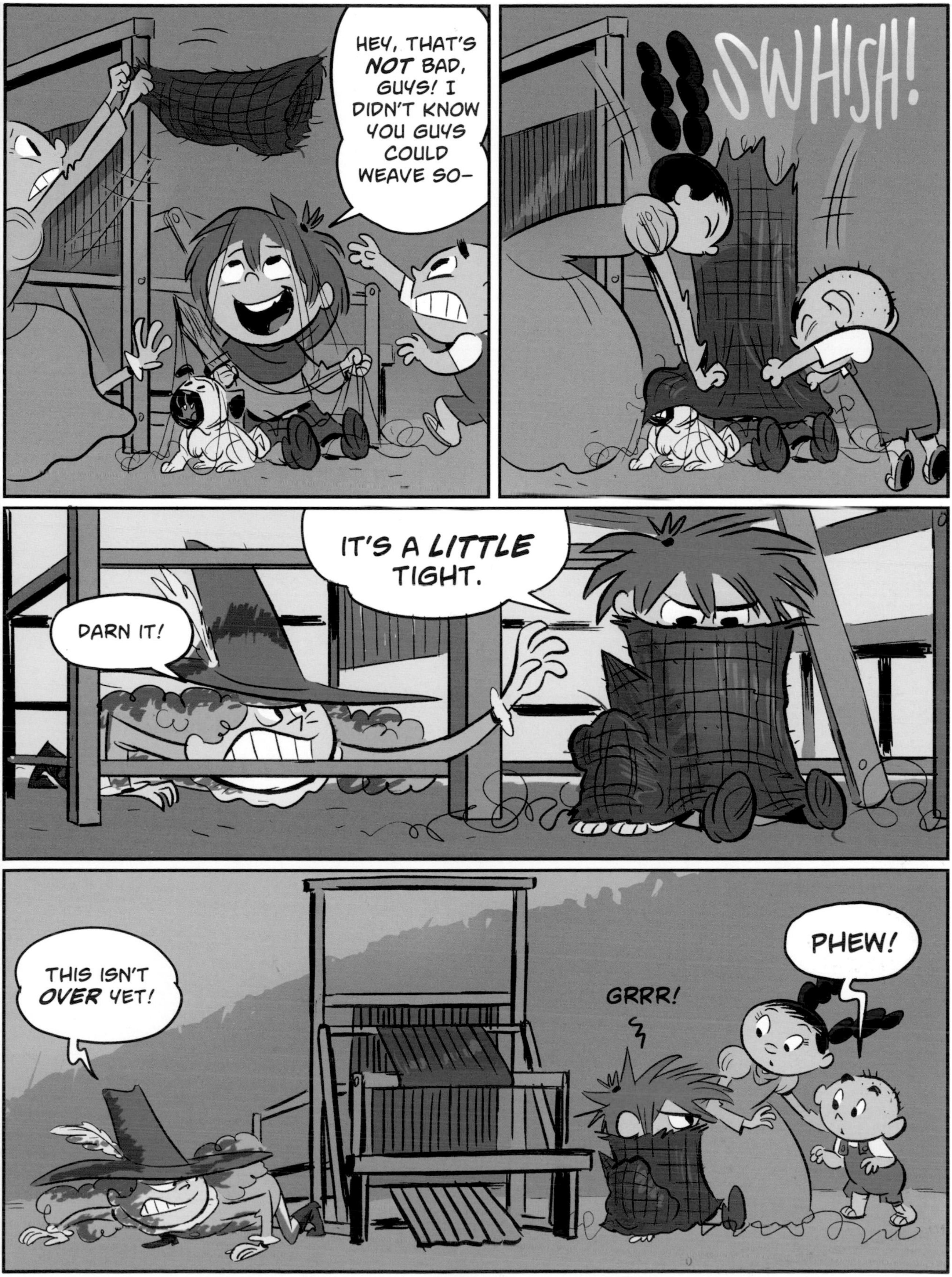
HEY, THAT'S NOT BAD, GUYS! I DIDN'T KNOW YOU GUYS COULD WEAVE SO-
SWHISH!
IT'S A LITTLE TIGHT.
DARN IT!
THIS ISN'T OVER YET!
GRRR!
PHEW!

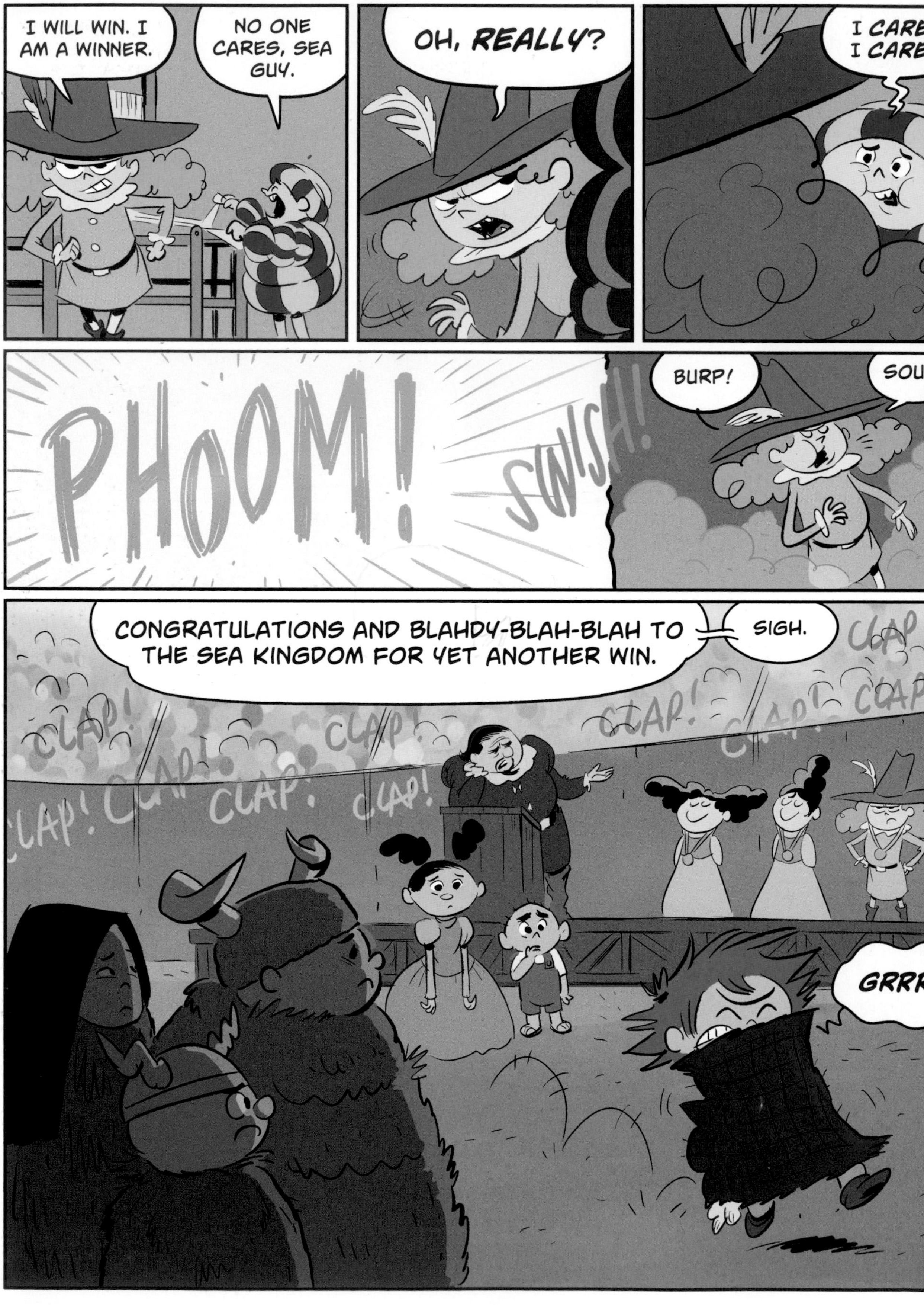
I WILL WIN. I AM A WINNER.
NO ONE CARES, SEA GUY.
OH, REALLY?
I CARE, I CARE!
PHOOM!
SWISH!
BURP!
SOUR.
CONGRATULATIONS AND BLAHDY-BLAH-BLAH TO THE SEA KINGDOM FOR YET ANOTHER WIN.
SIGH.
CLAP! CLAP! CLAP! CLAP! CLAP! CLAP! CLAP! CLAP! CLAP! CLAP! CLAP!
GRRR!

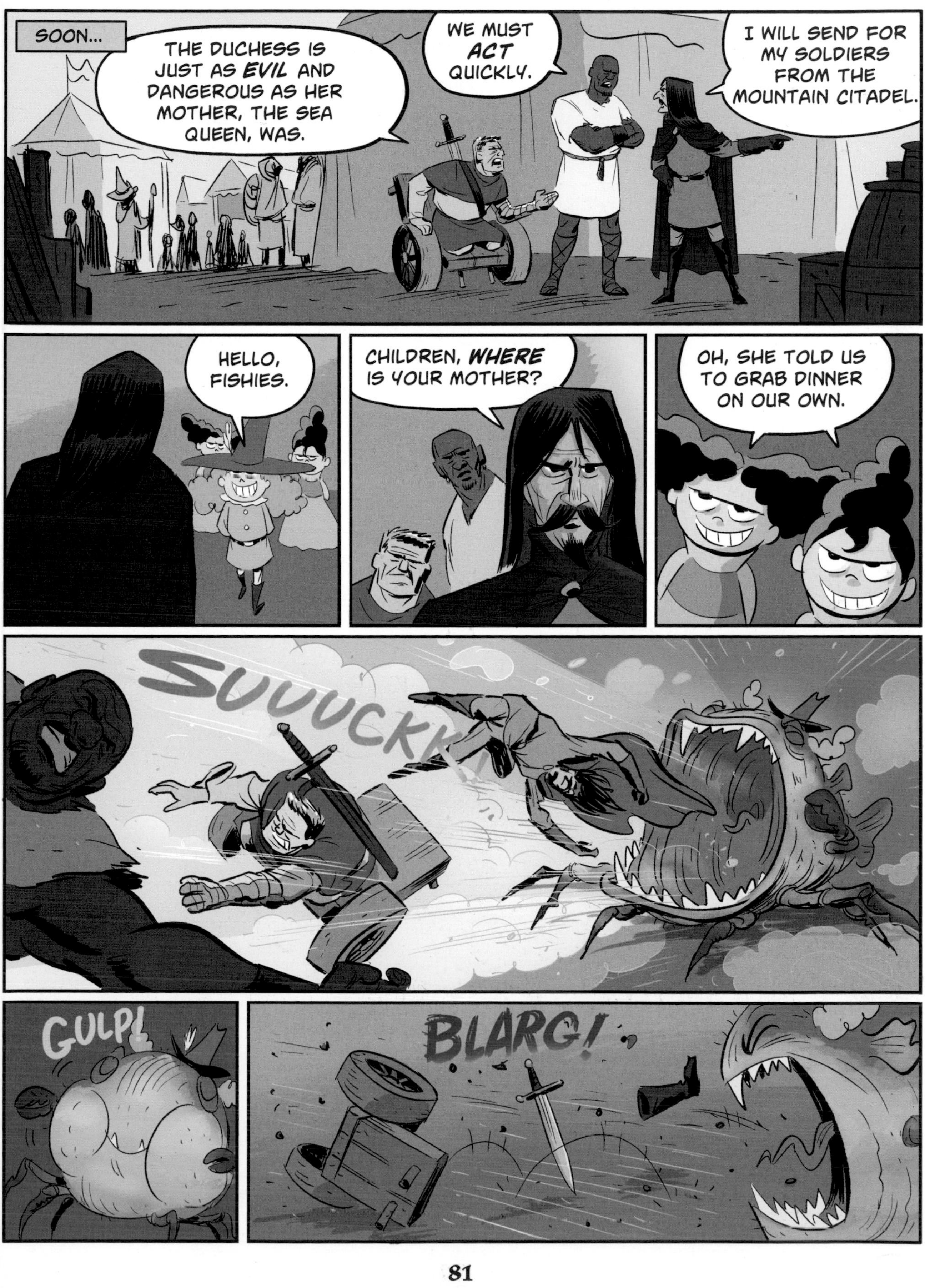
SOON...
THE DUCHESS IS JUST AS EVIL AND DANGEROUS AS HER MOTHER, THE SEA QUEEN, WAS.
WE MUST ACT QUICKLY.
I WILL SEND FOR MY SOLDIERS FROM THE MOUNTAIN CITADEL.
HELLO, FISHIES.
CHILDREN, WHERE IS YOUR MOTHER?
OH, SHE TOLD US TO GRAB DINNER ON OUR OWN.
SUUUCKK
GULP!
BLARG!

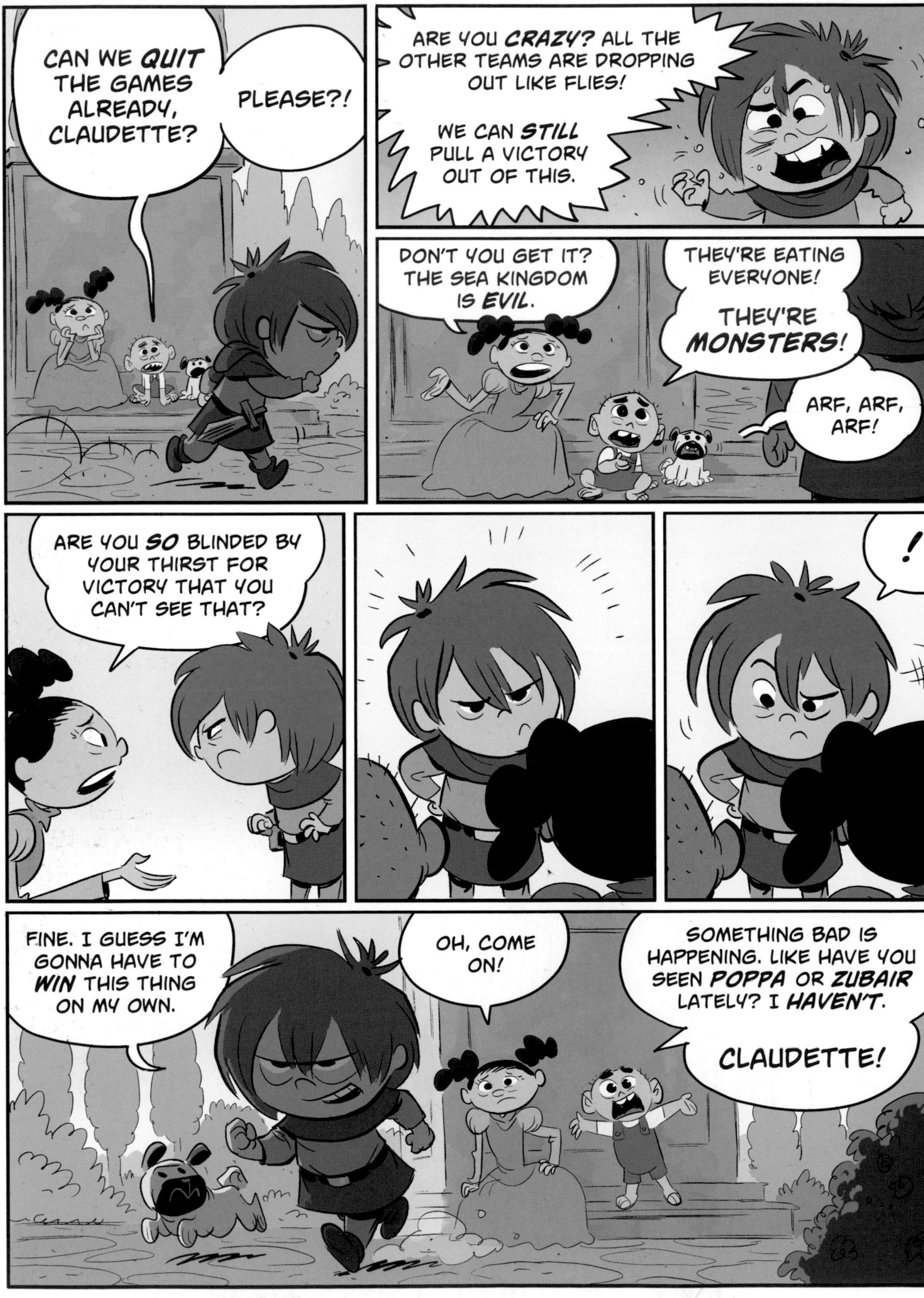
CAN WE QUIT THE GAMES ALREADY, CLAUDETTE?
PLEASE?!
ARE YOU CRAZY? ALL THE OTHER TEAMS ARE DROPPING OUT LIKE FLIES!
WE CAN STILL PULL A VICTORY OUT OF THIS.
DON'T YOU GET IT? THE SEA KINGDOM IS EVIL.
THEY'RE EATING EVERYONE!
THEY'RE MONSTERS!
ARF, ARF, ARF!
ARE YOU SO BLINDED BY YOUR THIRST FOR VICTORY THAT YOU CAN'T SEE THAT?
!
FINE. I GUESS I'M GONNA HAVE TO WIN THIS THING ON MY OWN.
OH, COME ON!
SOMETHING BAD IS HAPPENING. LIKE HAVE YOU SEEN POPPA OR ZUBAIR LATELY? I HAVEN'T.
CLAUDETTE!

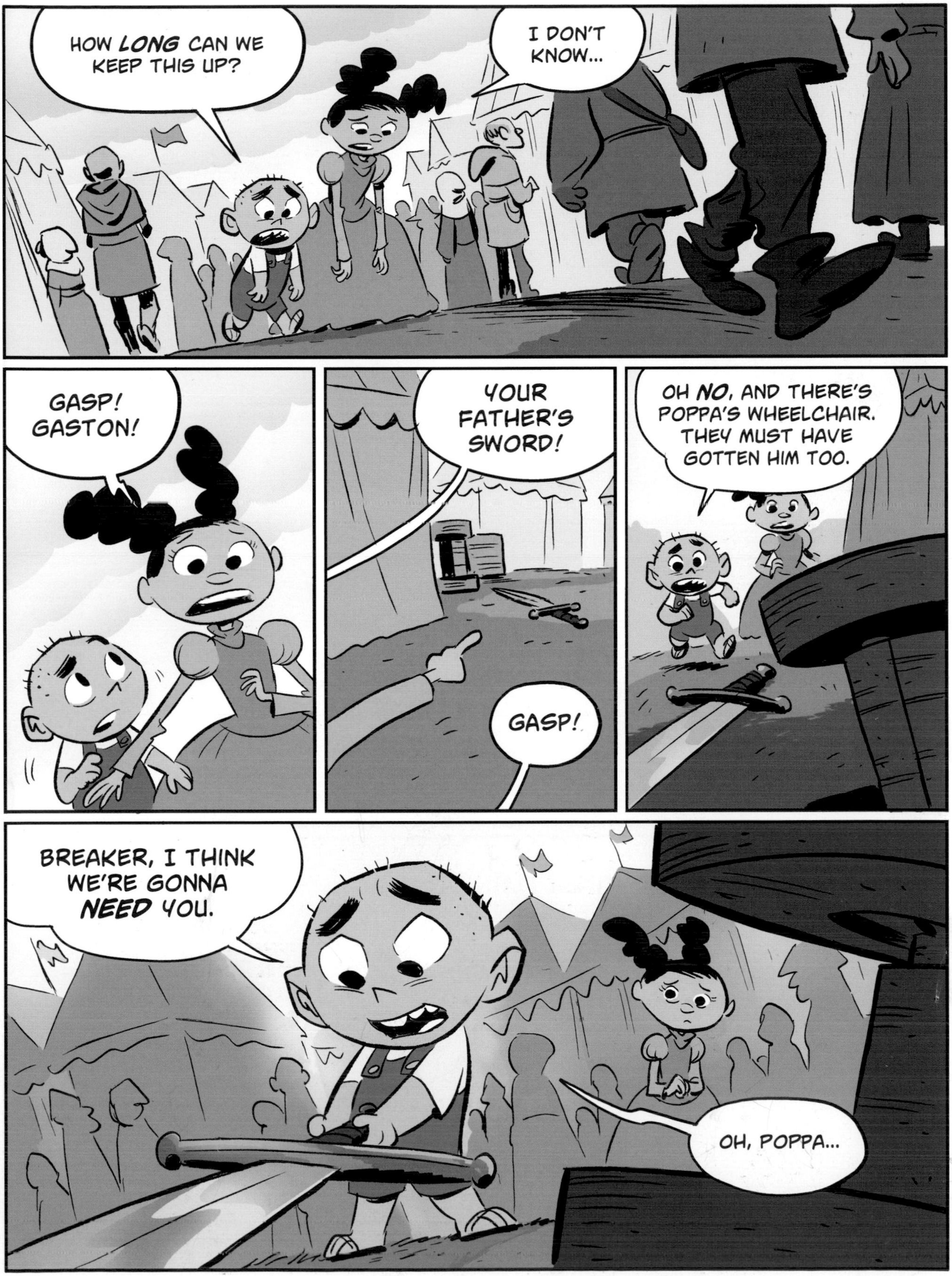
HOW *LONG* CAN WE KEEP THIS UP?
I DON'T KNOW...
GASP! GASTON!
YOUR FATHER'S SWORD!
GASP!
OH *NO*, AND THERE'S POPPA'S WHEELCHAIR. THEY MUST HAVE GOTTEN HIM TOO.
BREAKER, I THINK WE'RE GONNA *NEED* YOU.
OH, POPPA...

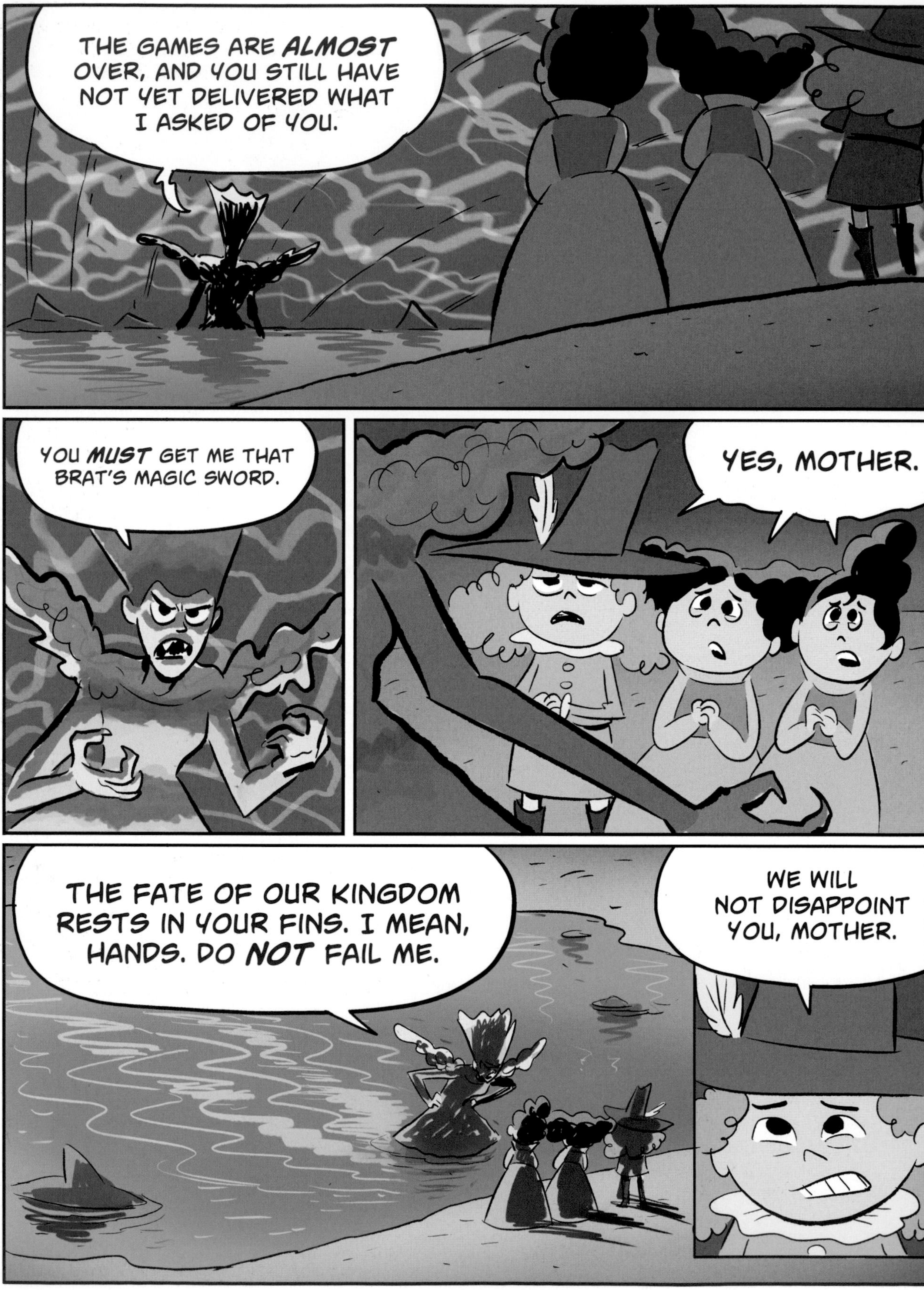
THE GAMES ARE ALMOST OVER, AND YOU STILL HAVE NOT YET DELIVERED WHAT I ASKED OF YOU.
YOU MUST GET ME THAT BRAT'S MAGIC SWORD.
YES, MOTHER.
THE FATE OF OUR KINGDOM RESTS IN YOUR FINS. I MEAN, HANDS. DO NOT FAIL ME.
WE WILL NOT DISAPPOINT YOU, MOTHER.

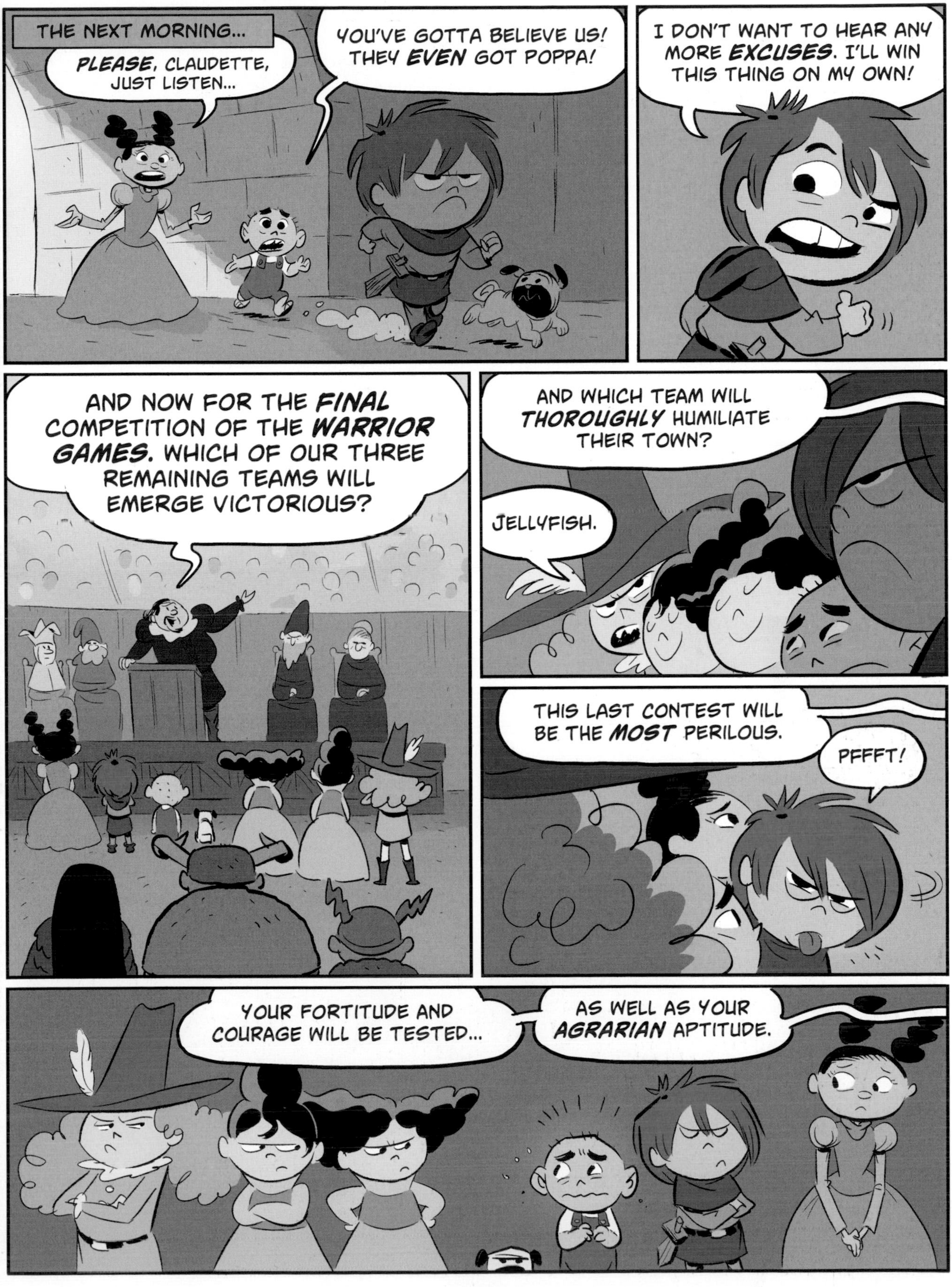
THE NEXT MORNING...
PLEASE, CLAUDETTE, JUST LISTEN...
YOU'VE GOTTA BELIEVE US! THEY EVEN GOT POPPA!
I DON'T WANT TO HEAR ANY MORE EXCUSES. I'LL WIN THIS THING ON MY OWN!
AND NOW FOR THE FINAL COMPETITION OF THE WARRIOR GAMES. WHICH OF OUR THREE REMAINING TEAMS WILL EMERGE VICTORIOUS?
AND WHICH TEAM WILL THOROUGHLY HUMILIATE THEIR TOWN?
JELLYFISH.
THIS LAST CONTEST WILL BE THE MOST PERILOUS.
PFFFT!
YOUR FORTITUDE AND COURAGE WILL BE TESTED...
AS WELL AS YOUR AGRARIAN APTITUDE.

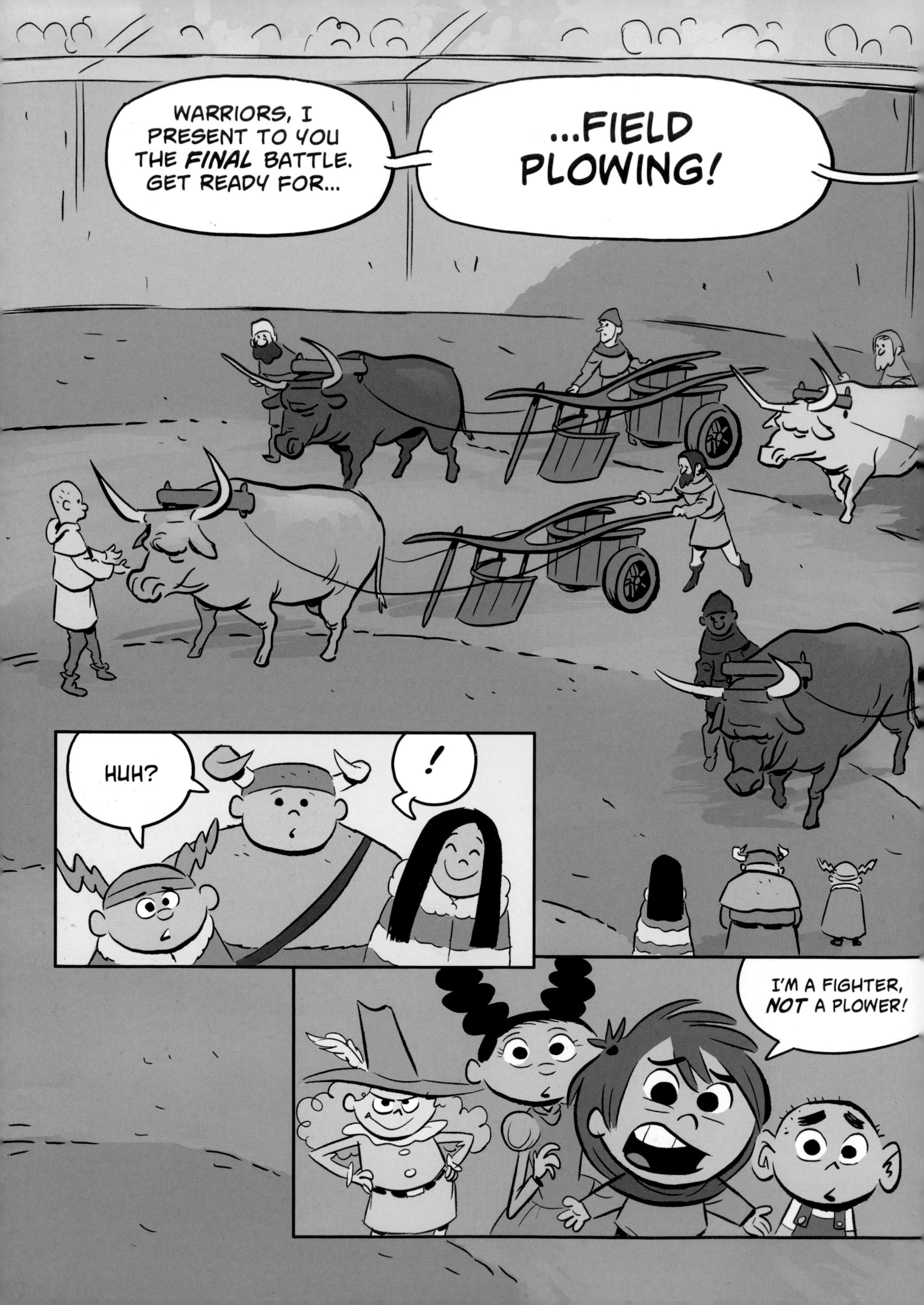
WARRIORS, I PRESENT TO YOU THE *FINAL* BATTLE. GET READY FOR...
...FIELD PLOWING!
HUH?
!
I'M A FIGHTER, *NOT* A PLOWER!

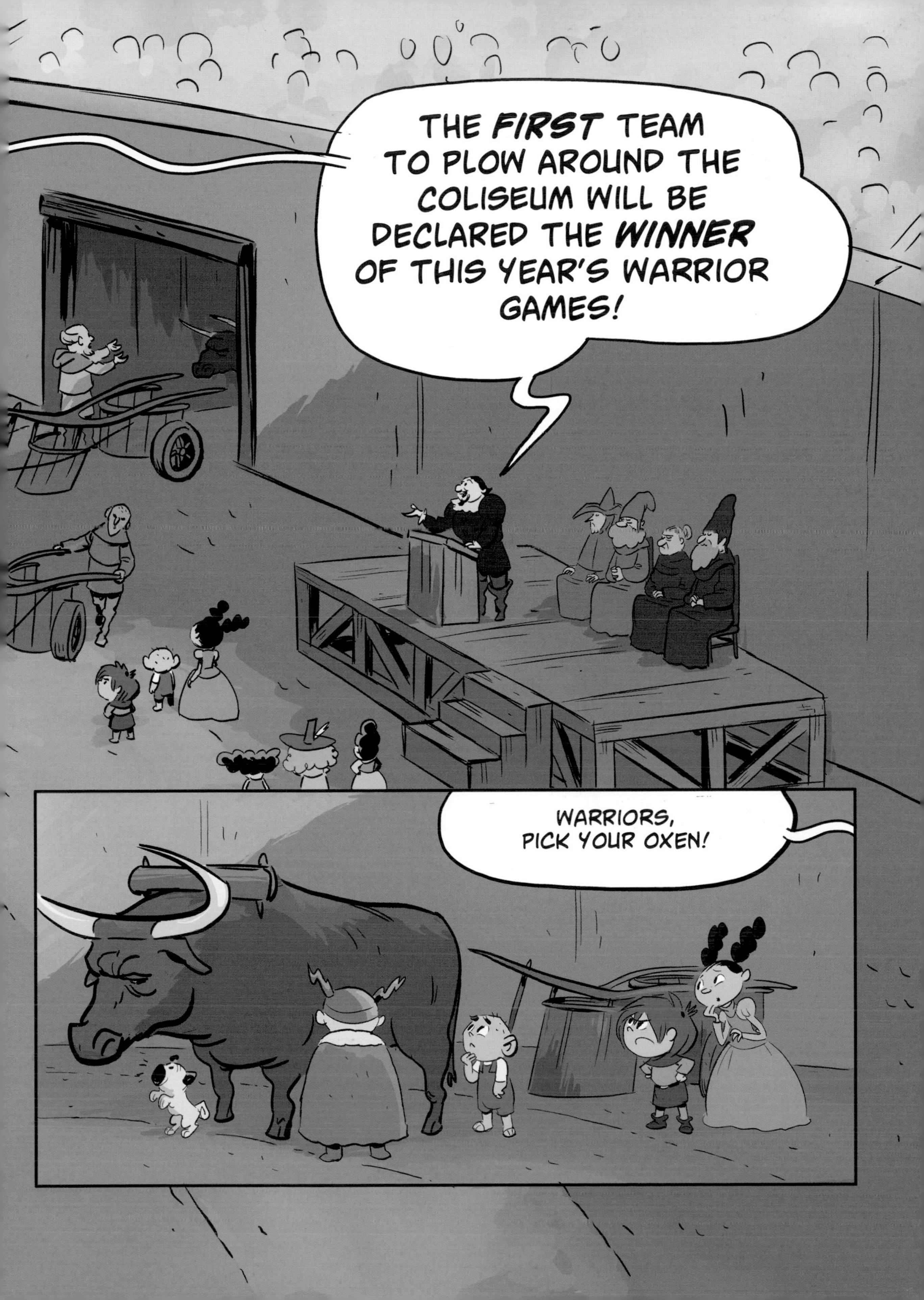

THE *FIRST* TEAM TO PLOW AROUND THE COLISEUM WILL BE DECLARED THE *WINNER* OF THIS YEAR'S WARRIOR GAMES!
WARRIORS, PICK YOUR OXEN!

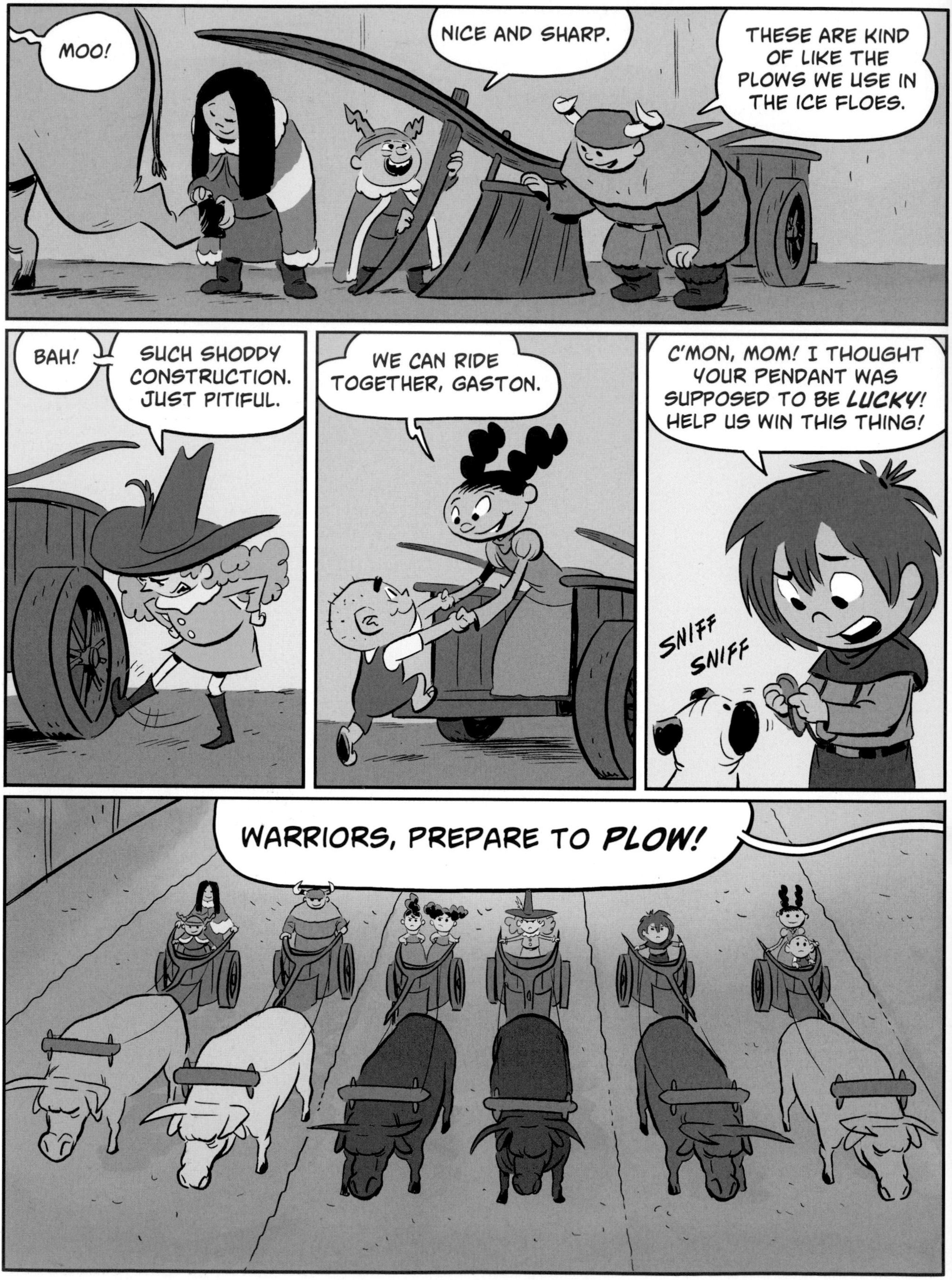
MOO!
NICE AND SHARP.
THESE ARE KIND OF LIKE THE PLOWS WE USE IN THE ICE FLOES.
BAH!
SUCH SHODDY CONSTRUCTION. JUST PITIFUL.
WE CAN RIDE TOGETHER, GASTON.
C'MON, MOM! I THOUGHT YOUR PENDANT WAS SUPPOSED TO BE LUCKY! HELP US WIN THIS THING!
SNIFF
SNIFF
WARRIORS, PREPARE TO PLOW!

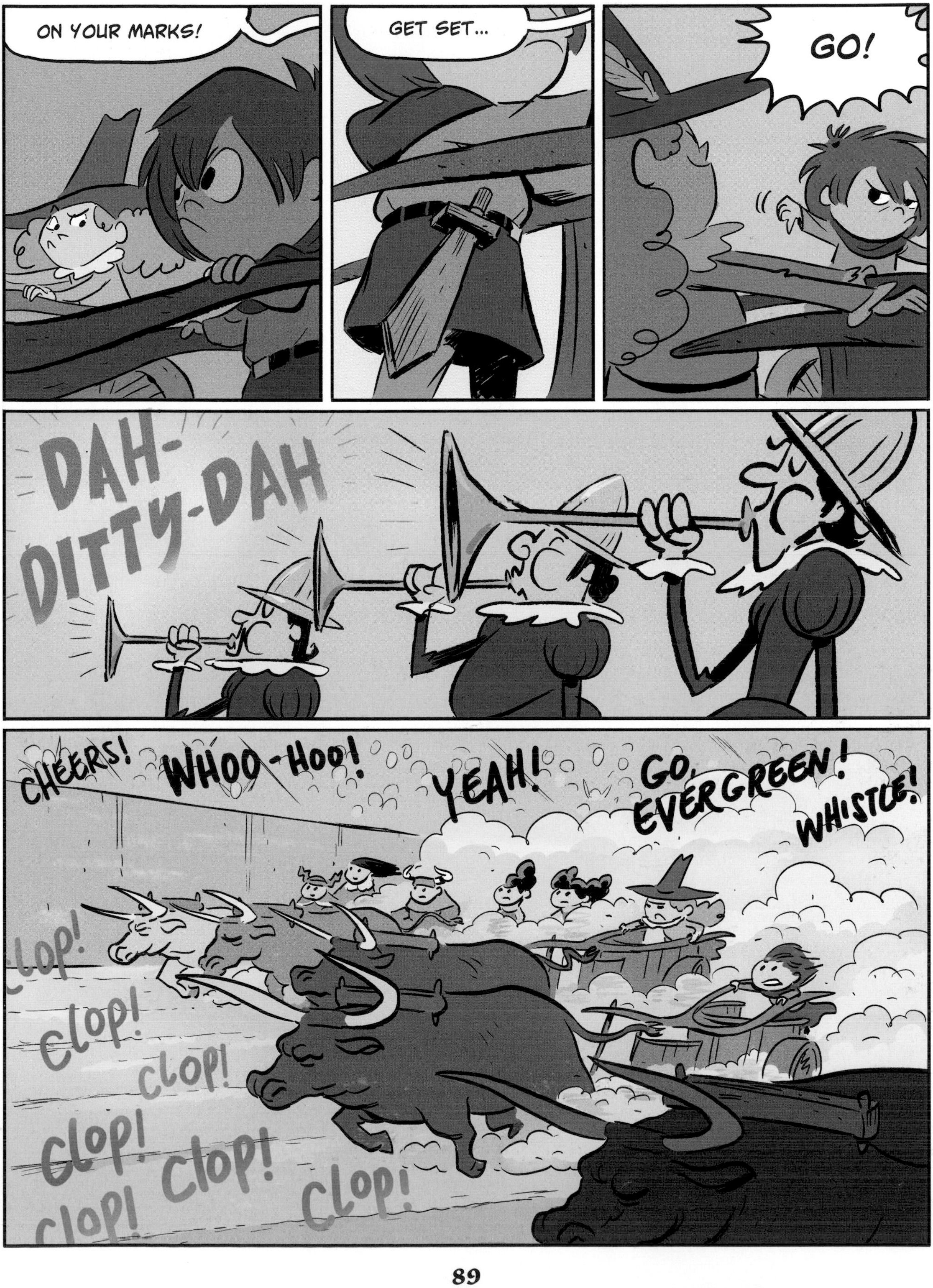
ON YOUR MARKS!
GET SET...
GO!
DAH-DITTY-DAH
CHEERS!
WHOO-HOO!
YEAH!
GO, EVERGREEN!
WHISTLE!
CLOP!
CLOP!
CLOP!
CLOP!
CLOP!
CLOP!
CLOP!

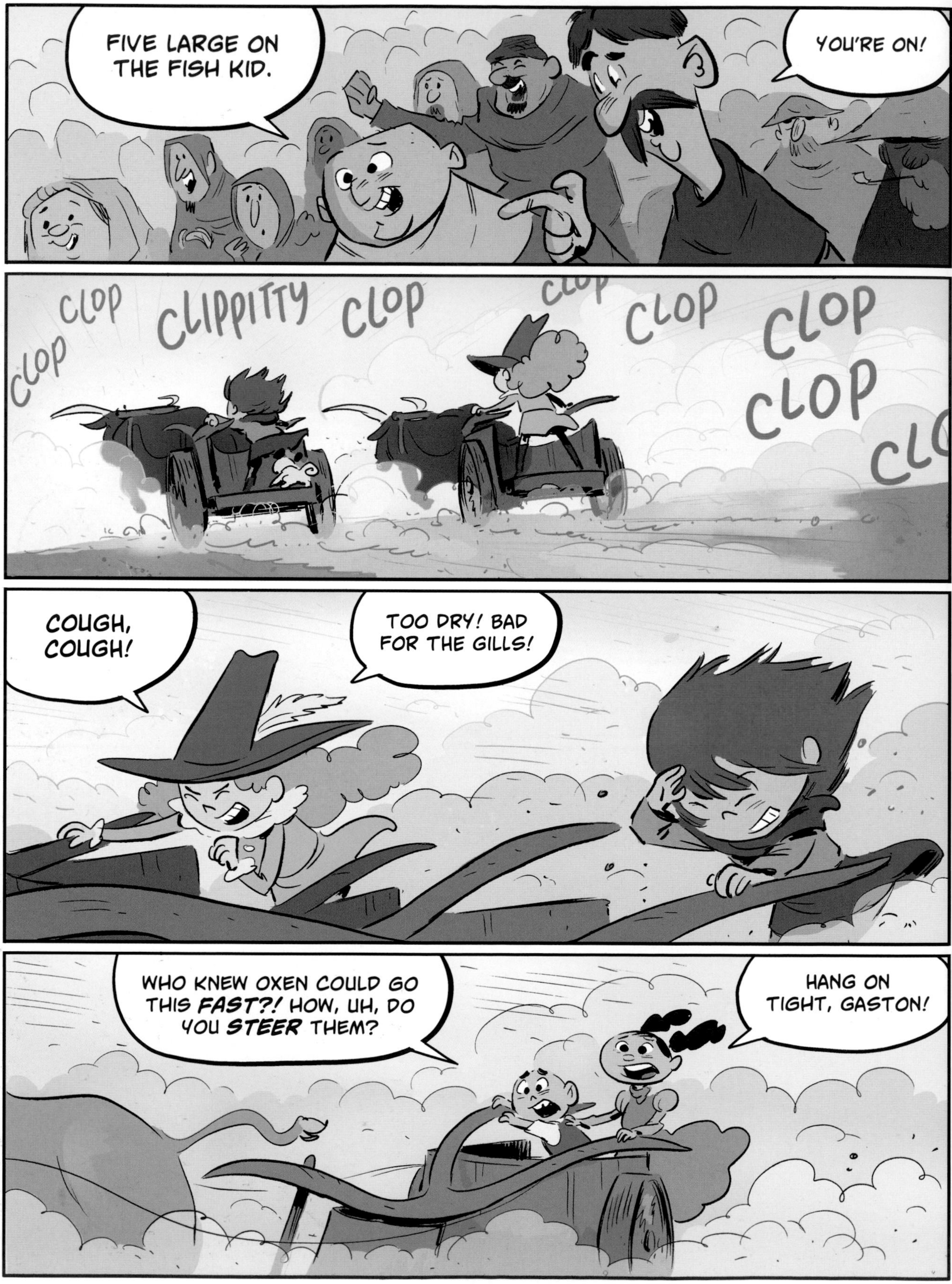

FIVE LARGE ON THE FISH KID.
YOU'RE ON!
CLOP CLOP CLIPPITTY CLOP
CLOP CLOP
CLOP CLOP
CLO
COUGH, COUGH!
TOO DRY! BAD FOR THE GILLS!
WHO KNEW OXEN COULD GO THIS *FAST?!* HOW, UH, DO YOU *STEER* THEM?
HANG ON TIGHT, GASTON!

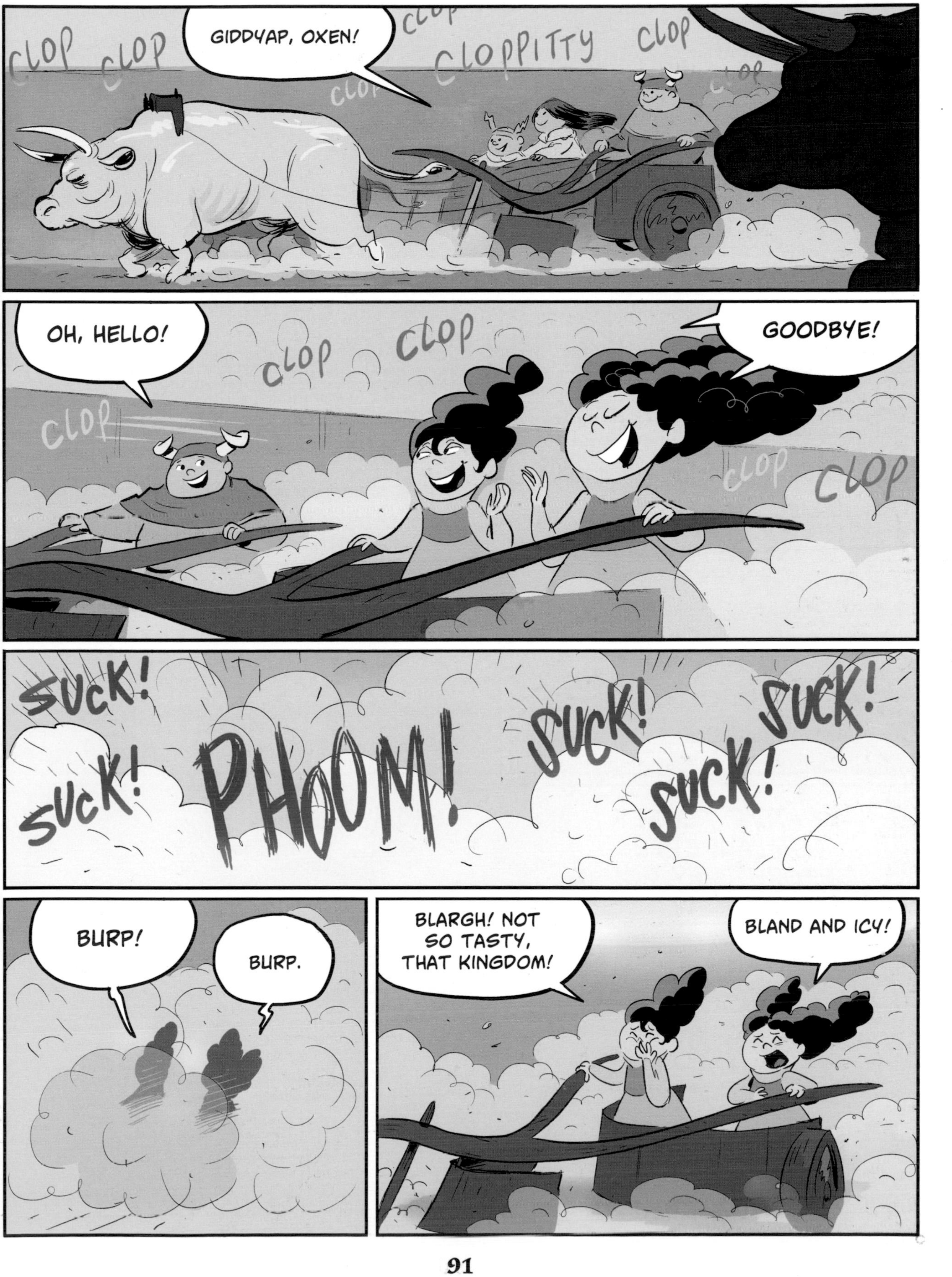
CLOP
CLOP
GIDDYAP, OXEN!
CLOP
CLOPPITTY
CLOP
OH, HELLO!
CLOP
CLOP
GOODBYE!
CLOP
CLOP
CLOP
SUCK!
SUCK!
PHOOM!
SUCK!
SUCK!
SUCK!
BURP!
BURP.
BLARGH! NOT SO TASTY, THAT KINGDOM!
BLAND AND ICY!

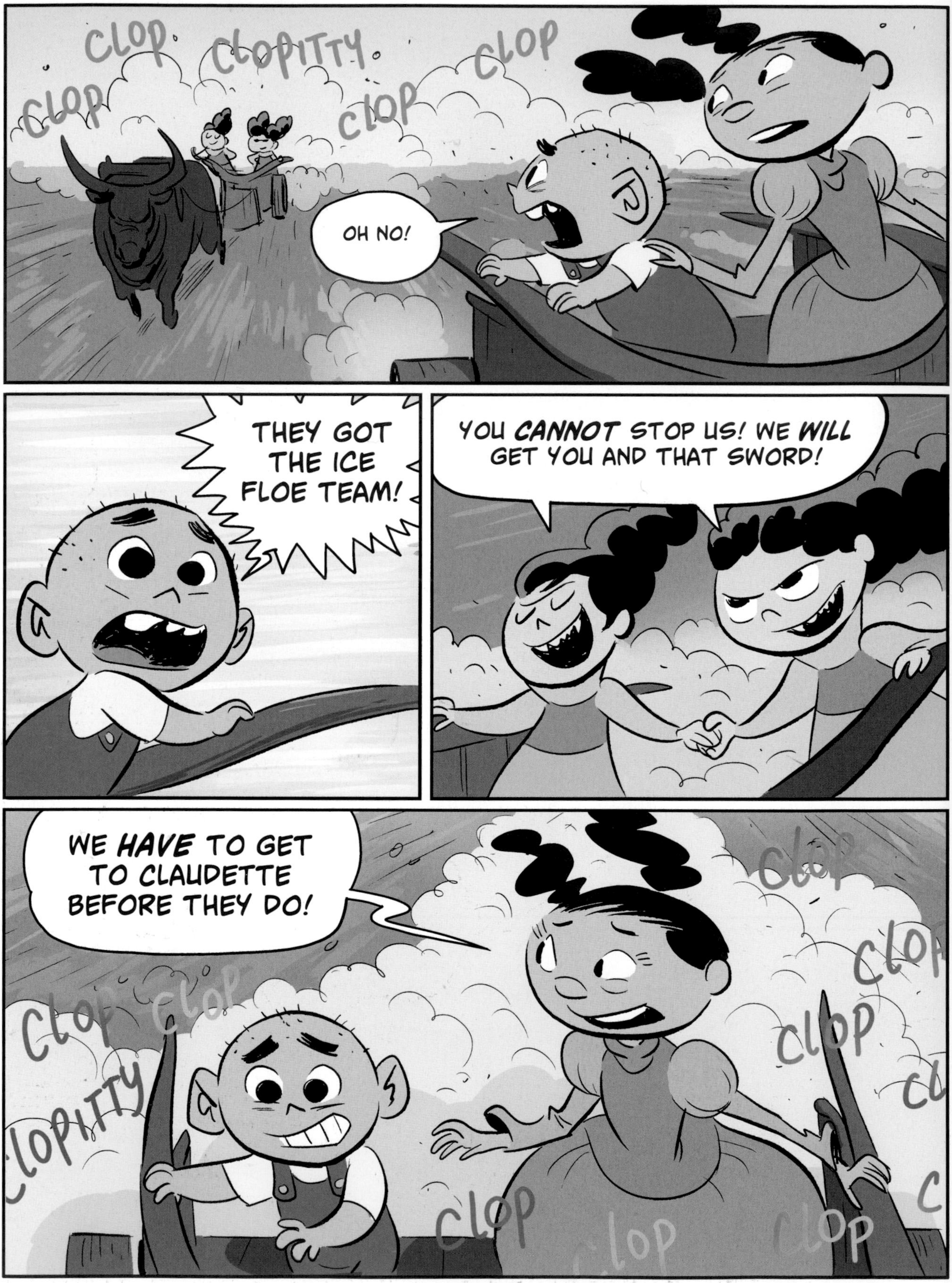
CLOP
CLOPITTY
CLOP
CLOP
CLOP
OH NO!
THEY GOT THE ICE FLOE TEAM!
YOU CANNOT STOP US! WE WILL GET YOU AND THAT SWORD!
WE HAVE TO GET TO CLAUDETTE BEFORE THEY DO!
CLOP
CLOP
CLOP
CLOP
CLOPITTY
CLOP
CLOP

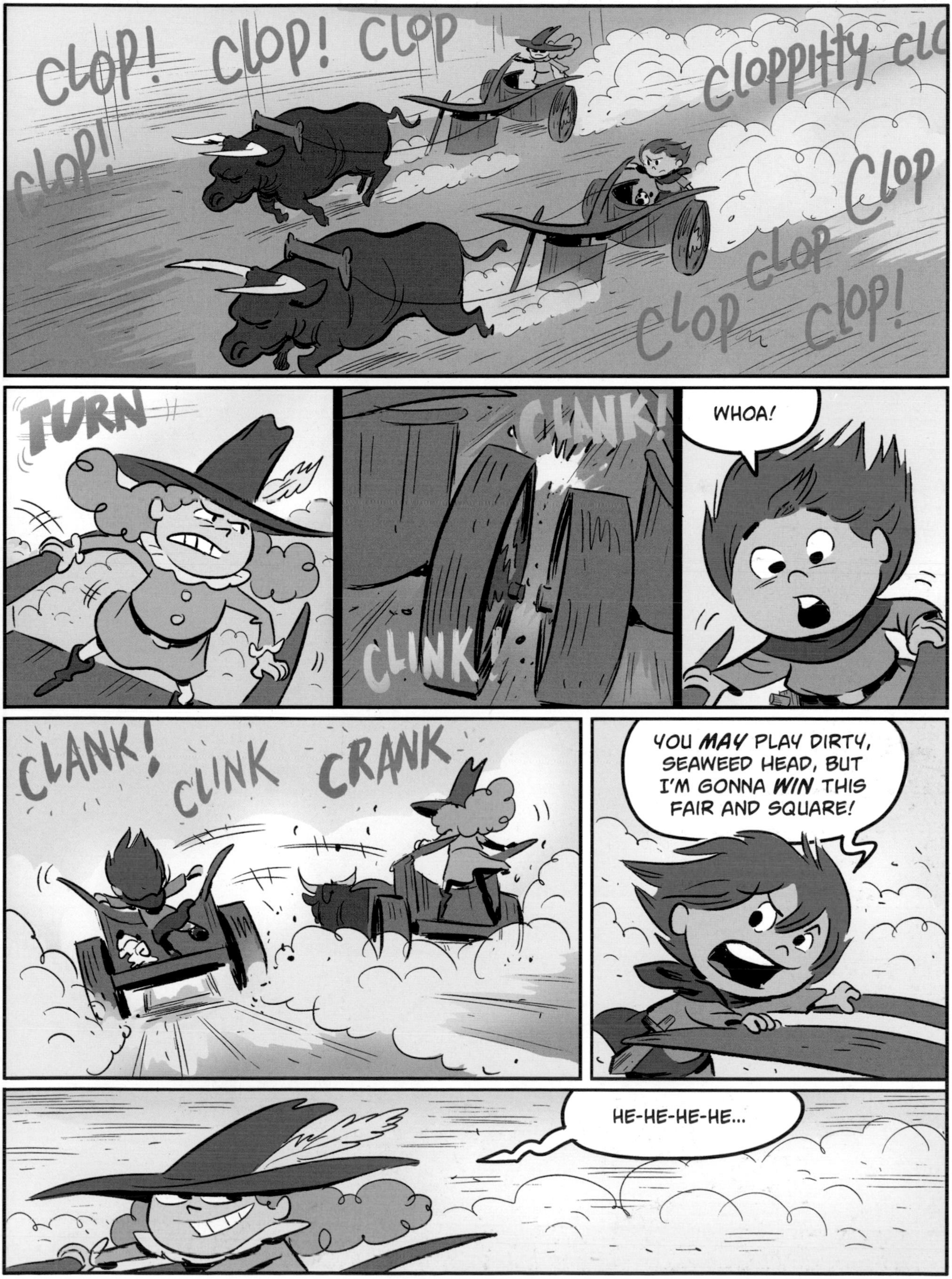

CLOP! CLOP! CLOP
CLOP!
CLOPPITTY CLO
CLOP
CLOP CLOP
CLOP!
TURN
CLANK!
CLINK!
WHOA!
CLANK! CLINK CRANK
YOU *MAY* PLAY DIRTY, SEAWEED HEAD, BUT I'M GONNA *WIN* THIS FAIR AND SQUARE!
HE-HE-HE-HE...

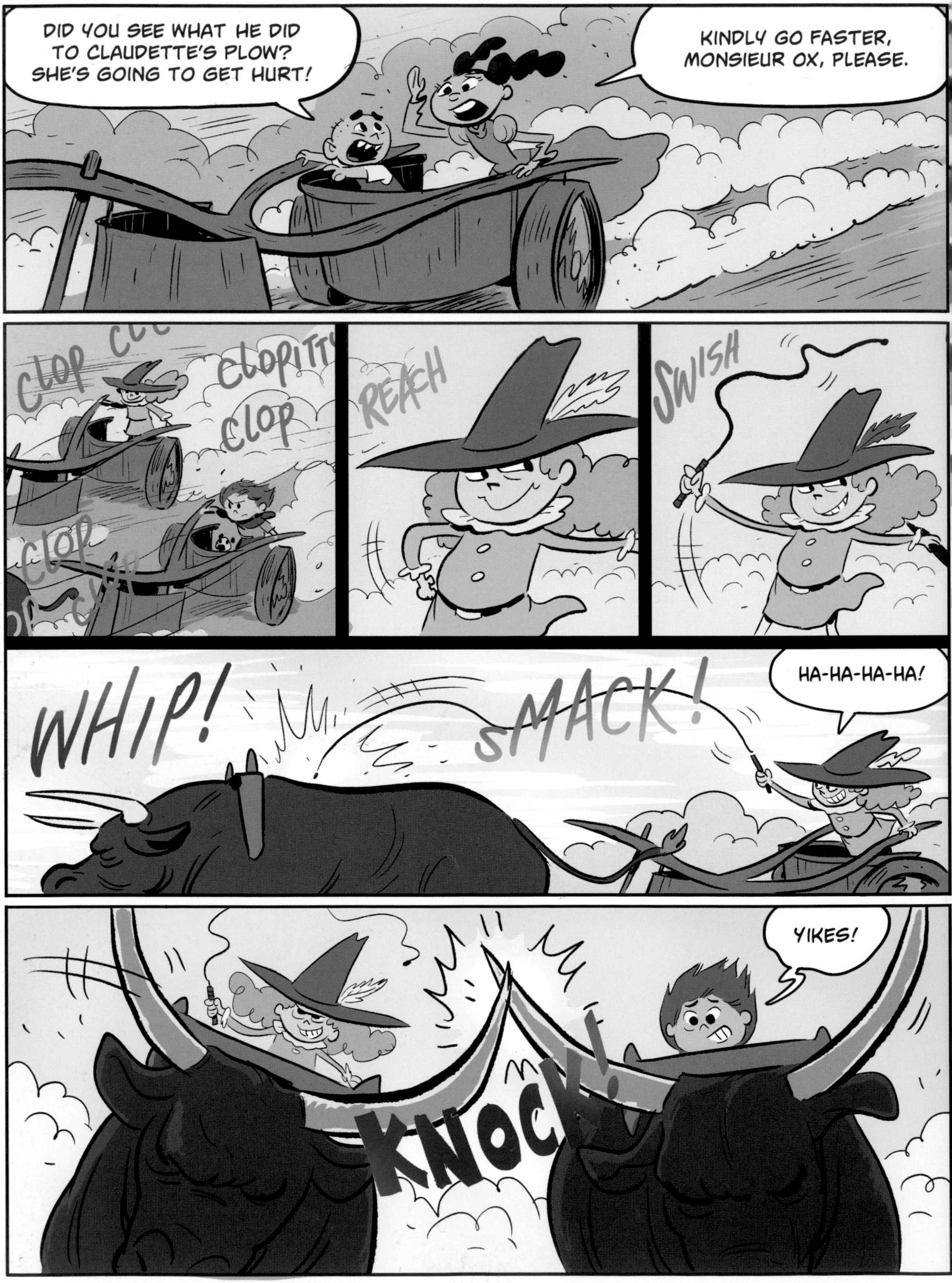
DID YOU SEE WHAT HE DID TO CLAUDETTE'S PLOW? SHE'S GOING TO GET HURT!
KINDLY GO FASTER, MONSIEUR OX, PLEASE.
CLOP
CLOPITTY
CLOP
CLOP
REACH
SWISH
WHIP!
SMACK!
HA-HA-HA-HA!
YIKES!
KNOCK!

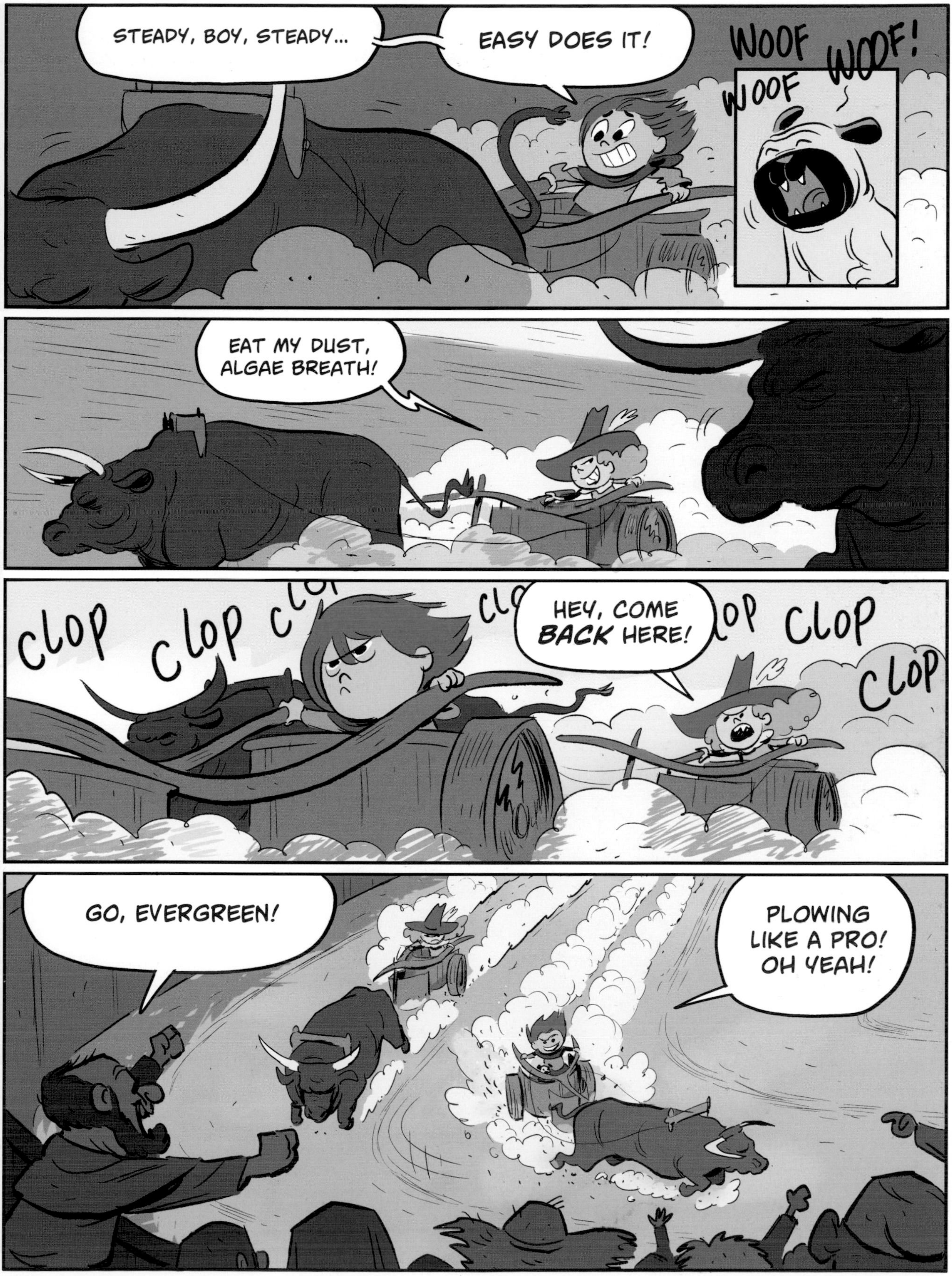
STEADY, BOY, STEADY...
EASY DOES IT!
WOOF WOOF WOOF!
EAT MY DUST, ALGAE BREATH!
CLOP CLOP CLOP
HEY, COME BACK HERE!
CLOP CLOP CLOP
GO, EVERGREEN!
PLOWING LIKE A PRO! OH YEAH!

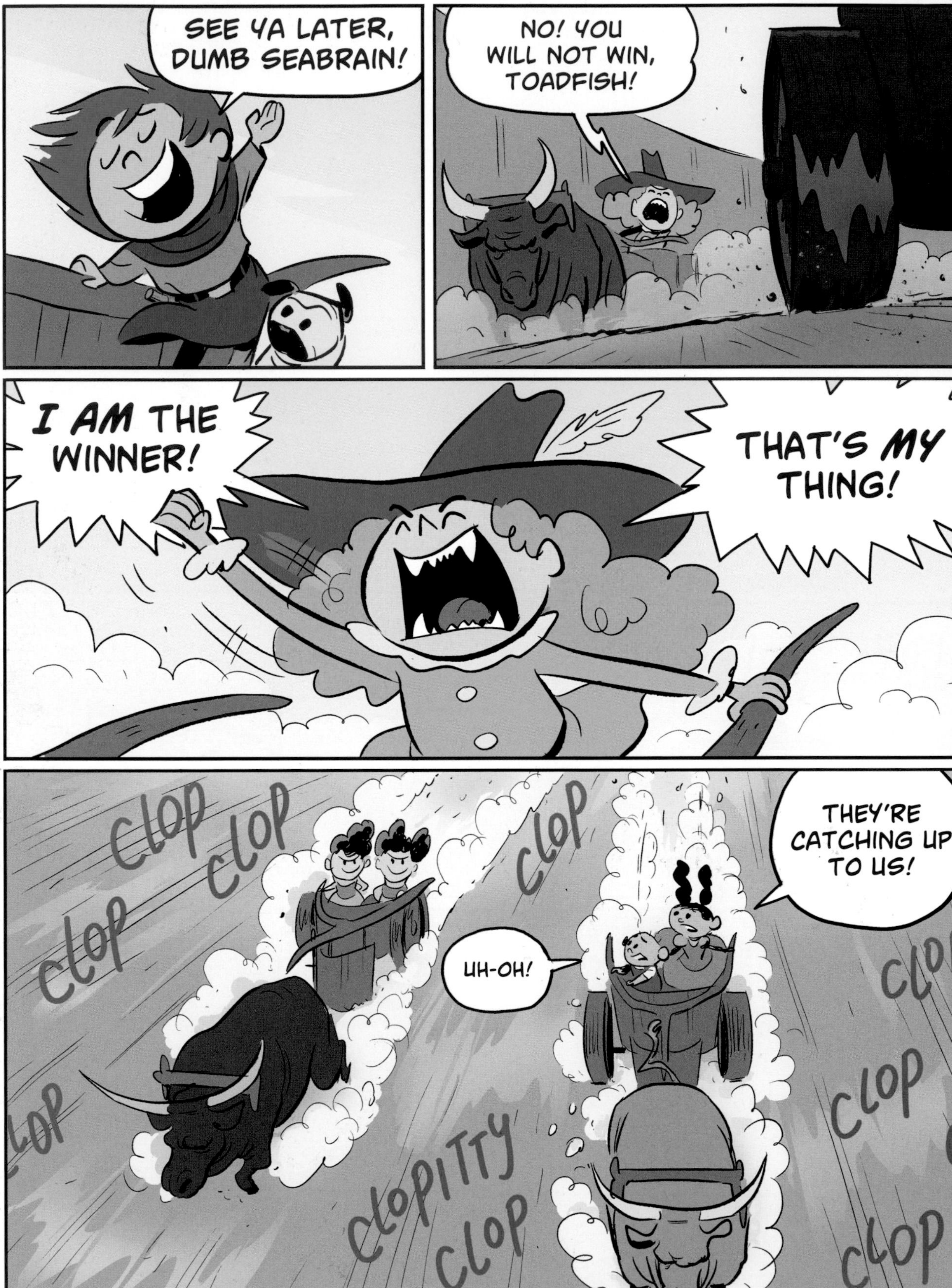

SEE YA LATER, DUMB SEABRAIN!
NO! YOU WILL NOT WIN, TOADFISH!
I AM THE WINNER!
THAT'S MY THING!
CLOP CLOP CLOP
CLOP
THEY'RE CATCHING UP TO US!
UH-OH!
CLOP
CLOP
CLOP
CLOPITTY CLOP
CLOP

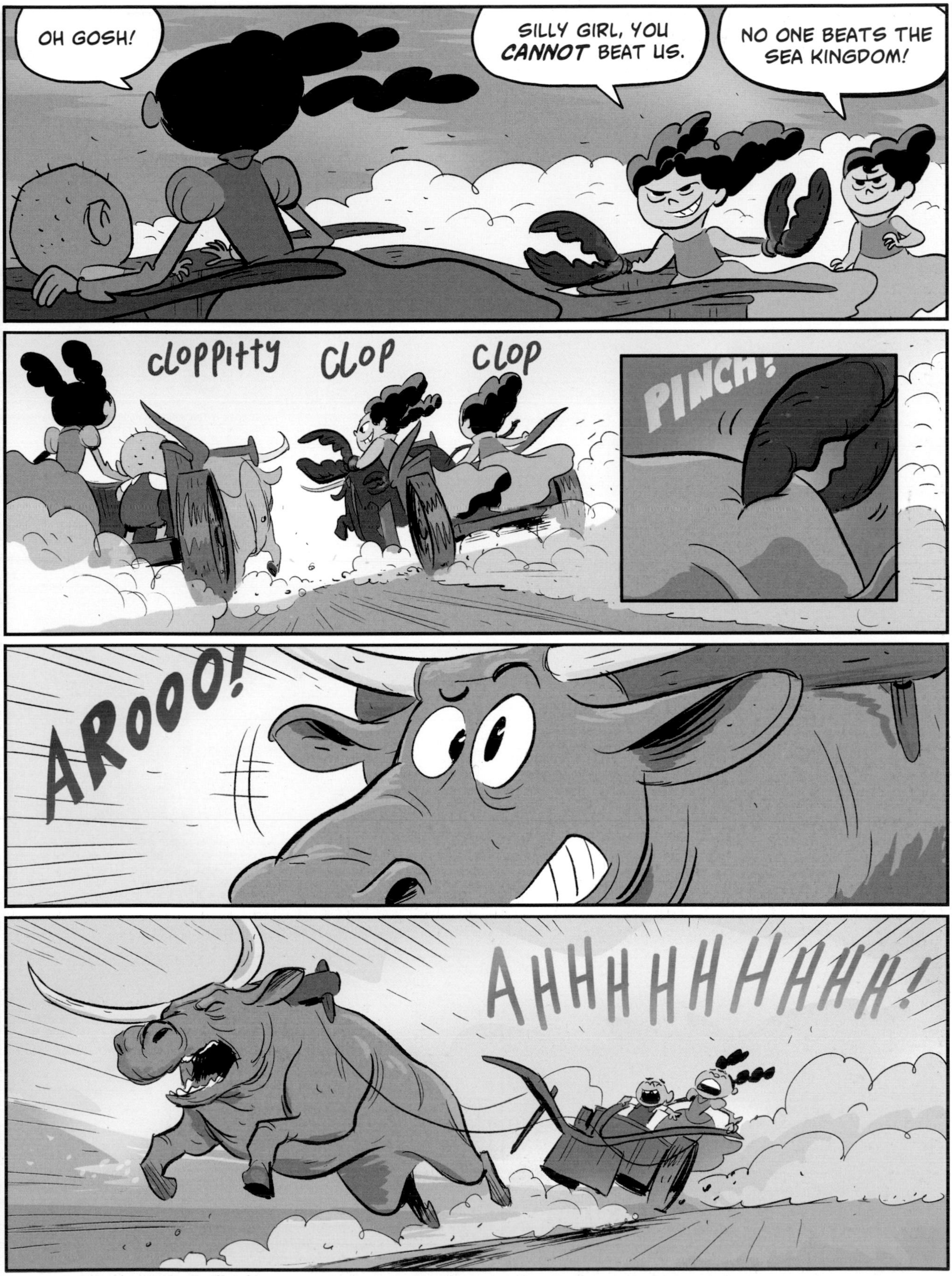
OH GOSH!
SILLY GIRL, YOU *CANNOT* BEAT US.
NO ONE BEATS THE SEA KINGDOM!
CLOPPITTY
CLOP
CLOP
PINCH!
AROOO!
AHHHHHHHHHH!

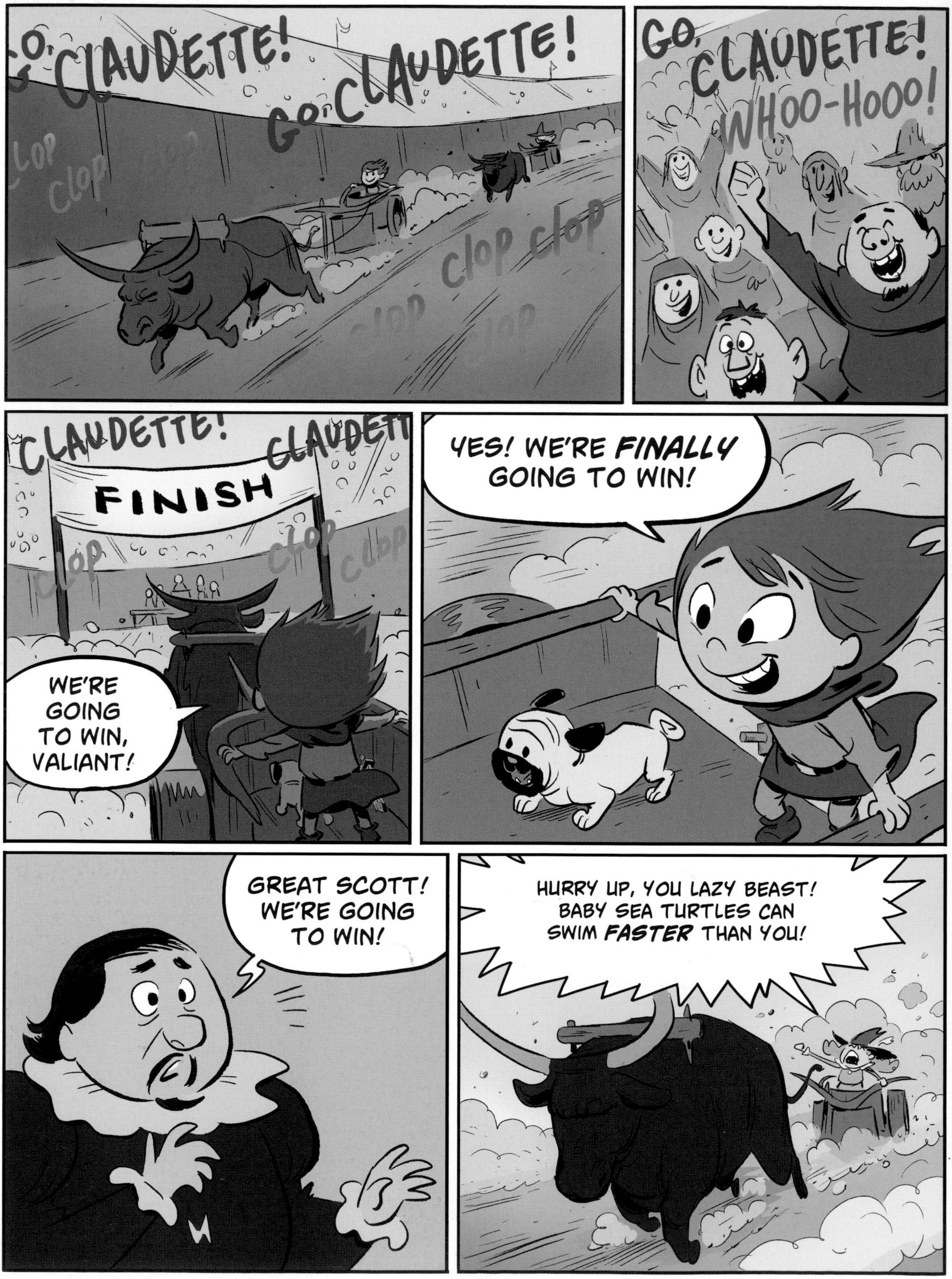
GO, CLAUDETTE!
GO, CLAUDETTE!
CLOP CLOP CLOP
CLOP CLOP CLOP CLOP
GO, CLAUDETTE!
WHOO-HOOO!
CLAUDETTE!
FINISH
CLOP CLOP CLOP
WE'RE GOING TO WIN, VALIANT!
YES! WE'RE *FINALLY* GOING TO WIN!
GREAT SCOTT! WE'RE GOING TO WIN!
HURRY UP, YOU LAZY BEAST! BABY SEA TURTLES CAN SWIM *FASTER* THAN YOU!

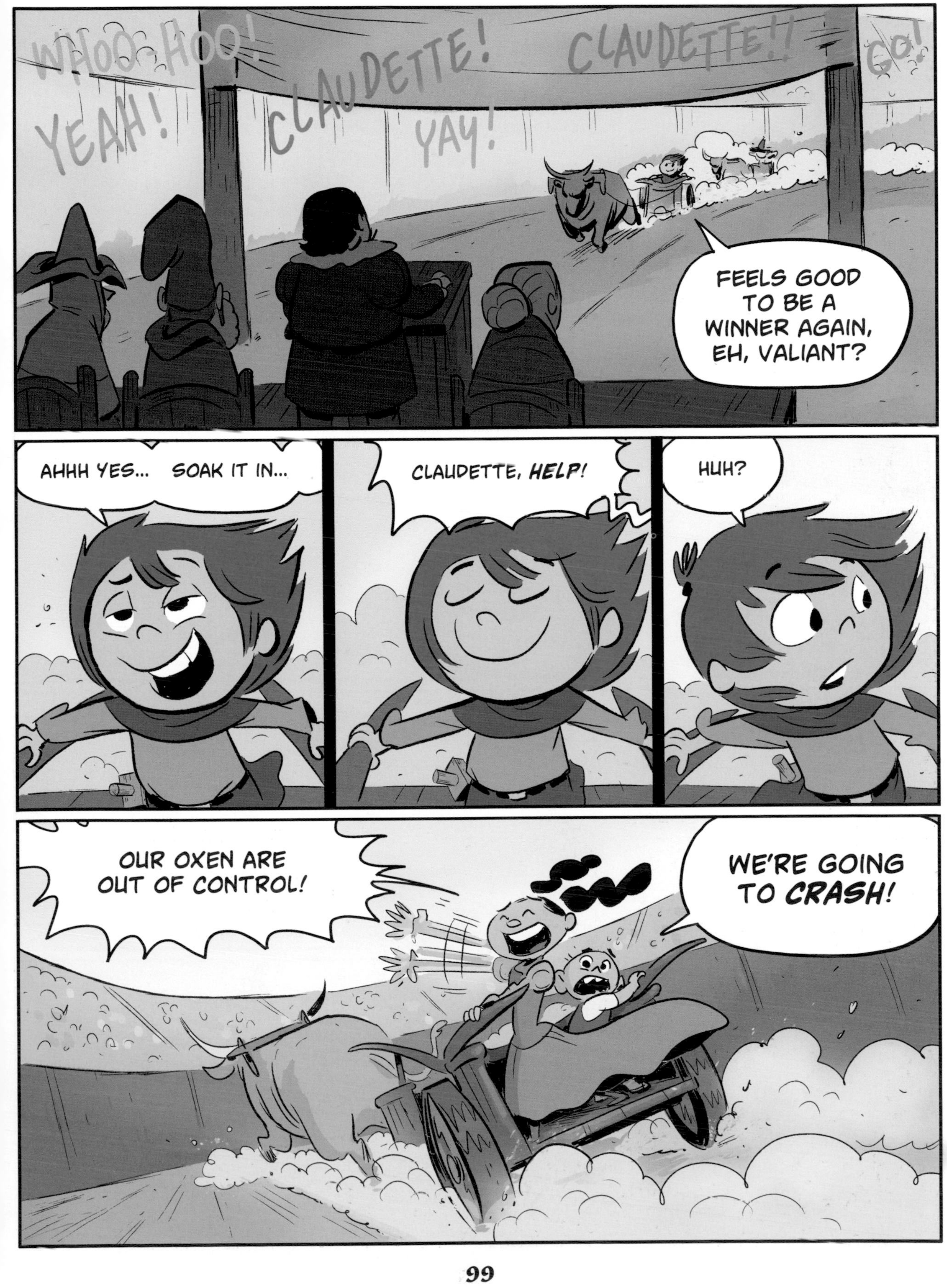
WHOO-HOO!
YEAH!
CLAUDETTE!
YAY!
CLAUDETTE!!
GO!
FEELS GOOD TO BE A WINNER AGAIN, EH, VALIANT?
AHHH YES... SOAK IT IN...
CLAUDETTE, HELP!
HUH?
OUR OXEN ARE OUT OF CONTROL!
WE'RE GOING TO CRASH!

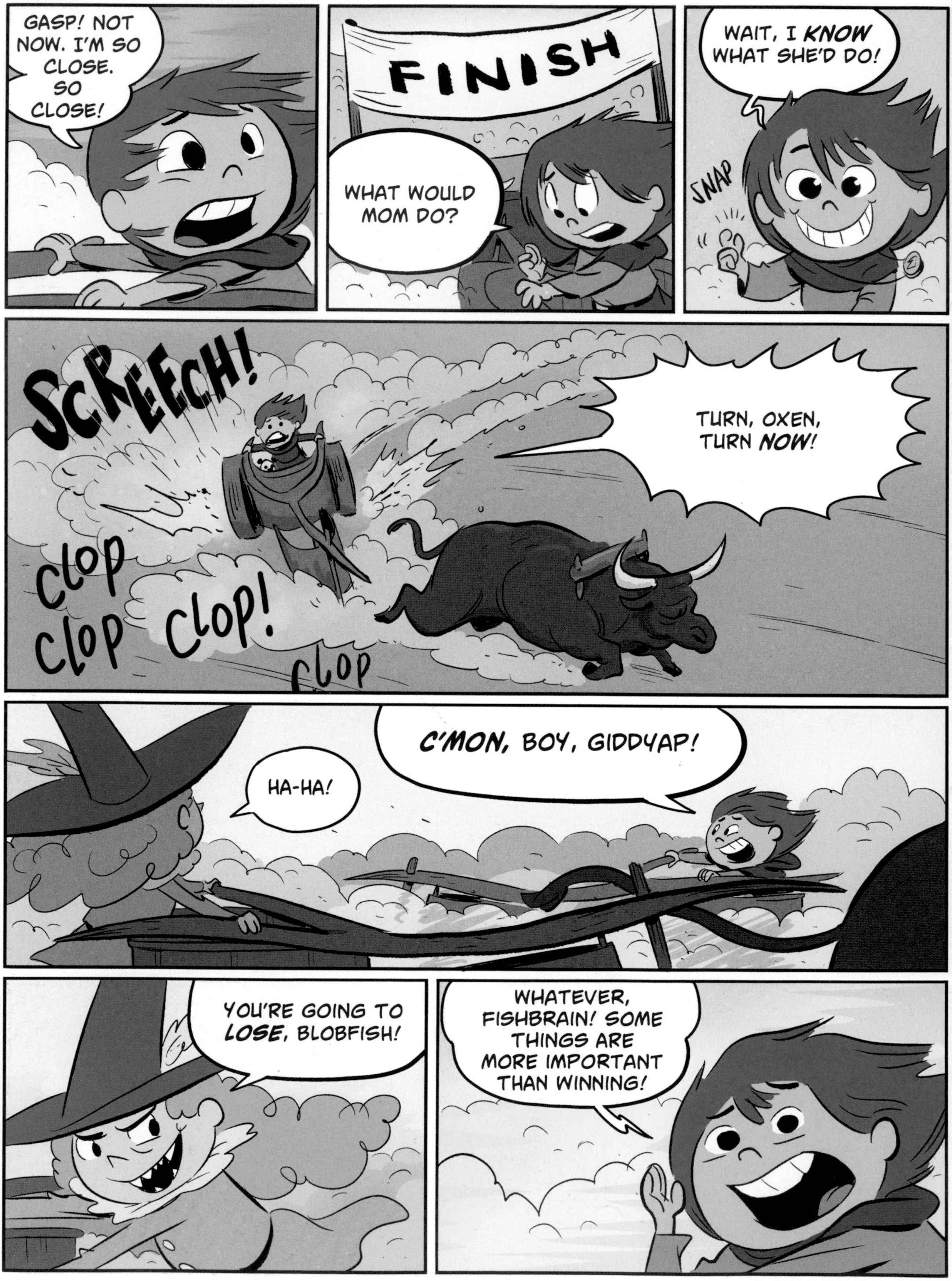
GASP! NOT NOW. I'M SO CLOSE. SO CLOSE!
FINISH
WHAT WOULD MOM DO?
WAIT, I KNOW WHAT SHE'D DO!
SNAP
SCREECH!
TURN, OXEN, TURN NOW!
CLOP
CLOP
CLOP!
CLOP
C'MON, BOY, GIDDYAP!
HA-HA!
YOU'RE GOING TO LOSE, BLOBFISH!
WHATEVER, FISHBRAIN! SOME THINGS ARE MORE IMPORTANT THAN WINNING!

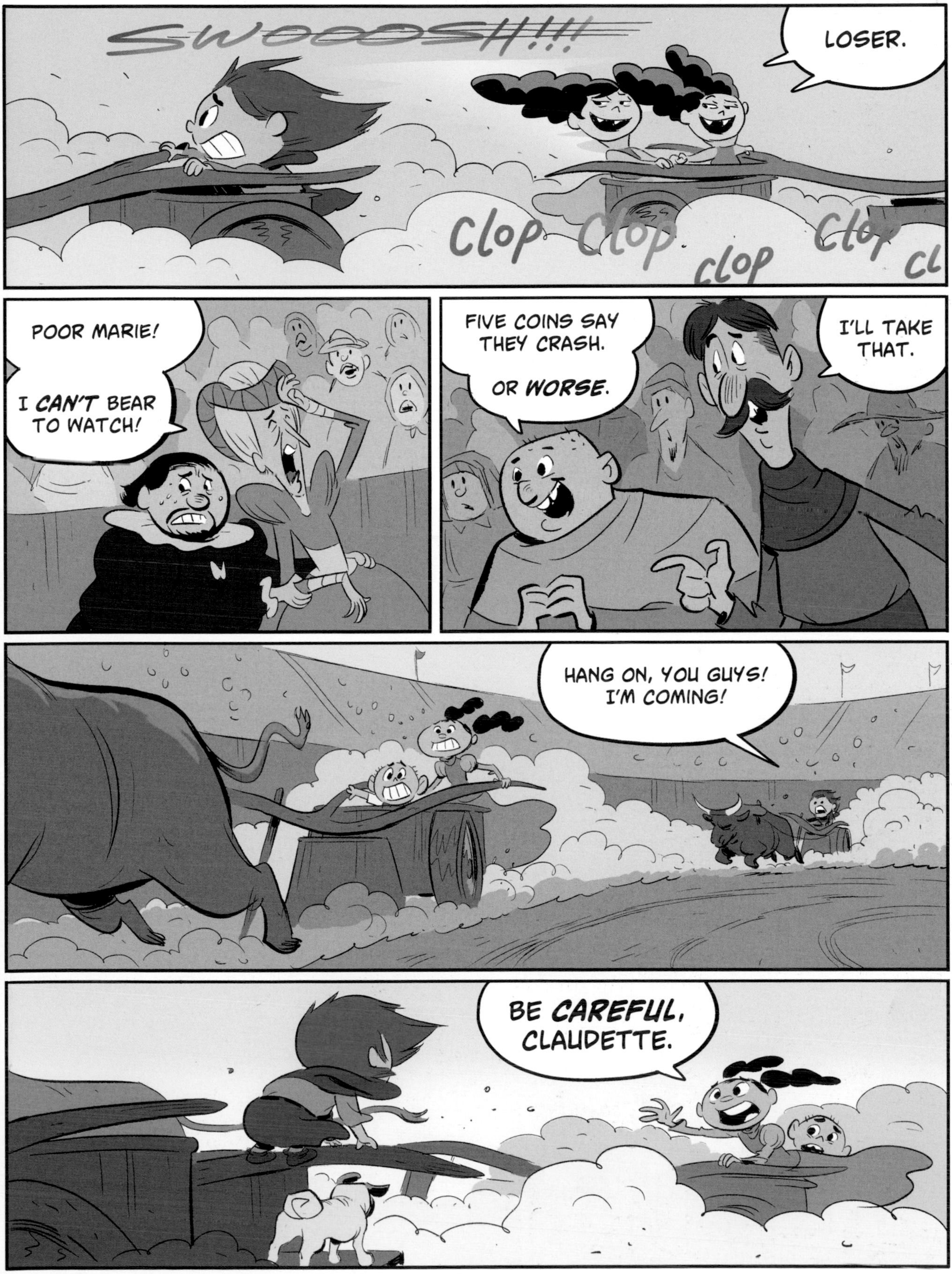
SWOOOOSH!!!
LOSER.
CLOP CLOP CLOP CLOP CL
POOR MARIE!
I *CAN'T* BEAR TO WATCH!
FIVE COINS SAY THEY CRASH.
OR *WORSE*.
I'LL TAKE THAT.
HANG ON, YOU GUYS! I'M COMING!
BE *CAREFUL*, CLAUDETTE.

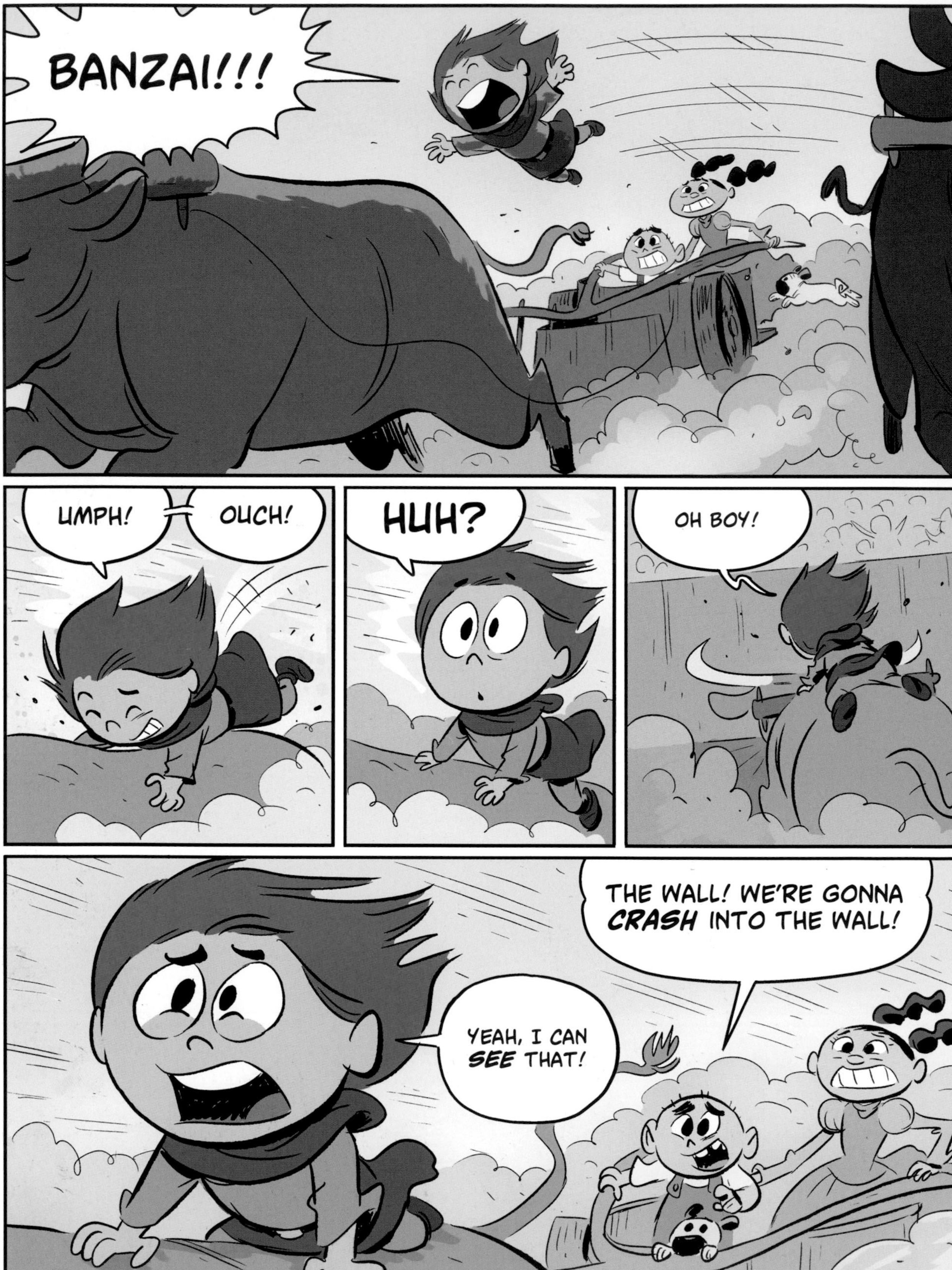

BANZAI!!!
UMPH!
OUCH!
HUH?
OH BOY!
THE WALL! WE'RE GONNA CRASH INTO THE WALL!
YEAH, I CAN SEE THAT!

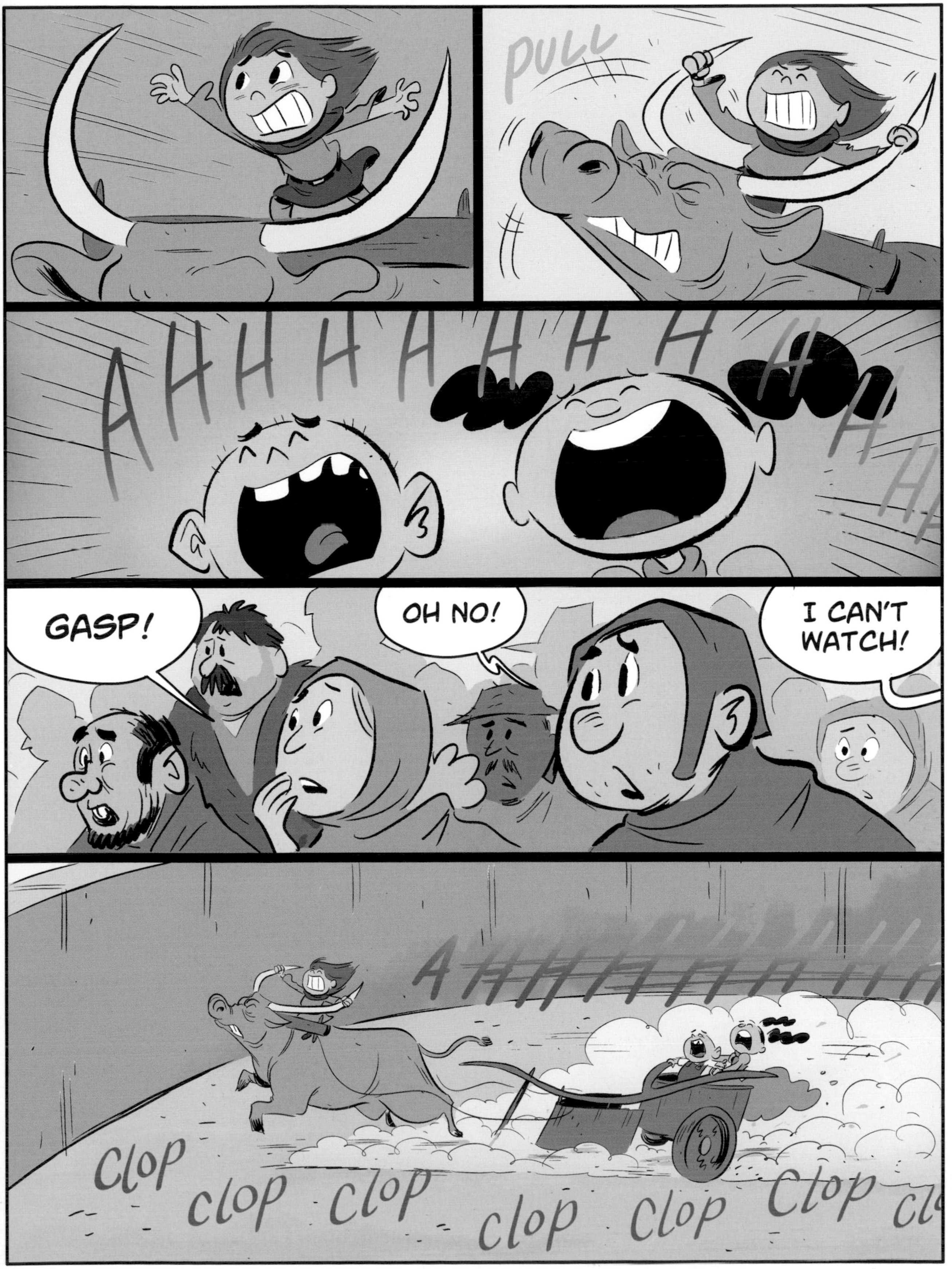
PULL
AHHHHHHHHHHH
GASP!
OH NO!
I CAN'T WATCH!
AHHHHHHHHHH
Clop clop clop clop Clop Clop

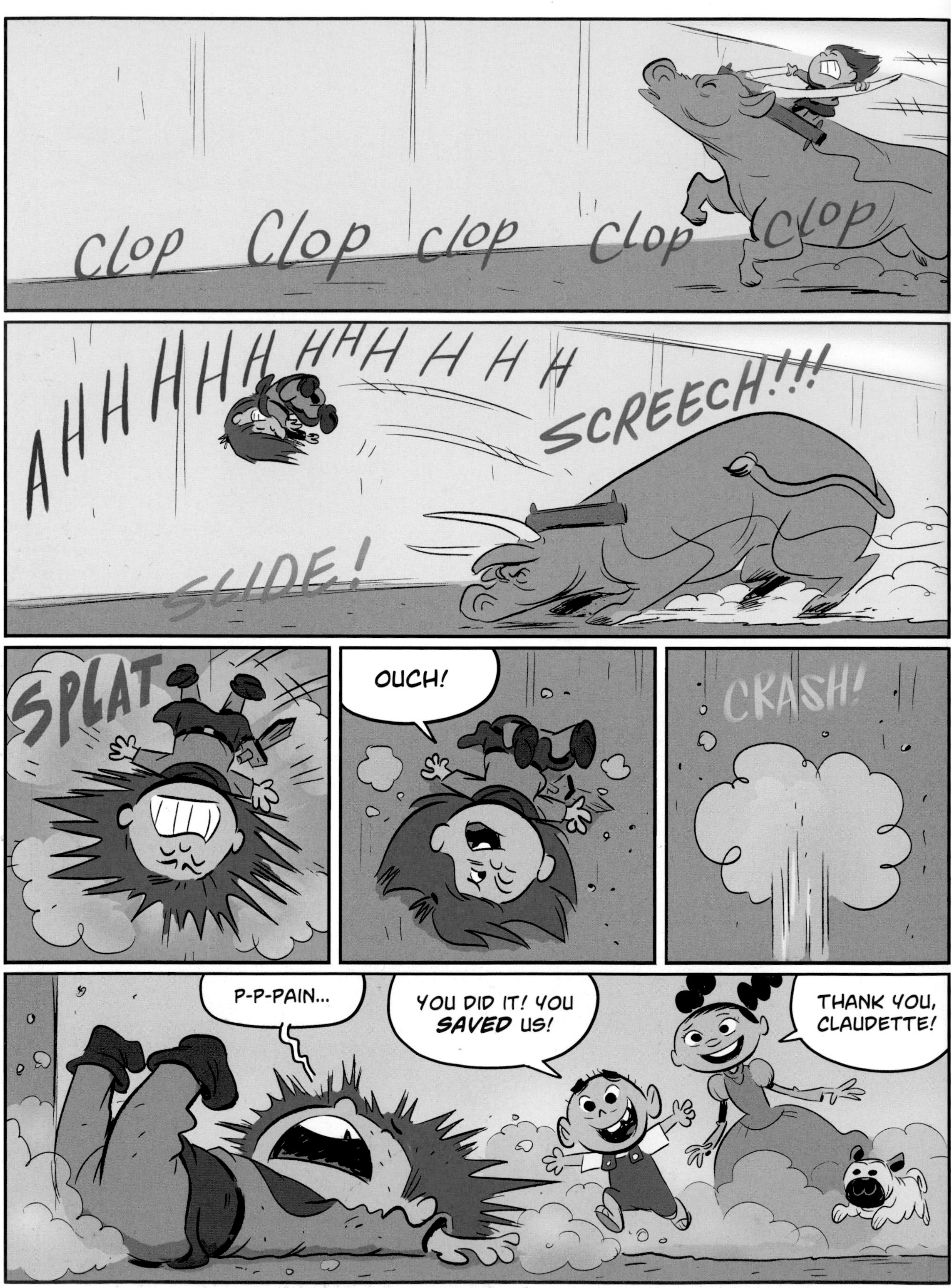
Clop Clop clop clop clop
AHHHHHHHHHH H H H
SCREECH!!!
SLIDE!
SPLAT
OUCH!
CRASH!
P-P-PAIN...
YOU DID IT! YOU SAVED US!
THANK YOU, CLAUDETTE!

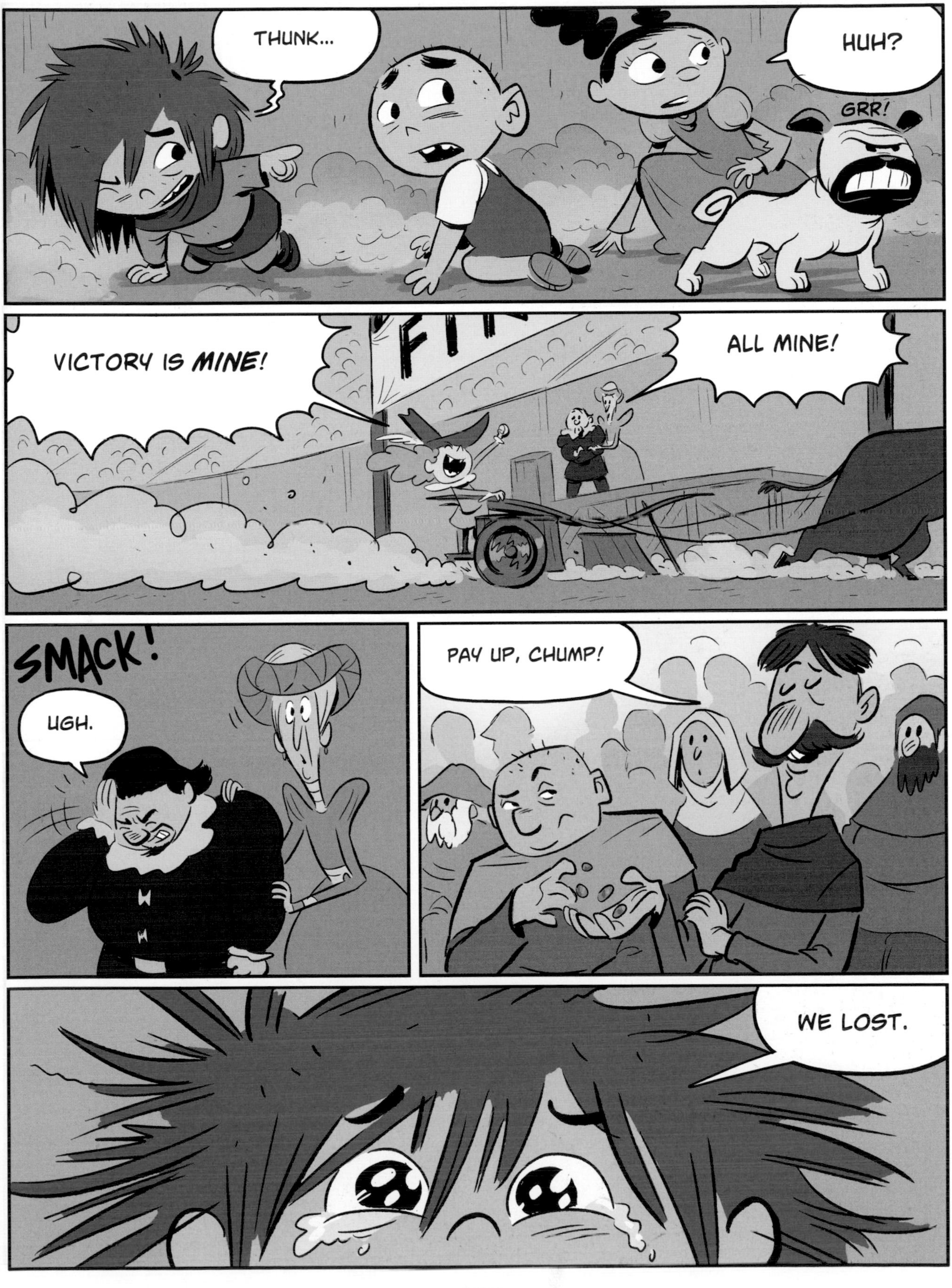
THUNK...
HUH?
GRR!
VICTORY IS ***MINE***!
ALL MINE!
SMACK!
UGH.
PAY UP, CHUMP!
WE LOST.

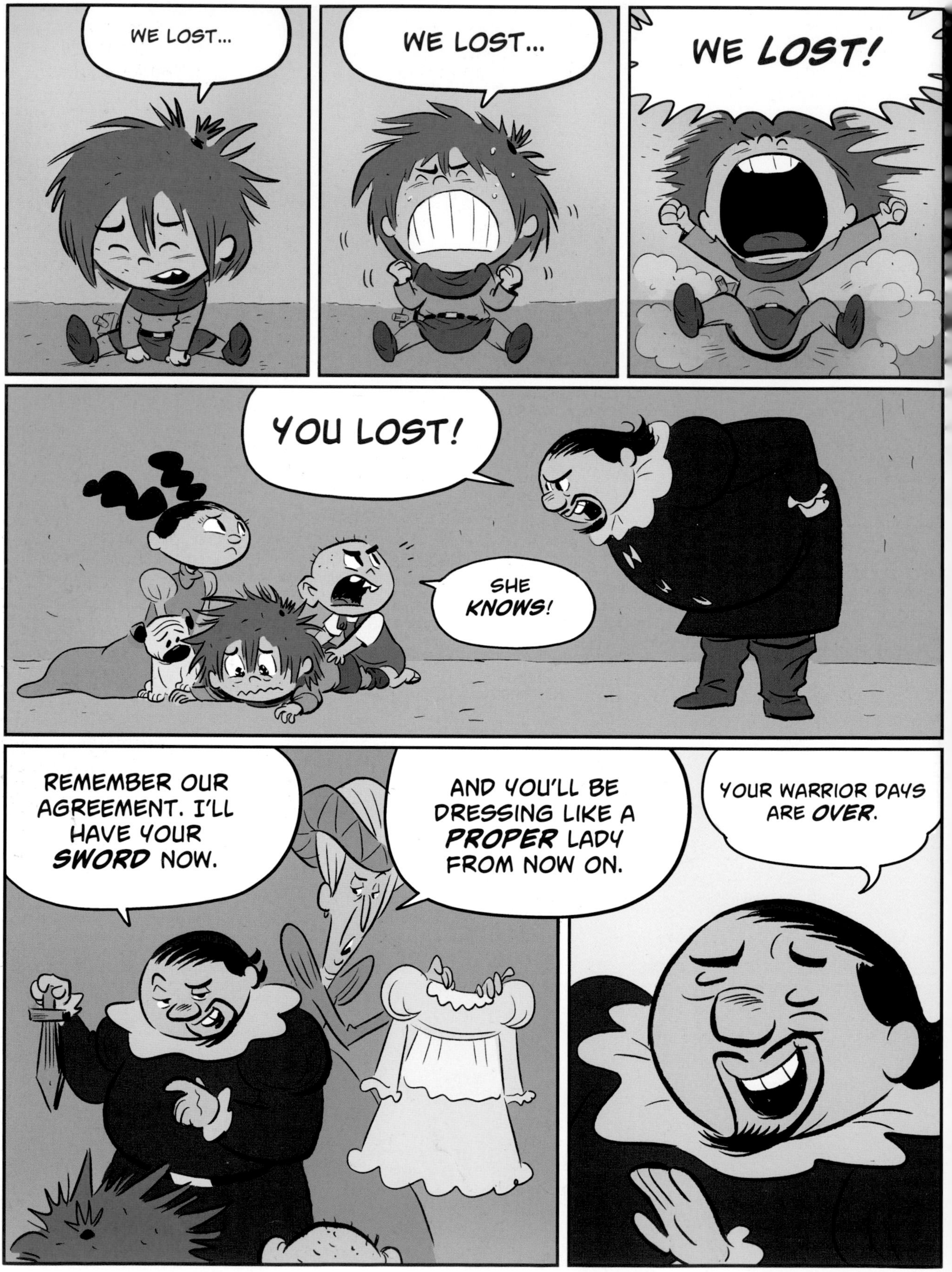
WE LOST...
WE LOST...
WE LOST!
YOU LOST!
SHE KNOWS!
REMEMBER OUR AGREEMENT. I'LL HAVE YOUR SWORD NOW.
AND YOU'LL BE DRESSING LIKE A PROPER LADY FROM NOW ON.
YOUR WARRIOR DAYS ARE OVER.

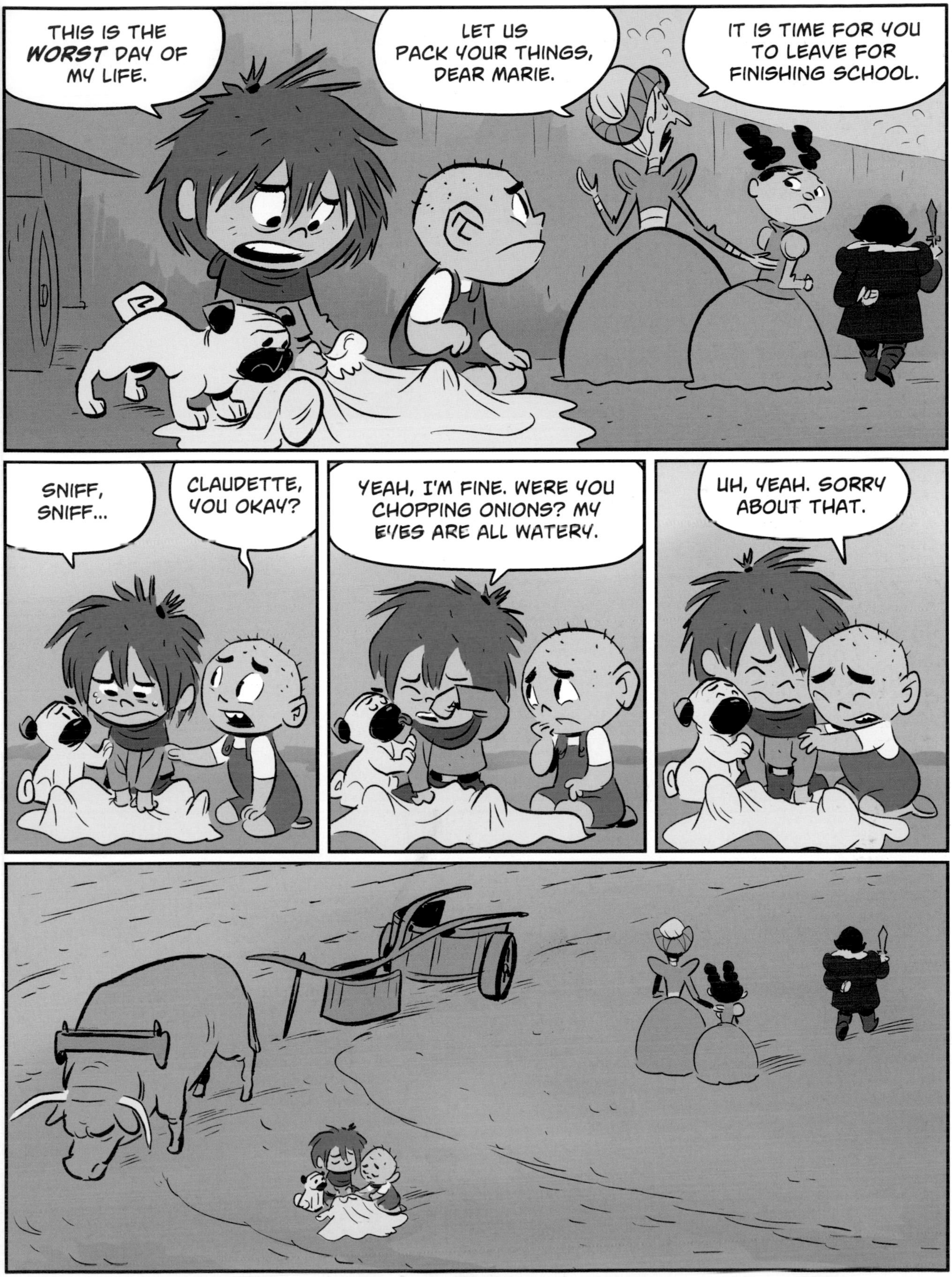
THIS IS THE WORST DAY OF MY LIFE.
LET US PACK YOUR THINGS, DEAR MARIE.
IT IS TIME FOR YOU TO LEAVE FOR FINISHING SCHOOL.
SNIFF, SNIFF...
CLAUDETTE, YOU OKAY?
YEAH, I'M FINE. WERE YOU CHOPPING ONIONS? MY EYES ARE ALL WATERY.
UH, YEAH. SORRY ABOUT THAT.

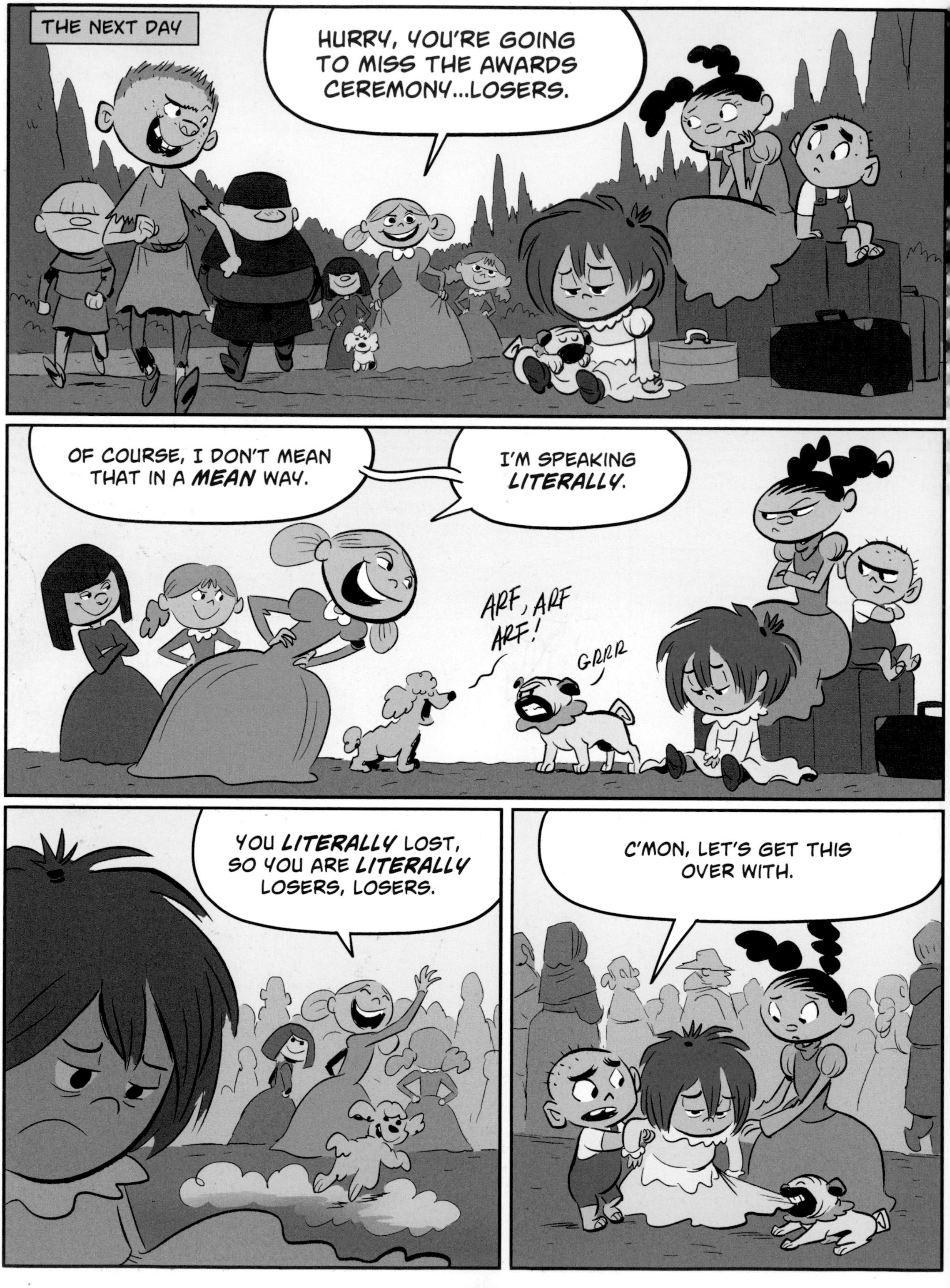
THE NEXT DAY
HURRY, YOU'RE GOING TO MISS THE AWARDS CEREMONY...LOSERS.
OF COURSE, I DON'T MEAN THAT IN A MEAN WAY.
I'M SPEAKING LITERALLY.
ARF, ARF ARF!
GRRR
YOU LITERALLY LOST, SO YOU ARE LITERALLY LOSERS, LOSERS.
C'MON, LET'S GET THIS OVER WITH.

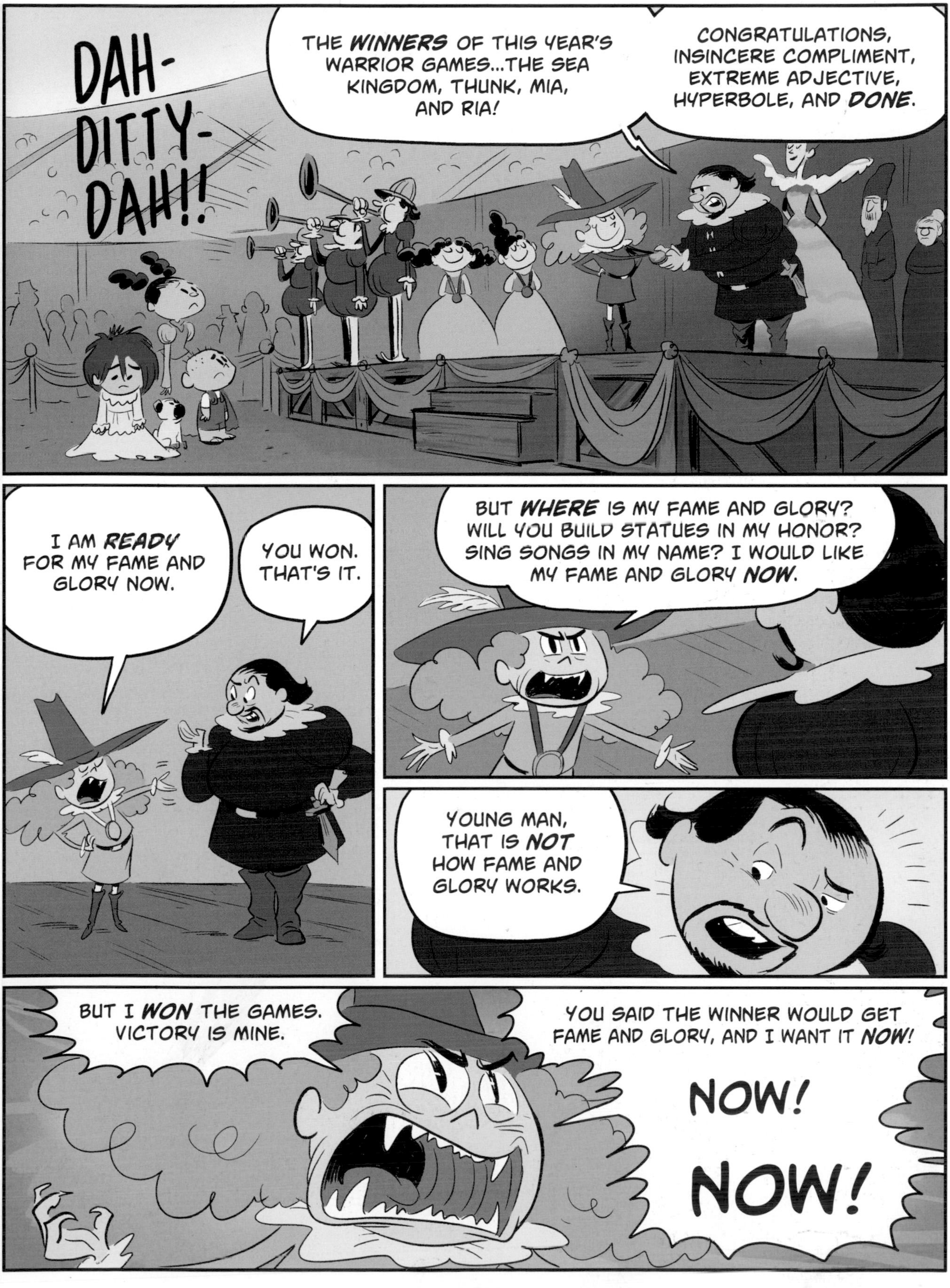
DAH-DITTY-DAH!!
THE WINNERS OF THIS YEAR'S WARRIOR GAMES...THE SEA KINGDOM, THUNK, MIA, AND RIA!
CONGRATULATIONS, INSINCERE COMPLIMENT, EXTREME ADJECTIVE, HYPERBOLE, AND DONE.
I AM READY FOR MY FAME AND GLORY NOW.
YOU WON. THAT'S IT.
BUT WHERE IS MY FAME AND GLORY? WILL YOU BUILD STATUES IN MY HONOR? SING SONGS IN MY NAME? I WOULD LIKE MY FAME AND GLORY NOW.
YOUNG MAN, THAT IS NOT HOW FAME AND GLORY WORKS.
BUT I WON THE GAMES. VICTORY IS MINE.
YOU SAID THE WINNER WOULD GET FAME AND GLORY, AND I WANT IT NOW!
NOW!
NOW!

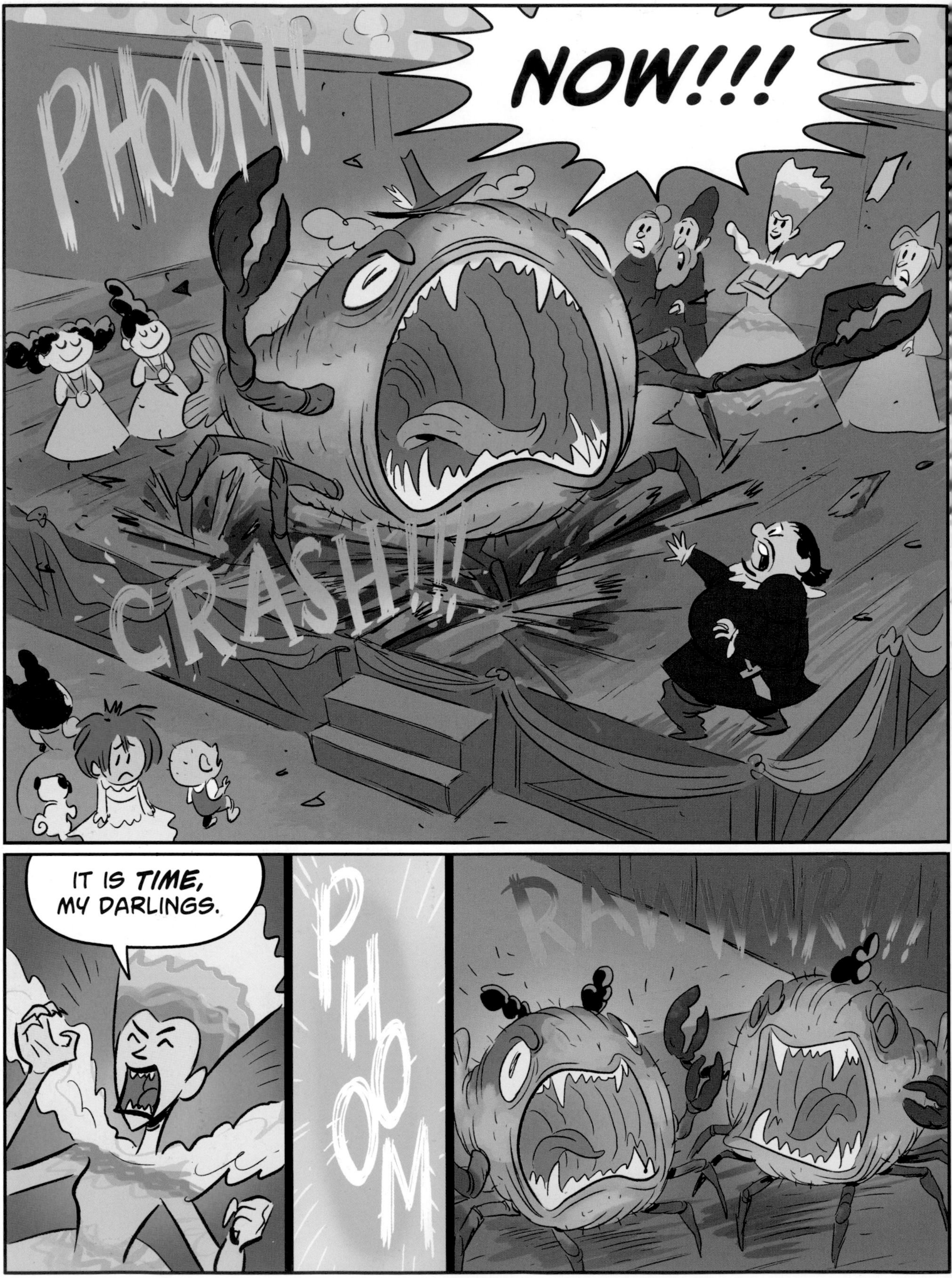
PHOOM!
NOW!!!
CRASH!!!!
IT IS TIME, MY DARLINGS.
PHOOM
RAWWR!!

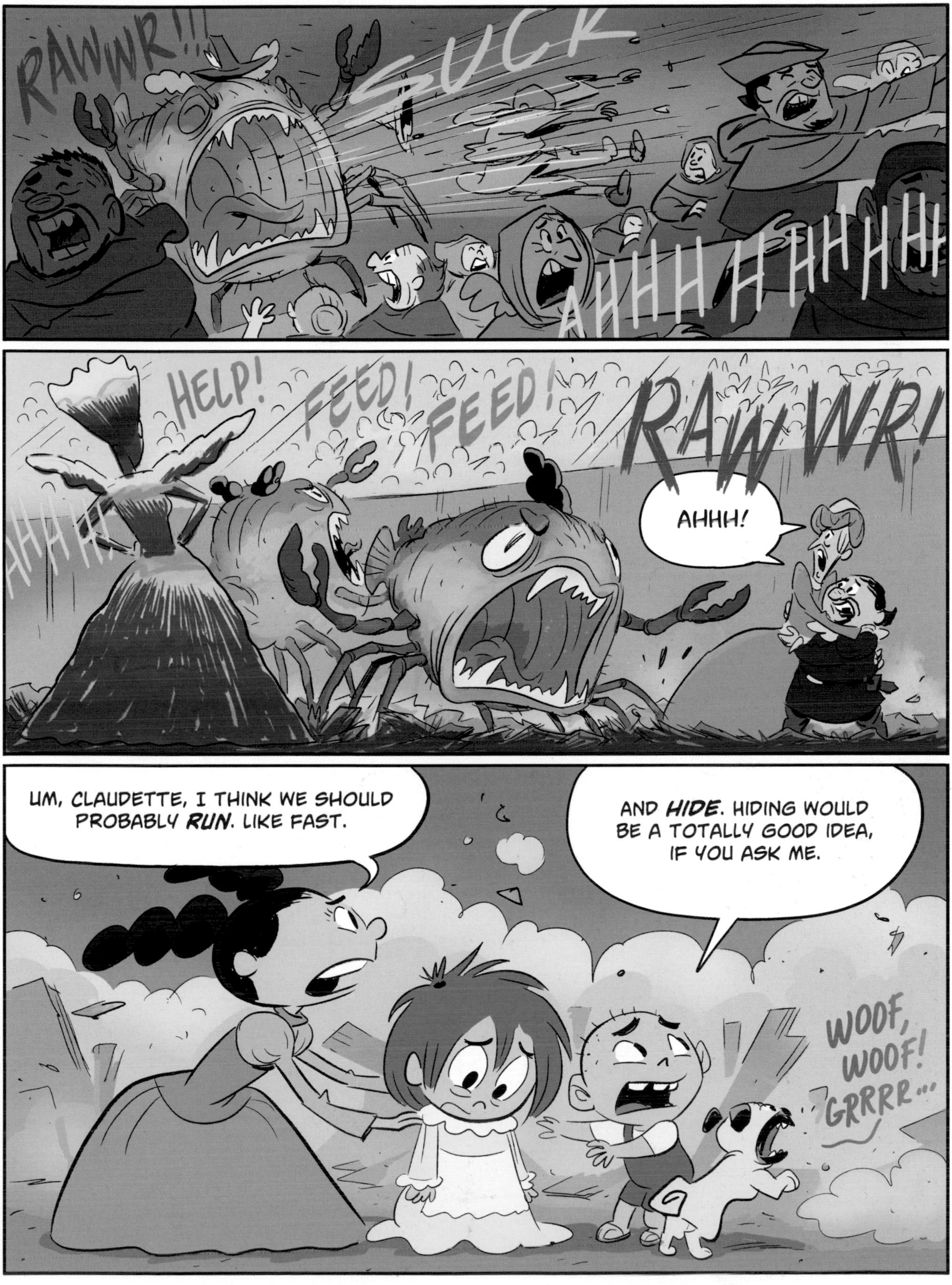
RAWWR!!!
SUCK
AHHHHHHHHHH
HELP!
FEED!
FEED!
RAWWR!
AHHH!
UM, CLAUDETTE, I THINK WE SHOULD PROBABLY RUN. LIKE FAST.
AND HIDE. HIDING WOULD BE A TOTALLY GOOD IDEA, IF YOU ASK ME.
WOOF, WOOF! GRRRR...

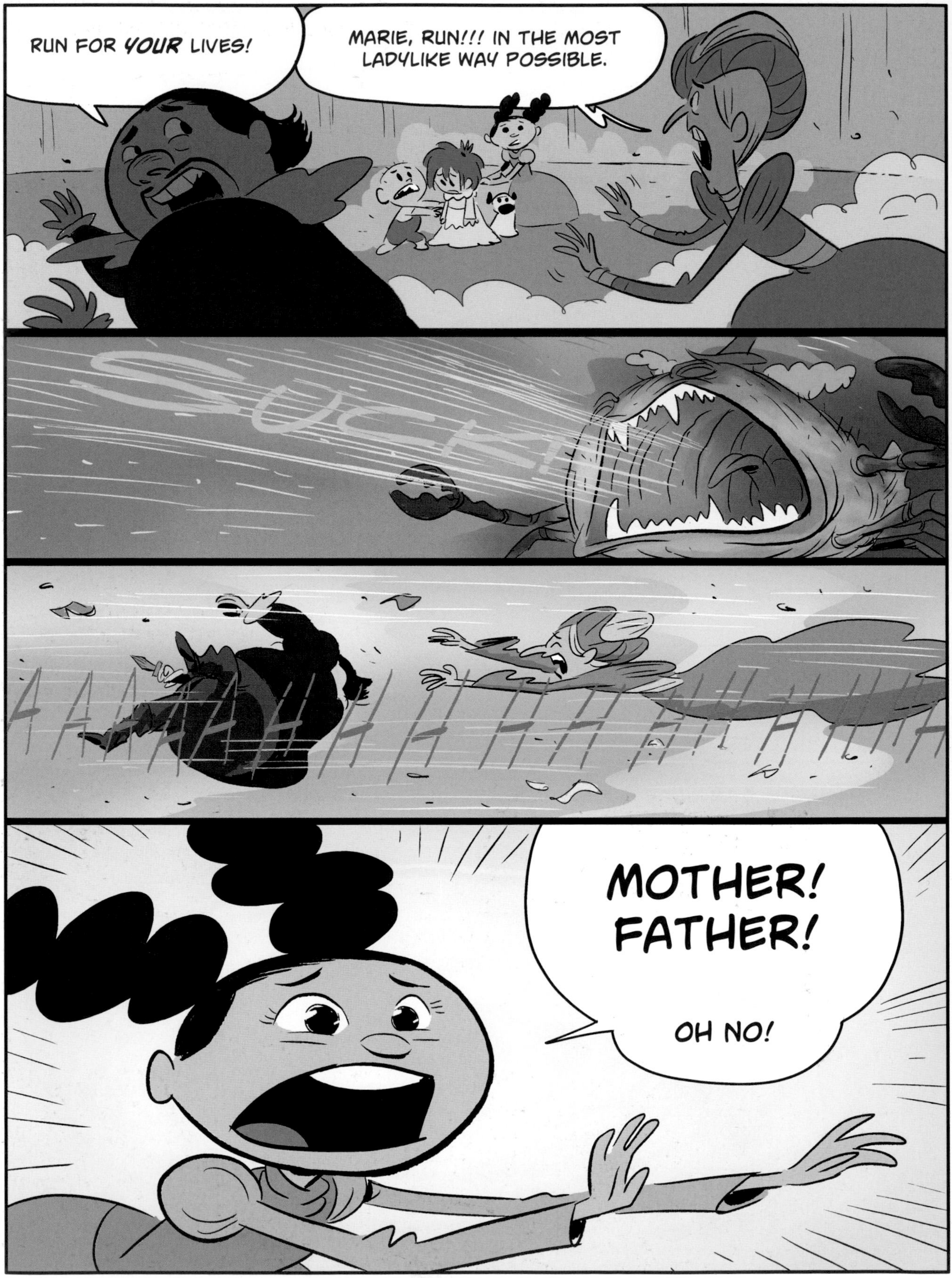
RUN FOR *YOUR* LIVES!
MARIE, RUN!!! IN THE MOST LADYLIKE WAY POSSIBLE.
SUCK!
AAAAAHHHHHHHHHHHHH
MOTHER! FATHER!
OH NO!

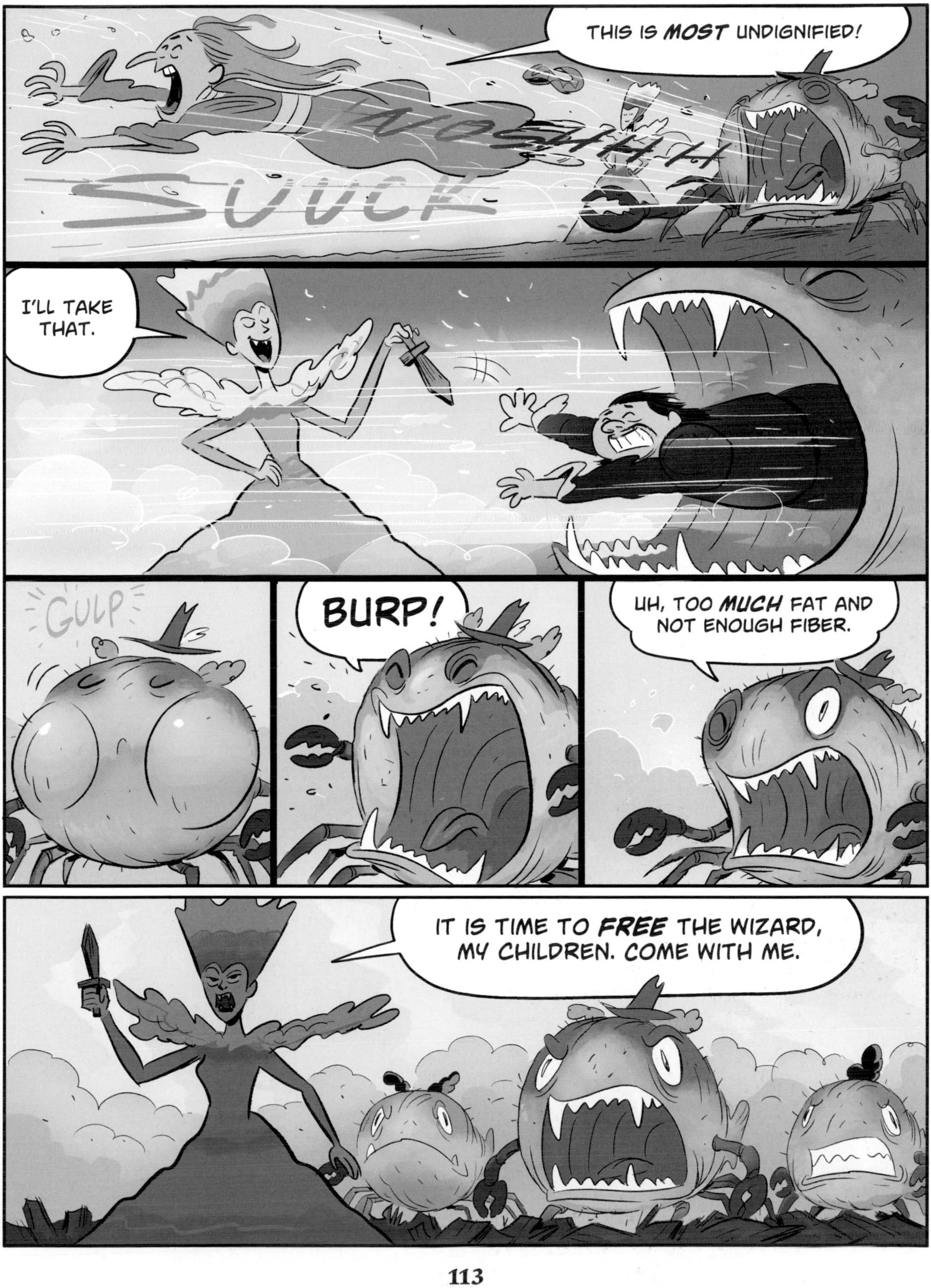
THIS IS MOST UNDIGNIFIED!
FWOOSHHHH
SUUCK
I'LL TAKE THAT.
GULP
BURP!
UH, TOO MUCH FAT AND NOT ENOUGH FIBER.
IT IS TIME TO FREE THE WIZARD, MY CHILDREN. COME WITH ME.

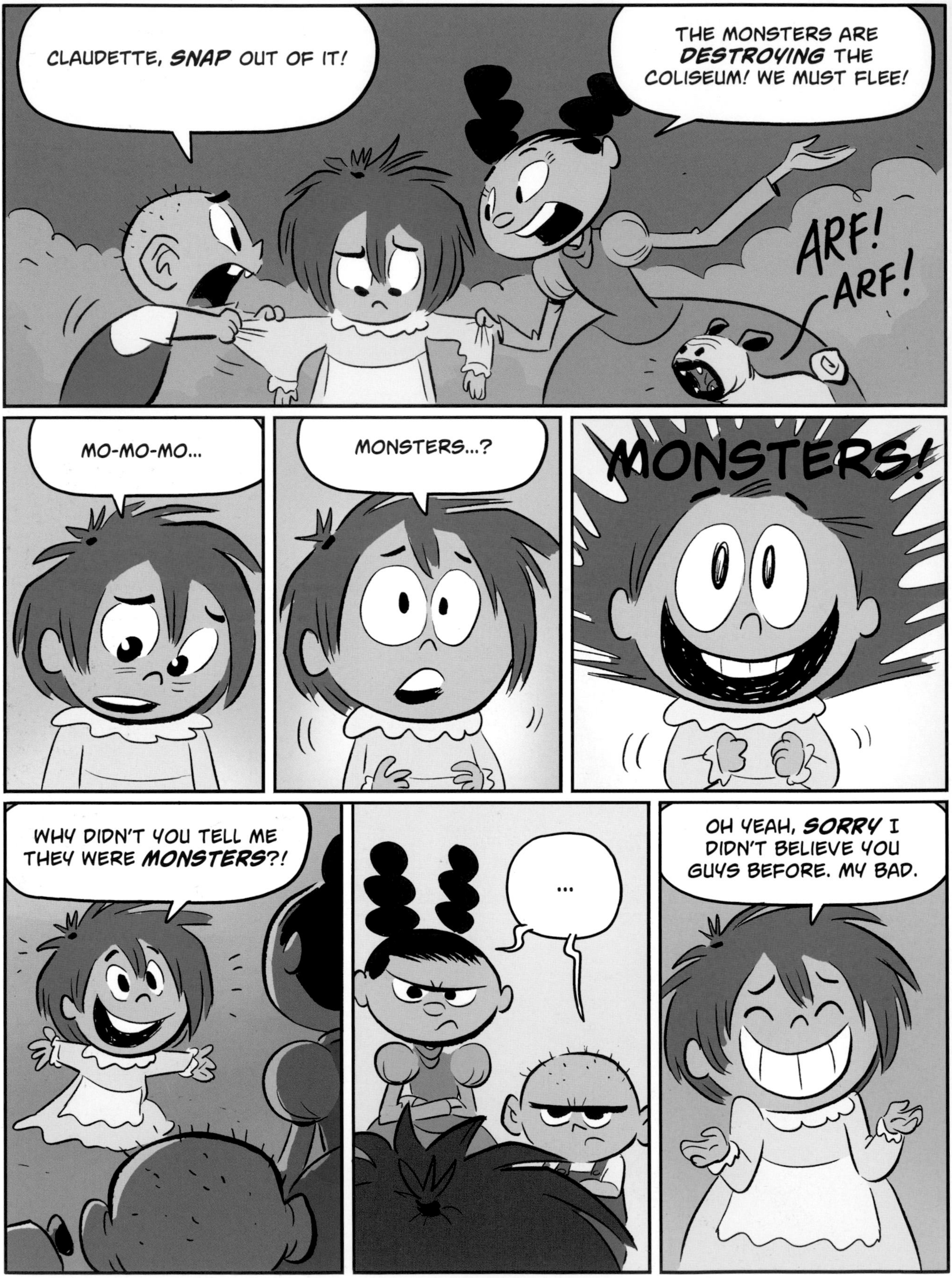

CLAUDETTE, SNAP OUT OF IT!
THE MONSTERS ARE DESTROYING THE COLISEUM! WE MUST FLEE!
ARF! ARF!
MO-MO-MO...
MONSTERS...?
MONSTERS!
WHY DIDN'T YOU TELL ME THEY WERE MONSTERS?!
...
OH YEAH, SORRY I DIDN'T BELIEVE YOU GUYS BEFORE. MY BAD.

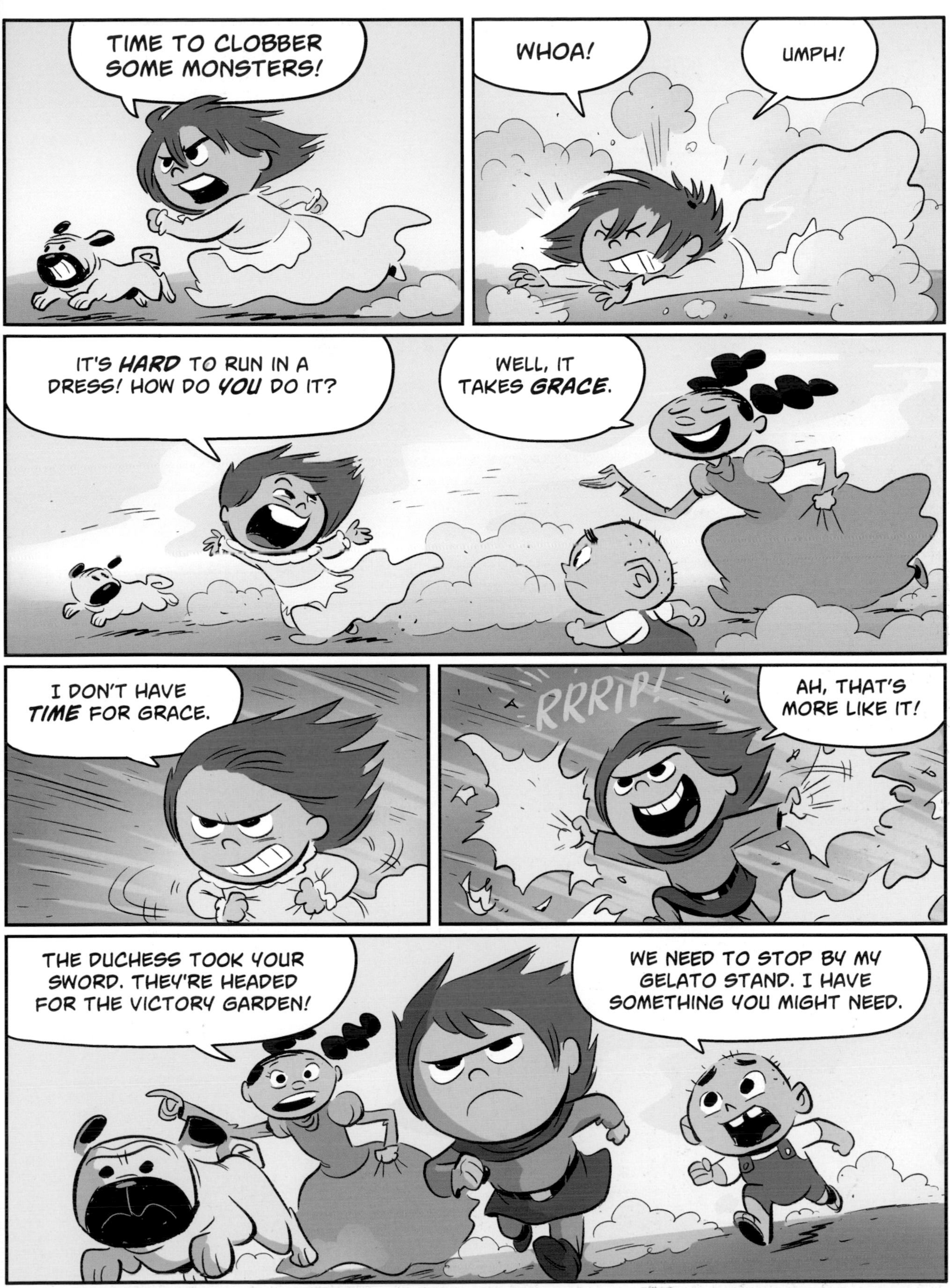
TIME TO CLOBBER SOME MONSTERS!
WHOA!
UMPH!
IT'S **HARD** TO RUN IN A DRESS! HOW DO **YOU** DO IT?
WELL, IT TAKES **GRACE**.
I DON'T HAVE **TIME** FOR GRACE.
RRRIP!
AH, THAT'S MORE LIKE IT!
THE DUCHESS TOOK YOUR SWORD. THEY'RE HEADED FOR THE VICTORY GARDEN!
WE NEED TO STOP BY MY GELATO STAND. I HAVE SOMETHING YOU MIGHT NEED.

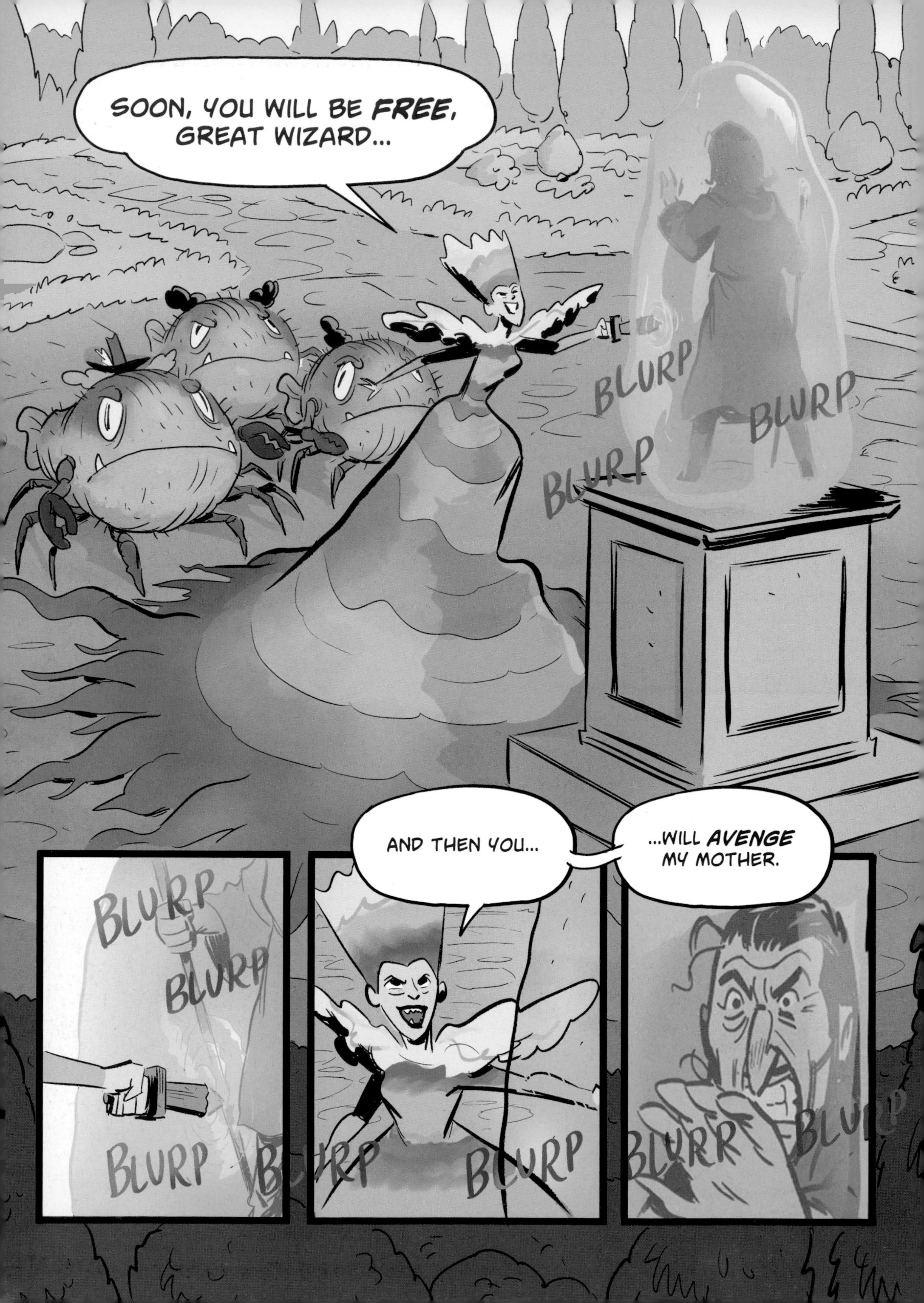
SOON, YOU WILL BE *FREE*, GREAT WIZARD...
BLURP
BLURP
BLURP
BLURP
BLURP
BLURP
AND THEN YOU...
BLURP
BLURP
...WILL *AVENGE* MY MOTHER.
BLURR

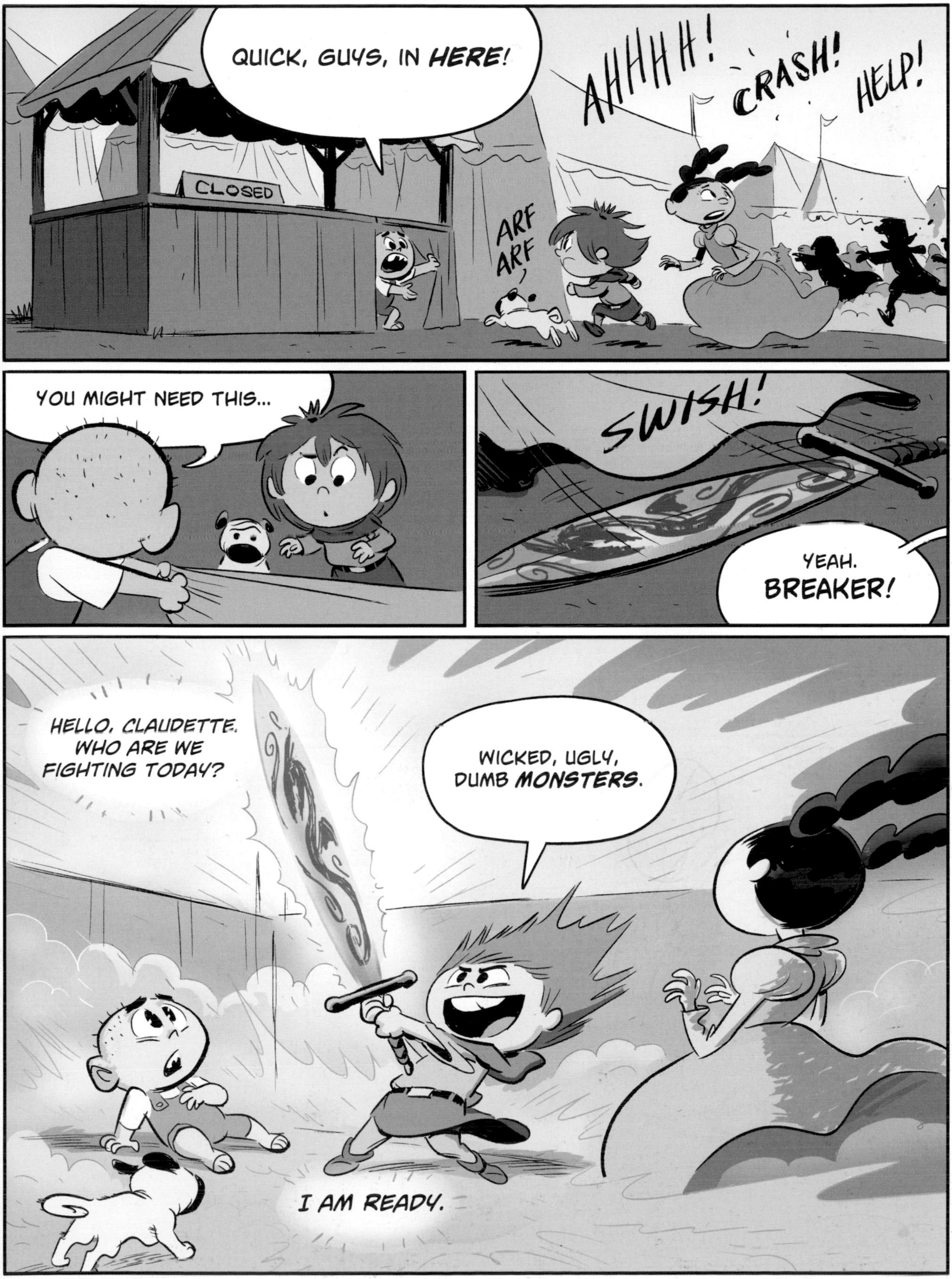
QUICK, GUYS, IN *HERE*!
AHHHH!
CRASH!
HELP!
ARF ARF
YOU MIGHT NEED THIS...
SWISH!
YEAH. **BREAKER!**
HELLO, CLAUDETTE. WHO ARE WE FIGHTING TODAY?
WICKED, UGLY, DUMB *MONSTERS*.
I AM READY.

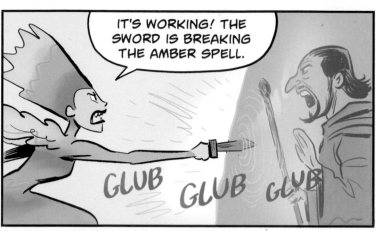

IT'S WORKING! THE SWORD IS BREAKING THE AMBER SPELL.

GLUB GLUB GLUB

STOP RIGHT *NOW*!

HUH?

THAT'S *MY* SWORD YOU GOT THERE.

AND I WANT IT BACK.

I MIGHT HAVE LOST THE WARRIOR GAMES...

BOING!

BUT I'M STILL THE *BEST* WARRIOR IN ALL THE KINGDOMS, OR ELSE...

BOUNCE

...MY NAME'S NOT *CLAUDETTE*!

SCHWING!!!

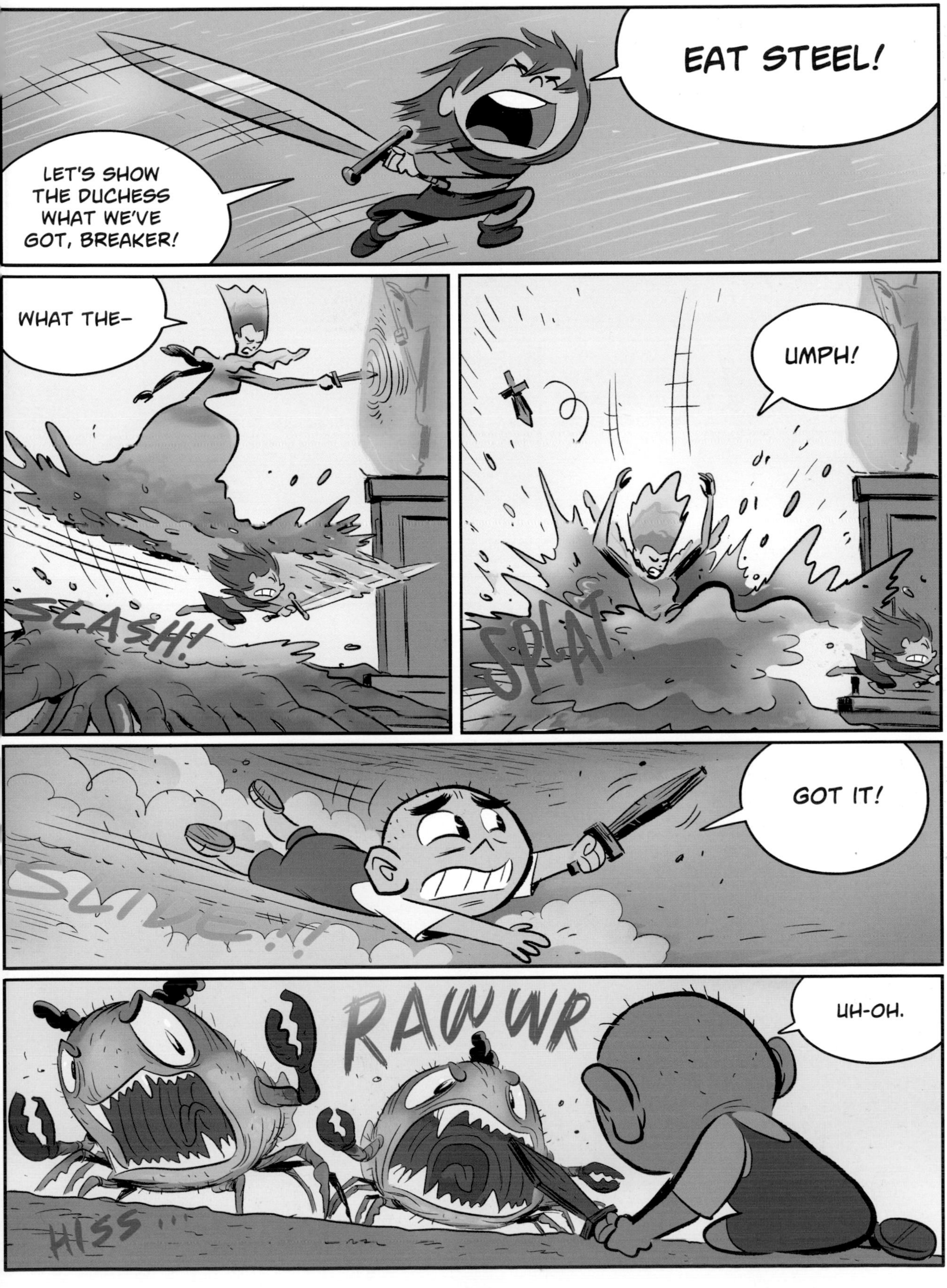

EAT STEEL!
LET'S SHOW THE DUCHESS WHAT WE'VE GOT, BREAKER!
WHAT THE-
SLASH!
UMPH!
SPLAT
GOT IT!
SLIDE!!
RAWWR
UH-OH.
HISS!!

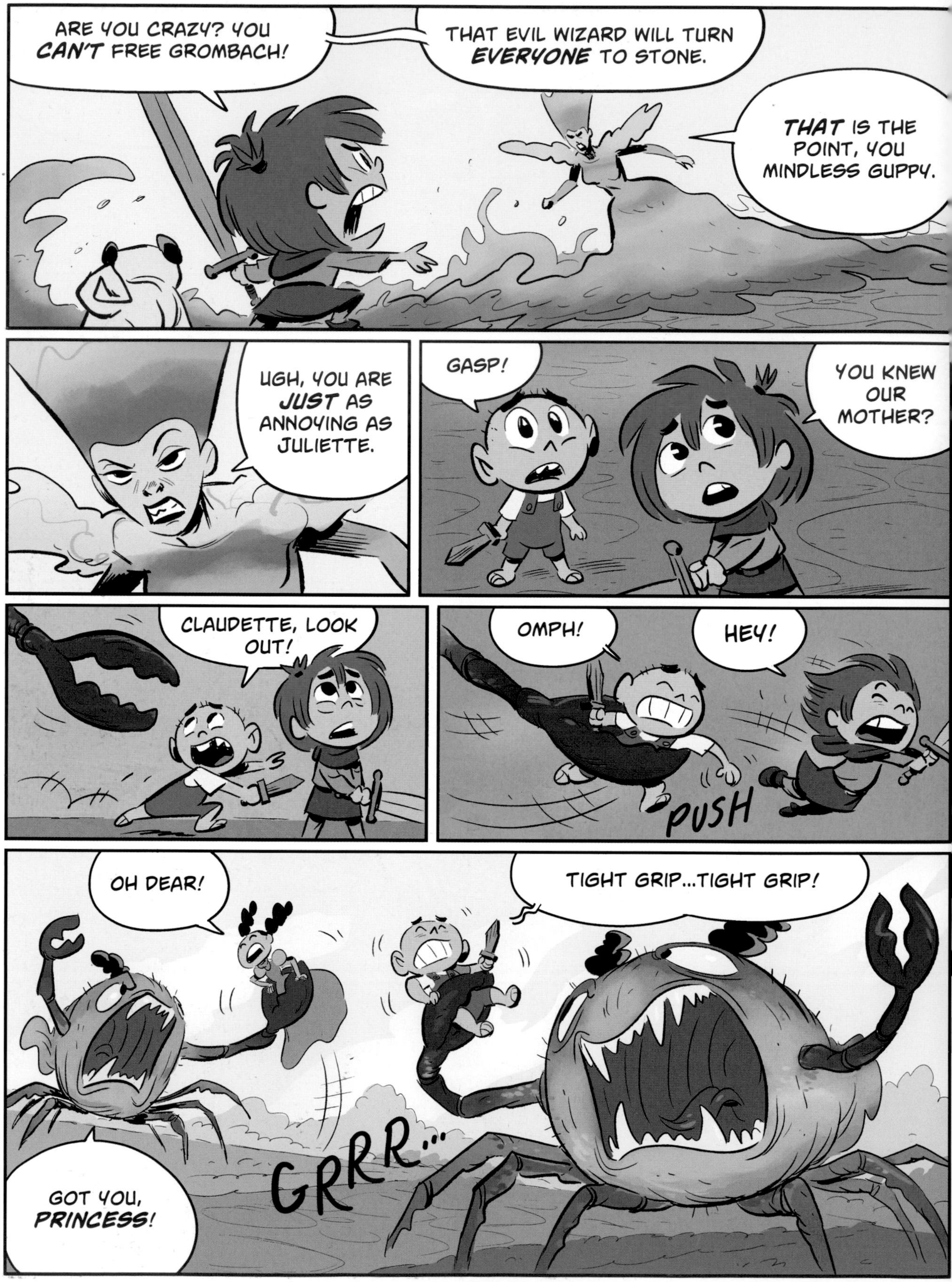
ARE YOU CRAZY? YOU CAN'T FREE GROMBACH!
THAT EVIL WIZARD WILL TURN EVERYONE TO STONE.
THAT IS THE POINT, YOU MINDLESS GUPPY.
UGH, YOU ARE JUST AS ANNOYING AS JULIETTE.
GASP!
YOU KNEW OUR MOTHER?
CLAUDETTE, LOOK OUT!
OMPH!
HEY!
PUSH
OH DEAR!
TIGHT GRIP...TIGHT GRIP!
GRRR...
GOT YOU, PRINCESS!

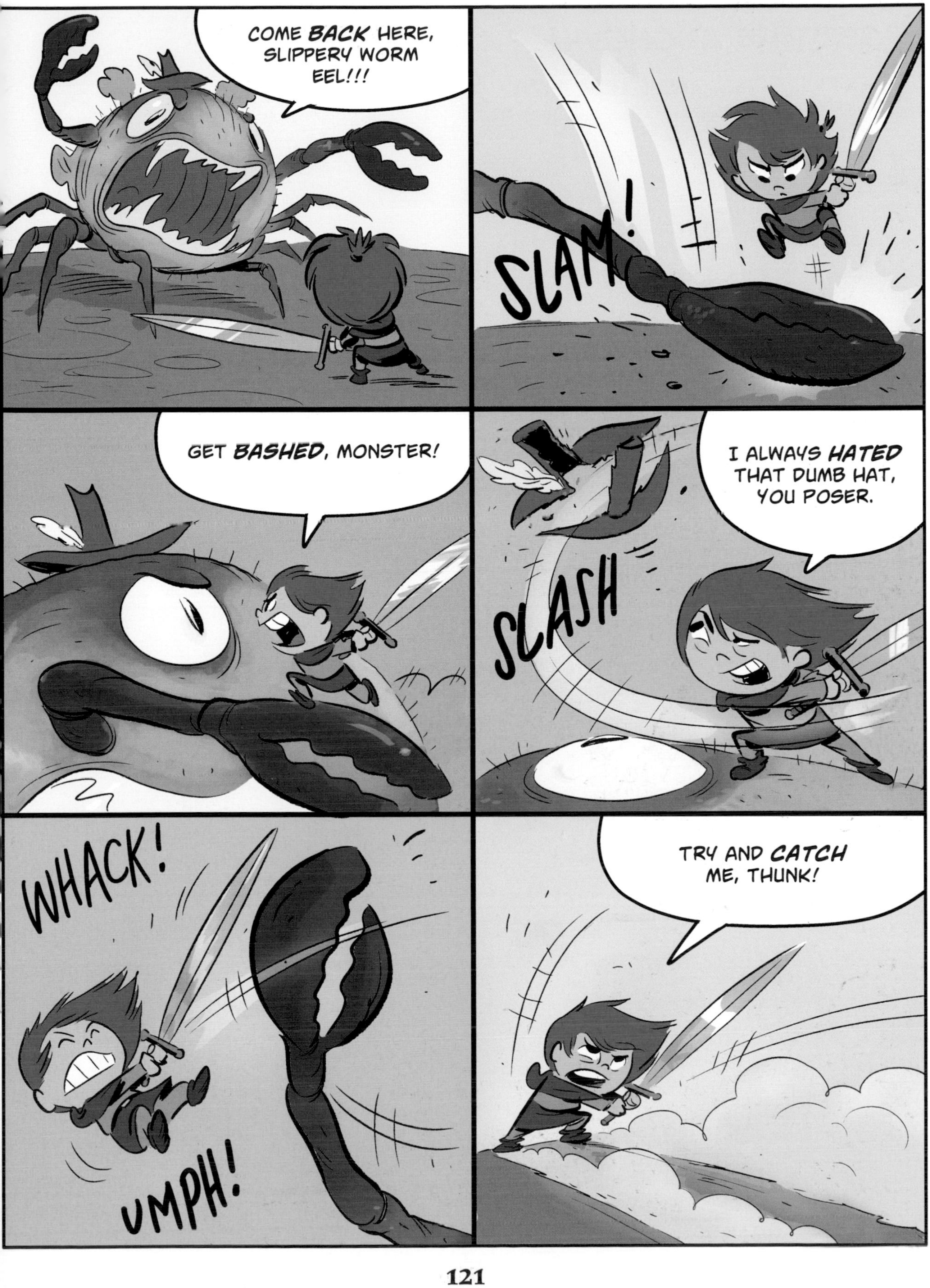
COME BACK HERE, SLIPPERY WORM EEL!!!
SLAM!
GET BASHED, MONSTER!
I ALWAYS HATED THAT DUMB HAT, YOU POSER.
SLASH
WHACK!
UMPH!
TRY AND CATCH ME, THUNK!

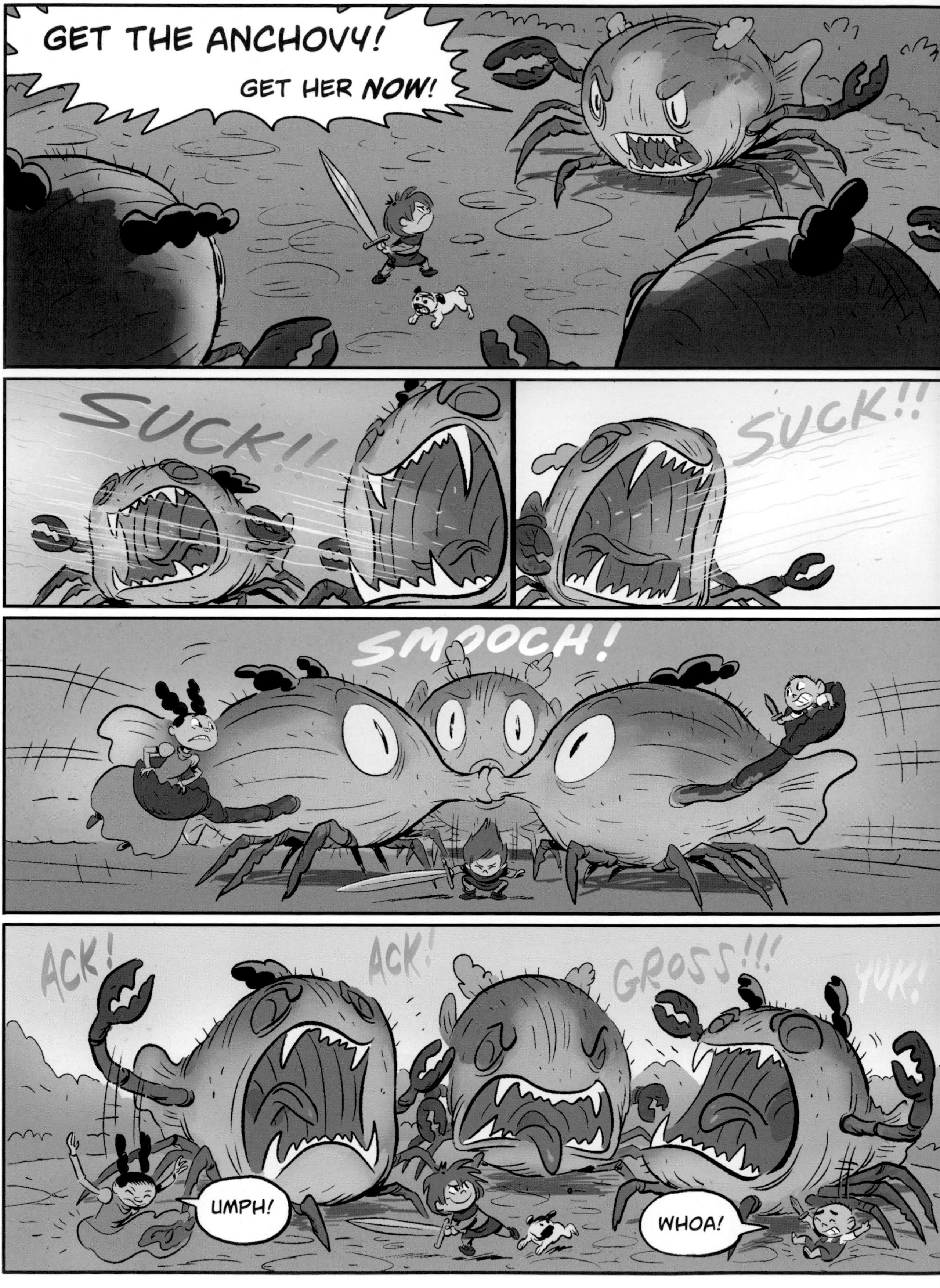
GET THE ANCHOVY!
GET HER NOW!
SUCK!!
SUCK!!
SMOOCH!
ACK!
ACK!
GROSS!!!
YUK!
UMPH!
WHOA!

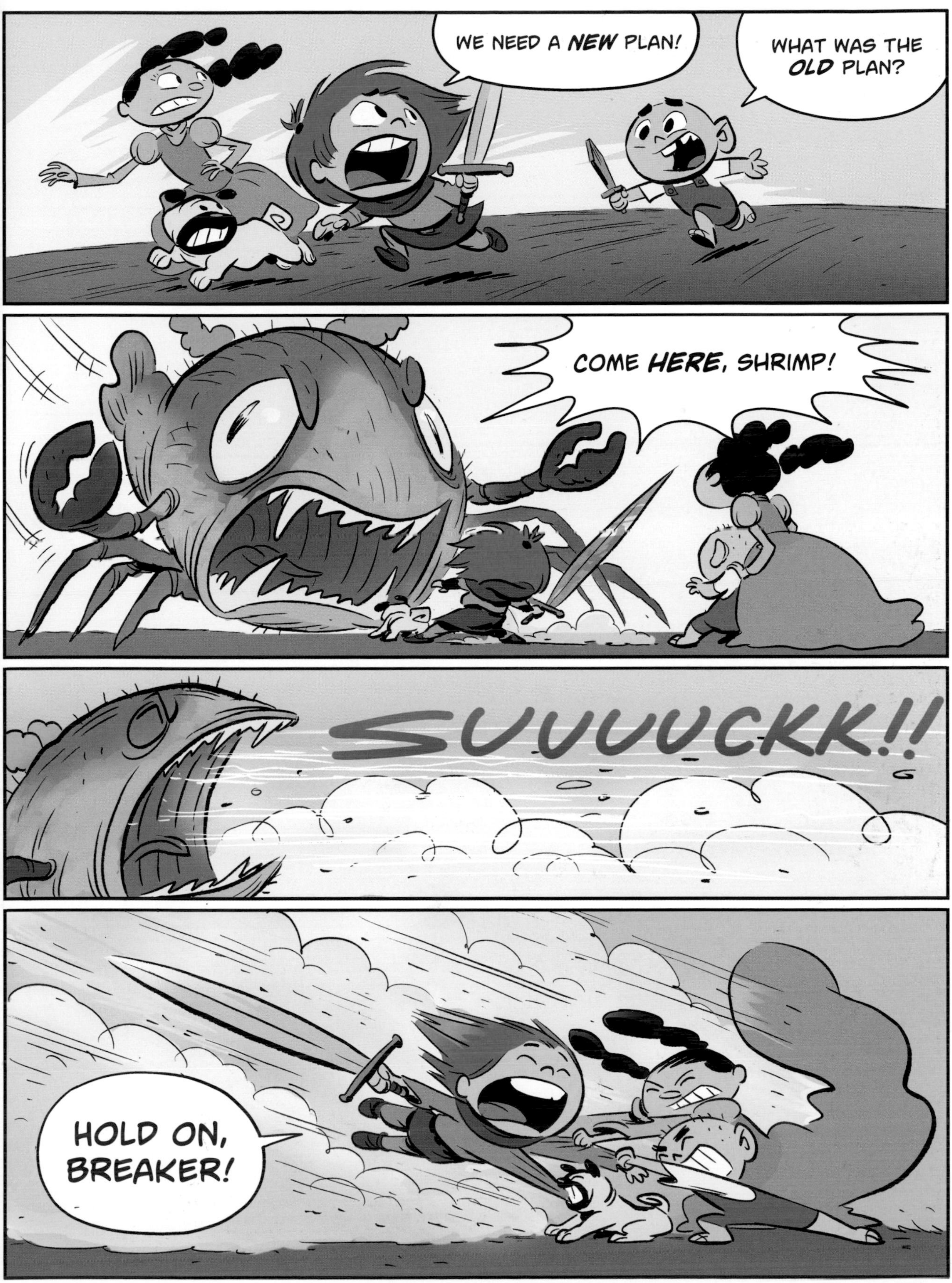
WE NEED A NEW PLAN!
WHAT WAS THE OLD PLAN?
COME HERE, SHRIMP!
SUUUUCKK!!
HOLD ON, BREAKER!

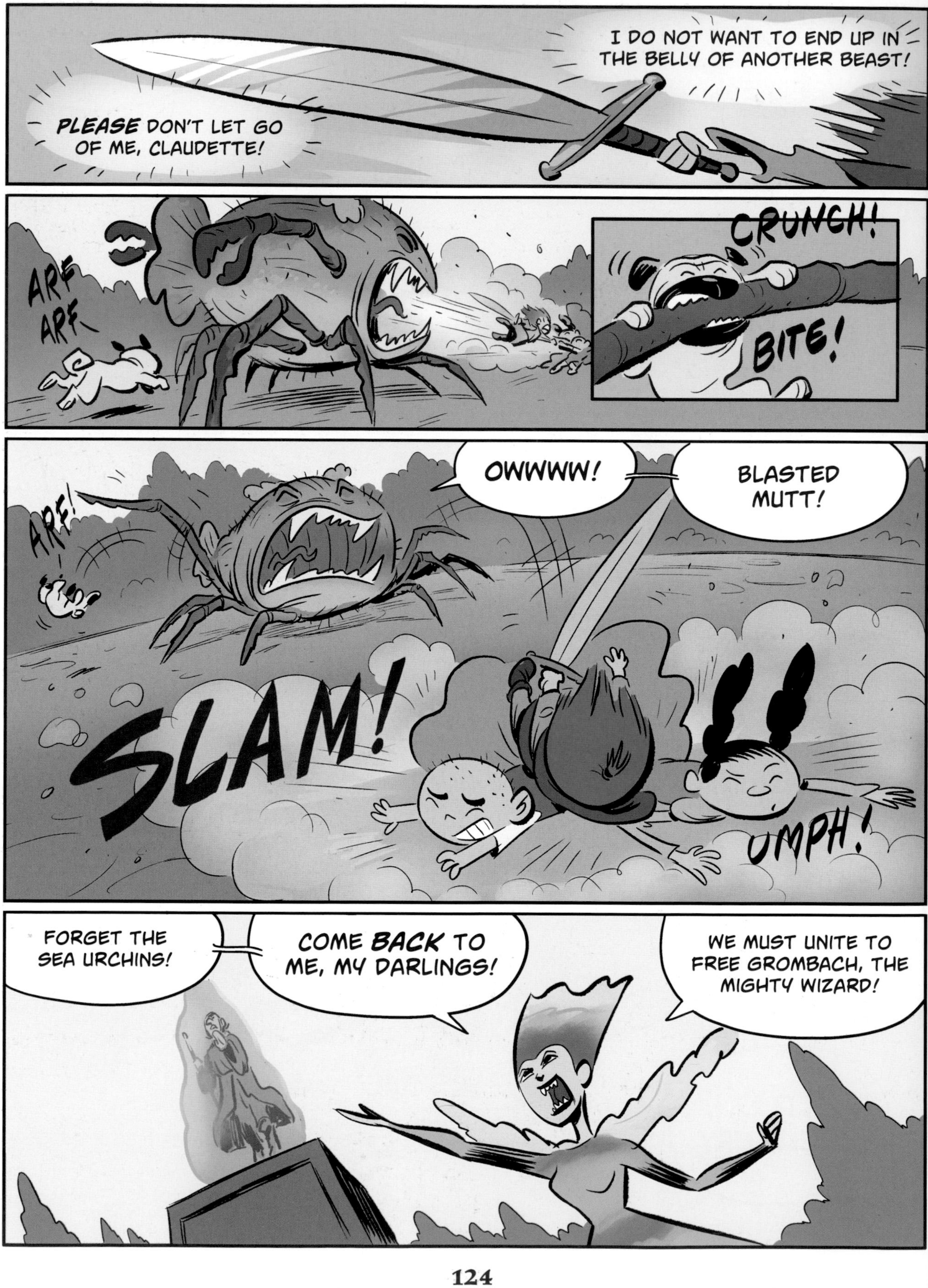
I DO NOT WANT TO END UP IN THE BELLY OF ANOTHER BEAST!
PLEASE DON'T LET GO OF ME, CLAUDETTE!
ARF ARF
CRUNCH!
BITE!
ARF!
OWWWW!
BLASTED MUTT!
SLAM!
UMPH!
FORGET THE SEA URCHINS!
COME BACK TO ME, MY DARLINGS!
WE MUST UNITE TO FREE GROMBACH, THE MIGHTY WIZARD!

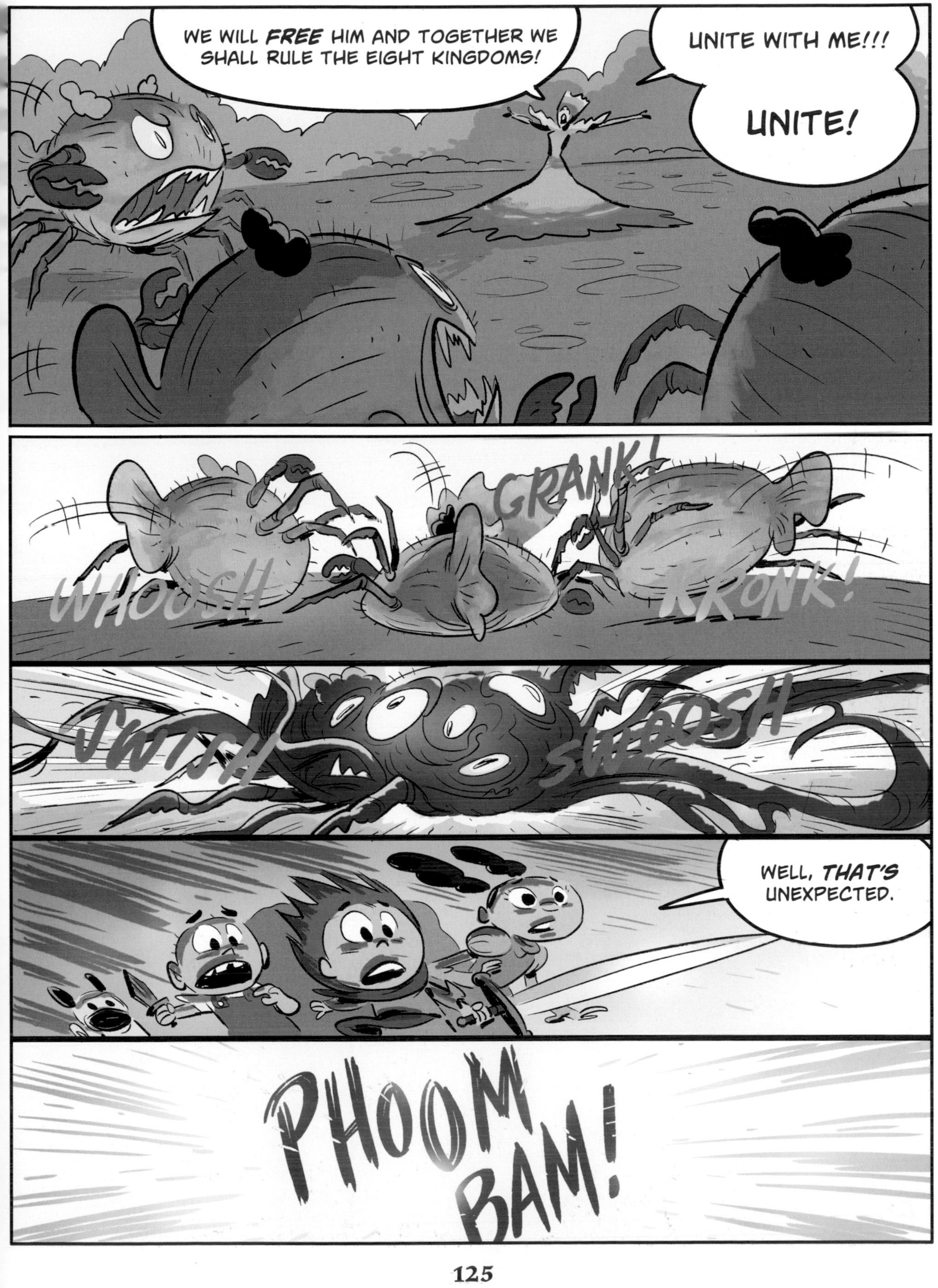

WE WILL FREE HIM AND TOGETHER WE SHALL RULE THE EIGHT KINGDOMS!
UNITE WITH ME!!!
UNITE!
GRANK!
WHOOSH
KRONK!
SWISH
SWOOSH
WELL, THAT'S UNEXPECTED.
PHOOM
BAM!

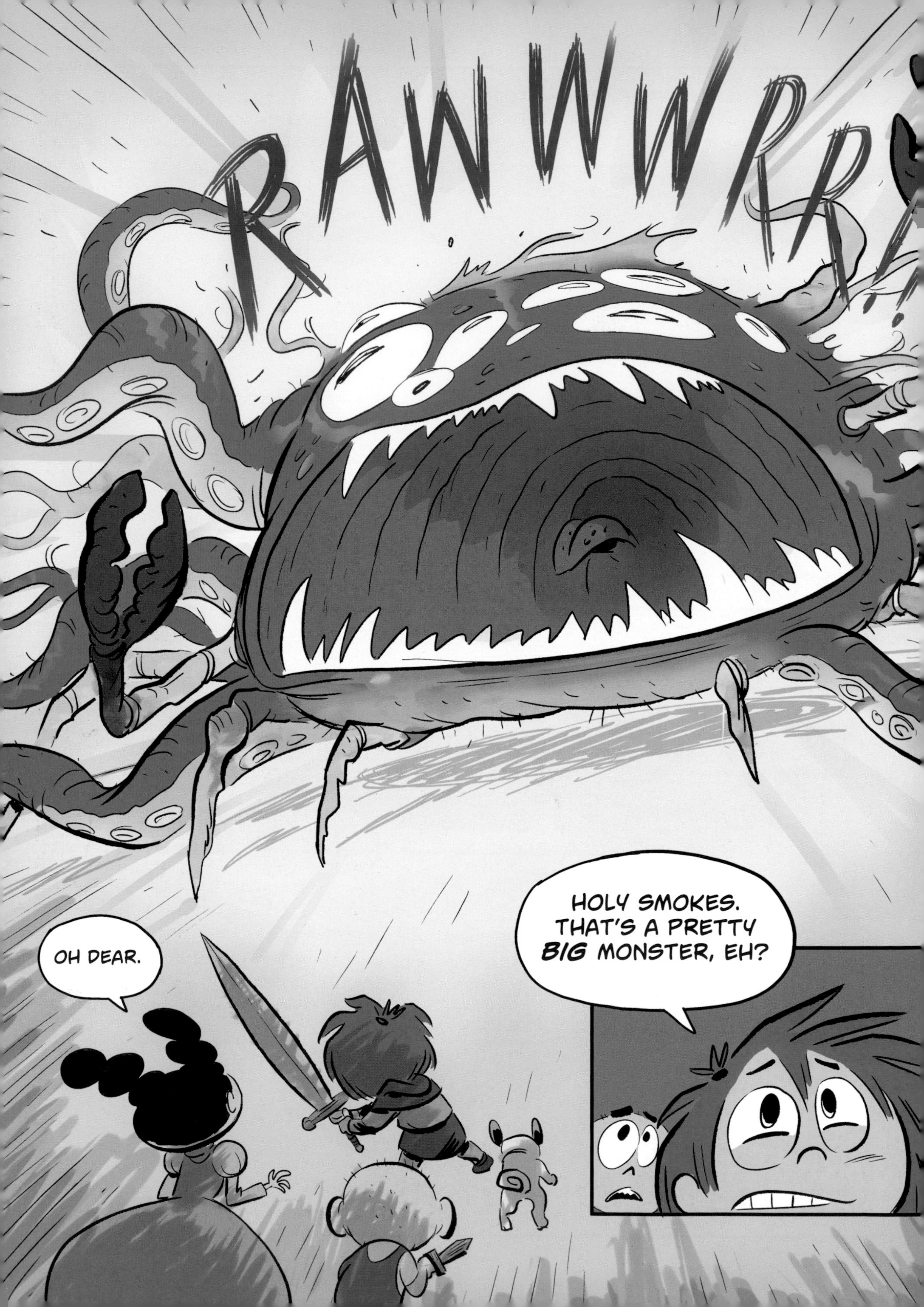
RAWWRR
OH DEAR.
HOLY SMOKES. THAT'S A PRETTY *BIG* MONSTER, EH?

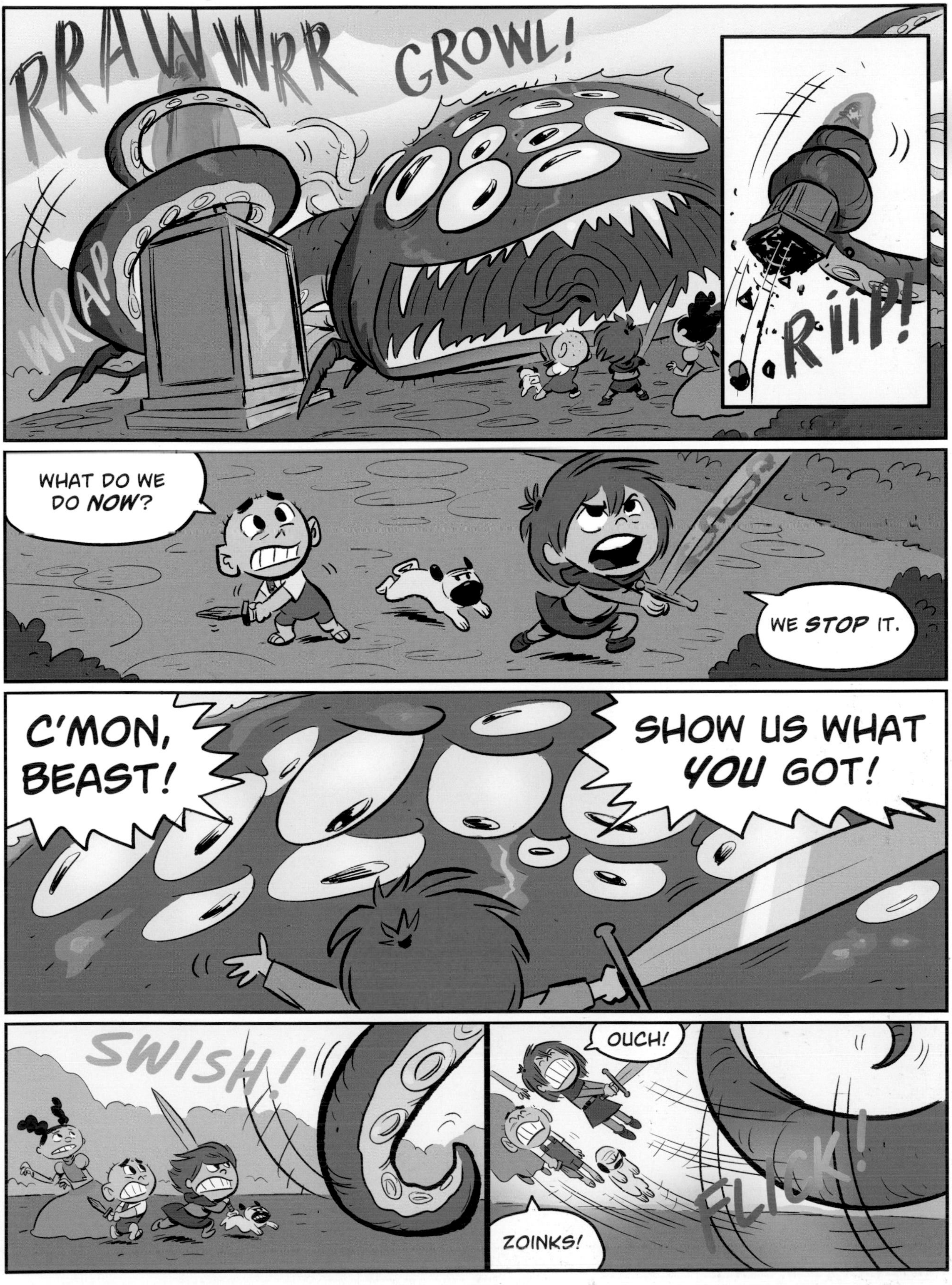
RRAWWRR
GROWL!
WRAP
RIIP!
WHAT DO WE DO NOW?
WE STOP IT.
C'MON, BEAST!
SHOW US WHAT YOU GOT!
SWISH!
OUCH!
ZOINKS!
FLICK!

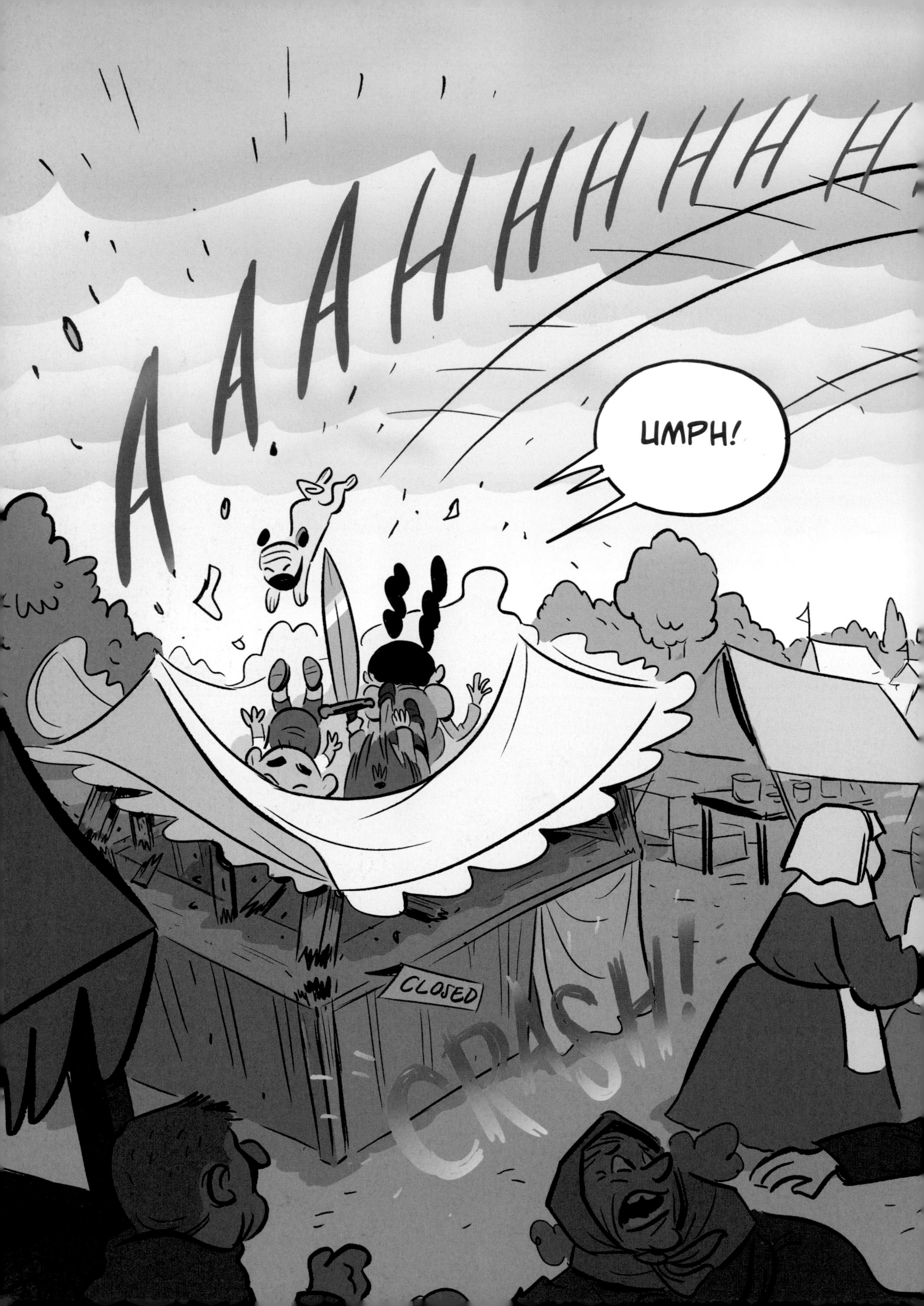
AAAHHHHHHHHH
UMPH!
CLOSED
CRASH!

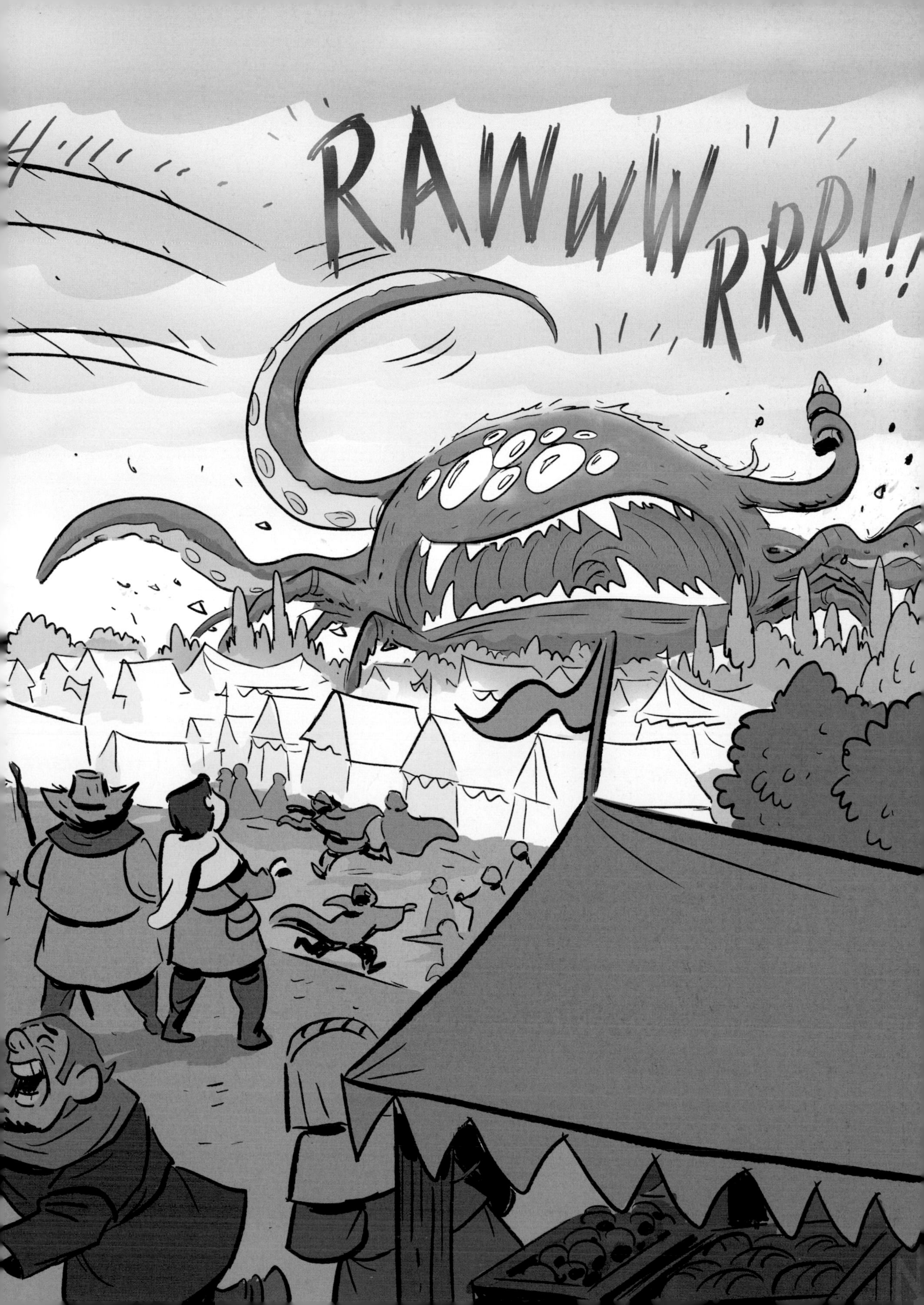
RAWWWRRR!!!

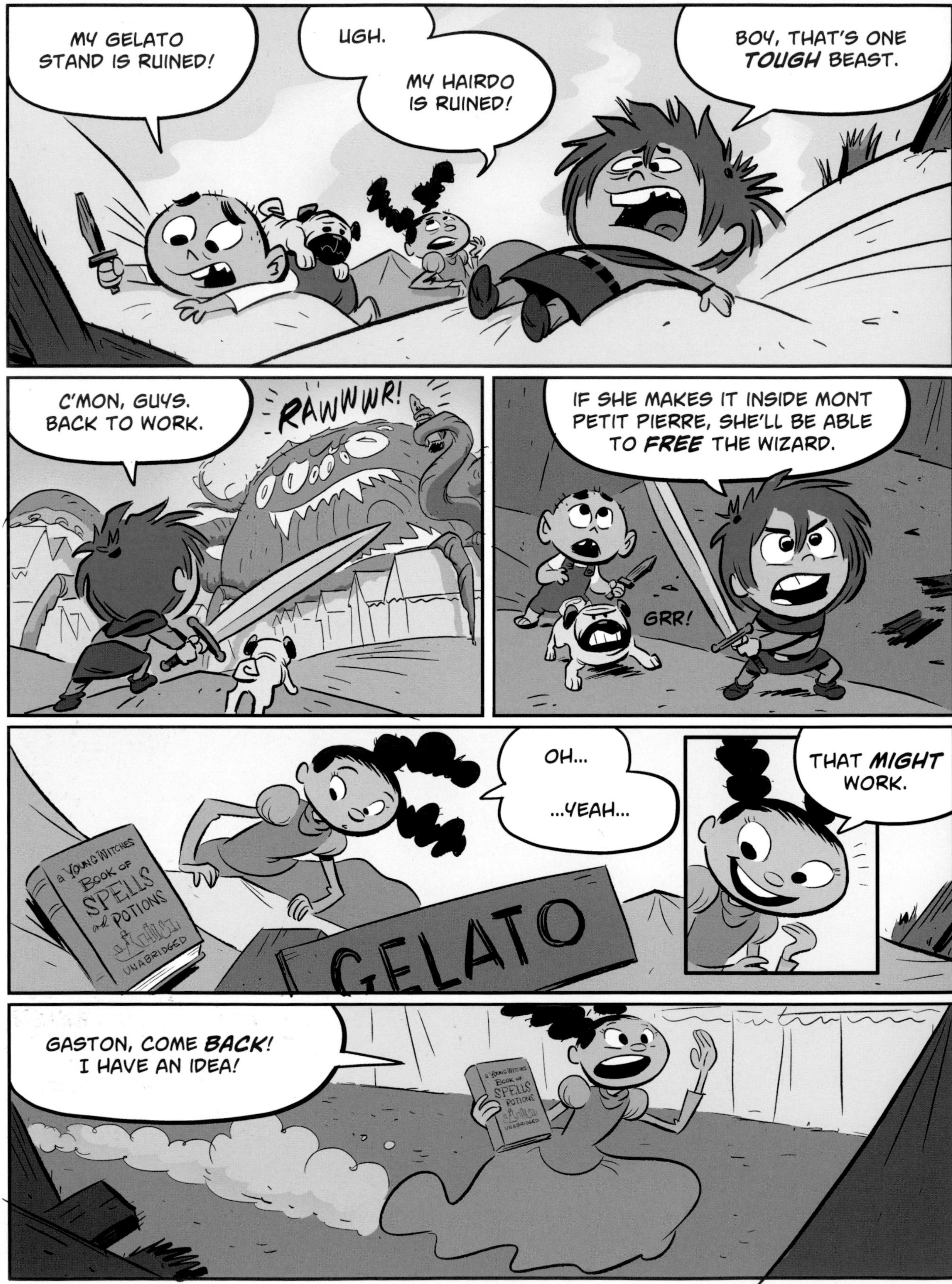
MY GELATO STAND IS RUINED!
UGH.
MY HAIRDO IS RUINED!
BOY, THAT'S ONE TOUGH BEAST.
C'MON, GUYS. BACK TO WORK.
RAWWWR!
IF SHE MAKES IT INSIDE MONT PETIT PIERRE, SHE'LL BE ABLE TO FREE THE WIZARD.
GRR!
a YOUNG WITCHES BOOK of SPELLS and POTIONS UNABRIDGED
GELATO
OH...
...YEAH...
THAT MIGHT WORK.
GASTON, COME BACK! I HAVE AN IDEA!

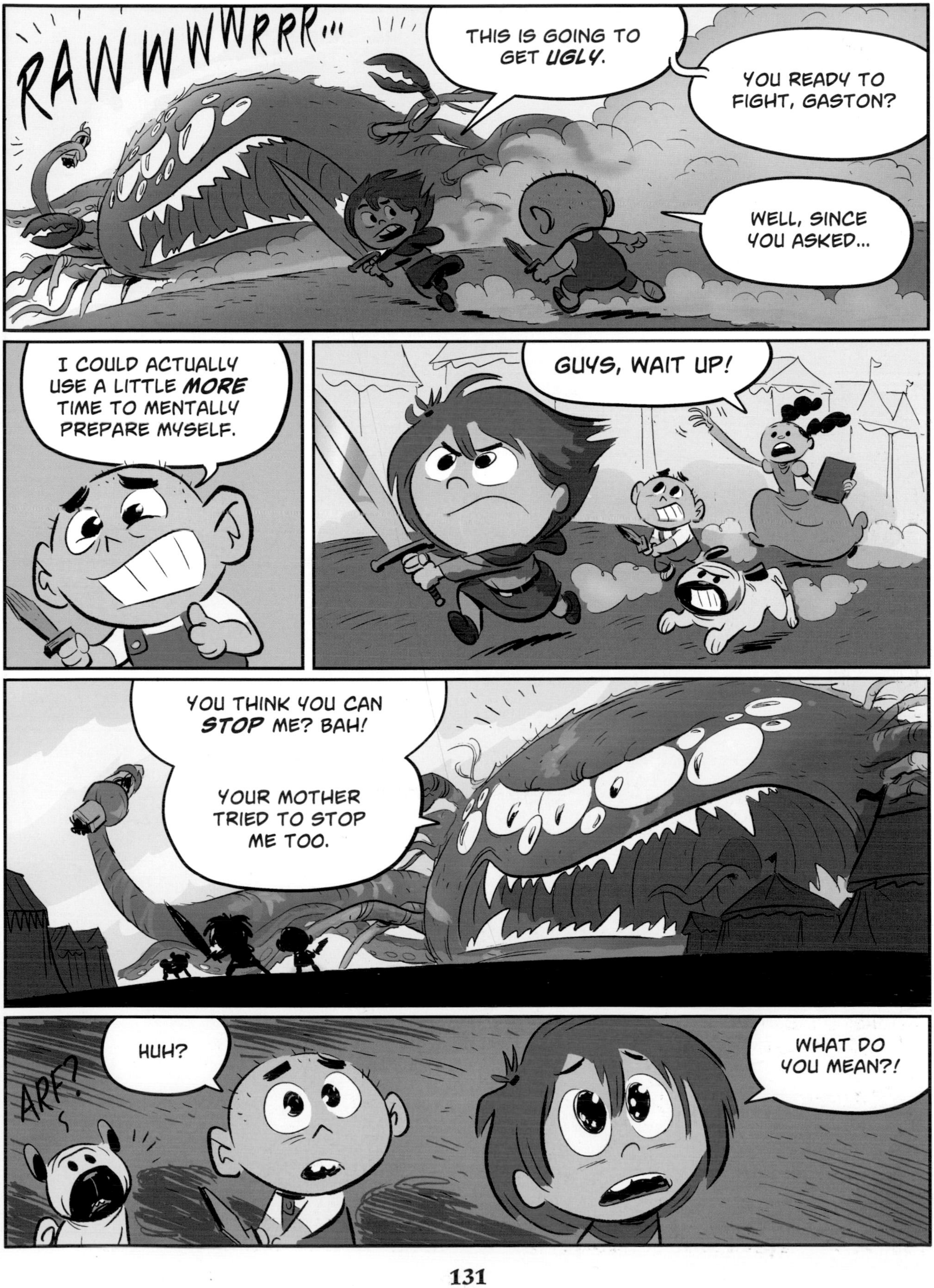
RAWWWWRRR!!!
THIS IS GOING TO GET UGLY.
YOU READY TO FIGHT, GASTON?
WELL, SINCE YOU ASKED...
I COULD ACTUALLY USE A LITTLE MORE TIME TO MENTALLY PREPARE MYSELF.
GUYS, WAIT UP!
YOU THINK YOU CAN STOP ME? BAH!
YOUR MOTHER TRIED TO STOP ME TOO.
ARF?
HUH?
WHAT DO YOU MEAN?!

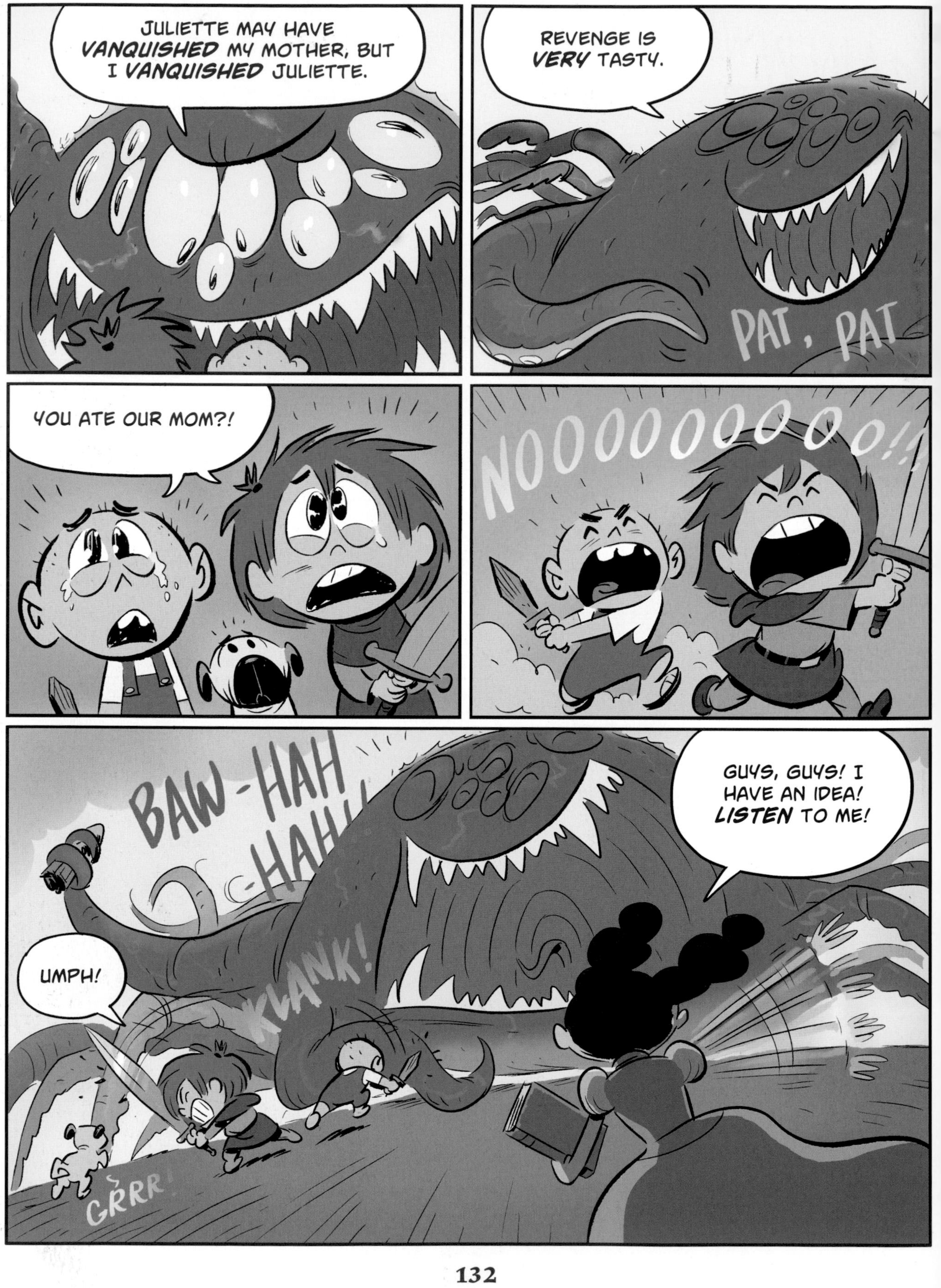
JULIETTE MAY HAVE VANQUISHED MY MOTHER, BUT I VANQUISHED JULIETTE.
REVENGE IS VERY TASTY.
PAT, PAT
YOU ATE OUR MOM?!
NOOOOOOOOO!!!
BAW-HAH-HAH!
GUYS, GUYS! I HAVE AN IDEA! LISTEN TO ME!
UMPH!
KLANK!
GRRR!

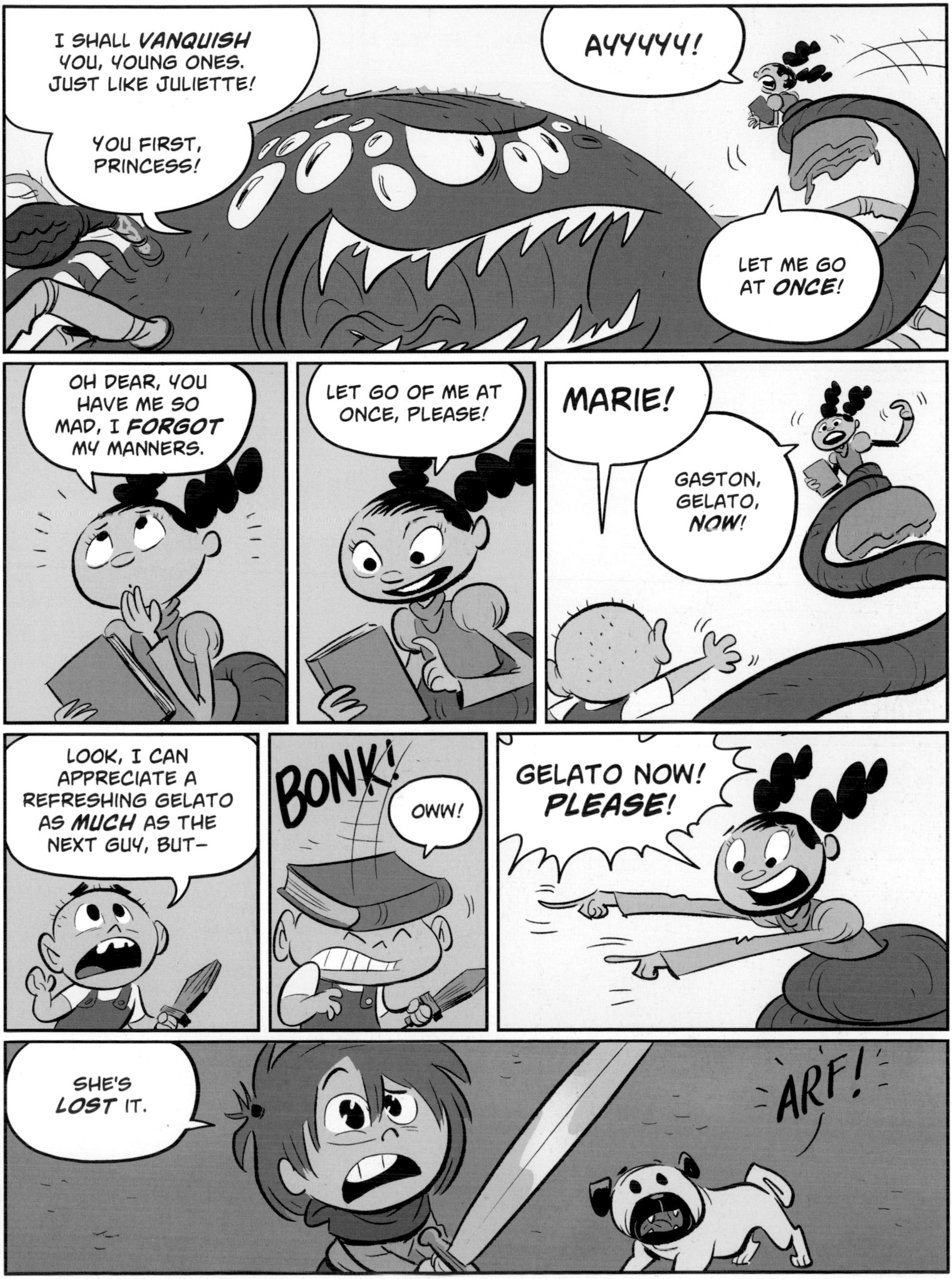
I SHALL VANQUISH YOU, YOUNG ONES. JUST LIKE JULIETTE!
YOU FIRST, PRINCESS!
AYYYYY!
LET ME GO AT ONCE!
OH DEAR, YOU HAVE ME SO MAD, I FORGOT MY MANNERS.
LET GO OF ME AT ONCE, PLEASE!
MARIE!
GASTON, GELATO, NOW!
LOOK, I CAN APPRECIATE A REFRESHING GELATO AS MUCH AS THE NEXT GUY, BUT–
BONK!
OWW!
GELATO NOW! PLEASE!
SHE'S LOST IT.
ARF!

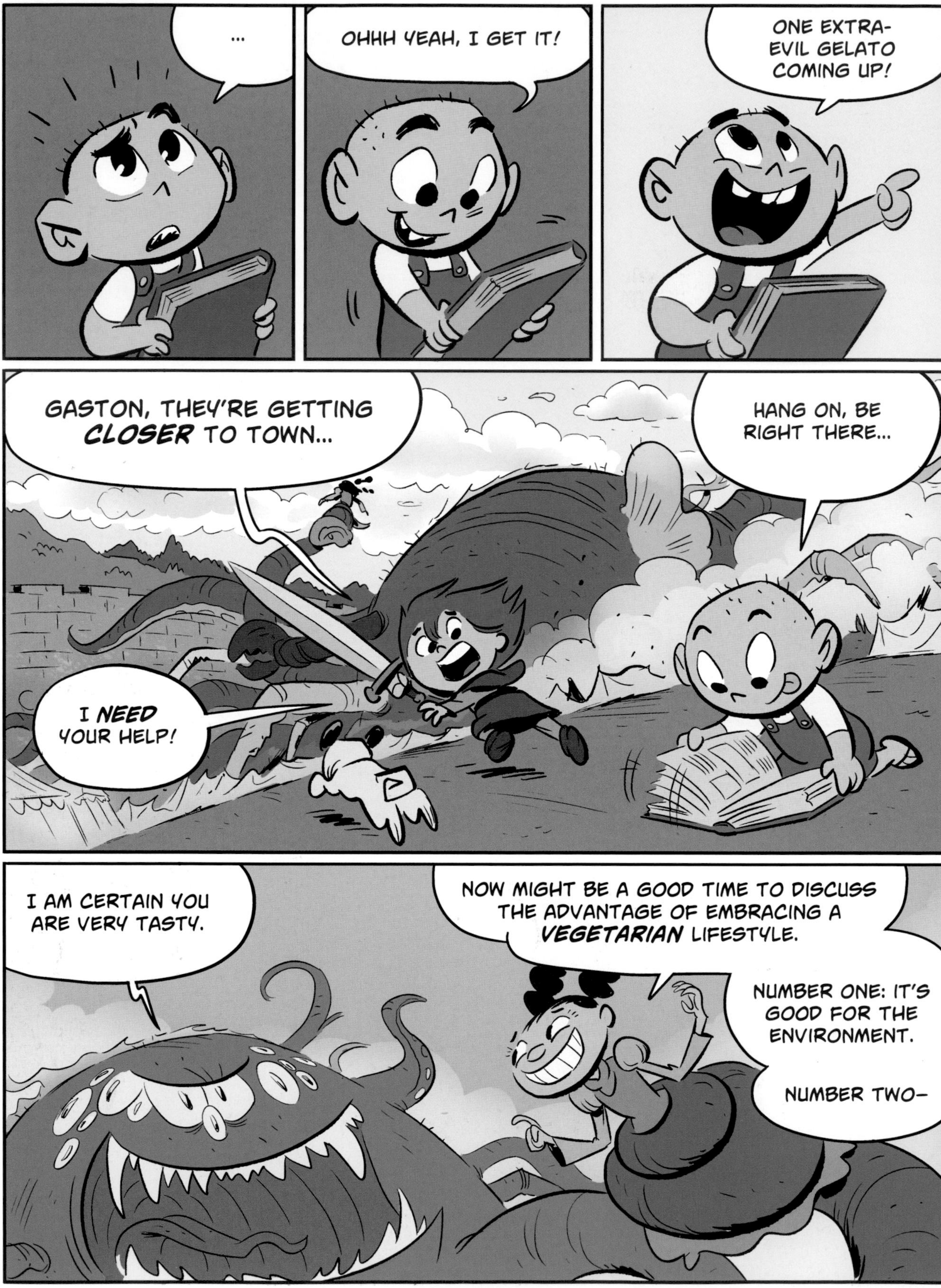
...
OHHH YEAH, I GET IT!
ONE EXTRA-EVIL GELATO COMING UP!
GASTON, THEY'RE GETTING CLOSER TO TOWN...
I NEED YOUR HELP!
HANG ON, BE RIGHT THERE...
I AM CERTAIN YOU ARE VERY TASTY.
NOW MIGHT BE A GOOD TIME TO DISCUSS THE ADVANTAGE OF EMBRACING A VEGETARIAN LIFESTYLE.
NUMBER ONE: IT'S GOOD FOR THE ENVIRONMENT.
NUMBER TWO-

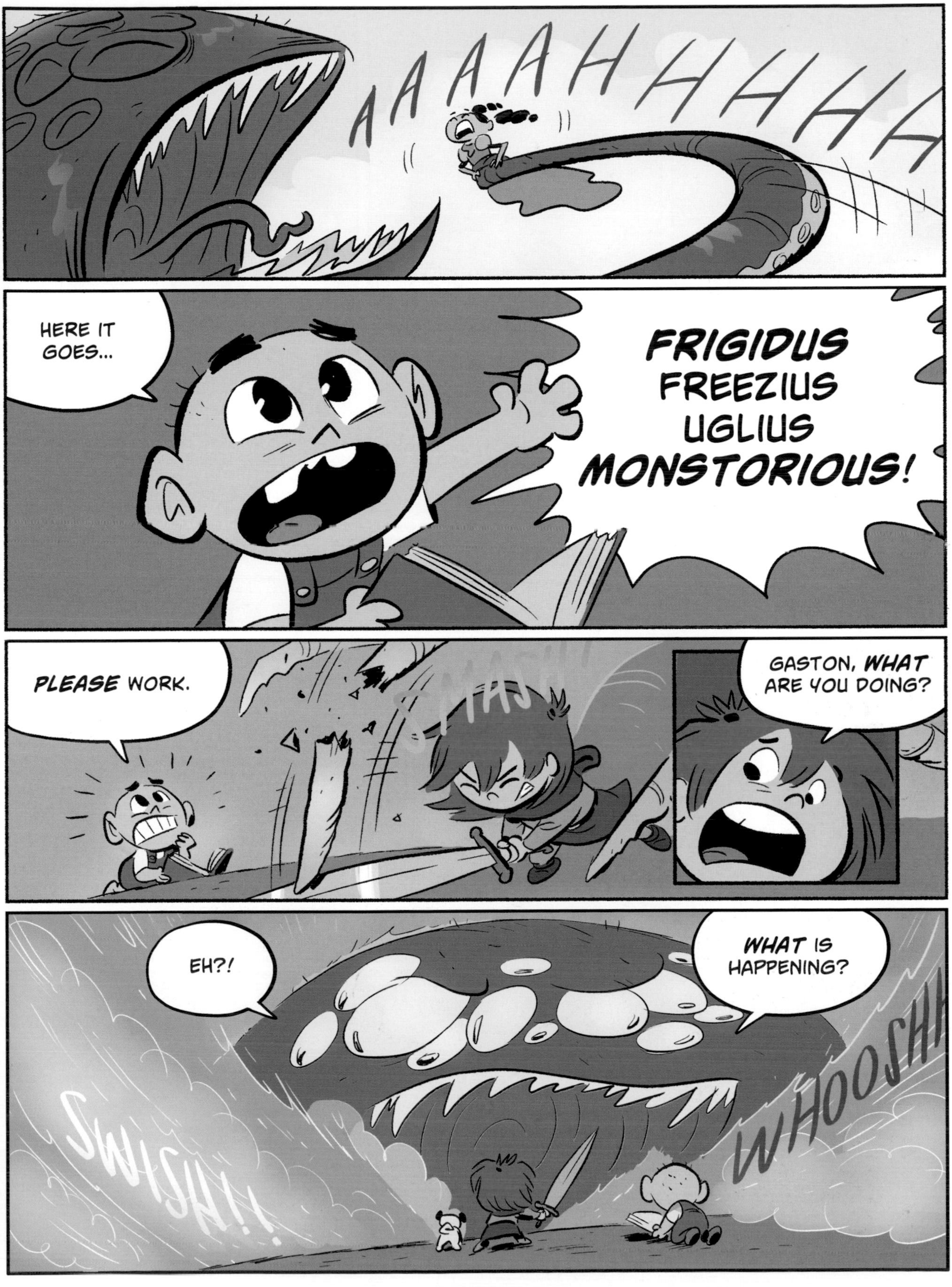
AAAAAHHHHHH
HERE IT GOES...
FRIGIDUS FREEZIUS UGLIUS MONSTORIOUS!
PLEASE WORK.
SMASH!
GASTON, WHAT ARE YOU DOING?
EH?!
WHAT IS HAPPENING?
SWISH!!
WHOOSH

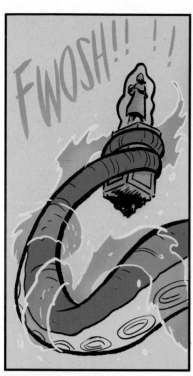

FWOSH!! !!

CREAK

CRACK!

NO, NO, NO, NO! THIS **CAN'T** BE HAPPENING. TURNING TO ICE...

SMASH!

ARGH!

CRACK!

EH?

WHAT THE—?

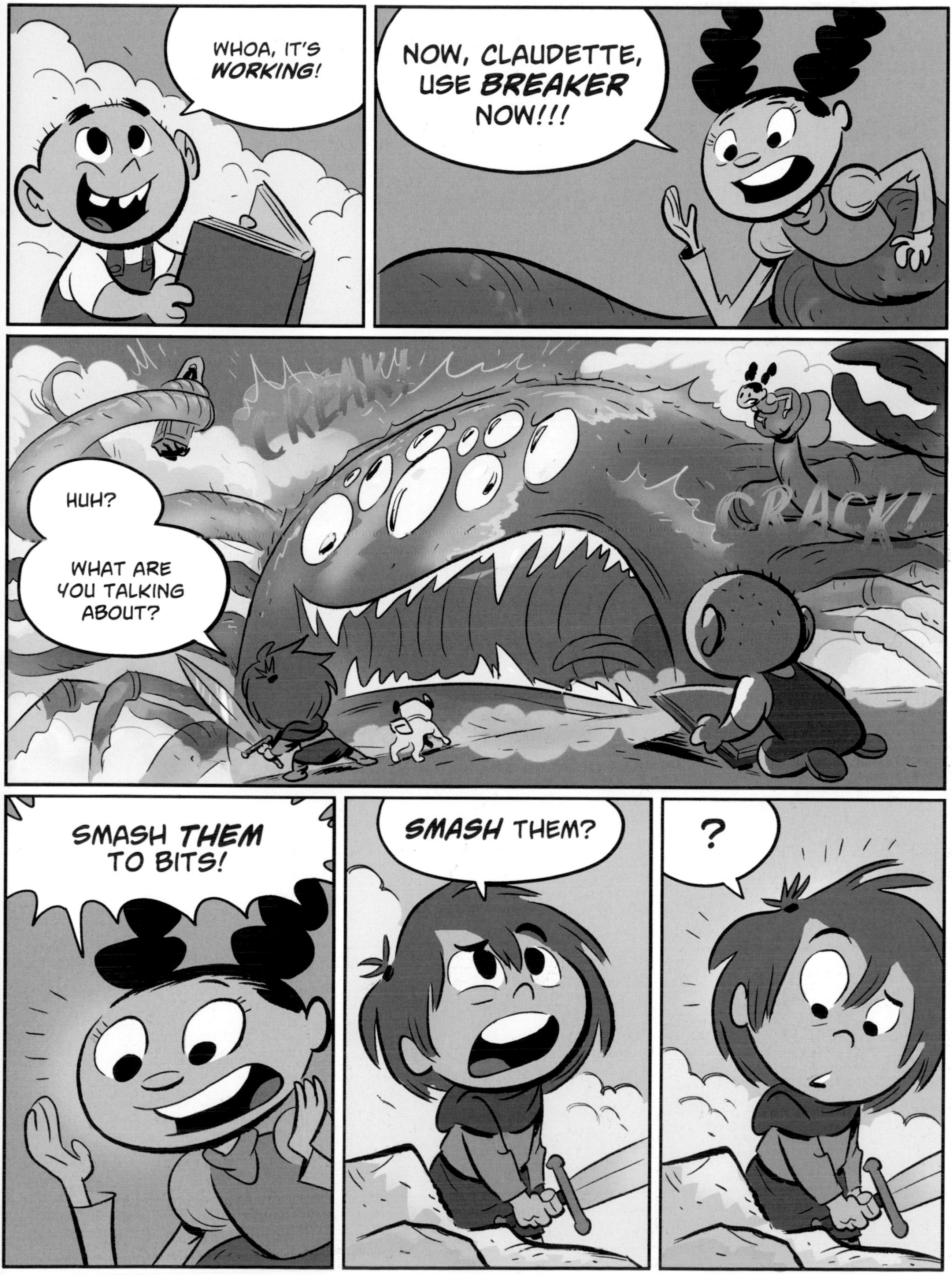
WHOA, IT'S *WORKING*!
NOW, CLAUDETTE, USE **BREAKER** NOW!!!
CREAK!
CRACK!
HUH?
WHAT ARE YOU TALKING ABOUT?
SMASH **THEM** TO BITS!
SMASH THEM?
?

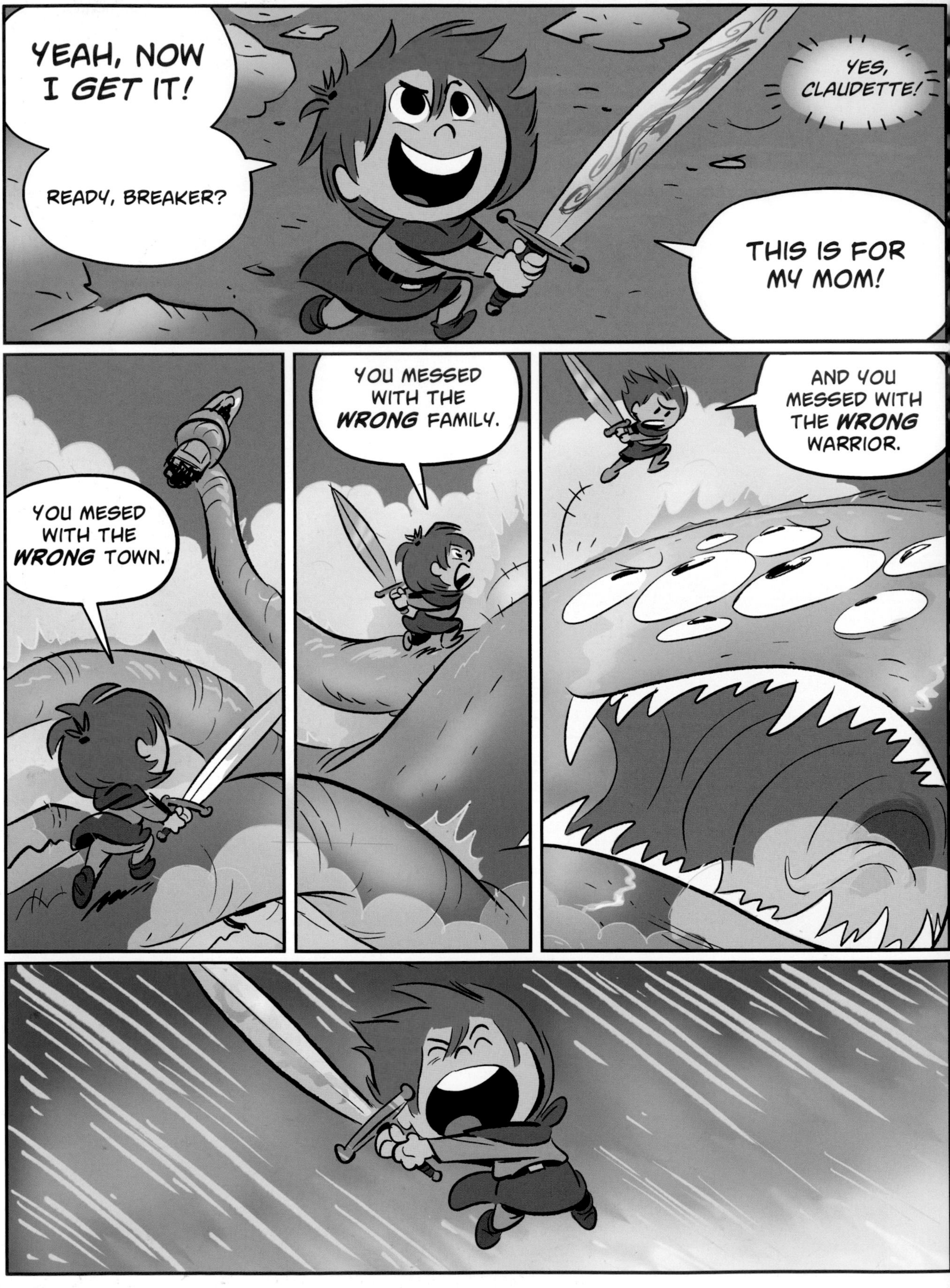

YEAH, NOW I GET IT!
READY, BREAKER?
YES, CLAUDETTE!
THIS IS FOR MY MOM!
YOU MESED WITH THE WRONG TOWN.
YOU MESSED WITH THE WRONG FAMILY.
AND YOU MESSED WITH THE WRONG WARRIOR.

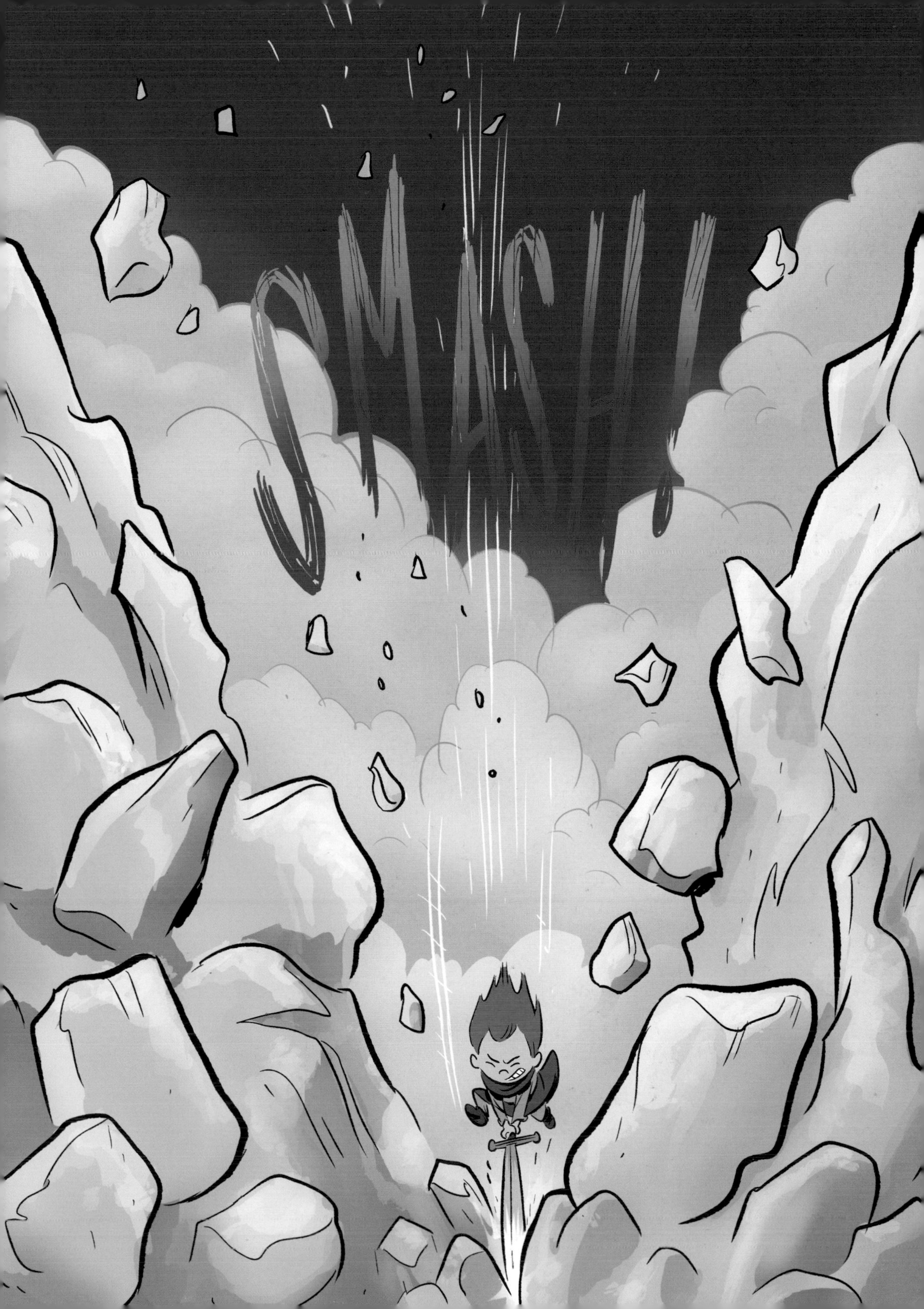
SMASH!

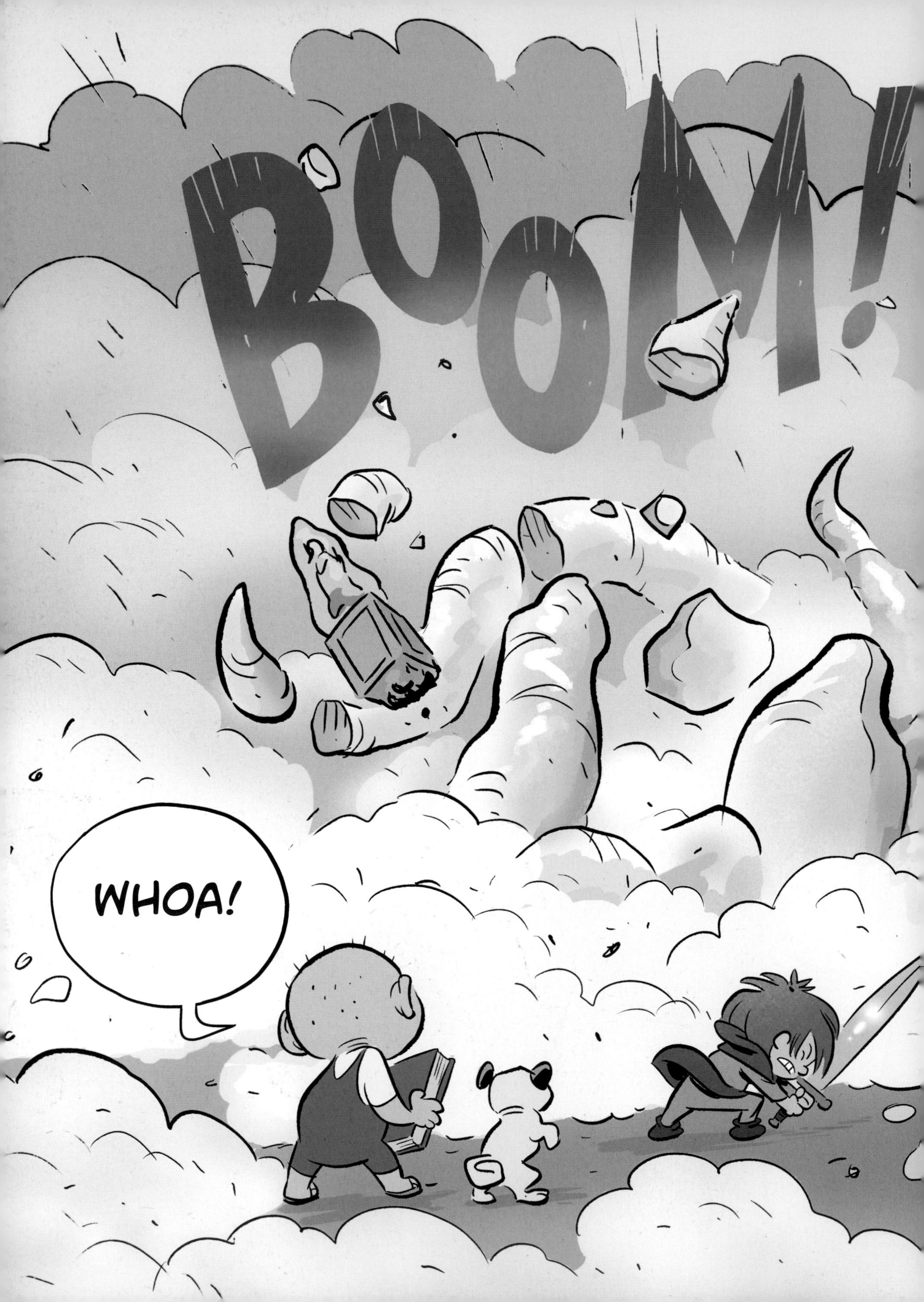
BOOM!
WHOA!

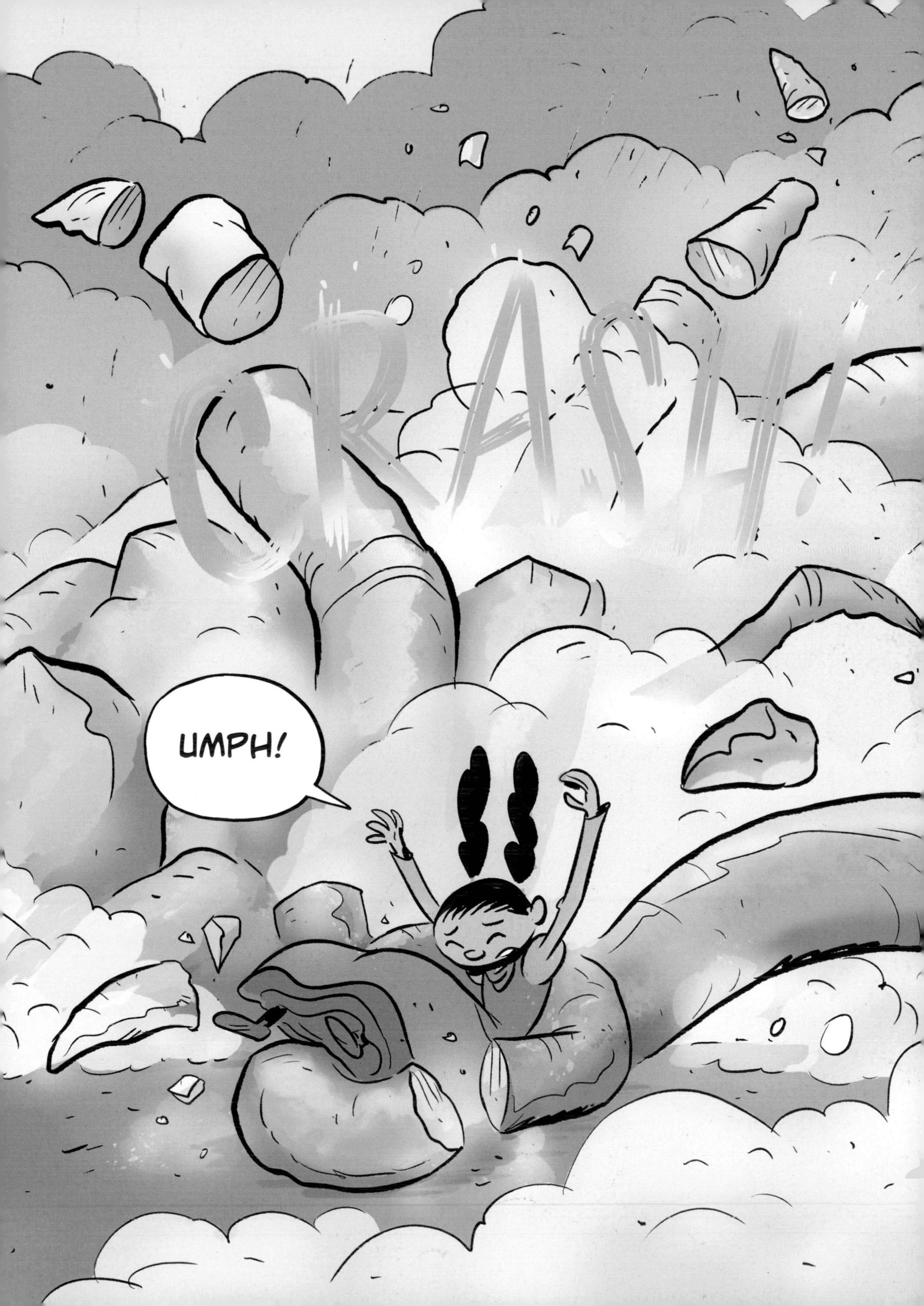
CRASH!
UMPH!

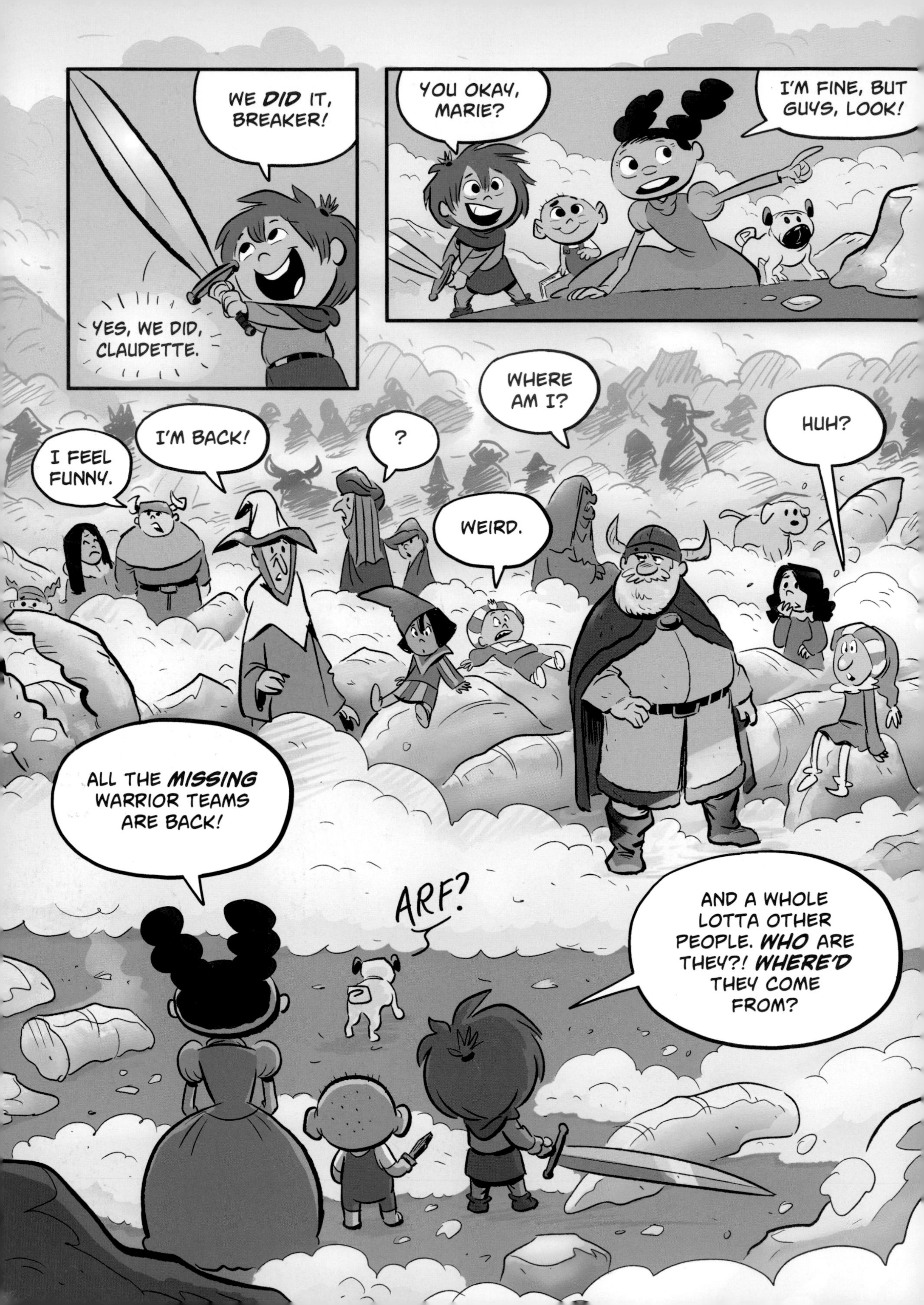

WE DID IT, BREAKER!
YES, WE DID, CLAUDETTE.
YOU OKAY, MARIE?
I'M FINE, BUT GUYS, LOOK!
I FEEL FUNNY.
I'M BACK!
?
WHERE AM I?
HUH?
WEIRD.
ALL THE MISSING WARRIOR TEAMS ARE BACK!
ARF?
AND A WHOLE LOTTA OTHER PEOPLE. WHO ARE THEY?! WHERE'D THEY COME FROM?

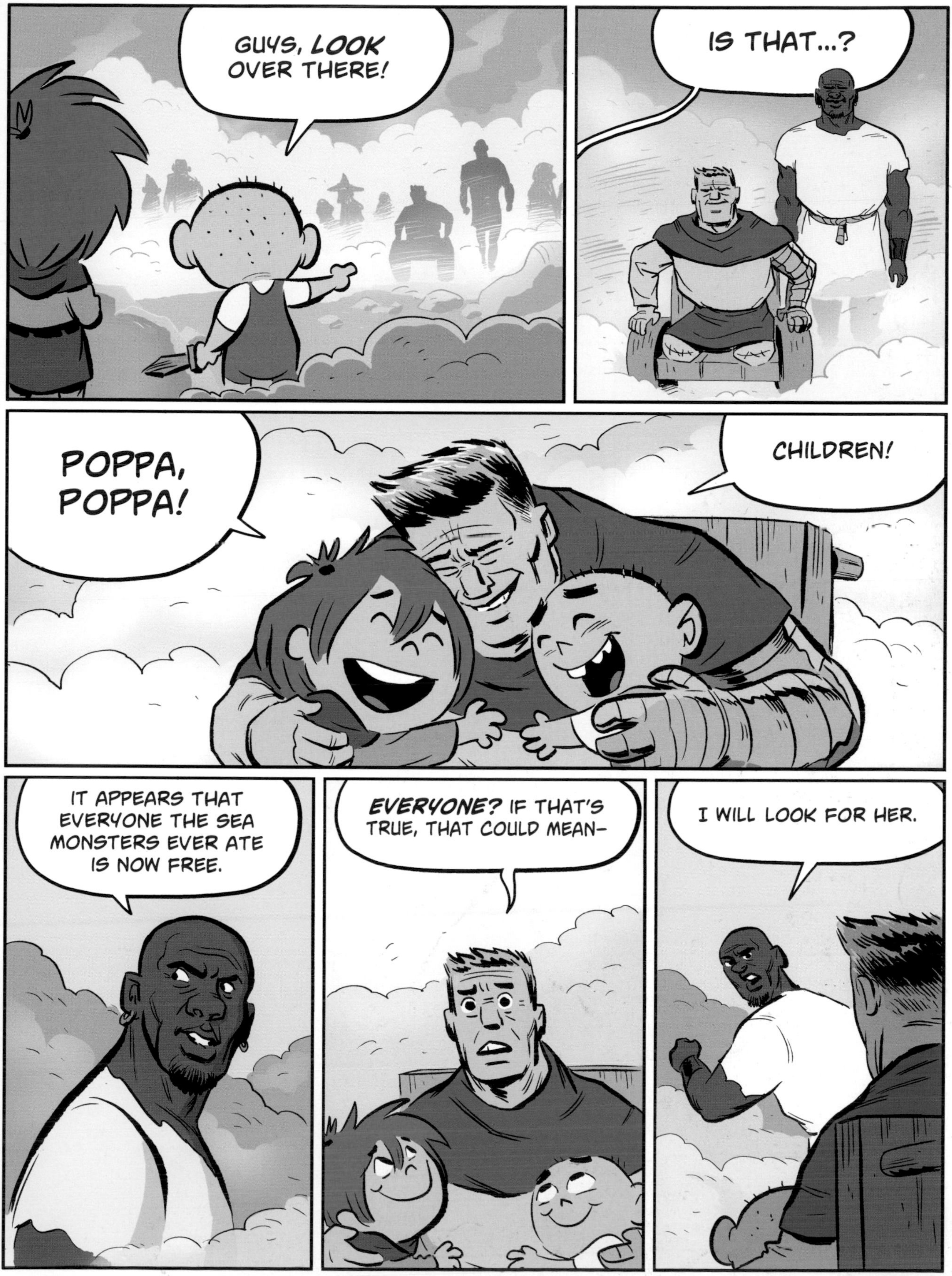
GUYS, LOOK OVER THERE!
IS THAT...?
POPPA, POPPA!
CHILDREN!
IT APPEARS THAT EVERYONE THE SEA MONSTERS EVER ATE IS NOW FREE.
EVERYONE? IF THAT'S TRUE, THAT COULD MEAN-
I WILL LOOK FOR HER.

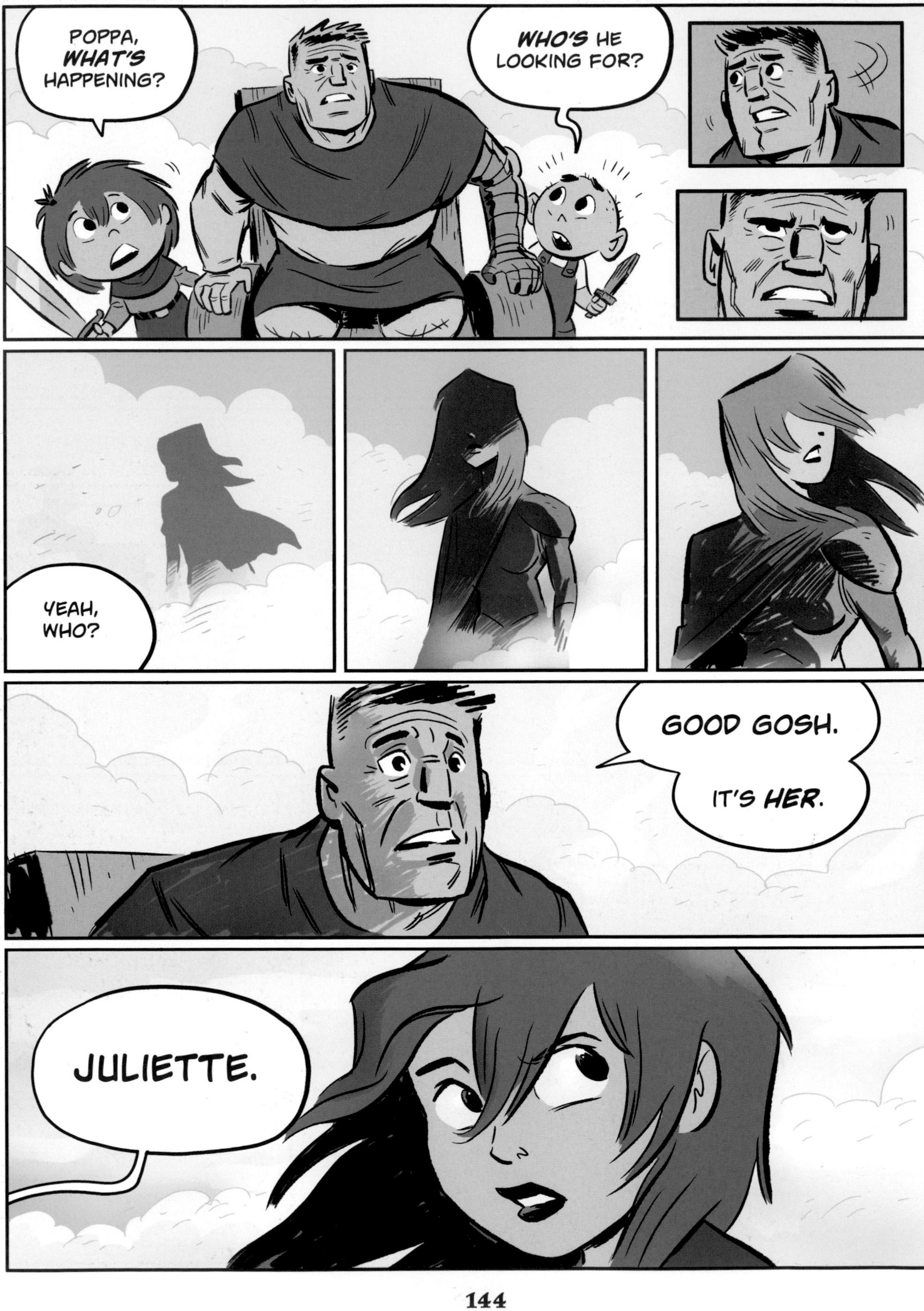
POPPA, WHAT'S HAPPENING?
WHO'S HE LOOKING FOR?
YEAH, WHO?
GOOD GOSH.
IT'S HER.
JULIETTE.

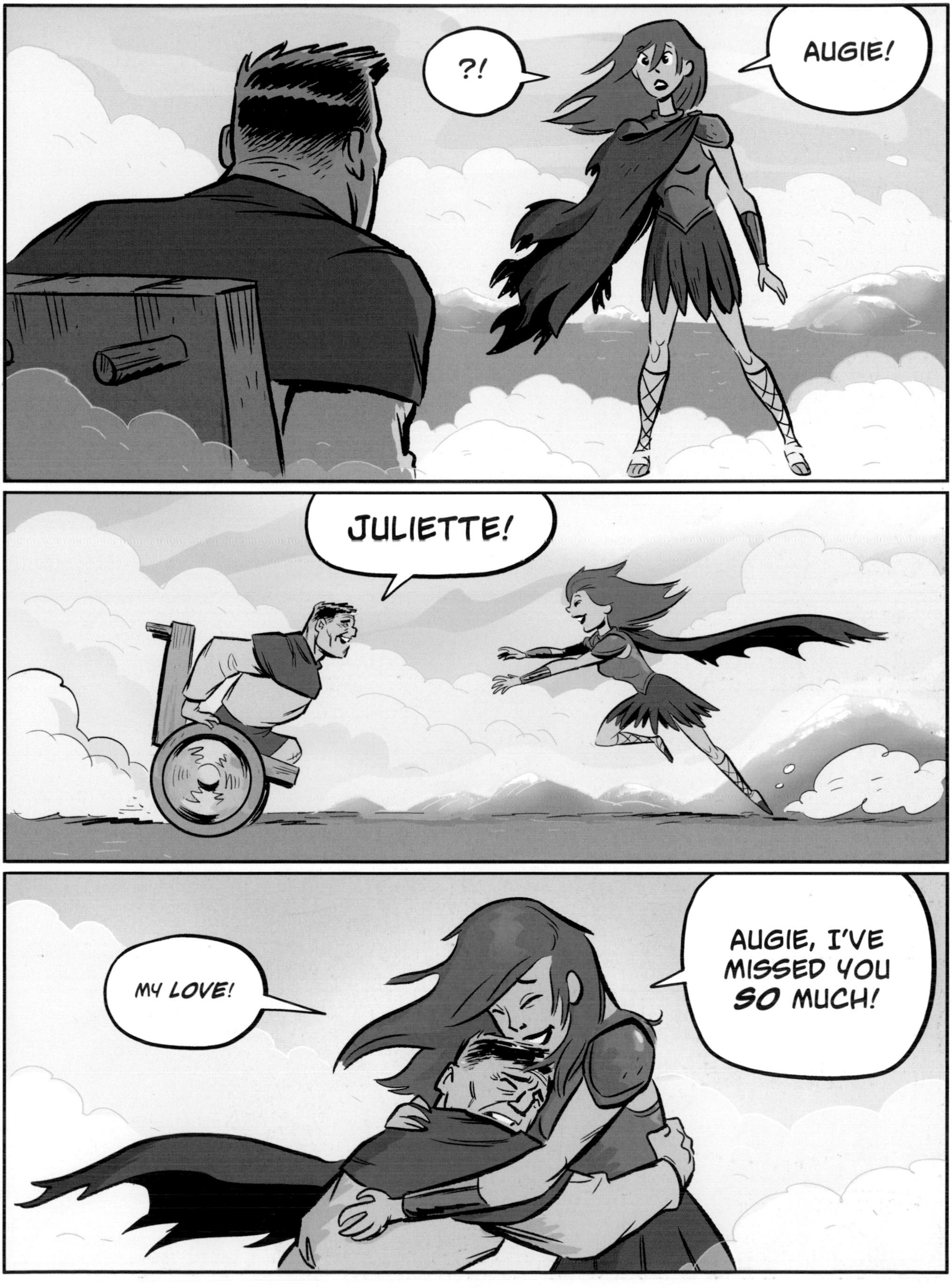
?!
AUGIE!
JULIETTE!
AUGIE, I'VE MISSED YOU SO MUCH!
MY LOVE!

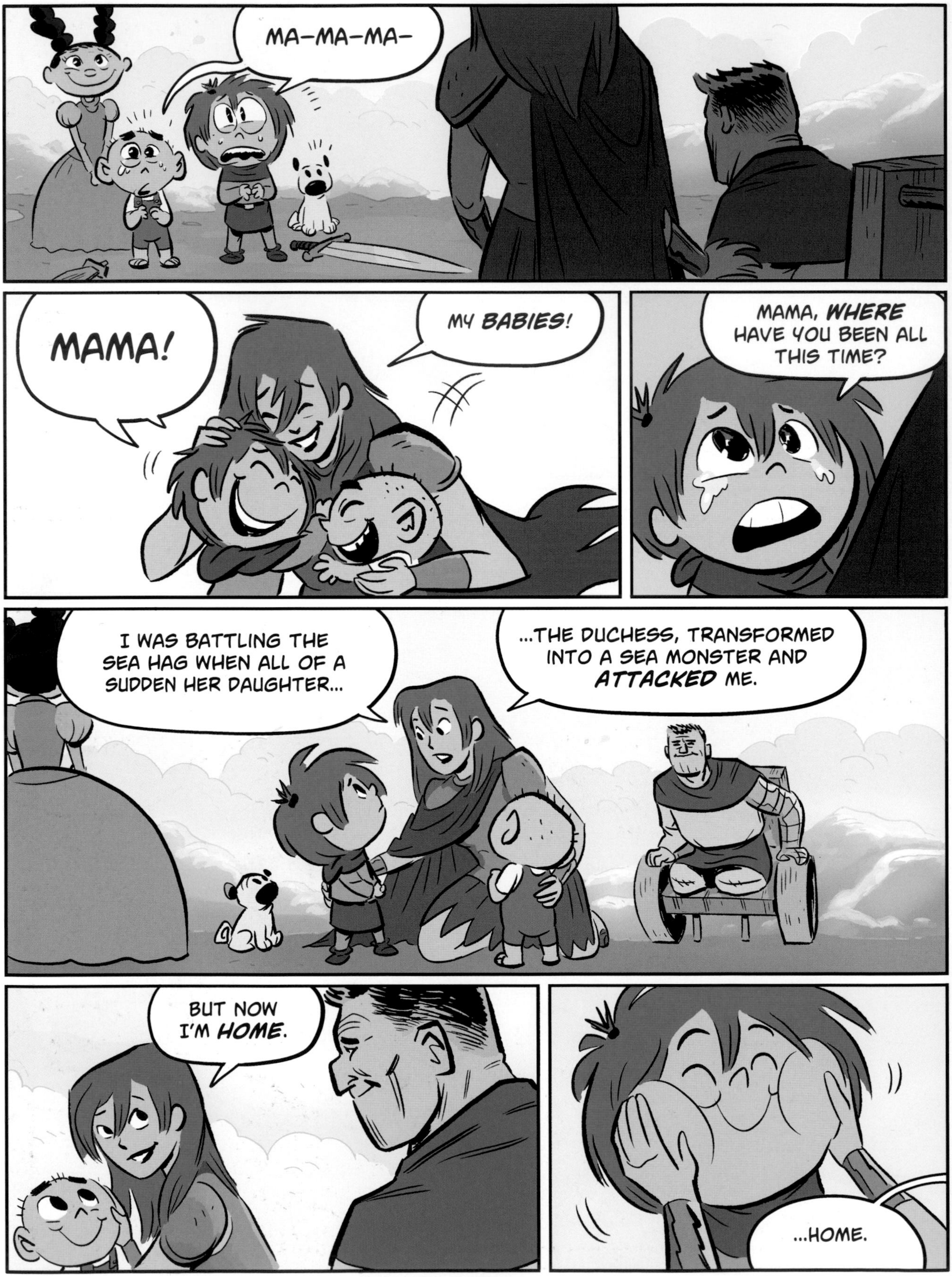
MA-MA-MA-
MAMA!
MY BABIES!
MAMA, WHERE HAVE YOU BEEN ALL THIS TIME?
I WAS BATTLING THE SEA HAG WHEN ALL OF A SUDDEN HER DAUGHTER...
...THE DUCHESS, TRANSFORMED INTO A SEA MONSTER AND ATTACKED ME.
BUT NOW I'M HOME.
...HOME.

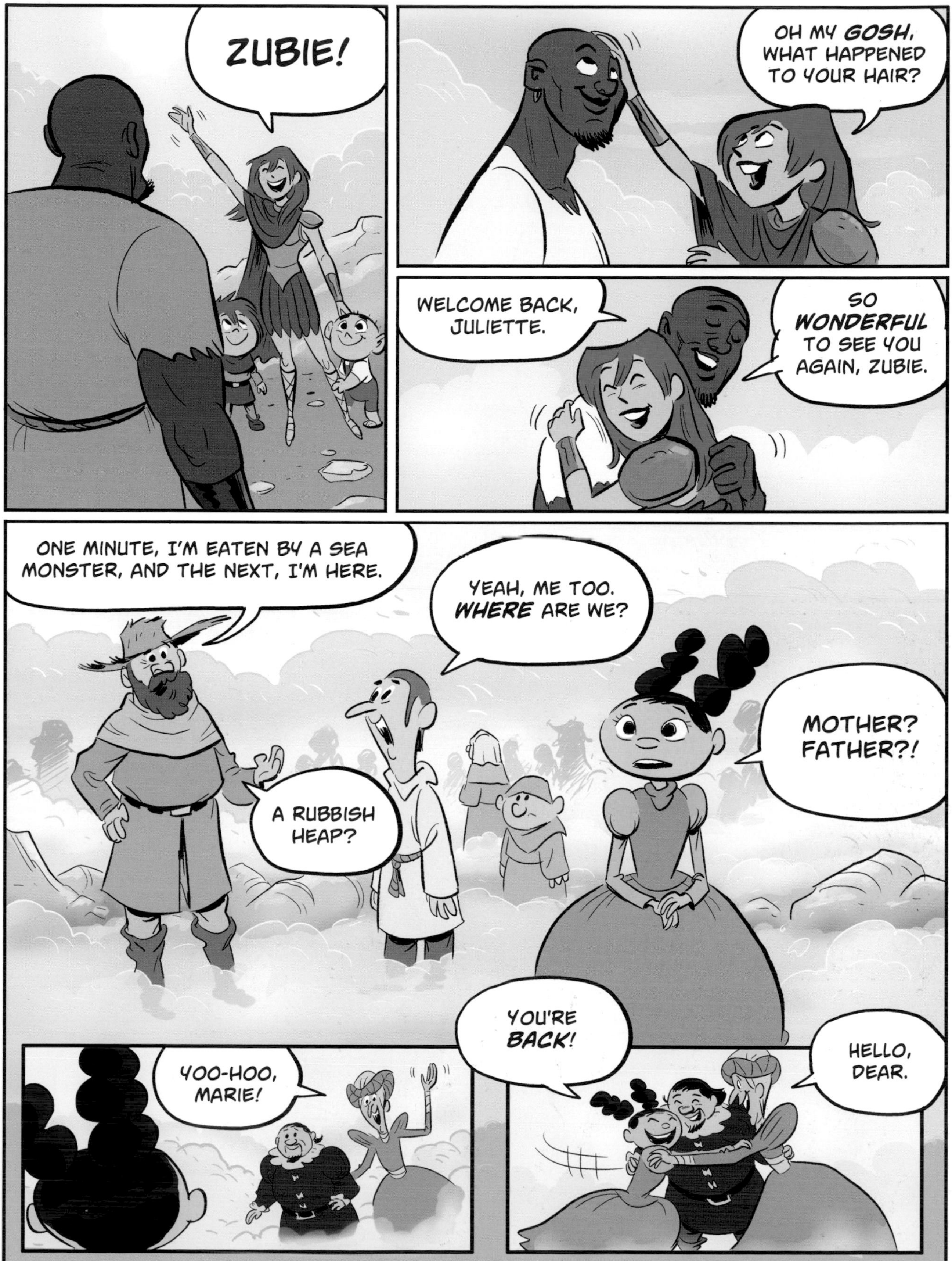
ZUBIE!
OH MY GOSH, WHAT HAPPENED TO YOUR HAIR?
WELCOME BACK, JULIETTE.
SO WONDERFUL TO SEE YOU AGAIN, ZUBIE.
ONE MINUTE, I'M EATEN BY A SEA MONSTER, AND THE NEXT, I'M HERE.
YEAH, ME TOO. WHERE ARE WE?
A RUBBISH HEAP?
MOTHER? FATHER?!
YOO-HOO, MARIE!
YOU'RE BACK!
HELLO, DEAR.

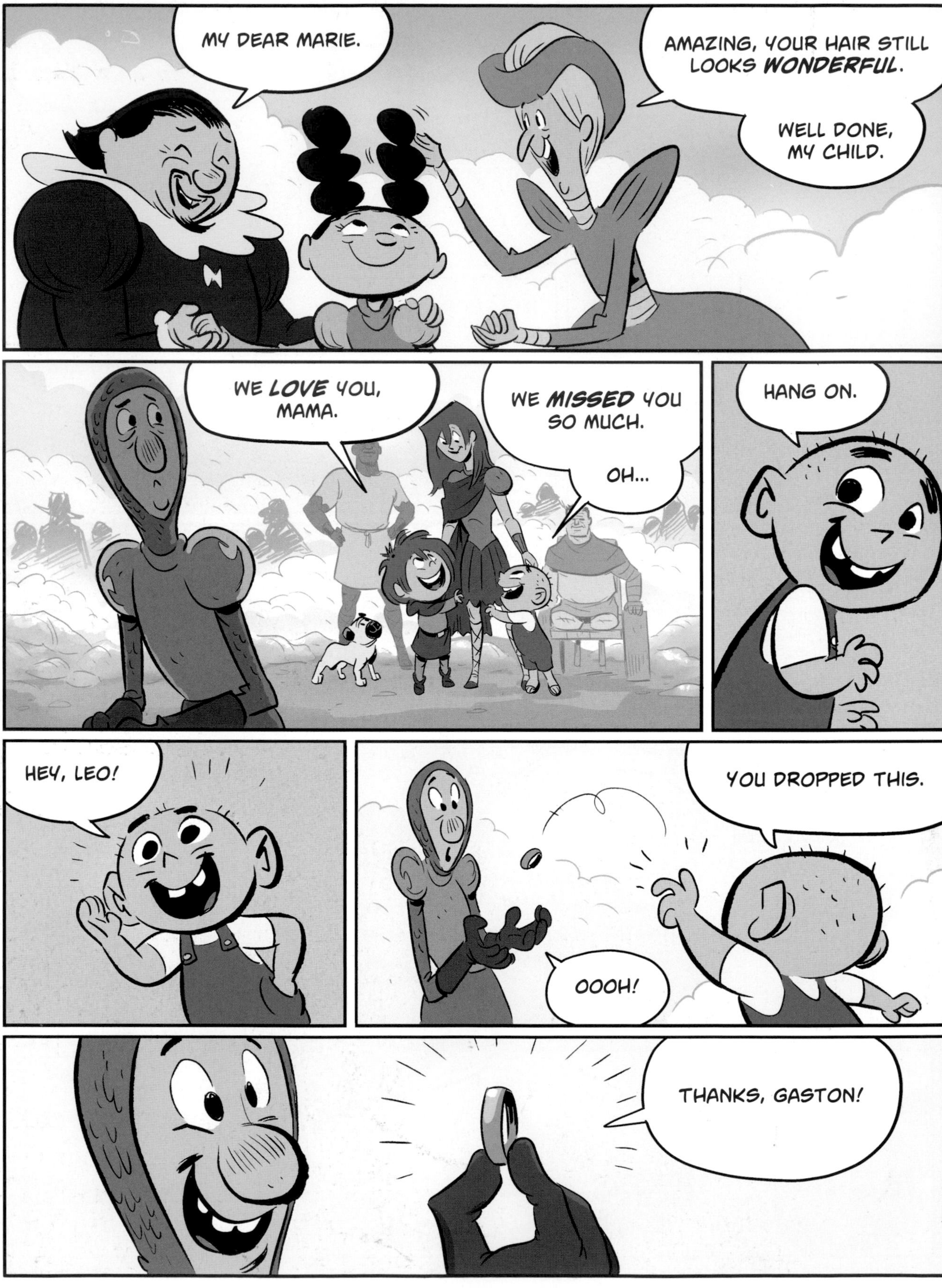
MY DEAR MARIE.
AMAZING, YOUR HAIR STILL LOOKS **WONDERFUL**.
WELL DONE, MY CHILD.
WE **LOVE** YOU, MAMA.
WE **MISSED** YOU SO MUCH.
OH...
HANG ON.
HEY, LEO!
YOU DROPPED THIS.
OOOH!
THANKS, GASTON!

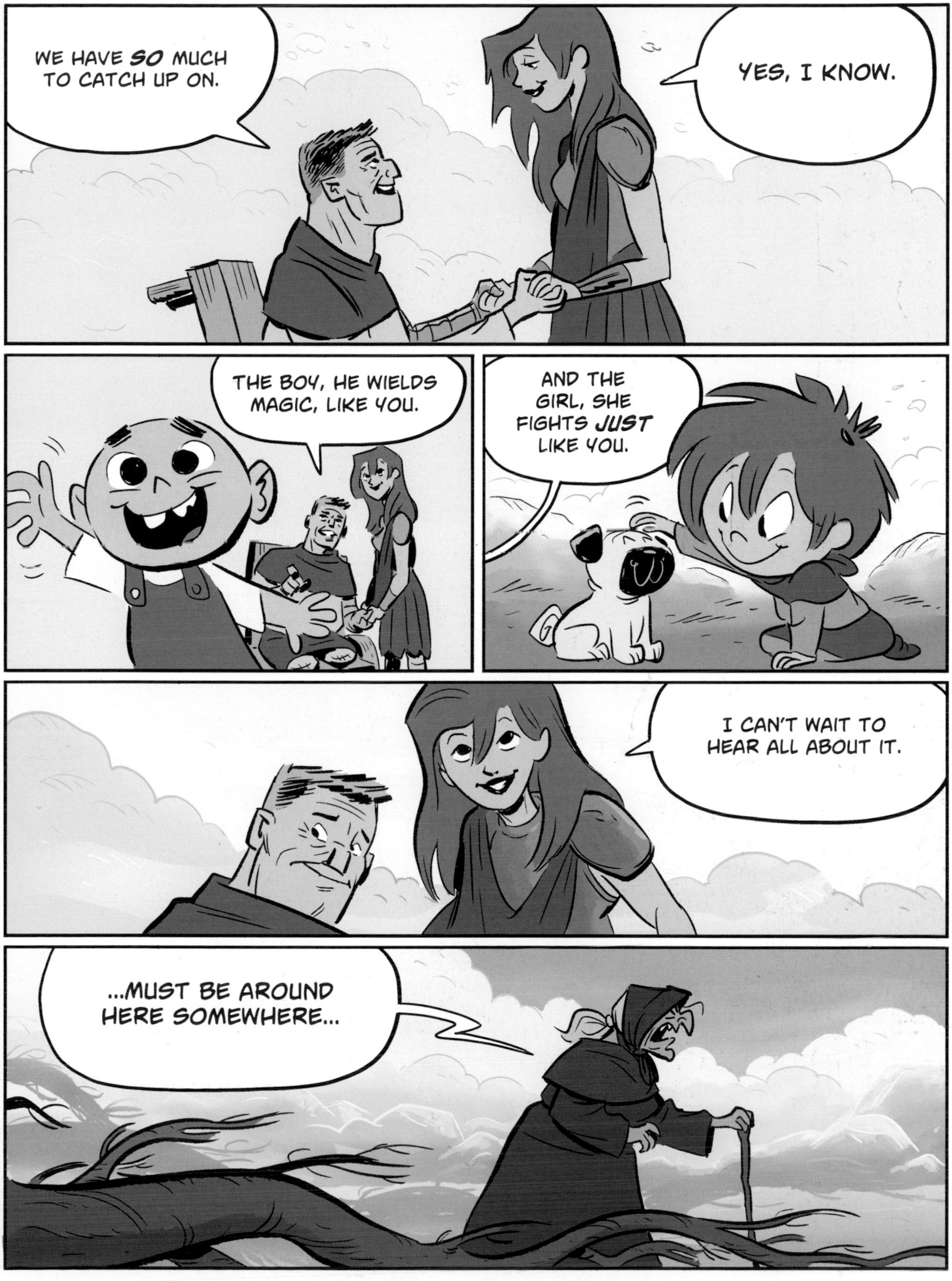

WE HAVE SO MUCH TO CATCH UP ON.
YES, I KNOW.
THE BOY, HE WIELDS MAGIC, LIKE YOU.
AND THE GIRL, SHE FIGHTS JUST LIKE YOU.
I CAN'T WAIT TO HEAR ALL ABOUT IT.
...MUST BE AROUND HERE SOMEWHERE...

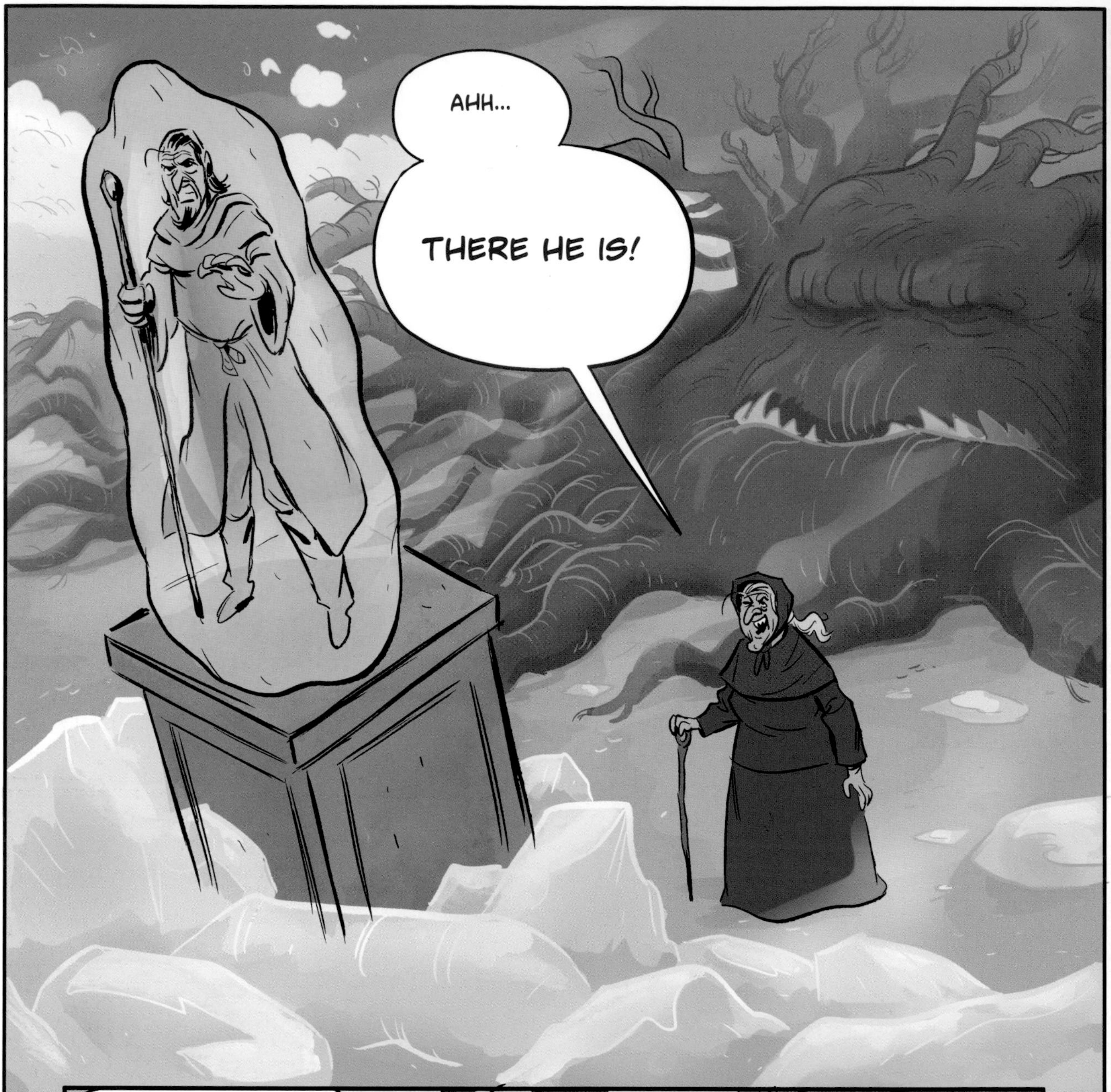
AHH...
THERE HE IS!

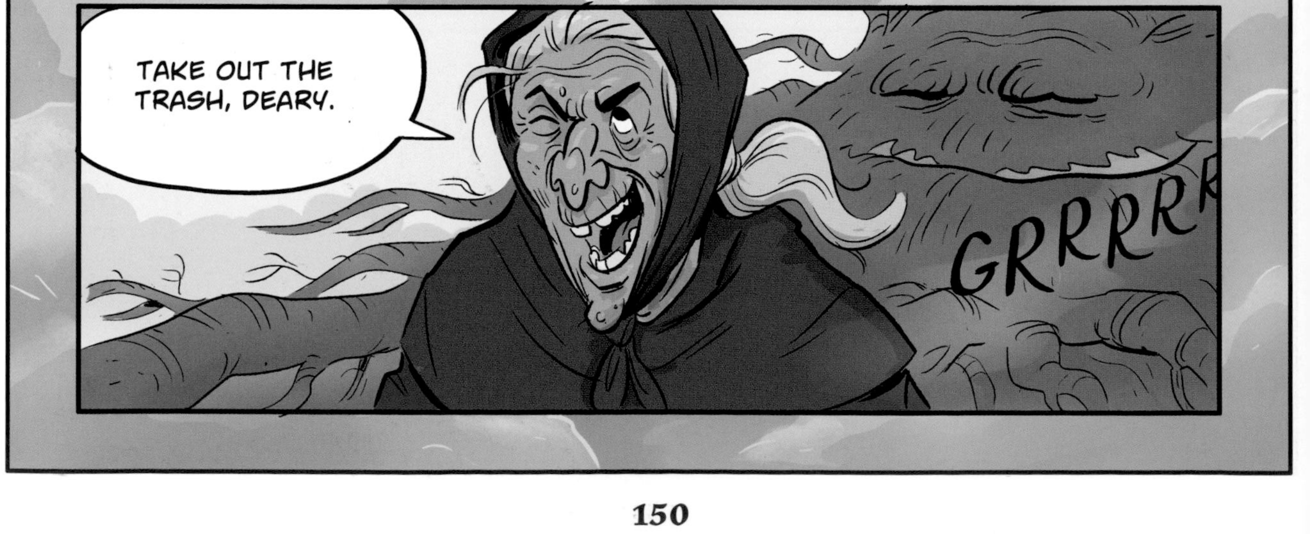
TAKE OUT THE TRASH, DEARY.
GRRRRR

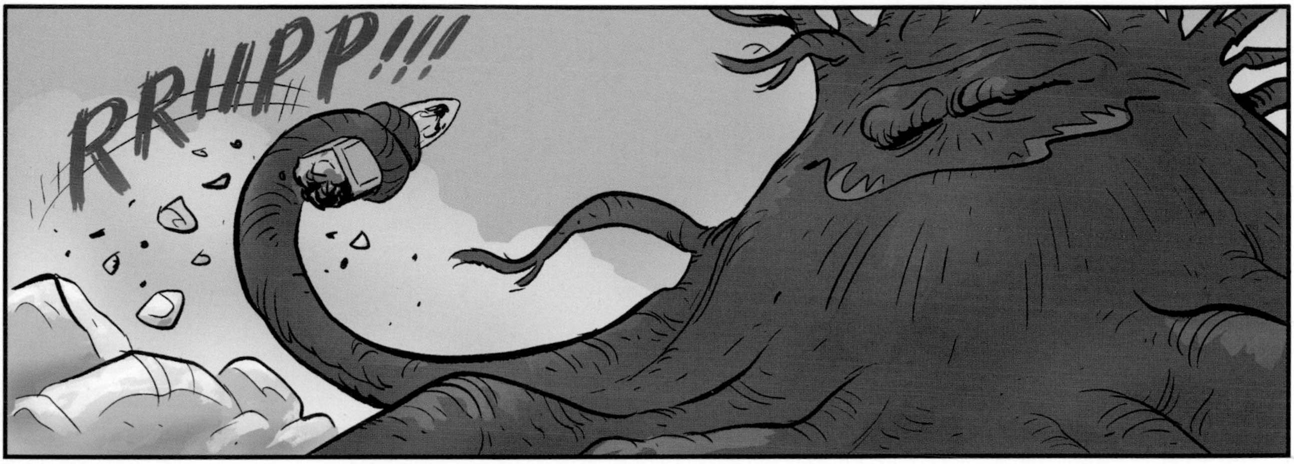
RRIIPP!!!

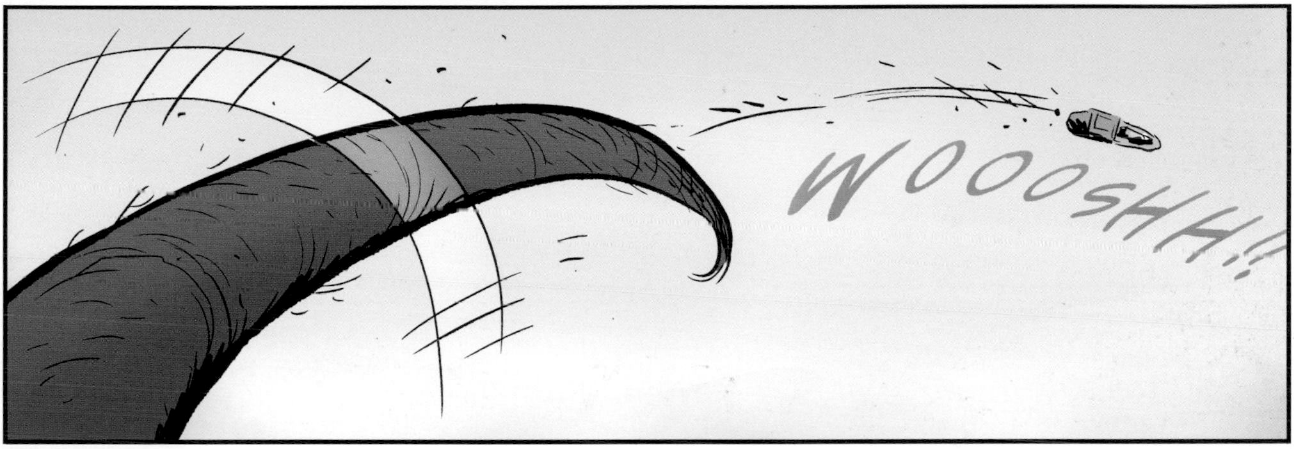
WOOOSHH!!

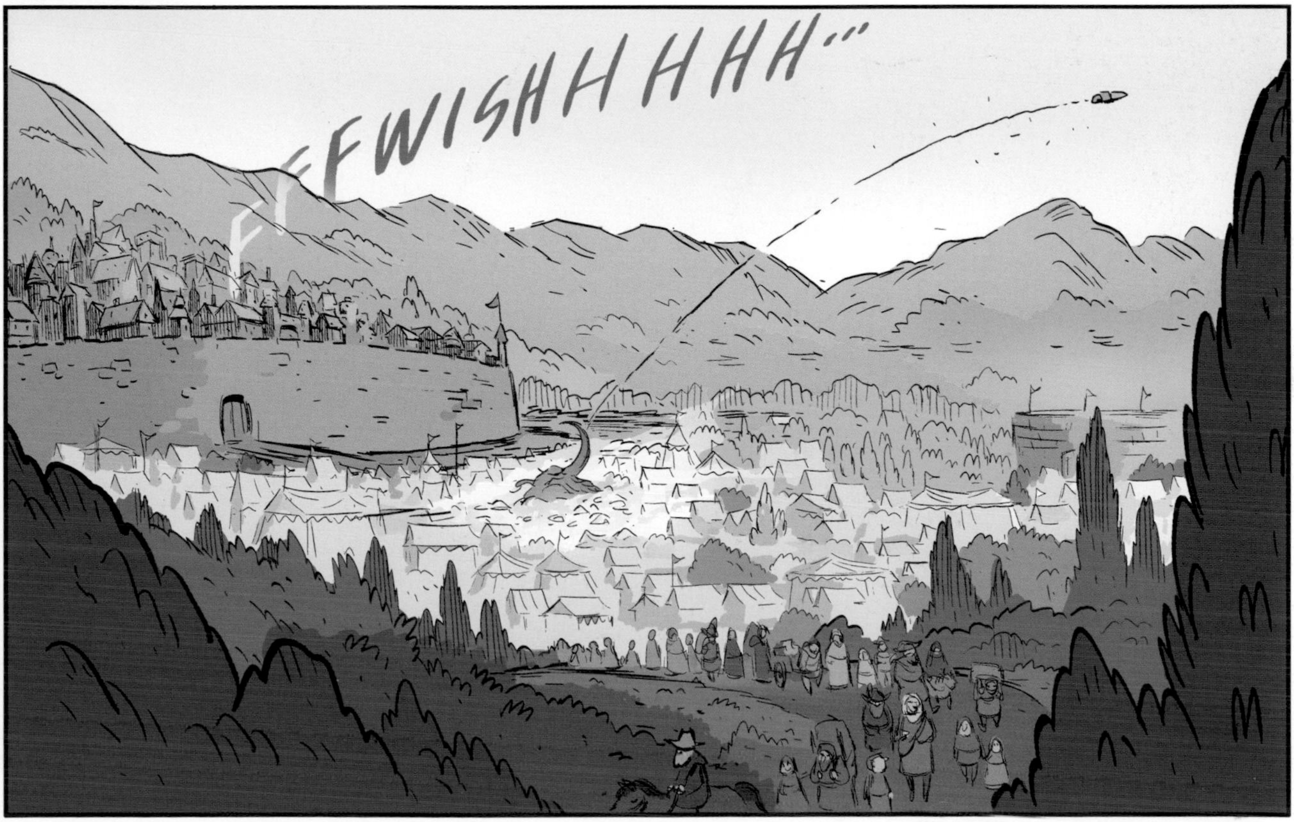
FFFWISHHHHH...

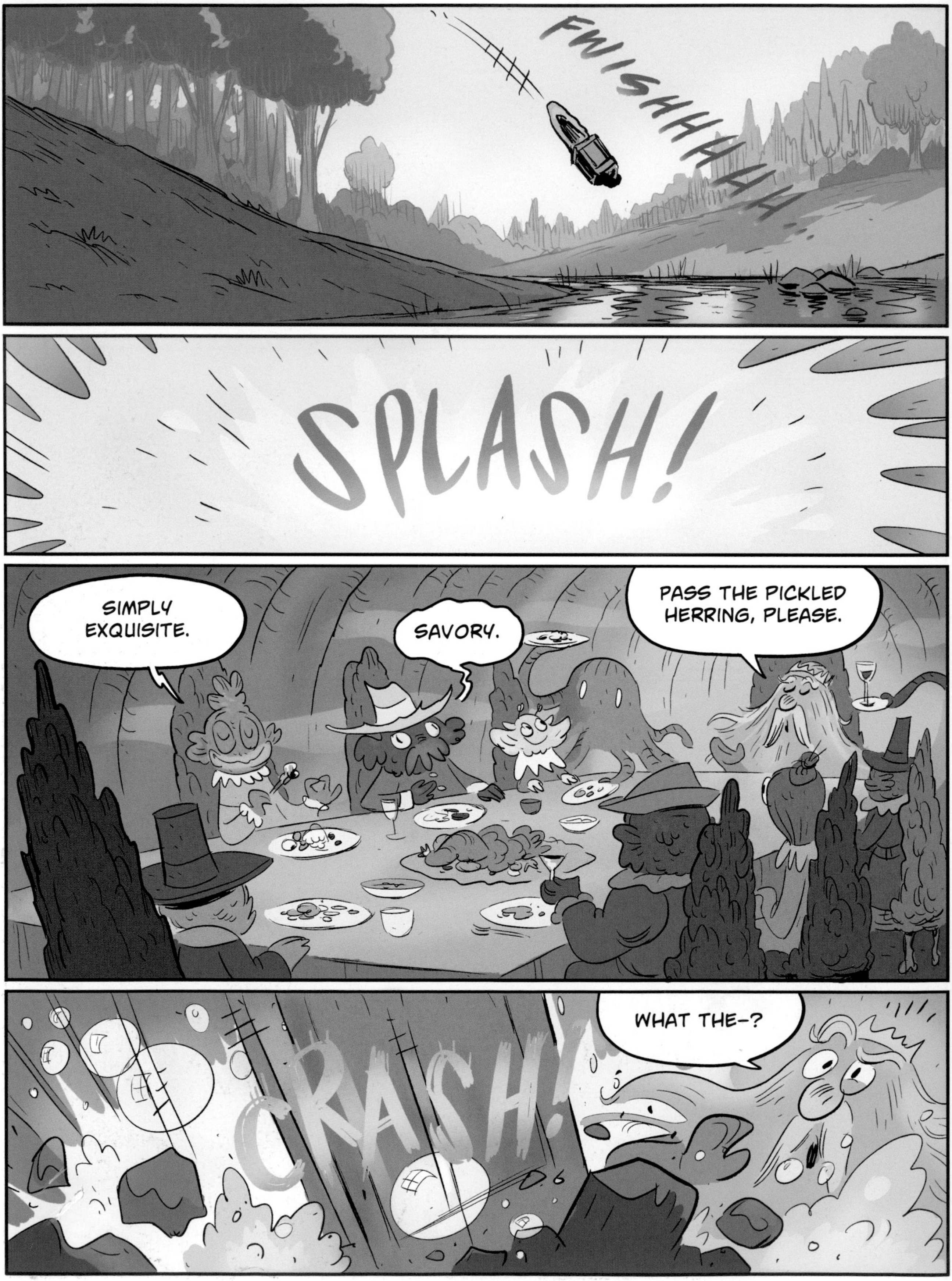
FWISHHHHH
SPLASH!
SIMPLY EXQUISITE.
SAVORY.
PASS THE PICKLED HERRING, PLEASE.
CRASH!
WHAT THE-?

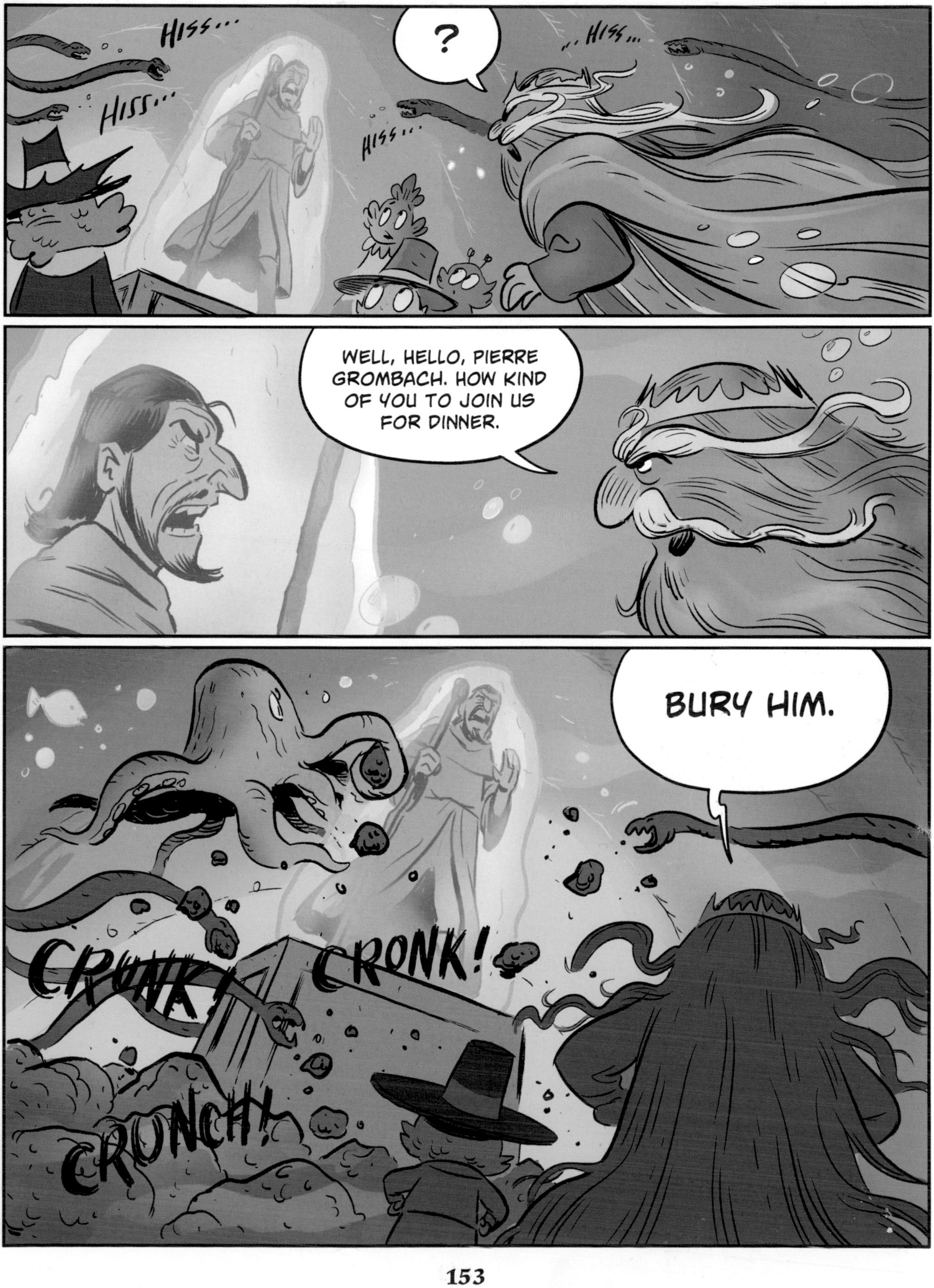
HISS...
HISS...
?
... HISS...
HISS...
WELL, HELLO, PIERRE GROMBACH. HOW KIND OF YOU TO JOIN US FOR DINNER.
BURY HIM.
CRONK!
CRONK!
CRUNCH!

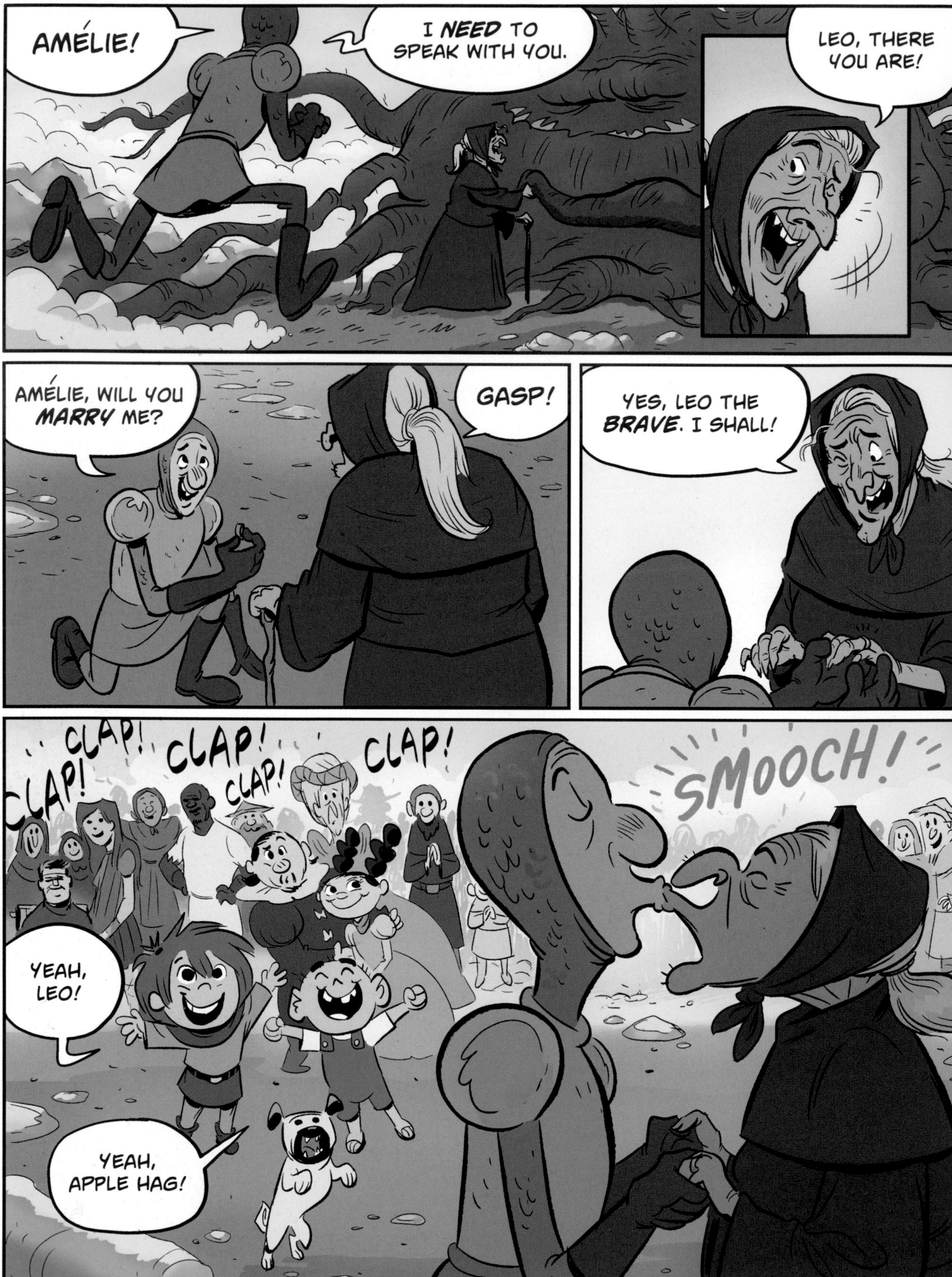
AMÉLIE!
I NEED TO SPEAK WITH YOU.
LEO, THERE YOU ARE!
AMÉLIE, WILL YOU MARRY ME?
GASP!
YES, LEO THE BRAVE. I SHALL!
CLAP! CLAP! CLAP! CLAP! CLAP!
SMOOCH!
YEAH, LEO!
YEAH, APPLE HAG!

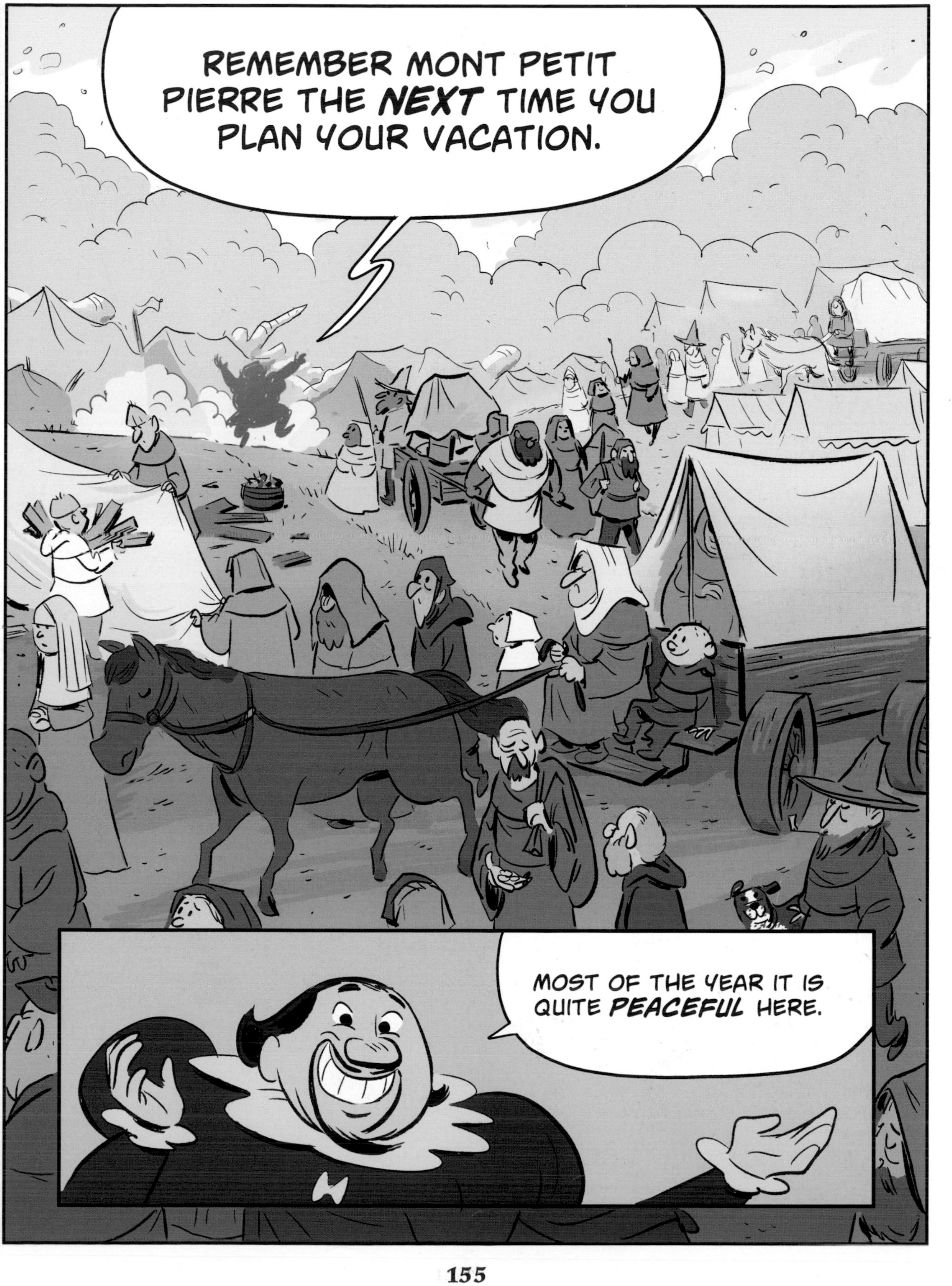
REMEMBER MONT PETIT PIERRE THE ***NEXT*** TIME YOU PLAN YOUR VACATION.
MOST OF THE YEAR IT IS QUITE ***PEACEFUL*** HERE.

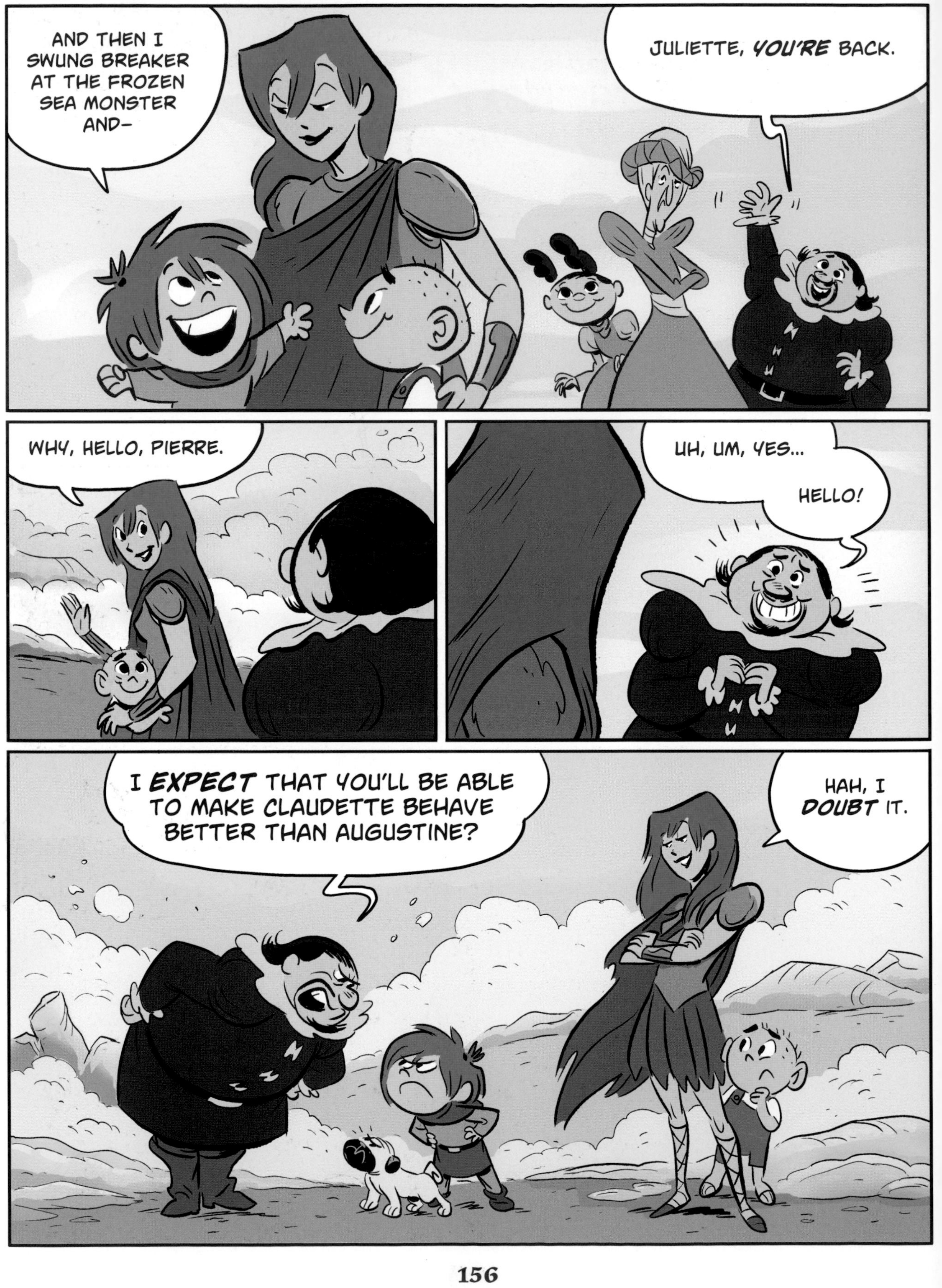
AND THEN I SWUNG BREAKER AT THE FROZEN SEA MONSTER AND–
JULIETTE, *YOU'RE* BACK.
WHY, HELLO, PIERRE.
UH, UM, YES...
HELLO!
I *EXPECT* THAT YOU'LL BE ABLE TO MAKE CLAUDETTE BEHAVE BETTER THAN AUGUSTINE?
HAH, I *DOUBT* IT.

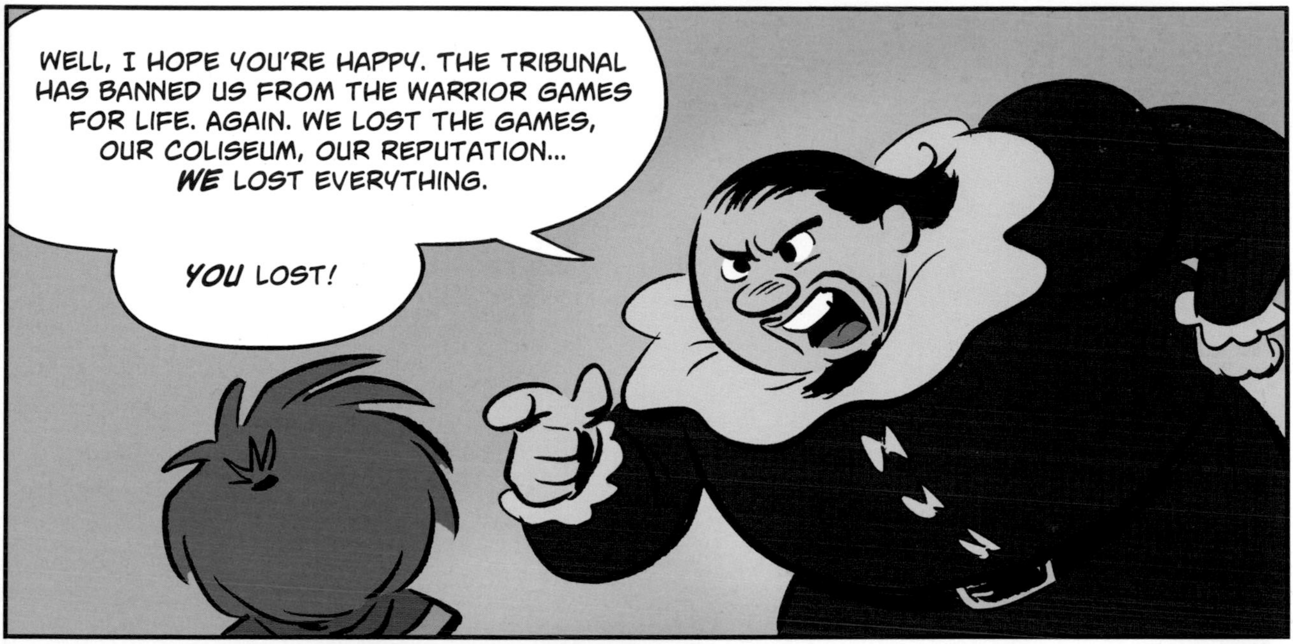
WELL, I HOPE YOU'RE HAPPY. THE TRIBUNAL HAS BANNED US FROM THE WARRIOR GAMES FOR LIFE. AGAIN. WE LOST THE GAMES, OUR COLISEUM, OUR REPUTATION... *WE* LOST EVERYTHING.
YOU LOST!

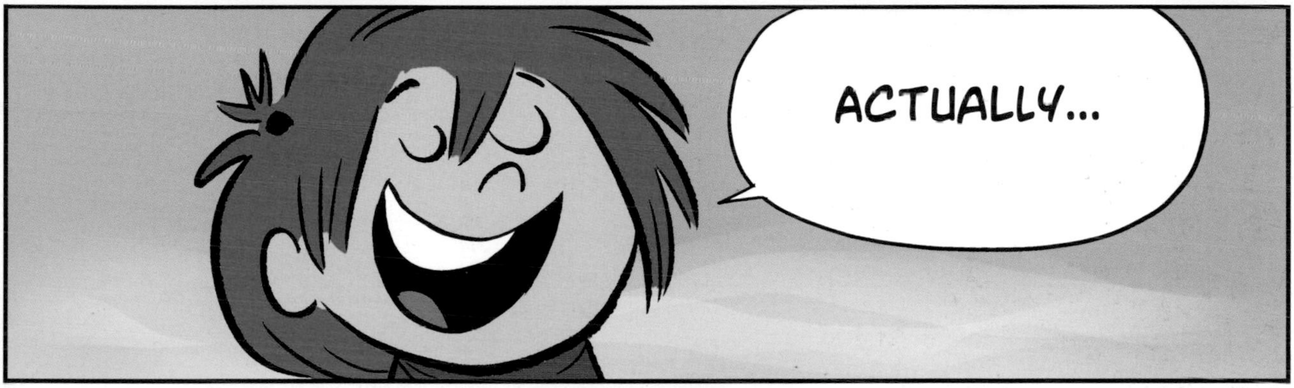
ACTUALLY...

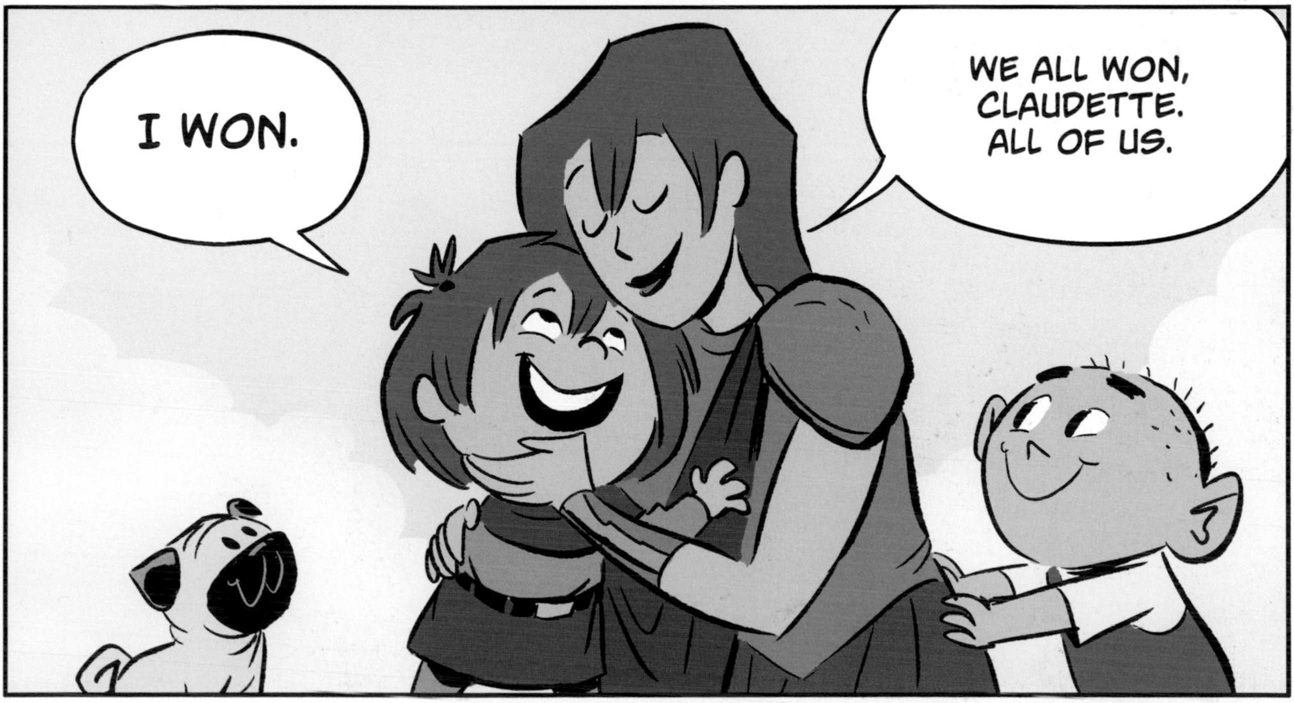
I WON.
WE ALL WON, CLAUDETTE. ALL OF US.

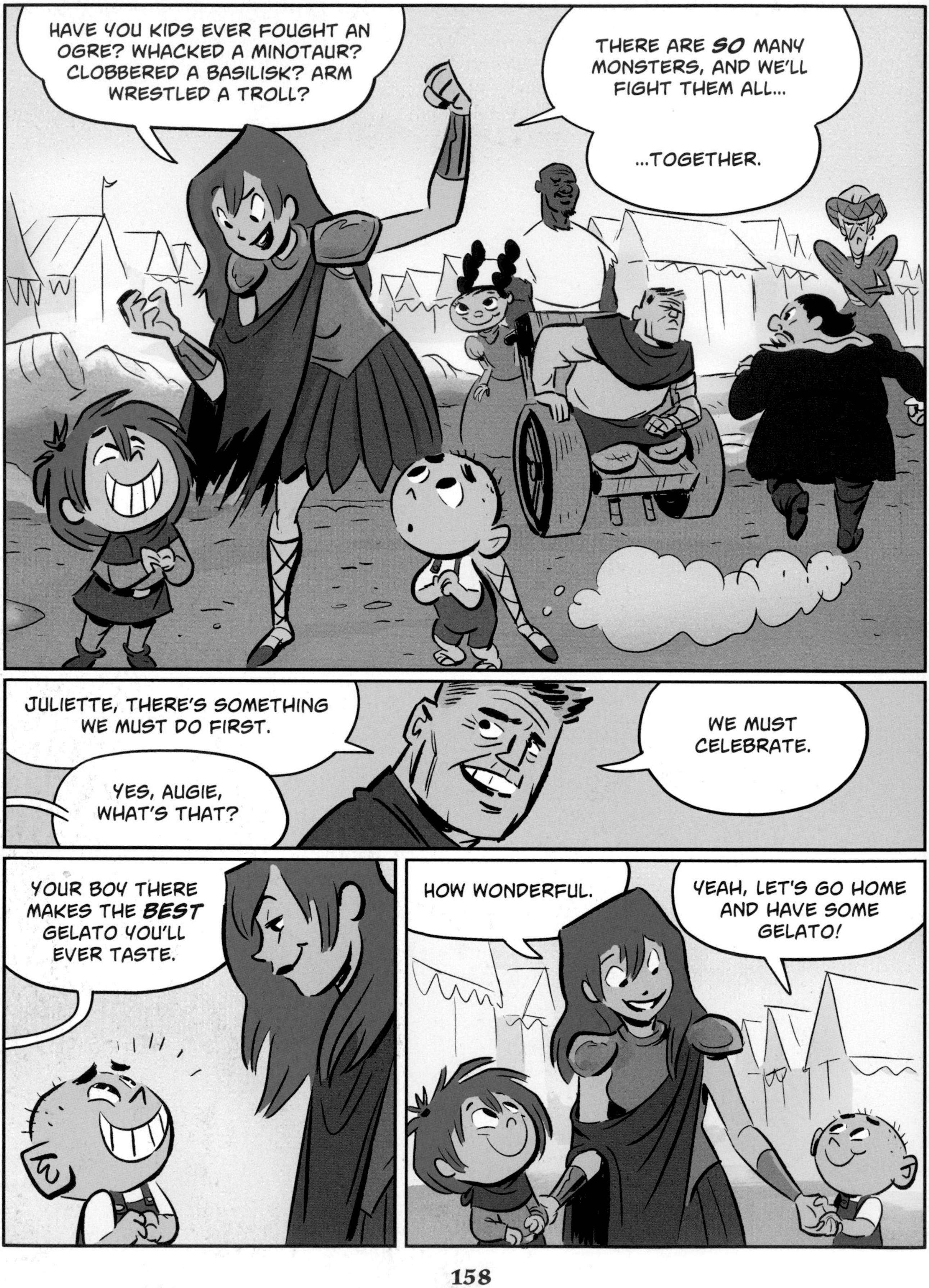
HAVE YOU KIDS EVER FOUGHT AN OGRE? WHACKED A MINOTAUR? CLOBBERED A BASILISK? ARM WRESTLED A TROLL?
THERE ARE SO MANY MONSTERS, AND WE'LL FIGHT THEM ALL...
...TOGETHER.
JULIETTE, THERE'S SOMETHING WE MUST DO FIRST.
YES, AUGIE, WHAT'S THAT?
WE MUST CELEBRATE.
YOUR BOY THERE MAKES THE BEST GELATO YOU'LL EVER TASTE.
HOW WONDERFUL.
YEAH, LET'S GO HOME AND HAVE SOME GELATO!

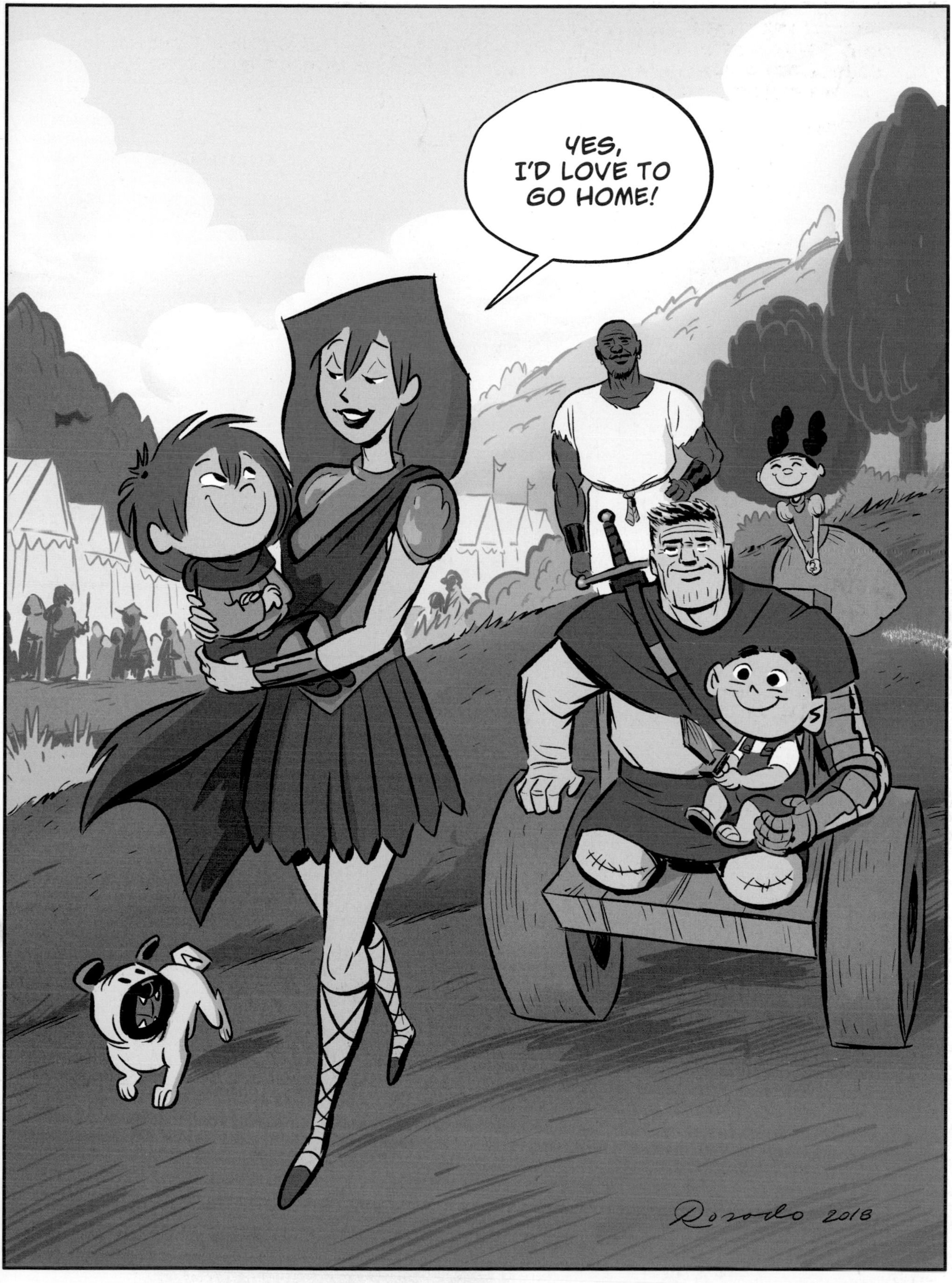
YES, I'D LOVE TO GO HOME!
2018

THE END

Rosado/Aguirre - 2018

NOTES FROM RAFAEL

Designing the kids from all the different kingdoms was a lot of fun. The Seven Lovelorn Princes return, this time as contestants in the Warrior Games. When designing the new characters from each kingdom, I tried to stick with the attitude and looks that had been established in *Dragons Beware!* So the kids from the Swamp Kingdom are all goofballs, the ones from the Northwest Kingdom are musicians, and so on.

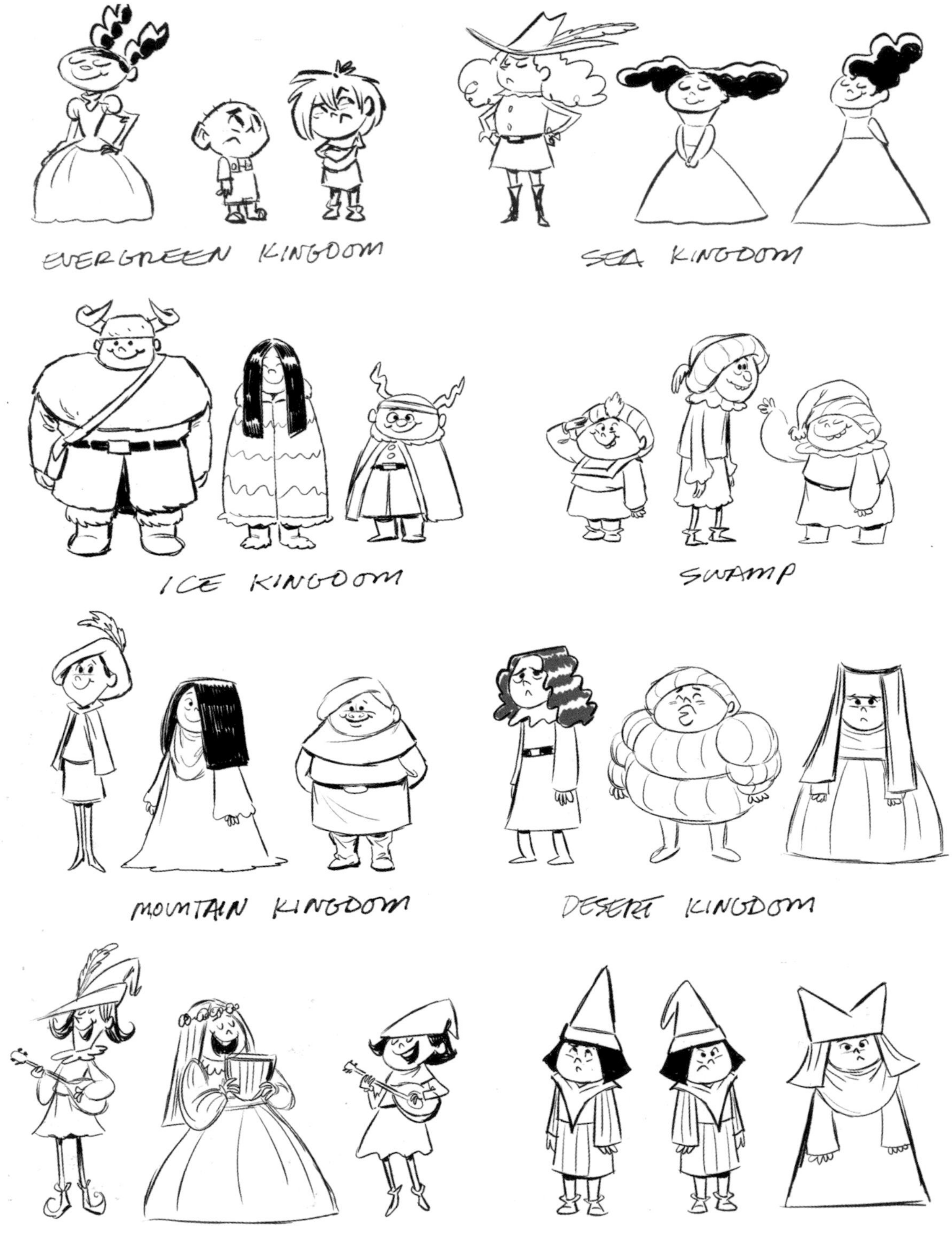

EVERGREEN KINGDOM
SEA KINGDOM
ICE KINGDOM
SWAMP
MOUNTAIN KINGDOM
DESERT KINGDOM
NORTHWEST KINGDOM
GREAT LAKES KINGDOM

For the color design of the teams, John Novak and I decided to keep it simple. Each team has a color palette all its own. It made John's job a bit easier, since there were so many group shots.

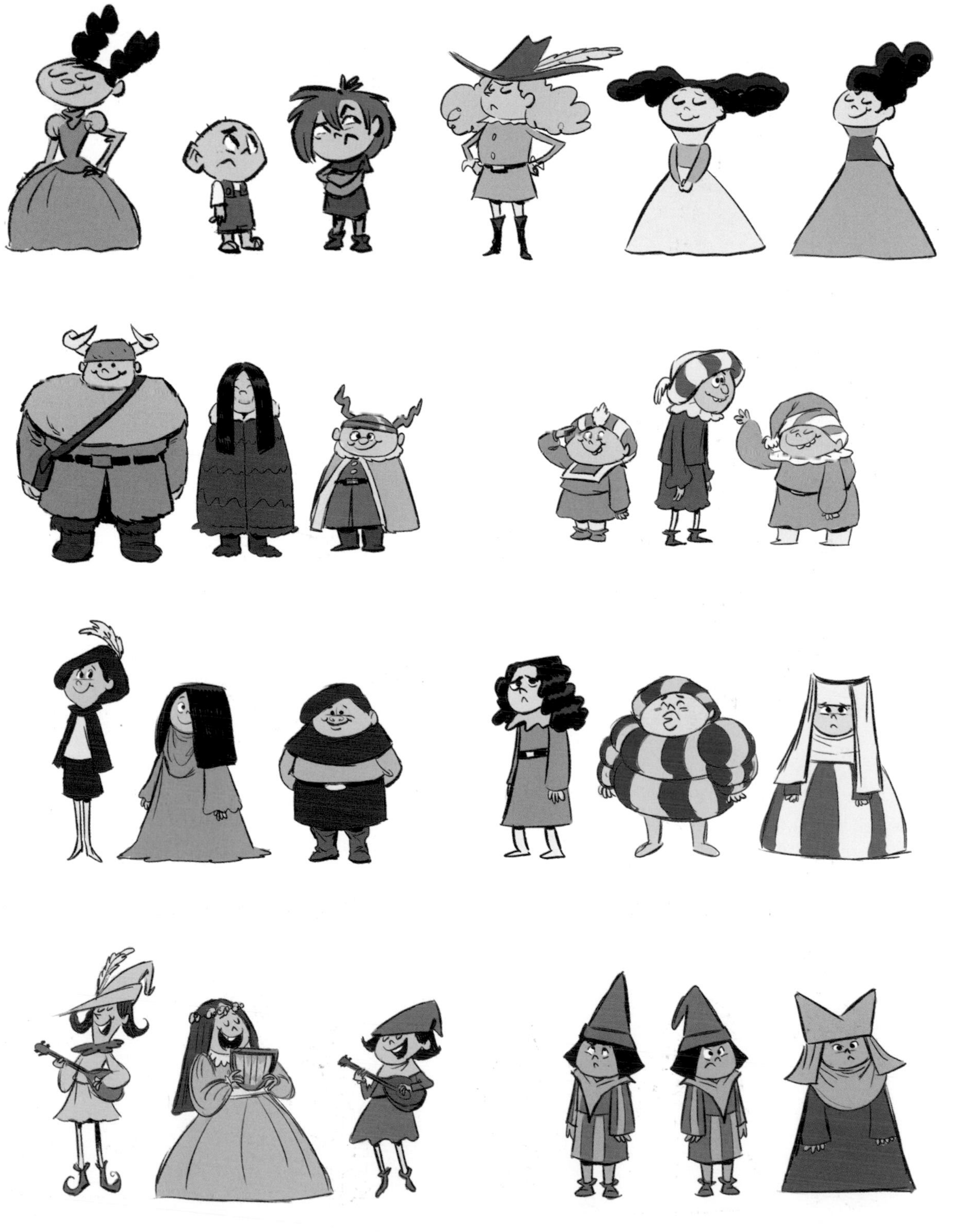

When designing Mia, Ria, and Thunk, I tried to somehow mirror Claudette and Marie. Mia and Ria's hair is sculptural and peculiar, like Marie's. Thunk's hair is wild and unruly, like Claudette's.

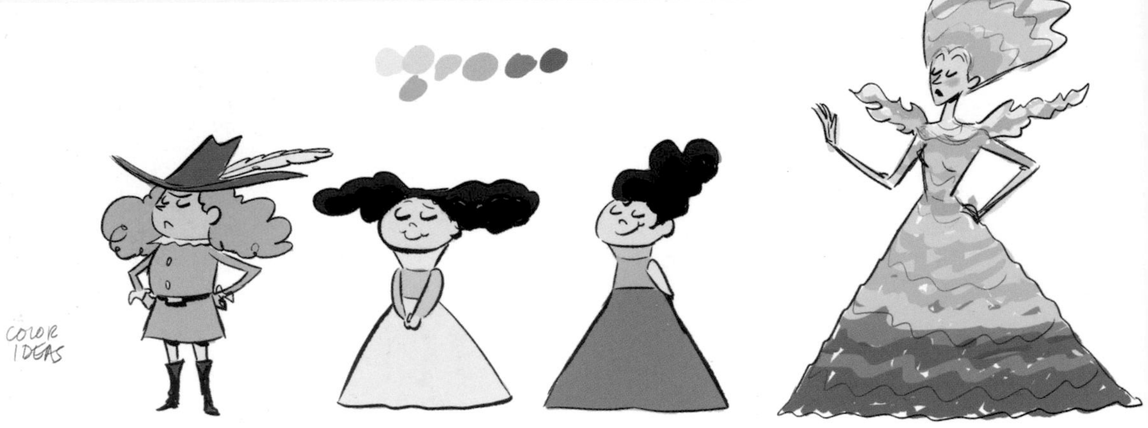
COLOR IDEAS

I had the idea of the coral motif for the Duchess's outfit right from the beginning. The final design is almost the same as my first doodle.

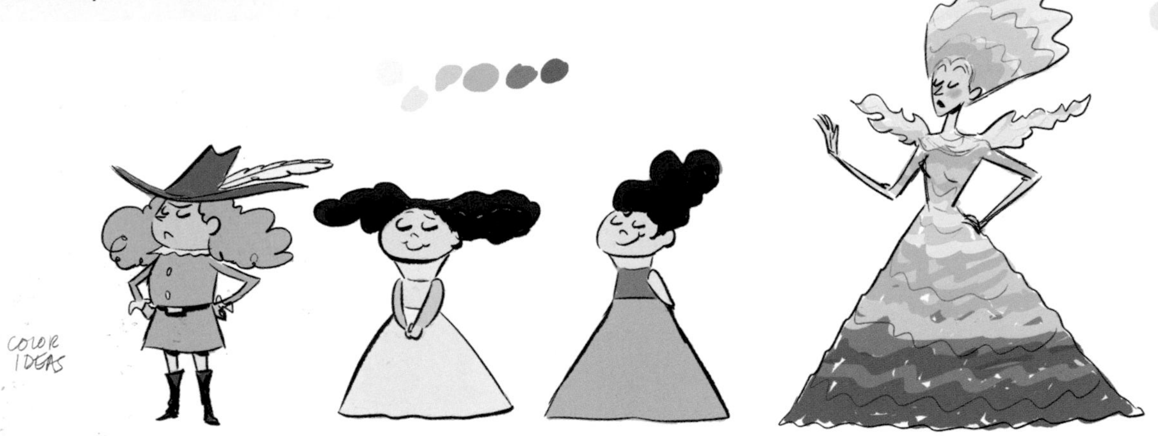
COLOR IDEAS

Since they hail from the Sea Kingdom, we decided to use cool colors in their design. Mia and Ria's color palette is similar to Marie's, and the color of Thunk's hair is close to Claudette's. The patterns on the Duchess's costume are suggestive of ocean waves.

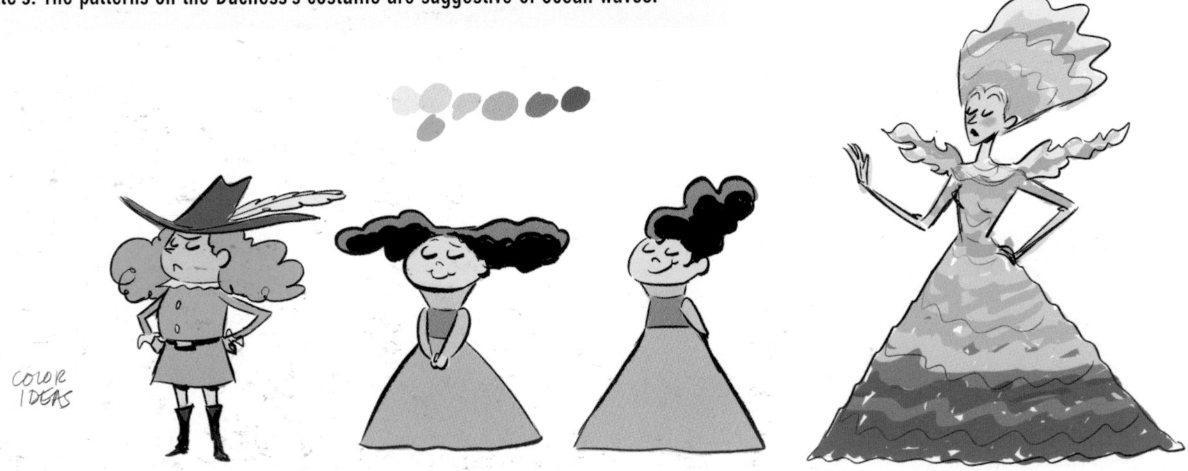
COLOR IDEAS

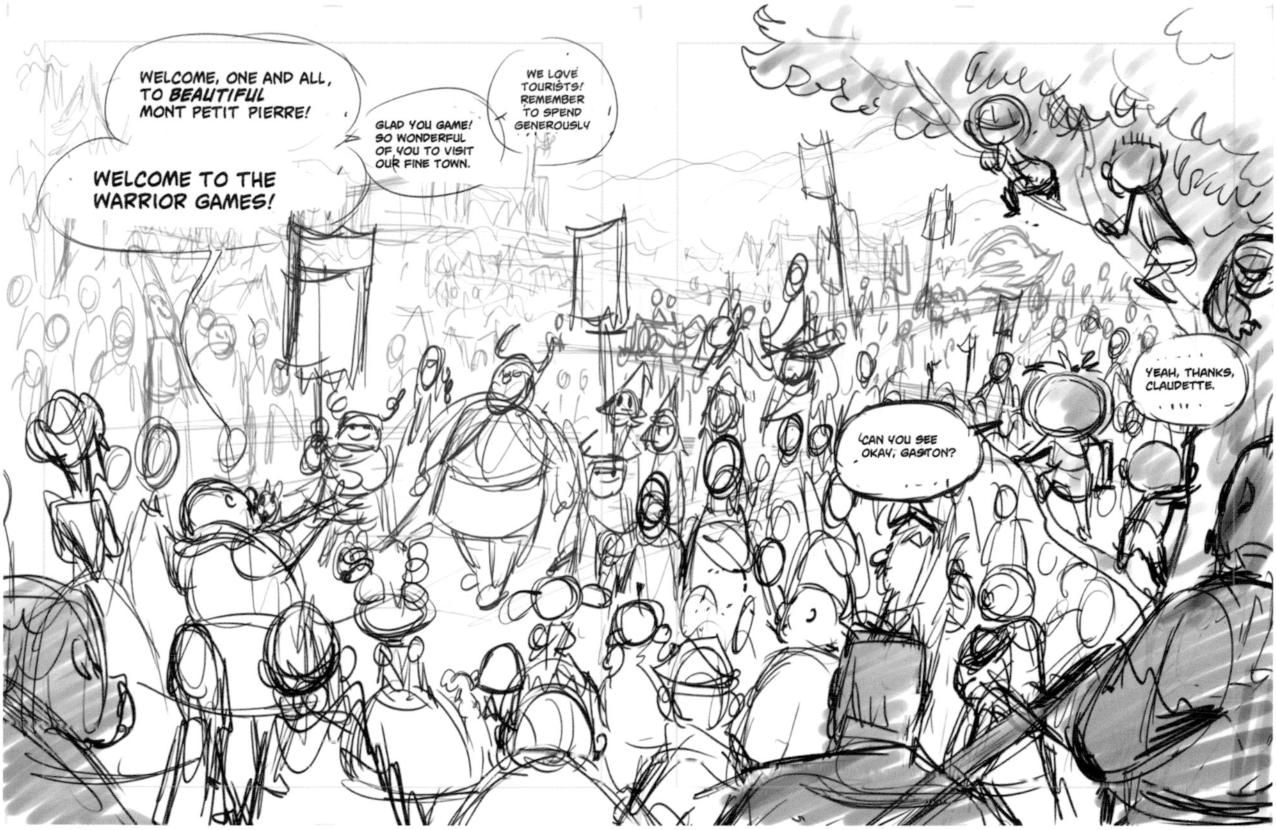
WELCOME, ONE AND ALL, TO BEAUTIFUL MONT PETIT PIERRE!
WELCOME TO THE WARRIOR GAMES!
GLAD YOU CAME! SO WONDERFUL OF YOU TO VISIT OUR FINE TOWN.
WE LOVE TOURISTS! REMEMBER TO SPEND GENEROUSLY
CAN YOU SEE OKAY, GASTON?
YEAH, THANKS, CLAUDETTE.

This two-page spread is probably the most detailed drawing I've ever done! I wanted the arrival of the delegations from all the different kingdoms to feel like a huge event, like every citizen in Mont Petit Pierre was there to see it.

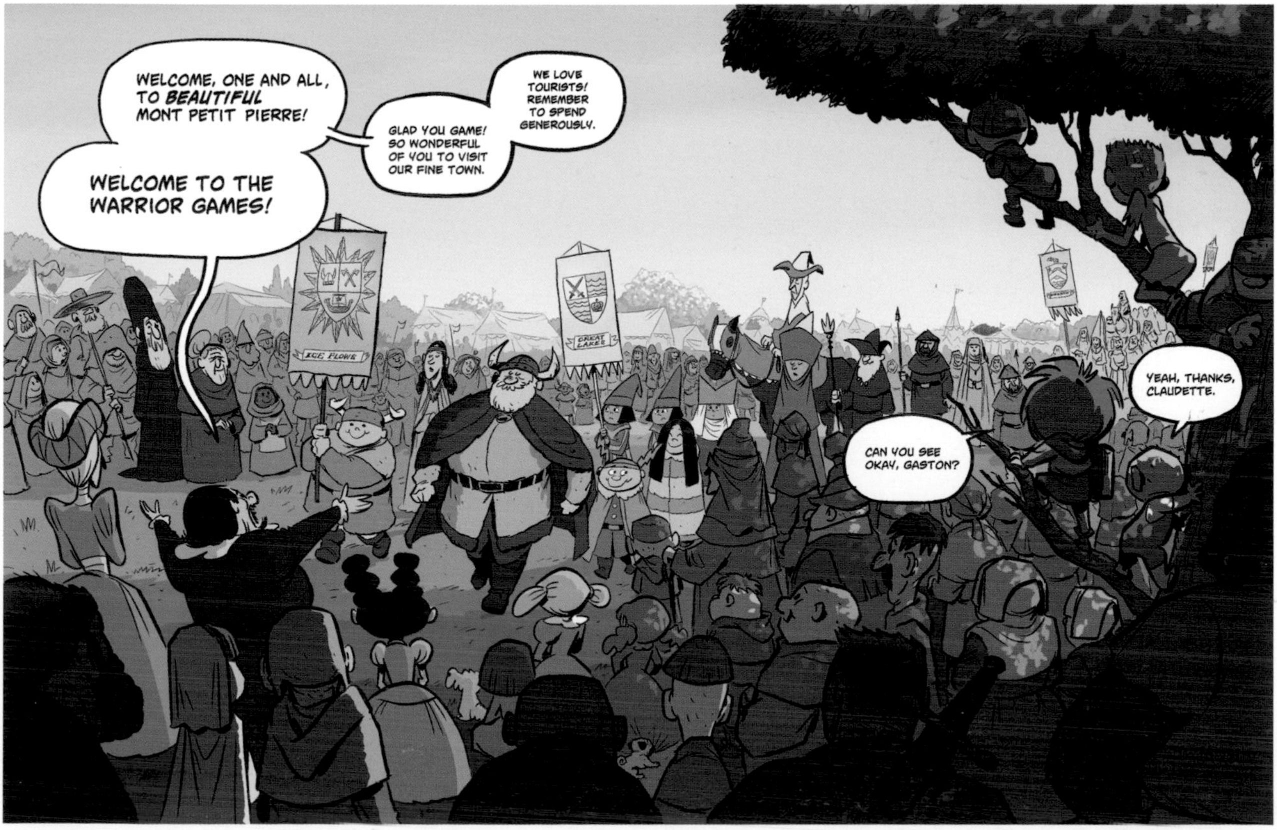
WELCOME, ONE AND ALL, TO BEAUTIFUL MONT PETIT PIERRE!
WELCOME TO THE WARRIOR GAMES!
GLAD YOU CAME! SO WONDERFUL OF YOU TO VISIT OUR FINE TOWN.
WE LOVE TOURISTS! REMEMBER TO SPEND GENEROUSLY.
CAN YOU SEE OKAY, GASTON?
YEAH, THANKS, CLAUDETTE.

My dad, Raul Rosado, has always been a big supporter of my work. He is an artist himself. There were a LOT of elements to figure out with the Warrior Games. My dad did a lot of initial research, then took it upon himself to design crests for each kingdom; the Victory Garden, including specific gardens for each kingdom; and the exterior of the coliseum, among many things. I couldn't have done it without him!

SIDE VIEW

MOUNTAIN KINGDOM GARDEN

SIDE VIEW

DESERT KINGDOM GARDEN

NORTHWEST KINGDOM

SWAMP KINGDOM

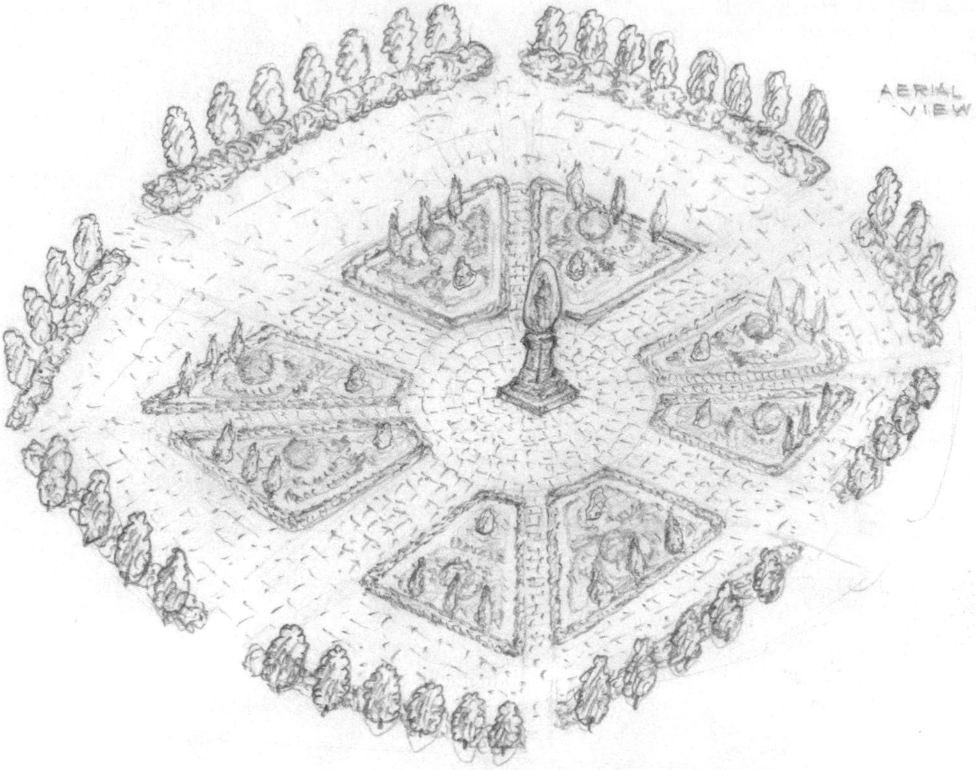
AERIAL VIEW

EVERGREEN KINGDOM
GARDEN

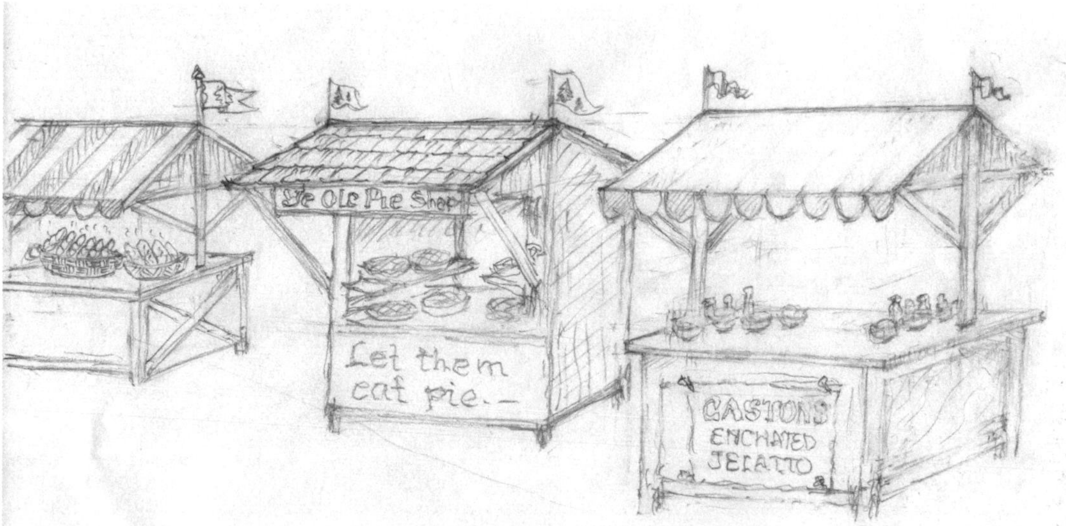
Ye Ole Pie Shop
Let them eat pie.
GASTONS ENCHATED JELATTO

GASTON'S
JELATTO
STAND

JORGE TEACHES: HOW DO YOU CHANGE A BOOK AFTER YOU'RE DONE? REWRITING!

WARNING: SPOILERS. Rafael and I work very closely on the stories of our books, and I do a lot of rewriting throughout the process. When we were nearing the very end of creating *Monsters Beware!*, our editor, Mark Siegel, suggested that we end this book with a really big bang.

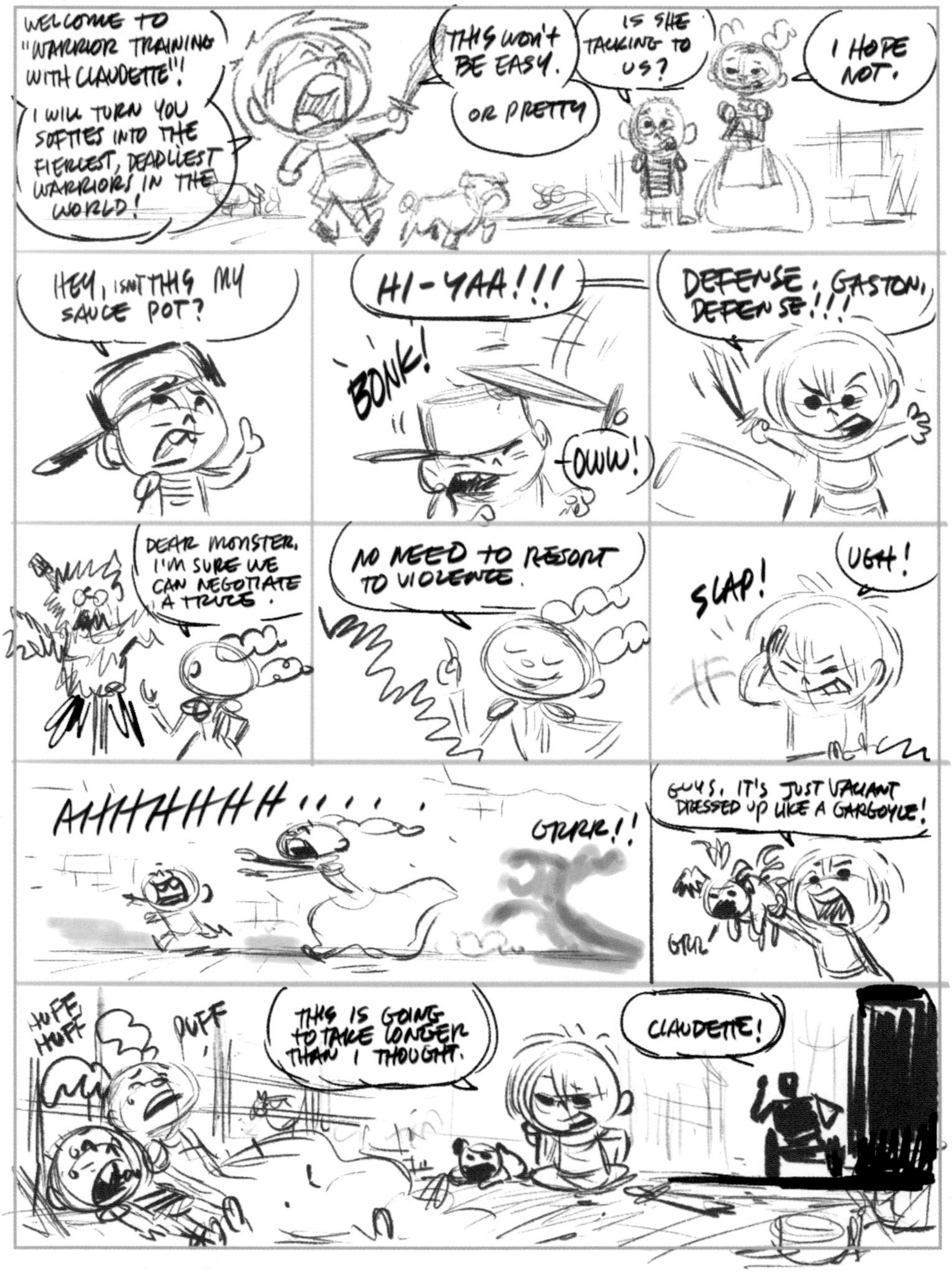
WELCOME TO "WARRIOR TRAINING WITH CLAUDETTE"!
I WILL TURN YOU SOFTIES INTO THE FIERCEST, DEADLIEST WARRIORS IN THE WORLD!
THIS WON'T BE EASY.
OR PRETTY
IS SHE TALKING TO US?
I HOPE NOT.
HEY, ISN'T THIS MY SAUCE POT?
HI-YAA!!!
BONK!
OWW!
DEFENSE, GASTON, DEFENSE!!!
DEAR MONSTER, I'M SURE WE CAN NEGOTIATE A TRUCE.
NO NEED TO RESORT TO VIOLENCE.
SLAP!
UGH!
AHHHHHHH.....
GRRR!!
GUYS, IT'S JUST VALIANT DRESSED UP LIKE A GARGOYLE!
GRR
HUFF, HUFF
PUFF
THIS IS GOING TO TAKE LONGER THAN I THOUGHT.
CLAUDETTE!

We came up with the idea of bringing back Claudette's mother, Juliette, at the end of the story. But Rafael was already done drawing the rough pages of most of the book. You can't just bring a major character back from the dead without some kind of setup. We decided that there would be a pendant, which Claudette would wear during the Warrior Games, that was once her mother's, and we'd refer back to it a few times. That would help make Juliette's presence felt during the book so that when she reappears at the end, it would feel organic. And so we came up with these two new pages.

Because of the way books are printed, you can't add just ONE page after it's drawn. Rafael had spent lots of time setting up page turns and timing. You have to add two pages at a time or else everything goes wonky. The new pages introduced Juliette's pendant, and just for laughs, we added a short training sequence.

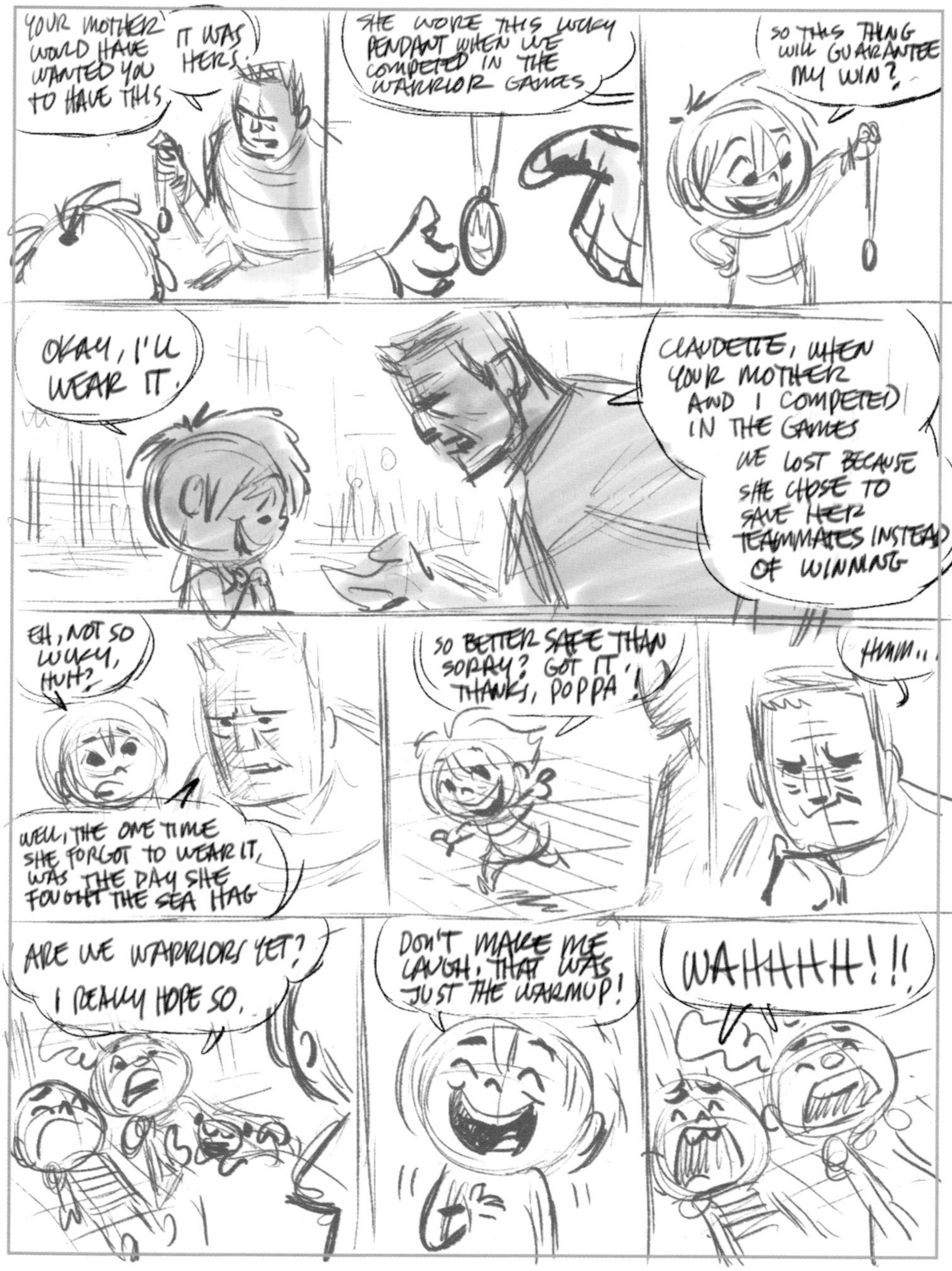
YOUR MOTHER WOULD HAVE WANTED YOU TO HAVE THIS.
IT WAS HERS.
SHE WORE THIS LUCKY PENDANT WHEN WE COMPETED IN THE WARRIOR GAMES
SO THIS THING WILL GUARANTEE MY WIN?
OKAY, I'LL WEAR IT.
CLAUDETTE, WHEN YOUR MOTHER AND I COMPETED IN THE GAMES
WE LOST BECAUSE SHE CHOSE TO SAVE HER TEAMMATES INSTEAD OF WINNING
EH, NOT SO LUCKY, HUH?
WELL, THE ONE TIME SHE FORGOT TO WEAR IT, WAS THE DAY SHE FOUGHT THE SEA HAG
SO BETTER SAFE THAN SORRY? GOT IT. THANKS, POPPA!
HMM..
ARE WE WARRIORS YET? I REALLY HOPE SO.
DON'T MAKE ME LAUGH, THAT WAS JUST THE WARMUP!
WAHHHH!!!

Now that we had laid the groundwork for the pendant and hinted at Juliette's presence, we still needed to hit that a little harder. So we reworked a couple pages in the book.

OLD PAGE

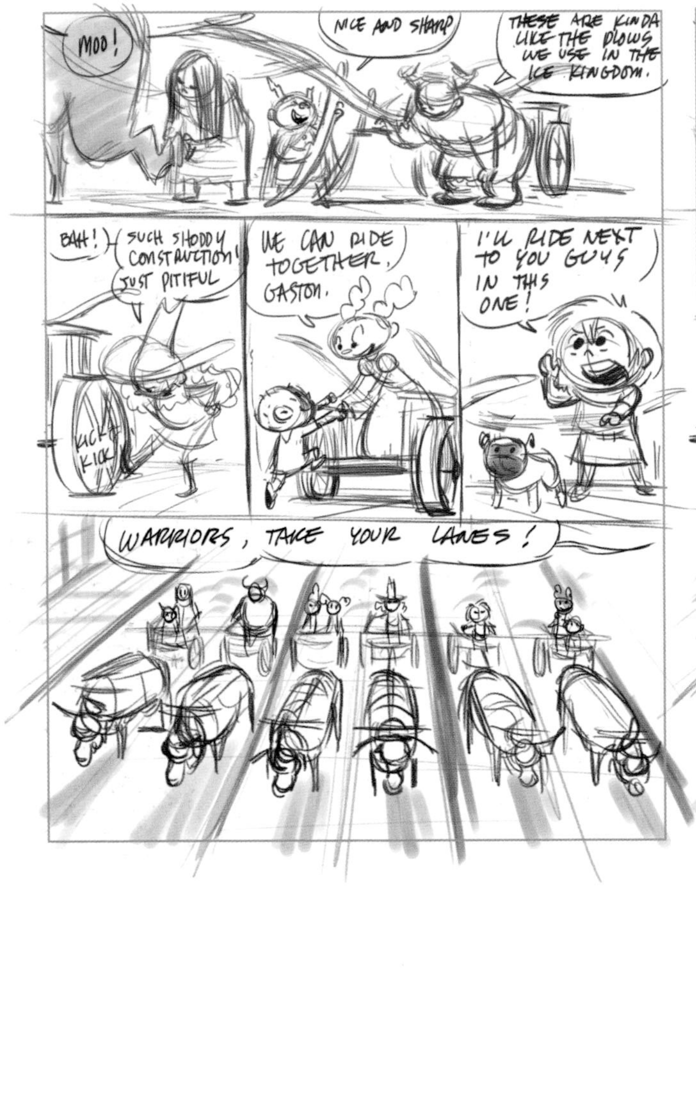

MOO!
NICE AND SHARP
THESE ARE KINDA LIKE THE PLOWS WE USE IN THE ICE KINGDOM.
BAH!
SUCH SHODDY CONSTRUCTION! JUST PITIFUL
KICK KICK
WE CAN RIDE TOGETHER, GASTON.
I'LL RIDE NEXT TO YOU GUYS IN THIS ONE!
WARRIORS, TAKE YOUR LANES!

NEW PAGE

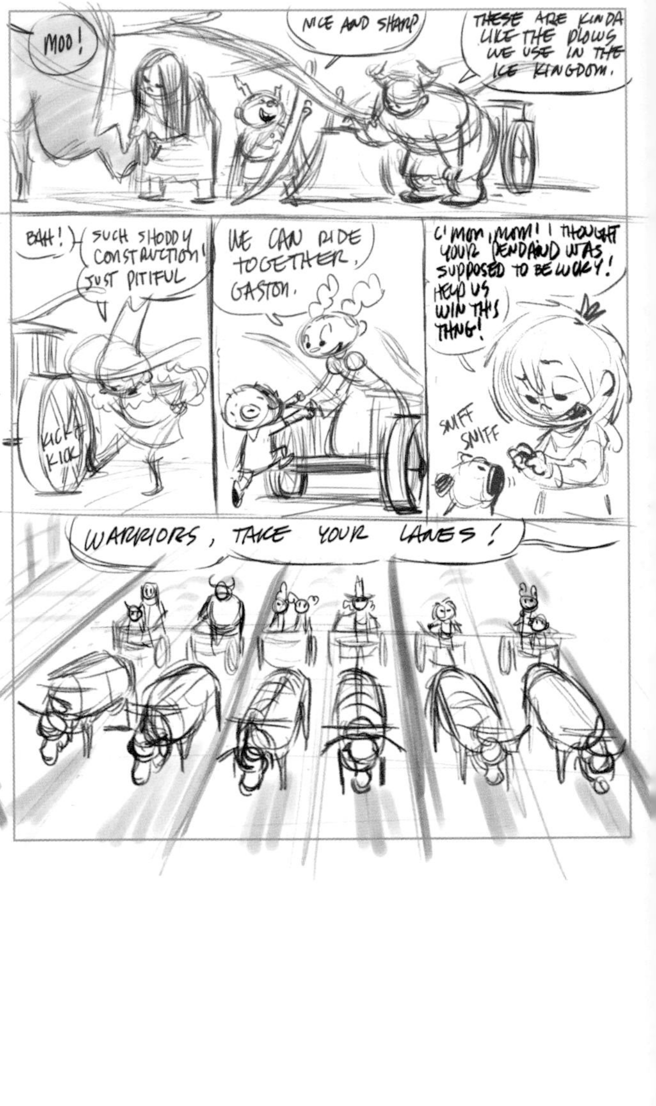

MOO!
NICE AND SHARP
THESE ARE KINDA LIKE THE PLOWS WE USE IN THE ICE KINGDOM.
BAH!
SUCH SHODDY CONSTRUCTION! JUST PITIFUL
KICK KICK
WE CAN RIDE TOGETHER, GASTON.
C'MON, MOM! I THOUGHT YOUR PENDANT WAS SUPPOSED TO BE LUCKY! HELP US WIN THIS THING!
SNIFF SNIFF
WARRIORS, TAKE YOUR LANES!

And that, folks, is how you add a major plot point to a book after it's already done. In other words, that's one way to rewrite.

OLD PAGE

GASP! OH, NO!
FINISH
DOGGONE IT.
ALRIGHT...
SCREECH!
TURN, OXEN, TURN!
CLOP
CLOP CLOP CLOP
HUH?
C'MON, BOY! GIDDY-UP!
YOU'RE GOING TO LOSE, ANCHOVY!
SOME THINGS ARE MORE IMPORTANT THAN WINNING.

NEW PAGE

GASP! OH, NO!
FINISH
WHAT WOULD MOM DO?
WAIT, I KNOW WHAT SHE' DO!
SNAP
SCREECH!
TURN, OXEN, TURN!
CLOP
CLOP CLOP CLOP
HUH?
C'MON, BOY! GIDDY-UP!
YOU'RE GOING TO LOSE, ANCHOVY!
SOME THINGS ARE MORE IMPORTANT THAN WINNING.

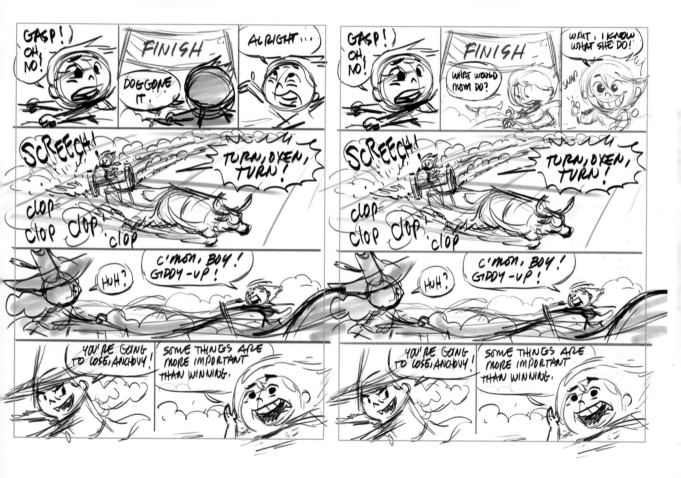